THE LOST ERWAIN

MARIAH STILLBROOK

ALSO BY MARIAH STILLBROOK

In The Pines

Published in the United States by Creative James Media.

www.creativejamesmedia.com

978-1-956183-46-7 (trade paperback) First U.S. Edition 2024

For Liv.

❧   I   ☙

This was my American Idol. My MasterChef. If I didn't do well here, then I didn't know what I would do, or what I would become. There was no other option—I couldn't fail.

I sat on a padded bench alongside the wooden corridor inside of The Harold, Stauffer, and Main Law Firm, acid filling the pit of my stomach. For longer than I could remember, there had always been a shadow of a queen looming over my shoulders, pushing me in the direction of greatness. As I sat with my back rigidly against the wall, my chin to my chest, and my breath as unsteady as a flimsy boat over choppy waters—all that I could hope for was that this ghostly imagery wouldn't fail me now.

My mom laid her warm hand over mine, causing my head to twitch. Her square chin was lifted and her brown eyes, per her usual, were astute. Naomi Wood was a headstrong woman who woke every morning with a cup of coffee in one hand, and a *People* magazine littered with meeting notes sticking out of it in the other; and though I had to forgive her terrible habit of trying to bake at least once a year—causing the house to smell of burnt mud cakes—she was the woman I strove to be someday.

"Don't be nervous, Makayla," she purred, her voice like melted caramel.

I inhaled a hasty breath and nodded quickly while my nose lifted too high into the air. She reached up and lowered my chin with a single finger.

"You've got this, baby."

I tried to pull from some of her easy energy, but her confidence wasn't proving to overshadow the fact that my respiratory system had pretty much ceased to work.

"I should've brought the *Forbes* magazine," I chattered, my words struggling to get through my crowded airways.

"I'm sure she's seen it, Lala."

"Mom!" I exclaimed in a hushed voice. "Do *not* call me that here—that is *so* not professional."

She rolled her eyes.

I should've brought the magazine. I just hadn't wanted to appear as though I was bragging. Seriously though, how many other seventeen-year-olds had been on the cover of *Forbes* because of their company?

In attempt to keep my heart from beating out of my chest, I exhaled a long, hot breath, tugging on my blouse as I did so. I blinked with purpose before allowing my gaze to float up to the name in gold letters on the white plaque next to the door. Lucy Armstrong. The name itself rendered excellence. I believed a name said a lot about a person. Makayla Wood, now that was a name you'd hear in court.

"Ms. Wood, would you kindly stand and plead your client's case . . ." I mean, it just worked.

Not often, but sometimes I allowed myself to drift away, to ponder over what my birth parents' names were, or are. Like Samantha for my mom. Maybe she has sparkly red hair like me, straight and thick. And my dad, perhaps he is named

Trevor. But then again, I don't let my thoughts deviate in that direction too often. Those people aren't my present, and as someone who's aspired to become a graduate of Harvard Law, daydreams have never been a luxury I have been able to afford.

The door of the office nearest me opened, cutting me off from my wandering thoughts—causing me to feel wound tight like a piece of licorice. Observing my reaction, my mom squeezed my hand reassuringly, but I quickly pulled it away, not wanting to appear dependent.

A second later, a tall thin woman, with blonde hair twisted into a low bun, appeared from the door of Lucy Armstrong's office. She curled herself around the door frame as she smiled down at me.

"Makayla Wood?"

I gulped, but the back of my throat was as dry as sand, so I swallowed an excess of air—an action that would later result in a very inappropriately timed belch.

"Yes," I said, uncrossing my ankles and rolling back my shoulders before coming to standing. My chest constricted, but I pushed through it.

"Great. So nice to meet you. I'm Lucy."

I looked down at her hand. This was it, the handshake I'd been waiting for since I was six-years-old. My first chance at a good impression for my Harvard interview. I wanted to throw up.

My mom kicked the back of my leg, and I quickly shot her a look.

"Breathe baby," she mouthed.

I nodded before returning my gaze to my interviewer.

"Of course," I exhaled, sliding my hand confidently into Lucy's. As soon as our skin touched, a flutter of pure ecstasy came over me like an enchanted mist. I couldn't believe it; this was really happening. "It is such a pleasure to meet you, Ms. Armstrong."

"Lucy, please," she corrected, her hand moving with mine. "Come on in. I have *really* been looking forward to meeting you."

I blinked a few times too many before letting my hand drop away from hers. My heart beat as quickly as a pair of hummingbird wings, and as I stepped into her office, I didn't even hear the door close behind me.

"Have a seat, Makayla," Lucy said, walking around her large mahogany desk. I tried not to appear too excited as I peered past her, out of her windows that looked out towards the nation's capital. This was where I wanted to be, right here, in this office. A Washington D.C. lawyer, just like my dad.

"Thank you, Ms. Armstrong," I said, flinching as I said her last name. "I mean Lucy."

She smiled and folded her hands over one another on top of her desk. "Don't be nervous, Makayla. We have all sat where you are sitting right now. And my goodness, a girl such as yourself has no reason to have any worries. You've already achieved so much in so little time." Her pink lips widened as she handed me the compliment.

I laughed anxiously and roped my hands together over my lap.

"So, tell me, what was it like starting a company at just twelve-years-old?"

My mind cleared itself. Shit, I knew this would happen. I had spent hours preparing for this, researching every possible question she could ask. Test scores, what kind of person I was, did I like to party—the answer was no. I'd never even had friends my own age, nor experienced any sort of romantic relationship. How else does a girl run a company and finish college before she can even legally make her own bad decisions? Another sharp pain in my chest.

I sifted through the silent echoes in my mind and remembered my rehearsed lines. "It was exhilarating. I was very fortunate to have parents who encouraged me to start achieving my life-long goals at such an early age—and not just that, but for my mom to get so actively involved. She took my baby, Sewn Back Together, and brought it full circle. Currently we have over ten thousand women under our employment, women who would never have been given the opportunity to work; and our handbags are made from one hundred percent recycled materials . . .”

Somehow, I did it. I freaking did it. I sat there in that chair and carried out an hour-long conversation with Lucy Armstrong. I don't even remember her asking the questions, I just know that I answered them; and as I did, it got easier and easier.

Before I knew it, the hour was up and she was escorting me back to where my mom was waiting for me, one hand on my lower back and the other reaching for the door.

I turned into her with a wide smile on my face just before I walked away, and this time I beat her to it. I held out my hand and raised my chest. “Thank you for your time, Lucy.”

She had a mystified look on her face as she hesitantly slipped her hand into mine. Who could blame her? She was probably dumbfounded by all my accomplishments.

“Well, Miss Wood. I—uh—you will be hearing from Harvard within a couple of weeks.”

“Thank you,” I said affirmatively. One last squeeze and then I let go of her hand, turning away from the Harvard rep and returning to my mother.

“How did it go?” she asked, once we'd started for the elevators.

“Really good,” I said. I'd never taken a single drug in my entire life, but I imagined this was what it was like to feel high. “I don't want to jinx anything, but I am pretty sure I'm in.”

My mom grabbed my hand and gave it another squeeze. “Good for you, sweetheart. I'm so proud of you.”

Neither one of us looked back before turning the corner that led us away from Lucy Armstrong's office. We smiled diligently as we walked on, nodding our heads at passersby. We didn't have a clue Lucy hadn't moved an inch from where she was standing just beside the door to her office, the odd expression on her face transforming into one of complete and utter bewilderment.

✤ 2 ✤

I've always prided myself on having a larger vocabulary than other kids my age. I read *The Complete Works of William Shakespeare* when I was four-years-old, and from there moved on to my parent's old college textbooks. I've even been accused from time to time of being a prodigy. But because of what ensued, after what I'd thought was an endearing and new relationship with Lucy Armstrong, there was only one word I knew of in the entire universe. Mortified.

After my interview my mom had called my dad and told him to meet us at Rogue, our family's favorite restaurant. It was super chic with a modern edge. Everything, even the walls and tables were made of glass. The plates were huge, the servings small, and there wasn't a single thing under forty dollars—but this was a night for celebration. We had only just stepped into the front door of our home, however, when my dad called us back and announced we would *not* be going out. That he would be leaving his office early and heading home as soon as he could.

"I just hope nothing is too terribly wrong," my mom had said after hanging up.

I was still high from the interview, and I'd believed that I'd nailed every aspect of it. I shouted down to her as I climbed the stairs to my bedroom, "I'm sure it's fine! Maybe he just wants to go somewhere else, a surprise maybe." Then I'd strolled into my room, picked up my Thursday notebook and flipped it to the current day. I skimmed through my checklist and lowered the tip of my freshly sharpened pencil to the heading, "Conquer Harvard Interview," and placed a check in the box.

I then changed out of my suit and hung it up next to the five others exactly like it, retrieving a pair of slacks and a nice crisp white button-up shirt in trade. The majority of my clothes were shipped directly to my doorstep via The Boxed Professional—an online subscription created for the modern workaholic who didn't have time to shop.

But when my dad arrived, it was immediately apparent that he had not rushed home to congratulate me, and he did not want to take us somewhere else for an exquisite dinner; as soon as I saw the look on his face, I knew exactly that. He was a vision of two different people lapped together as one. The first—someone who had just realized that the bridge under his feet, keeping him from falling into an endless ravine and his one and final death, was about to collapse. And the second— that of a father about to murder his child. Both personas were completely out of the norm for Philip Wood.

Only minutes later the three of us were sitting around our elegant dining room table, backs straight and hands laced over the smooth, spotless surface.

"I just don't understand, Makayla. What would inspire you to—"

"Dad, I already told you, I have no idea . . . I thought it went really well. I don't remember any of that."

He remained stiff. "How can you not remember saying those things?"

My lips were trembling. I literally had nothing to say back.

"I mean, really Makayla. 'I'm a little friggin' monkey and I like to eat bananas,'" he paraphrased, forcing me to close my eyes in shame. "'Nom, nom, nom, all day long.' Gibberish, and spouting off fables and nursery rhymes! What the hell were you thinking?"

I jumped in my seat at his outburst, then lowered my head until it was down over my hands. "I didn't say those things. I —I couldn't have."

"So, Lucy Armstrong just made that up, then?" His words were sharp. "Just put everything on the line to call me, against the rules, and ask me if you were on any kind of medication. If you were on *drugs*. Are you on drugs, Makayla?"

"No!" I lifted my face, which by now had to be the color of my hair. Two hot tears rolled like fire down my cheeks. "I've never even accidentally swallowed my mouthwash." I looked over at my mom, who unlike my dad didn't look pissed off, just worried. "I don't know what happened. I'm not saying she lied to you—I just don't understand—"

"Well understand this, young lady, you probably just blew your chance of getting into the one school you've been prepping for your entire life."

"Don't you think I know that!" I grabbed my temples and squeezed them. My head was pounding, and my breath was getting shorter. I could feel it, that something inside my body wanted out, but I simply attributed the feeling to anguish.

"Philip, let's just take it down a notch, all right," my mom said softly. The way she was looking at me, I could have sworn she was also waiting for something to erupt from my shell.

"What?" my dad snapped. "She's the one who has been killing herself over this interview—I just don't understand what she was thinking."

My mom looked at him as if she was pleading with him to understand something other than what she said next. "You're not helping things. We must keep calm, otherwise we could all just *explode*."

"Oh . . . right," he said, immediately pulling his chest backwards.

I couldn't take it anymore. My character had already been flattened out and streaked with the imprints of several burnt tires. I quickly looked from one parent to the other, before pushing away from the table and running back up to my room.

I hit my pillow hard, pulling the corners up around my head as I screamed into the stuffing. This wasn't happening. No, this was a nightmare and I was going to wake at any moment.

I remembered *everything* I said in that interview, it was just like I'd rehearsed. All my achievements and high-test scores, the college courses I'd taken even before graduating early from my prestigious private school; the fact that I'd already finished my first degree, and *my company*. The company I'd started so that it would look good for Harvard. I'd said all of it . . . I was sure of it. I mean, I had sort of blacked out a bit after Lucy had asked that initial question, but then I'd found myself again. Hadn't I?

A knock came at my door, and I lifted my head from the pillow. My mascara had run into my ivory sham, and now there were black smudges on the 3000 thread count Egyptian Cotton. But I didn't care. I didn't care about anything anymore.

"Lala," my mom said from the other side of the door.

I gritted my teeth. "What?"

"Can I come in?"

"Whatever," I retorted, letting my face fall back into the pillow.

The door opened and her soft footsteps padded across my room. The side of my bed lowered as she sat down, and when she laid a hand over my head and started stroking my hair I began to sob.

"Oh, come now, Lala, it's okay."

"It is *so* not okay, and don't call me that."

I hated it when she called me Lala. It was not a name that issued control, instead it was made of fluff and sporadic notes. I didn't have the patience for such a nickname. It was hard enough gaining respect as a teen, but when you add on trying to achieve greatness at this young age—it was nearly impossible. *Lala* wasn't someone who could be revered. I knew that from a very young age.

"Baby, this is life. These things happen. Perhaps it just wasn't meant to be."

As my temperature continued to rise, I flipped over, nostrils flared. "*Not meant to be?* Mom, I have been working towards this all my life."

"And your life has just begun." She smiled reassuringly, stroking my cheeks with the back of her hand.

My eyes darted down to her red painted fingernails before brushing them away; she'd picked the vibrant color the day before when we'd gone to get manicures. She'd said red was powerful. Perhaps I should've gone with that instead of the clear coat I'd pressed for.

"No, it's over," I snipped. "It is all over, because this was how I was going to get started."

I looked at my desk. Tidy and situated. Binders lined up in rows, each labeled appropriately. Color coordinated Post Its hanging in their predestined slots, waiting to be crumpled up and thrown away as soon as their assigned task was followed through. That desk was a symbol of how my life was run. Now it was all for nothing.

My mom grabbed my chin in her hand and forced me to look at her. "Lala, maybe it is time you take a vacation."

My eyeballs nearly popped out of my head. "A vacation?

Are you serious? I don't have time for that. I have to start reapplying—or, perhaps it's not too late. Maybe I can schedule an appointment with Lucy Armstrong and apologize —salvage what's left of my reputation."

She dropped her hand from my chin and looked down. "I shouldn't have let you get so involved with work. I told your father it was too much. I should have encouraged you to play more when you were little."

"Play?" I was beginning to sound a little delirious. "Are you crazy? People like *me* don't play."

She lifted her eyebrows, and for a second, I thought she was about to laugh, but instead she stood and patted me on the head. "Cry it out, then go to sleep. You haven't gotten rejected yet, so let's just wait until we get that letter in the mail to start reevaluating things. And don't forget, we still have the company."

I scoffed. "The only reason I came up with that idea was so I could get into Harvard. I needed something to set me apart, to show what I was made of."

My mom's expression changed from that of a scolded puppy into a fierce attack dog.

"Makayla Wood, why do you even want to be a lawyer?"

"What kind of stupid question is that?" I asked, wiping away a blackened tear.

"Those women we employ, do you think they even know what Harvard is? No. All they know is that they finally have a way to make enough money to support themselves and their children. A way to move out from abusive relationships, *dangerous* relationships." She shook her head at me. "If they heard what you just said, it would be devastating."

"Good thing they can't hear me then," I replied in a snotty tone. I wasn't sure how it had happened, but I'd found myself speaking like a juvenile.

"I hope you don't mean that. This whole time I had you

pegged as someone who was chasing equality of life. Someone who wanted to not only give these women a chance but find other ways to make the world a more livable place for people who grew up less fortunate than yourself."

"I can do without the victory speech right now, Naomi," I choked back bitterly.

Pressing her lips together, she hung back a moment before retorting. "I can see you aren't in the mood to listen so why don't you just sleep it off. We will discuss this in the morning, Lala."

I watched her back as she made her way out of my room, then clenching my teeth together until I heard the latch shut, I threw my pillow at the door, and screeched, "Don't call me that!"

The sound of a bird chirping made me turn and look out at the two birds who commonly took up vacancy on the branch outside my window. One was blue and the other was red, and they had been there off and on for as long as I could remember, singing to the sun rising and humming whenever the moon came out. Sometimes it felt like they were spying on me.

"Go away," I muttered, pulling my shades down. "I don't need anyone else judging me . . . and no, I didn't really mean those things."

Of course there was a reason I wanted to be a lawyer. My mom had been right, I'd been driven towards reformation of justice from the moment I could stand and lift my fist into the air. Our company elevated those values . . . I was just mad, that's all.

I marched over to my desk and pulled out my Thursday notebook . . . and then I lunged for my pencil and stood over the day's list as though I could stab it and make it bleed; but instead of doing that I flipped the pencil over in my hand and reluctantly laid the eraser down to the page, undoing the check I'd placed next to "Conquer Harvard Interview."

I could've sworn one of the birds began to cry.

⚜

The next morning, I woke up choking. It must have been loud because I had barely leaned over onto my side before my parents came rushing into my room.

"Call 911!" my mom yelled in straight up panic. "Philip? Don't just stand there, call them!"

"Is it happening?" he asked.

"I—I don't know. Just call them!"

"But what if she's—"

"Can't you see that she can't breathe? Call them *now!*"

The next thing I knew I was clutching my chest and gasping for air as the light went out around me.

When I reawakened, it was like I'd been abducted by aliens and taken into their ship, except that instead of aliens I was looking up at two desperately attractive firemen, and one equally gorgeous firewoman. Immediately something inside me flickered, the same sensation I'd felt only once before when my college professor looked my way during Biology for Non-Majors. I blame the crush on my complete lack of interest in the course, that and Professor Valerie Deitrick's electric blue eyes. They brought out an uncontrollable reaching desire inside me . . . like I wanted to find a reason to stay late and have secret teacher/student time. I'd just never thought my first crush would be on a grown woman.

I balled up my fists and curled my toes in an attempt to squash that feeling all over again—because I had much more important things to deal with than silly teenage hormones. I pushed past the ton of bricks lying over my chest and ventured to ask what was happening.

"Oh my god, is she awake?" my mom asked, as she bulldozed her way through the first responders to get to me.

"Looks like you had an anxiety attack, Makayla," the woman stated. I couldn't have been anymore humiliated. "Gave your parents quite a scare."

I started to sit up, but immediately felt dizzy and laid back down, gripping the space over my heart.

"Having chest pains?" a fireman with blond hair and hazel eyes asked.

"A little. Is that weird for someone my age?"

"Not when you lead the life of a forty-year-old. It's time to slow down, kiddo—"

Kiddo—ugh!

"—today you need to take it easy and rest." He turned towards my mom and dad. "She should be fine, but if her breathing becomes erratic again or any symptoms worsen, then take her in as soon as possible."

"Of course," my mom said.

I was forced to lie there as the three firefighters packed away their equipment and headed out, leaving me feeling debased and too weak to pull the covers over my face. As soon as it was just the three of us again, my parents went directly to their phones; my dad alerting his work to the fact that he'd be late, and my mother calling our office and telling them that neither of us would be coming in that day.

After she hung up, she walked over to my window and made a strange gesture to the two birds hanging out on the branch. I twisted up my features, asking in an accusatory manner, "Are you talking to them?"

"What? No." Fumbling with the blinds, she said distractedly, "Don't worry, baby, everything's going to be okay. We just need to get you to calm down a little."

My dad walked in, and she shot him a troubled look.

"What is it?" I asked, starting to feel panicky again. "Is it something worse? Did you hear from Harvard? Oh—oh my god, they're going to take me off the list. They— they—" I clenched my fist over my heart again and dug my head deeper into the pillow.

"Stop it!" my mom screeched, grabbing my face. "Forget about Harvard for god's sakes and just breathe. Breathe, Lala."

"Don't—call—me—that," I said through short breaths. There was a pang on my window, and I could've sworn I saw the red-feathered bird smash its face into the pane.

"She's not going to cooperate," my dad said, throwing his arms up in the air and walking out. My mom whispered something that I supposed to be vexing at the empty doorway, before handing me a paper bag and following him into the hall.

I took the bag and started breathing into it, heavily. Oh my god, this had happened. I was the person breathing into the bag. As I tried not to black out again, I listened to my parents fighting just outside my bedroom.

"I know what you're going to say, and the answer is no. Naomi, don't you think if we tell her it will just make her condition worse?"

Harvard. Was that what they were talking about?

"Well she's bound to find out sometime. I'm surprised it hasn't already happened—the girl has been fast tracking it since she tossed her diapers aside. The stress can't be good for her. Were you even watching her last night? She looked like she was going to explode."

My paper bag was shrinking and refilling rapidly.

When my father didn't reply, my mom ranted on. "I'm going to tell her."

My eyes widened. Tell me what?

"No. Naomi," my dad replied stiffly. "I'm sorry, but I can't let you do that. I'll take her with me to the office if that's what it takes, but you cannot tell her anything—not yet." There was a pause. "We promised when we took her that we would do it together when the time came. Remember?"

"We also had promised to tell her the truth when she was five."

"Don't you dare put that on me. We *all* agreed—"

"You just don't want her to find out, because you don't want the inevitable to happen! But it's who she is, Philip!"

"Don't you go putting words into my mouth that aren't there. I love our daughter and would be happy with whatever path she chooses to go down. I just think she's worked too hard to have to give it all up, that's all."

"Worked too hard, or forgotten what it's all about?"

Okay . . . what was going on? My breath remained shallow, and my bag was still working when my mom walked back into the room. She had a plastic smile on her face, the same one she wore during business matters when things weren't going her way.

"All right, baby. I'm going to go make a few more phone calls and then I'll come right back and check on you." I nodded my head, in an effort to pretend that I wasn't completely freaked out by what I'd just heard. "Keep doing that until your breath evens out, okay."

I watched her back as she disappeared from my room again. What was I—some sort of mutant? And I'm sorry, but had my mom and dad just said that they'd *taken* me?

Obviously, I knew I was adopted, they'd been more than forthcoming about that since I was little—I mean, between my dad's Latino heritage and my mother's Indian, I would have wondered how my skin came out as white as snow if they hadn't said anything. But I'd always imagined that they'd gone through the same excruciating process as every other infertile set of parents.

Suddenly I let out a breath so big that I almost popped my bag. What if my parents never adopted me, what if they'd stolen me? It could be like, oh, what was the name of that book—*The Face on the Milk Carton.*

No way. My parents were respectable people. Before she'd gotten involved with Sewn Back Together, my mom had worked for a string of environmental projects, and my dad was about as high powered as an attorney could get. Honestly, I'd always wondered why they'd wanted to get me in the first place, seeing as their careers were so important to them. I was simply overreacting, that's all. I wasn't stolen, nor was I a mutant, and Harvard was not yet off the table.

I continued to breathe into my bag, letting my thoughts settle until I'd finally calmed down enough to lower my eyelids and slowly drift away. Had I known what was in store for me, though, I would have done everything in my power not to wake back up.

❀   3   ❀

"What do you mean you are forcing me to take some time for myself?" I asked over take-out later that night.

My parents were digging into their Pad Thai while avoiding any verbal or visual contact with me at all costs. It was my dad who finally got up the guts to say something first.

"We just think that considering what happened this morning, it might be a good time to rest. You can reevaluate your plans later."

"This is complete bullshit."

"Makayla," my mom said in a low voice, holding a piece of shrimp tightly between her red chopsticks that we'd found in Thailand on a business trip years ago.

"What? You can't tell me what to do. I make my own money and am completely capable of supporting myself."

"It doesn't matter, you're still under our control until you're eighteen," my father retorted matter-of-factly. "To fight us on this would be more of a hassle than anything."

I narrowed my eyes at the both of them. They were right,

but I couldn't let them know that. I wasn't used to them speaking to me like this, and it brought out the child in me. The one I hadn't ever really introduced myself to before.

"They need me at the office," I stated.

"Rachel is ready to cover for you. She was going to be helping more once you went to law school, so now she's just stepping it up a little earlier. And besides, isn't this company just something you created so that you would look good for Harvard?" my mother questioned, raising a sharp, perfectly shaped brow.

I grumbled a curse word under my breath and shoved my chopsticks into my rice noodles. The table was quiet for a full minute before I exploded again.

"So, what do you expect me to do? Just curl up on the rug like a cat?"

They exchanged looks and then shrugged their shoulders. My dad didn't even appear to be really listening; he was sorting through emails on his iPad.

I scratched the area over my eye, a nervous habit of mine. "This can*not* be happening."

"Oh, give it up," my dad said, still mostly preoccupied with his tablet. "Believe me, I wanted you to get into Harvard as much as you did, but your mom's right. You worked through your childhood—you don't know what it's like to be a real teenager."

"I don't have time to be a *real teenager*," I snapped, before immediately rolling my shoulders back and into place. I was trying very hard to contain myself so what happened this morning wouldn't happen again. "I lead a professional life."

"Maybe it's time you try on a new life," my dad said. "Go get in trouble for once—meet some friends for god's sakes."

"Get in trouble? Make some friends? What are you asking me to do—go lace some Kool-Aid with vodka and throw a party in the backyard?"

"Stop it," my mom said, her eyes piercing. "You don't have to pull an attitude with us, Makayla. All we want is for you to relax."

Finally, my dad looked up from his work, and pushing away his plate, said, "Look, this is really easy. Take some time off, clear your head, and at the end of it you can go back to work. Got it?"

I just scowled at him. Because no, actually, I didn't *get it*.

❧

The next two weeks were excruciating. The day after my parents had informed me that I was to take a 'sanity break,' my mom came into my room with a big box which she proceeded to fill with anything work related, in and around my desk.

"You can't do this!" I screamed, as she began pulling Post It's from where they were carefully placed in order of tasks I needed to complete. "This is how I run my life, how I've always run my life. You expect me to get through a day without my lists!"

"Most teenagers don't use lists to get through their days, Lala."

"But you and Dad always said it was such a novel idea—you encouraged it!"

"Yes, but I think it's gotten a little out of hand." She let out an exasperated breath as she picked up Monday's notebook and began to read down what I had written. "'Lay out gray pants, white collared shirt with small square pocket, white kitten heels. Eat breakfast: steel cut oatmeal with strawberries and sliced almonds—only add maple syrup if there has been time for a brisk walk. Brush teeth. Copy yesterday's meeting notes about Brazil's location into folders C and F. Shower: don't wash hair, will do tomorrow'—I mean this is kind of intense, Makayla."

"It helps me," I argued. "You understand, I don't have a single second to waste. Every minute of my day is valuable."

She let the notebook close in her hands and stared at me like I was deranged.

"We never should have encouraged you to carry on with this Harvard thing."

"Why would you say that?"

Continuing as though I wasn't there, she whispered to herself, "It was selfish of us to keep you this way . . . this is all my fault."

My gaze hardened, but I chose not to question her further.

When my dad got home that night, he drilled a new lock on the door to the family office. A sorry look on his face, he explained that they couldn't take the chance that I wouldn't get in there and try to work while they were gone. Then he proceeded to say, as he made me turn in my phone and all internet devices, "This is for your own good. Believe me when I say you don't want any more stress in your life. Not if you like things the way they are."

Once more I was left feeling like there was something my parents weren't telling me . . . something possibly terrible. I began to worry the secret was that I was dying.

Without my computer, tablet, phone, or work binders, I was left with absolutely nothing to do except stew on my own frustrations. Every day I sat on the couch by the window, staring out at the road like a dog, wondering if I had some kind of rare disease that would kill me any day now, while waiting for the mail man to bring me any news from Harvard. And every day all that came were catalogues, bills, and junk mail. I wasted time by making origami cranes out of pizza coupon fliers.

I'd called Lucy Armstrong's assistant the day after my interview and tried to get in to see her, but all that I'd received in return was a message from her office stating that she was not allowed to speak to interviewees after the initial interview. There was nothing I could do to undo what I'd done. So far, all this time off was proving to do was cause me to stress out more.

"Good news," my mom said one day, as she walked into the kitchen with an arm full of take-out.

I didn't bother to look up from where I was sulking on a stool, tucked into the kitchen island. "What?" I asked stubbornly from my pile of cranes.

"You and I are going on a girl's trip!"

Her overstated smile stayed frozen on her face as I curled my lip up into an unsavory expression.

"A girl's trip, really?"

She unloaded an armful of magazines and set down her bag before walking over to where I was perched, picking up one of my cranes and inspecting the workmanship. "I think it will be easier for you to relax if we get you out of here. So, the two of us are going to head out—maybe we could even go see the redwoods of California. I think being back in nature could be really good for—"

"Ew. I hate forests."

Her lips twitched and she dropped the crane.

"Well, you don't have a choice in the matter. We are going to leave in a few days, so if I were you, I would start packing."

I immediately began arguing with her, but she stuck a finger in the air and stopped me. "This is non-negotiable, Makayla," she said, before grabbing a magazine from the counter and stalking off upstairs.

I waited a few minutes before following her, planning my argument. When I'd decided I had a convincing testimony, I jumped off the kitchen stool and rolled back my shoulders, marching up the stairs to where I was sure she had plopped on her bed and was knee deep into reading about celebrities. It was how she liked to unwind every day after work.

But as I neared my parents' bedroom door, I could've sworn that I heard her speaking to someone. And as I paused, my hand on the doorframe, I was sure of it. There was another voice in there. Female.

". . . I'm telling you, Naomi, she's coming undone. Has there been any more gibberish?"

"No, but she doesn't even remember using it during her interview. It's like she blacked out."

"I don't know about this. I know we agreed to let her live her own life, but this just feels wrong. She should have a choice."

"I realize this is hard for the two of you, but Philip and I know Lala. She doesn't belong in—"

I'd been resting my hands against the door, pressing my ear into the small crack made between it and the wall, when my feet slipped over one another and I fell into the door—pushing it wide open and performing one hell of a nosedive into the carpet.

A strange popping noise issued from somewhere in the room, and when I looked up my mother was frowning down at me, trying to appear unfazed by the commotion. Was that purple glitter falling onto the carpet?

"What are you doing?" she asked.

"Is there someone in here with you?"

"Does it look like there's someone in here with me? What do you want, Lala?"

I crawled up to my knees and then stood slowly up, scanning the room for signs of someone else's existence. But there was no one in there except for the two of us.

"Never mind," I said.

"Do me a favor and set the table for dinner then, would you. Your father will be home any minute."

"Right," I said, still eyeing the corners of the room suspiciously.

It wasn't until I'd laid out all the silverware and plates for our rotisserie chicken, mashed potatoes, and green beans, that I remembered I'd completely forgotten to plead my case.

$$\mathfrak{H} \quad 4 \quad \mathfrak{H}$$

Luckily for me I hadn't needed to fight my mother on her ludicrous girl's trip idea because it backfired on her the very next day. She came home in a huff, proclaiming that there was a problem down in Kenya with one of our factories. They needed someone out there pronto.

"*Okay!*" I said, jumping off the couch with my new stolen notebook. I'd smuggled it out from one of my hidden storage places I used for emergencies—because you never know when you might think of something you need to write down. I immediately began recording a weekly list of tasks. Unfortunately, what I had written down so far for the following day lacked any substantial amount of motivation:

•Don't shower . . . what's the point.

•Wear purple Sewn Back Together T-shirt and gray shorts.

•Eat breakfast: 1/4 cup Mueslix and—screw it, make pancakes.

•Stare out window and wait for the mail.

"I'll run right upstairs and start packing!" I was already revising the next day's list as I skipped past my mom.

She snagged the back of my shirt as I walked by and pulled

me into to her like I was on a retractable leash. "Whoa, whoa, whoa," she said, pecking the notebook from my hand. "Where did you get this?"

"It was stuck in between some magazines in the end table." I held my hand out for it. "Can I please have it? I need it to pack."

She appeared both amused and flustered as she tore at what was left of my dignity. "Makayla, you are not going to Kenya."

"What do you mean? It's my company."

"It's *our* company, and I'm not going either. I'm sending Rachel, which means I have to put off our trip for a little longer."

"Wait—but—"

"No buts, Makayla. Look, your dad and I aren't doing this to punish you. We are seriously worried about your health, sweetie."

"Ugh, do not call me ridiculous things like sweetie," I said, as I crossed my arms over my chest. "Listen *mother*, you removing me from my position is only pushing me further away from my goals. You might not have the ambition to further your career, but I do, and the company is all I have right now. Until I hear back from Harvard—" I stopped, suddenly aware of the look on my mom's face. Never had I noticed how sharp those dark and pointy eyes of hers could get. "What?" I asked innocently.

"Makayla Wood, don't you ever speak to me in that manner ever again, do you hear me? I am your mother, not your *mother*, and the way this works is we respect one another. You do not run things around here. *You* are still a child."

My face was suddenly on fire as all the blood rushed up into my head. It was the first time my mom had ever scolded me in my entire life, and I had to say, it did not feel awesome. In fact, she might as well have stripped me naked and struck out her finger and laughed. I felt—I felt *insignificant.*

Reaching down deep inside I grabbed for my fighting words and stood up taller as I rolled back my shoulders, and stated defiantly, "After the raccoon roller derby on Thursday I would really like to go the Knight's Club for a fish dinner." She furrowed her eyebrows. Wait, what had I just said? I pointed a finger at her and prepared for a do over. "Because they also have karaoke and Marge the beaver sings "I Will Survive" every night."

"Makayla," my mom said, a worried look washing over her.

What was happening? Had I just said Marge the beaver?

"I think you need to go upstairs and rest," she said, setting down my notebook behind her and laying a hand over my shoulder.

I stared down at her hand for only a second before I gruffly wiped it away. "Don't touch me! I might have Zappyweed infection from galivanting in the forest last night!" I couldn't stop. I could hear the words, but I couldn't stop. I twisted my face, listening to myself fight whatever was happening. "I was hunting Jelly Worms and a Doohicky jumped out and rubbed Zappyweed all over my skin. He thought it was funny, but I didn't think it was funny."

"I know, honey," my mom said, grabbing me by both shoulders and leading me towards the stairs.

"Zappyweeds are known to grow next to the place where Jelly Worms nest though, so I must have been close. I doubt it was a Gummi Bear breeding ground because they hate the water and there's a creek that flows next to the Jelly Worm roost." Oh my god, why wouldn't it stop? Is this what happened during my Harvard interview?

Once we got to my bedroom, my mom gently pushed me inside as I continued to ramble about nonsense. "I can only eat fish on Thursdays because that's when Mr. Groverplain brings in the fish from the neighboring land. The fish here are inedible because they are intellectuals and have families and so we can't eat them."

"I know, baby." She reached through the door and petted my head. "Why don't you lay down and get some rest."

I scratched my shoulder as though it really itched. "Zappyweed."

"I know," she said, retrieving her hand and closing the door, leaving me to stand there in my room, confounded and quite frankly, feeling rather dumb for the first time ever.

Two hours later I sat on my bed, staring out my window. I hadn't ever really noticed how many kids lived in my neighborhood—it's not like I ever had time to get to know any of them. Plus, I'd always preferred the company of adults.

A pair of teenagers about my age came walking up from the other side of the road. One of them was a dark-skinned girl with an emerald strip mixed in with the rest of her curly black hair. She was wearing a red and black kilt with platform army boots and was sipping on a coffee. Her friend was a tall white kid with short brown hair. He was fairly thin and had thick black nerd glasses. He seemed more preppy. As they crossed the street, the boy looked up just in time to catch me staring down at them.

Shit, I cursed in my head, scrunching back down away from the window.

That looked bad, like I was some sort of shut-in freak. Too curious to let it go, I slowly lifted my head back up and attempted to peer back down at them but became instantly mortified when the girl pointed up at me.

Again, I silently cursed myself, ducking low once more.

That was it, I had probably just started a rumor that there was a crazy person living in the Woods' house. I waited two full minutes, counting to one hundred and twenty before lifting my head again. When I did, they were gone.

I wiped at a bead of sweat that had accrued just over my brow line, then jumped from my bed and headed straight to my vanity where I sat down and stared at myself in the mirror.

Very slowly, I repeated, "My name is Makayla Wood." Oh, thank god, it came out right. Just twenty minutes ago I'd held a conversation with myself about last Friday night's gerbil knitting club. Apparently, the hamsters weren't invited and that caused a feud, and now the hamsters were kicking the gerbils out of their Tuesday night book club.

"I am the Co-Founder of Sewn Back Together. I plan to win my first law case by the time I'm twenty-two. If I don't get into Harvard I will reevaluate and graduate from Yale instead." Yale was better anyway, I just wanted to go to Harvard because that's where my parents went.

Feeling better, I turned around and stared at my desk. Perhaps this was a good time to pull out those old applications from the other schools. I hadn't done it before because I was a shoo-in for Harvard, but considering the situation it didn't seem like a terrible idea.

On the other hand, I really shouldn't have been stressing about it; with my background and my father's contacts, I would be able to get in wherever I wanted. Right? I mean, I *should* still be able to get into Harvard. My freak out couldn't have been bad enough to undo all my other accomplishments —surely, they would see that. In any case, I decided it was still smart to have a back-up plan.

Over the next two days I worked on what I could, attempting to get through the few hard copy applications I'd had stored away, but without the use of the internet or my phone it was nearly impossible.

"How about you just let me use the internet while you are home then?" I'd argued with my parents over dinner. "That way you can make sure I'm only using it for school preparations."

But instead of seeing my perfectly reasonable point, my father, rather rudely shoveled the rest of his deli made chicken cordon bleu and bacon wrapped asparagus together onto his fork, and responded with his mouth full. "We've been over this—no."

"But Dad—"

"No Makayla," he'd said, wiping his mouth with his napkin on his way out of the dining room.

Appalled, I looked to my mom, who was slowly chewing a piece of bread and leafing through a clothes magazine that had come for her in the mail. There still hadn't been any traces of a Harvard letter.

"Really?" I said, my hands up on either side of my head. "How much longer do I have to endure this, *Mom*? You two get to work, you get to eat your dinner and head back to your schedules—but I'm supposed to sit here with my hands tucked under my rear end and do what?"

"Relax," she said, her attention occupied by that of a coral sweater. She lifted her red wine and took a sip.

"I'm tired of relaxing!"

Her gaze shifted to mine. "You aren't to go back to work, nor are you to lift a finger in the direction of any other school until you can prove to us that you can chill out. And don't try getting into the neighbor's houses again. I got the strangest phone call from Mrs. Emerson that you tried to smuggle yourself into their library."

"Oh whatever, that woman is totally insane."

All I'd done was ask to use her internet, explaining that ours was down. Which she'd been completely cool with, but then the old bat freaked out because I'd requested a salad, and perhaps a coffee with three packets of stevia and a bit of almond milk—on the side. Totally reasonable. But she wasn't my secretary, she'd said. To which I had pointed out that she could be if she applied herself.

My mother gave me a stern look. "Also, your little outburst the other day was slightly alarming."

"I agree," I said, nodding my head profusely. "Why don't you take me to see someone?"

She set her wine glass down on the table and sat back in her chair. "You want to see someone?"

"I think I should, don't you?"

She didn't say anything right away, instead she seemed to be mulling over whatever was going on in her head. Then she scooted forward in her chair again and began looking through the magazine, dog earring the page with the coral sweater.

"No. I think this is simply a case of you needing to learn to relax."

The anger began to well up in my chest again . . . it was traveling up towards my head . . . I could feel the words getting jumbled inside me. But I refused to let whatever this was get the best of me again, therefore there was only one option: continue to act stubborn.

Without saying another word, I stood, leaned forward, and reached for my mother's wine glass, downing what was left—which was only a sip really. When I was done, I simply smirked at her, daring her to overreact. However, I couldn't gauge her reaction, for it was immediately clouded over from the lighting in the room growing brighter. First around the edges and then illuminating the entire room with a bright yellow light.

I steadied myself, trying with all my might *not* to show any evidence of how I was feeling. But the longer I stood there, the stranger I felt.

My mom pulled away from her magazine and crossed her arms over her chest. "Happy?"

"Very. Can I have more?"

"No. Go to your room. You're grounded."

"Whatever," I said, strolling away. It was somewhat difficult to find the stairs through the crystals that were falling from the ceiling, but the rainbow belt I was holding onto really helped to steady me along the way.

5

The next day I woke up late. The house was almost too quiet when I strolled down the stairs into the kitchen. The first thing I noticed was that the wine had been removed from the counter as well as the fridge, and that the liquor cabinet had been locked for the first time ever.

"God," I muttered. "Ask me to act like a kid, and then I do, and then I get into trouble. This is the stupidest . . ." I grumbled all the way through making eggs, pancakes, and hash browns.

After I'd eaten my very large breakfast, I meandered through the house a few times, made three more cranes, and stared at the wall for about an hour, until I finally wound my way back into one of our rooms that had a fairly full library. It had occurred to me earlier in the week that I should perhaps pick up a reading habit, but it wasn't in my nature to read anything that wasn't in need of a highlighter. In fact, as I rummaged through the various titles taking up space on the shelves, I realized I couldn't remember the last time I'd read for pleasure.

I ran my fingers over the spines, absorbing the titles—

fishing for one that could keep my mind at bay. *Nymphology, Sprites of the Forest, Mythology for the Mundane, Learning to Live with Magic* . . . what was all this? I counted thirteen titles about magic and myth. That was weird. Naomi and Philip Wood were the last two people on earth I would have suspected of owning these sorts of books.

Not curious in the very least about educating myself on imaginary creatures, I walked a few paces to the right and found a gold mine of classics. Settling on *Great Expectations*, because the title defined me as an individual, I took the book and walked outside so that I could watch for the mail as I read.

I'd barely gotten seated on the front stoop, however, when I heard a boy's voice say, "Hey, isn't that our little creeper from the other day?"

Immediately I looked up to find the same girl and boy who I had been spying on a few days ago standing in front of my house.

"Oh my goodness, that *is* her," the girl said. She elbowed him in the ribs. "I told you she wasn't a damn ghost."

Ghost? Oh god, that was worse than recluse.

My face burned from embarrassment. I wanted nothing more than to disappear, or go inside, because to be honest I'd never really figured out how to interact with humans my own age—but they were already crossing my parent's beautifully manicured yard in order to get to me.

"Hey, what's your name?" the girl asked, sipping on a bright green straw, the same color as the strip in her hair.

"I-It's Makayla."

"You new here or something? I didn't think there was anyone else our age living on this block."

"You know what Cee-Cee, I bet she a privy. Look what she reading," the boy said flamboyantly.

I looked down at the book in my hands. "What's a privy?"

"Private school, honey," the girl said.

"Oh, yeah. I, uh, I did go there, but I finished a long time ago."

"So, you one of them smart kids who's already started college?" she asked.

"Oh, well, I sort of already finished my first degree. Now I'm applying for another college."

"Shit girl, you already finished college! How old are you?" she exclaimed.

"She can't be more than fifteen, look at that complexion. Flawless."

"I'm, um, I'm seventeen actually."

"Wheweee! You *are* smart!" the girl said. "We gonna sit down with you." She looked up at her guy friend and nodded at him. "You mind if we sit down with you, honey?"

"Well, I—I was just going to—" but there was no point, they'd already made themselves comfortable. Was this normal? Was this how the younger population socialized—they just invaded each other's privacy?

"I'm Jeremy," the skinny boy said, scrunching up his nose and sticking his hand out from where he'd sat cross-legged on the concrete before the stoop.

Shaking his hand, a much less formal shake than I was used to, I said, "Nice to meet you."

"Cee-Cee," the girl said, digging her straw into what appeared to be one of those coffee milkshakes. "And I don't shake hands."

I raised my eyebrows.

"My parents named me Anastacia, isn't that awful?" She asked the question as though she assumed I would answer yes. My immediate reaction to this person was that she was someone who tested others before letting them in, which was interesting seeing as she'd crashed *my* party *for one*.

"Actually," I replied, "I think it's really nice. In fact, yes, I like it." I looked up at the sky, thinking how it would sound in court. "What's your last name?"

"Montgomery."

I stared down at her in disbelief. "Anastacia Montgomery is your name? Why that is—that is fabulous. I would kill for a name like that."

The boy named Jeremy started laughing. "This girl's a trip, Cee-Cee."

"Yeah, she all right." I guess I'd passed the initial test. "Hey, so you wanna be our friend? We was just gonna go to my house and watch some Netflix."

These guys moved fast. I couldn't remember ever being asked to be someone's friend.

I immediately reached out for my excuse. "I really need to wait for the mail. I'm expecting something important."

"Oh yeah, what's that?" Jeremy asked.

"A letter."

They really were intrusive.

"From who?" they asked at the same time.

"Harvard."

At that Cee-Cee exploded. "Shit! This is girl is cray! Smart *and* pretty!"

"Damn right she is. Hey, which way you swing?"

I leaned my head forward. "Which way do I what?"

"Swing girl," Cee-Cee clarified. "Like what kind you like?" Reading my super confused expression, she rolled her eyes. "I like boys. Jeremy here likes boys and sometimes girls—"

"But mostly boys," he said with a grin.

"So, what do you like?" she repeated.

"Oh! Well, I guess I've never really thought about it. Um, boys, I guess. But I mean, girls are pretty . . . too. I think maybe I don't see gender as much as the person, but I haven't ever really—"

Jeremy and Cee-Cee shared a look and then repeated at the same time, "Pan."

I frowned, unsure of what to even say. I'd never ever even thought about it that much. Romance wasn't something that got one into Harvard.

Placating my thoughts, Jeremy reached up with his long arm and felt a piece of my hair between his fingers. "Girl, how you get your hair that color?"

"It's natural," I retorted, feeling my personal space bubble pop.

"Nuh-uh, this color red? You serious?" he asked in disbelief.

"She's lying," Cee-Cee volunteered for me. "My cousin did that color. You have to buy it to get it all sparkly like that."

"Uh no, I'm not lying," I retorted, offended. "It's always been like this." And I'd always been proud of my red sparkly hair. No one else had it.

"Anyway," Cee-Cee said, sounding bored, "you're gonna come with us. You can check the mail later, smart girl." Then she stood up and so did Jeremy, and before I had a chance to argue, they each took one of my arms and lifted me up. "You like *Grey's Anatomy*? Cause we just started season one."

"What—what's that?"

They looked at each other.

"Oh lord," Cee-Cee sighed. "Well Jeremy, looks like we gotta start over. She gotta see it from the beginning."

As I was dragged over my parent's lawn back onto the sidewalk, I realized something. "Wait, so if you have Netflix, then you must have the internet."

"Uh, duh," Cee-Cee said. "We ain't livin' in the stone ages. And are you really telling me you don't got it in that big ol' house of yours?"

"No, we do . . . it's just . . . well I'm sort of grounded and my parents took everything away."

"Ooooooo," Jeremy cooed. "It appears that we caught ourselves a rebel, Miss Anastacia Montgomery."

"I believe we did, Mr. Jeremy Love."

My ears perked up. "Jeremy Love?"

"Yes. It's great, huh," he said.

"It is. You two have wonderful names."

Two hours later the three of us were camped out in Cee-Cee's basement. I had Cee-Cee's laptop in front of me, Jeremy's phone in one hand, and an iPad in the other; but I hadn't gotten any further than typing Yale into the laptop because of that stupid show.

"I just love the music they're playing," I said, my voice trance-like, following the characters of Seattle Grace's new surgical intern team.

"I know, right," Jeremy said, a piece of licorice sticking out of his mouth. "You want one," he asked, offering me a Twizzler.

"Oh, no thank you. I try not to eat candy."

At that, both Cee-Cee and Jeremy looked at me as though I'd just said something incriminating. Then it occurred to me, if I was going to splurge...

"Hey, do you guys know where we could get some wine?"

Unsure of how it had happened, the day had passed us by, and so had the entire first season of *Grey's Anatomy*. As I laid there, my head on Jeremy Love's leg—my new best friend—and my legs on Anastacia Montgomery's stomach—my other new best friend, I lost my breath as—spoiler alert! Meredith Grey got her heart slandered as McDreamy's wife walked up to the two of them and made her presence known. The more I drank, the more I felt like I was actually inside of the show—that I *was* Meredith Grey. My heart ached so badly.

"It's not fair!" I bellowed, sitting up as the credits rolled, leaning over and throwing back the rest of the wine that was in my glass.

Cee-Cee had stolen two bottles from her dad's stash. Her and Jeremy had polished off a bottle together, but I'd only had about a glass and a half. Still, though, the whole room was sparkling like there were diamonds everywhere. If I wasn't so heartbroken from finding out McDreamy had a wife, I would have felt invincible.

A grasshopper landed on my stomach and stared up at me. I swatted away the insect—ignoring it as it turned into a green bunny and flew away—then grabbed a piece of strawberry licorice from the table and stuffed it into my mouth.

"She has, like, no one—and then she met *him*—and now they can't even be together. Do you have any black licorice? Man, that sounds really good right now."

"He gotta pick Meredith over that wife of his. No offense, but you can't trust no red head," Cee-Cee said.

"Oh shoot, Cee-Cee, she's ruined your name," Jeremy said half-heartedly. Then repeating the name of Meredith's new adversary, he said, "Addison Montgomery."

A look of horror washed over the three of us as we took in that terrible truth, but we were quickly interrupted by the sound of footsteps thumping down into our lair.

"Is that your *dad*?" Jeremy asked, clearly in shock. "He never comes down here."

I was too lost in my own world to notice the panic setting in to my two new best friends. I was, in fact, still lifting magazines and candy wrappers looking for anything that tasted of dark licorice.

Cee-Cee cursed, grabbing the wine bottles from the coffee table. Seeing that mine was still practically full before stuffing them under a cover, she whispered, "Girl, you a light weight."

"Anastacia?" A deep man's voice bellowed from up the stairs.

"Oh, hey pops. Whatcha doin?" she yelled back; her voice shaky.

As soon as *I* saw Mr. Montgomery, though, I felt something tingle inside me. He was a tall, muscular man, wearing a striking grey suit. He had a beaver's tail, but that was all right.

Before my friends could snag me and pull me down, I was up and walking towards him. Paying no attention to the off-putting expression on the man's face, I swatted at a swarm of flying lady bugs and pushed the rainbow curtains out of my way and held out my hand. I just knew it, that he would have to have a firm, professional handshake. That was all I really needed to feel whole again.

"Mr. Montgomery?" I asked, looking up at him as though he was the president of Harvard.

"Yes?"

"It's so nice to meet you. I'm Makayla Wood."

Mr. Montgomery looked down at my hand and then over at his daughter, the corners of his mouth turning even further down. "Anastacia, is this girl drunk? Have you all been drinking?"

"Um . . . well, sir—"

He didn't let her finish, instead he pointed at me. "This girl's parents are upstairs right now. Most worried folks I've ever seen in my life—they've been looking for her for hours." Grabbing my hand, he directed me up the stairs. "I'll be having words with you later," he said to his daughter. "Jeremy, time for you to go home."

Oblivious to the fact that we were all in trouble, I stumbled up the steps to the landing—maybe this was where they kept the good candy. I laughed at myself as I took a bit of a trip, letting Cee-Cee's dad steady me, and I looked up to find my own dad with a scowl knitted into his face, and my mother nervously biting down over her fist.

"Oh my god, there you are," she said, lunging past the

kitchen island to get to me, immediately pulling me into her arms. My dad simply leaned down and sniffed me.

"Makayla Wood, have you been drinking?"

"I do apologize," Cee-Cee's dad was saying. "I had no idea my child was into this sort of thing. Since my wife passed a few years back I haven't been able to watch over Cee-Cee as much as I want to, but I assure you there will be consequences."

"Oh no, Rick." My dad shook his head. "This is not your fault. We've been having some problems with Makayla lately."

"Yeah, they sure have," I snickered.

I had forgotten all about why my cheeks were stained with tears, and now I was simply concerned with how bright and shiny everything was in this room.

"Wow," I said, breaking away from my mom and reaching for the stainless-steel doors of the refrigerator. "This is *so* pretty." I couldn't help it, I had to push the water dispenser. "Oh my god, look at that!" I pointed as a pink waterfall began to form, rocks and grass growing around it. "Whoa."

My head jerked to the side as my mom yanked me back towards her. "This is not funny! We have been worried sick about you!"

I snorted under my breath. "You told me to relax, so I did." I couldn't help but think that my voice sounded very far away. I looked up at Rick and snickered as I asked, "Do you think I could take home some of that fine Peanut Gringo you've all been serving tonight?"

"Makayla!" my dad shouted.

"What?"

"I am so sorry—my apologies, Rick," my dad said, grabbing my arm and pulling me towards the front door.

"It's not your fault, Philip. See you around," he said, as my parents dragged me outside.

I woke up in my bed later that night, fully dressed and

with a pounding headache. It was only then that I realized what I'd done.

"Oh my god, no!" I exclaimed, horrified, jumping out of my bed and running to my bedroom door. When I opened it, I could hear the muffled sound of my parents talking downstairs.

Moving very slowly so that the floorboards didn't creak, I rounded the corner and came halfway down the stairs so I could better hear what they were saying.

"I told you this was going to happen," my mom said with a sharp tongue. "That's why I wanted to say something to her after that interview. You can't tell me you didn't think something terrible had happened when we came home to find her missing tonight."

Silence.

My mom continued. "They said if she was going to transition there would most likely be signs first. Maude told me the gibberish was just the beginning. I mean we can't deny it, she's subconsciously remembering where she's from."

What? Where was I from? *Transition?*

"Naomi, this is something that has to be dealt with very cautiously. My god, would you believe somebody if they told you what we were going to tell her?"

More silence.

"No."

"Here's the problem, you've been around them all of your life, but to someone like me or her, it's not rational."

"It *is* rational to *them*, Philip, and it is something that is going to happen if we don't get her to calm down."

It was quiet for a long time, and then my dad said, "I just can't believe she got into Mr. Montgomery's wine."

"She took a swig from my glass last night."

"What?"

"It was just a small bit; I didn't think anything of it."

"Isn't that the one thing they said to keep her away from—"

"Philip! We've had open wine bottles out the entire time she's lived here! She's never made the slightest move toward the stuff."

"Well, if our kid develops a drinking problem this is on you!"

"Me?"

Okay, this was weird. I couldn't decide whether to stay where I was or interrupt them and ask what in the world they were talking about. Finally, I decided to head down, but as I grew closer to them it occurred to me that maybe I was supposed to stay away from alcohol because my real parents were alcoholics. I came to a halt. I didn't know if that was true, but it would destroy me if it was. I'd already created little portfolios with what I decided my birth parents would be like. Simpletons, but nice. They'd just had me too early, that was all. I didn't want to know otherwise.

I quickly changed my mind and retracted my steps back into my room, where I decided to throw a pillow over my head and wait until morning to feel my parents' wrath. I wasn't worried about getting in that much trouble, I mean I was the perfect daughter, really. Smart, important, and this was the first time I'd ever done anything super wrong. And honestly, what was the big deal? I'd had a few swigs of wine—barely more than a glass. Most people wouldn't even have had a reaction to that. I did, though, for whatever reason.

Whatever . . . I would worry about all that in the morning. I flipped over and stared at my ceiling, and allowed my thoughts to wander in the direction of what would happen with Meredith and McDreamy in season two of *Grey's Anatomy*.

As I drifted to sleep, I speculated for the first time what it would feel like to fall in love. Before watching that show the prospect of ever comprehending the emotion seemed like a distant, unknown land. But for whatever reason, that night I'd felt like I was *inside* that television; and the emotions of Meredith's character, as fictional as she was, were real inside me. I still felt a little forlorn. Was this what love was like? Achingly, frustratingly painful . . . yet somehow euphoric at the same time.

I couldn't help but feel, as I closed my thoughts from the world until the next morning, that all this work I had been doing all my life had kept me away from one of the most substantial feelings there was, ever, in existence. I couldn't decide what was more frightening: feeling the way Meredith had because of love, or never feeling that way *ever* because love never found me. It wasn't a question that I could write down and outline. It was undefinable, unpredictable, and that alone set my heart on fire. Unbeknownst to me, this was just the first of many unexplored paths I was destined to find myself walking down.

6

The next morning all my romantic notions of what love might taste like were forgotten, and I was once more a prisoner in the house of Wood. The idea I had conjured up that my parents would let me off the hook because I was a stellar child was nothing more than a fantasy; instead they did the opposite—they hooked up a nanny cam. Not literally, but they said they'd be watching me over the security cameras from their tablets while at work. It was just the most humiliating thing that could happen to someone like me.

"Sorry about this, Lala, but you gave us no choice," my mom said on her way out the door.

"Don't call me that! And oh my god, I won't ever do it again!"

She bit down on the inside of her cheek while raising her left brow. She didn't believe me.

An hour later, I'd finally calmed down and was starting to begin my rounds of walking senselessly around the house, when our house phone rang.

"Hello?"

"Girl, you straight up *crazy*. I got in so much shit cause a you. My dad seriously thought you were on drugs."

"Cee-Cee?"

She laughed. "Yeah girl, your number's on our fridge. Neighborhood connection or some shit like that. Anyway, you coming over to watch the second season today? Jeremy's on his way."

"My parents have me on lock down. I'm sorry, I want to." I really did want to. I liked Jeremy and Cee-Cee. It felt surprisingly nice to be around kids my own age, and we'd clicked so well.

"Aw, that's all right. Well call me when you get out of jail. We'll wait to watch the second season till you can come over."

"Really? You'd, like, wait for me?"

"Course we would. All right, we gonna go get some coffee. My head hurts from that nasty wine."

"Yeah, it was gross," I lied. I toyed with the idea of having her bring me some more, but quickly decided against it. "I'll call you later, I guess."

"Later," she said, hanging up.

An hour later the doorbell rang, and when I answered it there was no one there; but when I looked down there was an iced coffee drink with whip cream on top and a note scribbled on the cup in black marker: *To Makayla Wood, future lawyer extraordinaire. From your new besties, Anastacia Montgomery and Jeremy Love. Don't worry, if they don't let you out soon, we will bust you out!*

I smiled as I bent down and picked it up. I'd only known those two for a day, but it felt like we'd been friends for most of our lives. People usually liked me because they were paid to —employees, assistants—it was kind of nice to have Jeremy and Cee-Cee like me just because.

My mom didn't get home as early as she'd wanted, and because I was mad at them and knew they were watching me, I pulled out all my secret notepads and sorted them out on the kitchen table. As I started each new day of the week, color coded of course, I stared up at the camera hiding inside one of the paintings.

"Let's see," I said very loudly. "Tuesday. Hm, well, normally I would list Fabric Meeting at 10 because we always have a fabric meeting at 10 but seeing as I'm a prisoner in my own home, away from the business I helped *create*—I guess I'll be ironing my socks at ten on Tuesday."

By three o'clock that afternoon I had my entire boring week mapped out, and by the time my mom got home at five, I had managed to clean my room three times over. I'd found three extra notebooks in the process.

"Makayla!" my mother yelled as she entered the house. "Where are you?"

"Up here!" I shouted back. "Still doing nothing!"

"Can you come down here, please!"

Setting down a sketch I'd been working on for a new backpack line for Sewn Back Together (I'd been leafing through my mother's fashion magazines and had gotten some ideas for new designs), I scoffed as I marched out of my room and down the stairs. When I got down there, I was displeased to find both my parents standing side by side, that was until I noticed a very thin letter in my father's hands. Thin as a recently sharpened filet knife.

"What is that?" I asked.

He looked at my mother and whispered, "I really don't think this is a good idea right now."

"Don't you think we've kept enough from her already," she stammered back. Then, returning her attention to me, she said, "Baby, I think you should sit down."

"What *is* that?"

She looked at my dad and took a deep breath. I squinted so I could see the Harvard emblem staring back at me from the corner of the envelope. Suddenly I couldn't wait another second.

With my heart pounding, I lunged for the letter and snagged it from my dad, escaping with it into the living room. I stood in the middle of the floor, tearing it open as though I was starved and it was the last food ration left on Earth. All the while my mom was holding my dad back from following me and yanking it from my hands, as if she already knew I would bark and snap like a rabid beast if anyone dared come near me.

"There's still a chance," I said, pieces of envelope falling to the floor. "There's still a chance that they took me. I'm a child prodigy. I mean, I was practically born from the Harvard mold." I was panting by the time I got the letter out, and my hands were shaking as I held it in front of me as though I'd just located the last golden ticket. But it was, it was the last golden ticket. There would never be another Harvard . . . ever. Sure, I'd said Yale was better, but I still wanted Harvard more than anything in the world.

As soon as I got past, "Dear Ms. Wood," though, I knew that this was not a letter of acceptance, but a death sentence.

"Honey, Lala, what's it say?"

My mom's voice was but a blur in the background as I stood still as stone.

Dear Ms. Wood,

We regret to inform you that after careful consideration we have had to deny you admittance to Harvard. We were very impressed by your tremendous accomplishments

achieved at such a young age, but we must admit that after your interview we were a bit frazzled.

As I am sure you are aware, the ability to work well under pressure is a vital strategy that we expect our students to adhere by. We are afraid that after your strange interview with Ms.

Armstrong we cannot possibly allow you into our program. Please do understand this is nothing against you, your collection of knitted snail hats, or your ability to relay the alphabet forwards and backwards in five different languages. We are simply thinking of your mental health.

Here is to hoping you are well,
Dean of Admissions,
Becky Rutabaga

"That name is just the worst," I whispered.

My fate had just been handed to me by a vegetable that half of the human race didn't even know about.

The house was too quiet. I could hear my dad breathing, my mom silently stepping forward and then back again. They already knew the answer, I mean—they knew as soon as my dad received that phone call from Lucy Armstrong—they knew my dreams were shattered.

"Lala?"

My cheeks burning, my hands shaking, I turned my head very slowly towards my mother. Mental health. They had actually mentioned my mental health in my Harvard letter. No, no it couldn't be real. I'd worked far too hard all my life to ensure that the letter I received from this particular esteemed institution was an acceptance letter. Every morning as soon as I opened my eyes, ever since I was a child, I'd imagined checking off 'Get into Harvard,' into one of my notebooks. No, this couldn't be happening.

"Please say something," my dad said.

I just stared at him, and as I did, I felt something snap.

"It's a bit turbulent in here, isn't it?" I said in a British accent.

My mom's face fell and my father's hand met his forehead. It was happening again.

Too mentally exhausted to fight it off, I simply followed the static humming in my ears. Looking around at the ceiling and surrounding walls, I continued to vomit out nonsense. "I think we have cactuses growing in the walls again."

"Lala—"

And then I felt it. A fist inside my chest, reaching over the madness. It grabbed at my heart and yanked down, pulling away all the fluff. My insides wretched, and I screamed at my mother, "QUIT CALLING ME THAT! MY NAME IS MAKAYLA!!!!!!"

And then something very awful happened. Worse, even, than the hurt look on my mom's face. The room started shaking, or at least it appeared to be.

The letter in my hand dropped to the ground, and as I stared from the walls back to my parents' faces, I realized all the sound had turned off, except for the buzzing going on inside my head. I could see their mouths moving, but I couldn't hear anything they were saying.

"What's going on?" I said, hearing my own muffled voice echo against the buzz.

I closed my eyes and reached my hands over my ears, trying to make everything stop, but the sensation of shaking just grew more violent. When I reopened my eyes, I saw my parents backing away, and a strange whiteness filling in around me. Not like a cloud, but like strips of white light circling my body.

"Mom? Dad?" But they weren't helping me. They looked —they looked afraid.

I stretched my arms out to the sides, feeling the white strips of light; they were thick, electric. I lifted my gaze to meet that of my parents. "What's happening to me?"

And then I was pulled against the wall.

All I heard for the next five minutes was wood smashing and glass shattering. Family pictures, the giant green and yellow antique fan my mother and I had brought back from Japan, a tower of CDs, the slender bookshelf that held a bunch of books none of us ever read, the coffee table—all of it smashed, broken, torn to pieces as my back and shoulders hit against every surface, including the ceiling and floor for what felt like eternity.

There was shouting from my parents, my dad telling my mom to get away while reaching for me—but I was like some sort of bouncy ball, springing violently from one surface to the other.

"HEL—P—ME! WH—AT'S—HAP—PEN—ING—TO—-ME!" I shouted as I bounced from floor to wall.

"It's okay, baby!" my mom yelled from where she stood in the other room, her hands cupped around her mouth. "It's going to be okay!"

"Makayla! Stop, drop, and roll!" My father was cranking his arm through the air in a circular motion, hollering at me as though he were my coach.

"THA—T'S—FIRE—STU—PID!" I yelled back—the breath knocked out of me as my back came down against the floor.

As my chest tried like mad to rise against the invisible set of bricks lying on top of it, I glimpsed a chair that had fallen on its side. Before I was pulled back up only to be smashed into the corner again, I grabbed for the edge of it and held on with all my might. And even though something was pulling me backwards, like a pair of giant hands attached to my shoulder blades, I crammed my eyes shut and started counting backwards from ten, visualizing a paper bag attached to my mouth.

". . . 3,2,1," I said, reopening my eyes to find that I was still clinging to the chair.

The whirlwind had stopped.

Slowly, confused and terrified, I gingerly let go of the chair and looked up at my parents. The look on their faces was unexplainable.

I took a moment to catch my breath, then uttered, "I will ask you one more time, what is going on?"

"Baby," my mom said, treading carefully as she took very small steps back into the now destroyed family room. "Now, I don't want you to freak out—"

"Makayla," my dad said, standing still, his hands out in front of him as though he were blocking my wrath.

I touched my forehead and brought it down to see blood trickling down from my fingertips.

"God, what is with you guys," I said, holding out my arm for balance while trying to push up to standing. "I mean, shouldn't you be, like, calling 911—" And that's when I stopped, but not because of the horrific looks coloring their faces. I stopped because coming to my feet wasn't as easy as it should've been; something was pulling me backwards, affecting my balance.

I fell back down onto my knees, and something soft fell over my shoulders. It was then that I felt something inside shift. An 'aha' moment, if you will.

Scooping up what looked like an enormous sheer, sparkling blue and purple butterfly wing from where it was draped over my shoulder and onto the ground, I stared from my mother to my father.

"Okay, explain."

My mom, looking like a child who had just soiled her pants, mumbled quietly under breath, "I'll go make the mud cakes."

❧ 7 ❧

Once again, we found ourselves sitting around the dining room table, our hands crossed carefully over the wooden surface. The house smelled of burnt mud batter and my *wings* were draped behind me, falling off the sides of the chair.

I had four wings, all sprouting from the same part of my back. Two on top and two on bottom. As for the mud cakes, as my mother topped the disgusting earth pastries with moss as though it was frosting, I was told they were to be used as a bribe. Evidently in order to get into the world I was from—*the world I was from*—they had to bribe Mort, the gnome who guarded our mailbox. This very unclear explanation had only left me with more questions, that of which my parents were trying to give me.

"I'm a faery," I repeated for what must have been the twentieth time.

My parents nodded solemnly.

"My biological mom and dad are also faeries."

"Yes," said my dad. "Great people, uh, strange, but very nice. In fact, Tanker and I went to a Steeler's game just last—"

"Stop." I brought my hands up to cover my face. "Please quit saying their names."

It was just awful . . . Tanker and Maude. And if that wasn't bad enough, their last name was Abberwockey.

Apparently, my parents were on really good terms with the Abberwockeys. They went to see them at least once a year and occasionally met up with them in our world.

"How do you get away with going out with them in public?" I asked, staring over my shoulder at one of my wings.

"They can make people see what they want them to see," my mom said quietly.

"So, they can hide their wings?"

"Yes."

"They are wonderful people, baby," my mom was saying. "They never wanted to leave you—" she paused, her face growing redder by the second as she wiped a tear from the corner of her eye. "They were scared, and it was with the heaviest of hearts that they explained they had to give you up —send you to live someplace safe—because it was dangerous for you to be in Garlandia any longer."

I bit the inside of my cheek to keep from scowling. Garlandia. I was from a place called freaking Garlandia.

As my mom began losing the battle of fighting off her emotions, I grew rather annoyed. Why was *she* crying? I was the one who had just found out that my entire life was a lie.

"Why was it dangerous?" I asked curtly. "Was there a dark wizard out to get me or something?"

"Makayla, stop it," my dad scolded, reaching over and taking my mom's hand.

"What? Until about an hour ago faeries didn't exist, so excuse me for asking."

"We shouldn't have kept her so hidden from the truth," my mother mumbled.

"You guys still haven't answered my question. Why did my birth parents bring me here?"

My father took a deep breath. "You are what is called an Erwain faery." He ignored my eye roll. "It is an ancient race of fey, and one that is dwindling off. You were the first Erwain faery born in two hundred years. We think, as do Maude and Tanker, that someone was after you because of this rarity."

"What? That doesn't make any sense. And explain to me how if I was the only one of my kind born in two hundred years, how I would have parents that were even alive to give birth to me?"

"Your kind ages differently," said my mom. "You age quickly through your adolescence, much like a human, then you slow down. You will live a very long life, sweetie."

"And when you were a baby," my dad continued, "someone or something came after you and tried to cut off your wings."

"What? That is just—you know what—whatever."

"This is serious, Makayla." my dad warned. "This is your life. When Tanker and Maude found you after the incident, all they saw was a shadow as it jumped from your window. To this day nobody knows who it was."

"So how do they know this person, place, or thing was after my wings then, if they didn't know they were there till after they had escaped."

"You wouldn't have hidden your wings if they weren't in trouble," my dad said.

It was very hard to believe, just then, that my dad was a Harvard graduate—that he was a Washington D.C. lawyer. If it wasn't for the atrocities hanging down from my shoulder blades, I would have been very disappointed in him.

Meanwhile, my mother was off in her own world, rambling on. "You had the funniest little look on your face, one that you were still wearing when they showed up here.

They believe you used magic to protect your wings from whoever it was who was trying to steal them. They couldn't break the spell, though, and for better or worse they believed it was just as well. It was safer for your wings to be hidden."

"You're telling me I used magic when I was just a little baby?"

"Yes," my parents said at the same time.

"I can use magic?"

"Yes, you are a faery," my father answered earnestly.

"O—kay," I said. "And this is all, like, judicious to you guys?"

"We've had plenty of time to digest it, Lala," my mom said.

I opened my mouth to yell at her for calling me that, but quickly decided the childish nickname was the least of my problems.

"So how come my wings have never come out before? How—how have I not ever been able to cast a spell, or whatever?"

My parents looked at each other and my mother sighed. "Maude and Tanker explained to us that the spell you cast when your wings went away was most likely a defensive act of magic, one that was instinctive, but seeing as you were just a baby you wouldn't know how to reverse it until you were shown, or until it came back to you on its own." She paused. "Since they'd decided it was too dangerous to keep you in Garlandia they thought it best to leave it alone. To let you grow up as a human until you were old enough to learn how to defend yourself; but when that moment came, they couldn't bear to take you back. The three of us had already bonded, and you were so happy. You had goals and dreams." She looked like she was going to cry again. "We all decided it was best to leave things as they were, and when the time came, we would deal with it then."

"Wait." I clenched my fists over the table. "You are telling me these people not only left me in the hands of strangers, but that they decided it was best to leave me ignorant? That all of you thought that that was the best solution."

"They weren't really strangers," my mom said, sniffing and wiping her left eye with one of her knuckles.

I glared at her.

"I've known Maude all my life. I wandered into Garlandia when I was a little girl."

"Um, how?" I asked, throwing my hands to the sides.

"It's not uncommon for small children to see between the worlds. I was simply talking to a tree, running my hand over its trunk, and when I turned around, I was staring at Maude and Tanker's house. She found me and took me home, but I made her promise to find me again."

"Let me guess," I said rather rudely, "the two of you became the best of friends."

"Yes," my mom said, pursing her lips together.

"This is why you've been encouraging me to relax, is it? Because you knew if I was pushed to my emotional breaking point, I would come unhinged and turn back into a faery."

"You've always been a faery," my dad corrected. "Your wings just haven't been attached."

"Right . . . so what were you going to do if I never freaked out and found them again. Just wait until I was fifty years old and still looked like a teenager? Or if I, I don't know, met someone and actually fell in love and had a child, and that child was born with butterfly wings—would you have told me then?" I was starting to feel a little crazy, like I wanted to stick my fist through the wall, crazy.

"Take it down a notch, Makayla," my dad said.

I visibly fumed in his direction.

"Look," he continued, "if you want to blame someone, then blame me, all right. Your mother—mothers—thought we should tell you a long time ago. It was I who convinced everyone that you wouldn't be able to handle the truth about who you really were and where you came from."

"That's just great. Lovely of you to make such life altering decisions for me," I scoffed, shaking my head.

Suddenly I realized I didn't want to handle any of this anymore. I would rather deal with what was hanging off my backside later. Verbalizing my frustrations, I stood up and pushed away from the table. "I can't do this right now. I just— you know what, I'm going to go work on my college applications."

"Makayla," my dad said, looking thoroughly exhausted. "You can't—"

But I had heard enough. This was not a world I wanted to belong to. I was Makayla Wood, entrepreneur, child prodigy, and someday the best damn lawyer to arrive. Not Makayla Abberwockey from Garlandia. That was the most ridiculous thing I had ever heard. No—it—it wasn't possible.

Shielding my ears from my parents' protests that I sit back down, I prepared to march off to my room, but unfortunately I didn't make it more than a step or two before my wings started fluttering, lifting me off the ground so that I was levitating over their heads. I began to panic, shouting out, "Help me! Make it stop!"

Immediately they stood, my dad grabbing my legs and trying to steady me, but my wings were beating harder, causing a great deal of wind in the small room—it was like these wings had a life of their own. Grabbing for the swinging chandelier, I desperately tried to keep from flying away.

"You need to calm down, Lala!" my mom was shouting over the ruckus. "Count to ten, baby!"

"Get the bag!" my dad yelled, now holding my legs, trying with all his might to pull me down.

My mom disappeared and my wings began beating more

violently—I felt like I was about to shoot across the room and through the wall. Continuing to scream for help, my mom returned with a brown paper bag and handed it to my dad who then held it up for me.

With no other options, I accepted the bag and put it up to my mouth, hyperventilating. After another minute or two, my breath slowed down and so did the beating of my wings. Finally, my feet touched the ground again.

Once they had me sitting back in my chair, my mother's hand grasping my own, she said to my dad, "I don't think we can wait any longer. Tanker and Maude need to know about this, and we can't risk anyone seeing her in this condition. Only they can help her right now."

Just the idea of meeting my birth parents made my stomach flip, and not in an excited way. I had been fine with never meeting them when I thought they were normal people.

I buried my head in my arms, and when I came up, both red-faced and fighting another bout of anxiety, I said, "Can't you just ask them to write down a spell for me to reverse this? I don't want to meet them . . . I don't want to be a faery."

My parents exchanged a look. My mom maintained the same guilty look she'd had since this debacle began, while my dad appeared to be seriously contemplating my request. Even though he seemed to have accepted all this, I could tell he wished maybe as much as I did, that he had never known any of this fantasy crap to be real.

"Seriously, this is *my* life. I'm less than a year away from being able to make my own decisions—"

"But that is here, not there," my mom said very seriously.

"Wait—what?" A shadow moved across my chest.

"Garlandia has its own laws, baby. The moment you exploded—"

"The moment I what?"

My dad was rubbing his temples with the pads of his fingers. "When your wings returned to you."

"Yes," my mom said, "the moment that happened, your name would've registered back on the list under the Erwain population. We have no choice; we must take you back." Seeing the look of horror wash over my face, she continued quickly, "But that doesn't mean you have to stay. Maude has told me that there are some fey who live primarily in our world —you may just have to return every now and again. I've never been very clear on the rules."

There was a burning in my chest unlike any sensation I'd ever had. "*You have never been very clear on the rules?* You were raising an illegal faery in your house for seventeen years and you weren't very clear on the rules? Seriously!" I stared up at the chandelier and screamed inside, so loud in fact that I imagined pulling down the crystal hanging and smashing it onto the table. And then it came crashing down.

"Makayla Wood! No magic in the house!" my father screamed at me.

My mom and dad had backed away from the table, but I was just sitting there, staring at what I'd done. Then, in my typical teenage angst I just looked at them. "Yeah, okay, like I even know how I did that. Maybe if you'd been clearer on what kind of creature you had living with you—"

"Go to your room!"

"Philip, she can't. She doesn't know how to control her wings yet," my mom said quietly.

"Oh yes, right." He grasped his chin with his hand, staring around the room at the shattered crystals lying on the table and floor. "Well, this isn't very safe."

Trying to sound practical even under the bizarre circumstances, my mom said in a level voice, "Why don't you clean this up, and I will take her."

"Hang on," I said, formulating a desperate plan. "You said

this Garlandia place would only know I was alive if my wings had exploded, or whatever."

"Yes," my mom said. "The way Tanker and Maude explained it to us was that whatever spell you'd conjured totally wiped your wings away . . . like you'd tucked them into a space that nobody would ever find, except for you." She paused. "Anyway, it's your wings they can track. Now that they've returned, you'll be on their radar."

"So, I could do it again?"

My mom looked at my dad, who raised his eyebrows. I could tell that at least *he* was thinking it wasn't a bad idea.

"Well, perhaps," she said after a moment's deliberation. "But this is who you are, and it doesn't mean—"

"No, it's not. You said it yourselves, even my birth parents thought it was best to leave me here once *whatever was after me*"— I rolled my eyes— "was gone. You all decided I was happier this way, and guess what, you were right. Now, I'd really like you to take me to this Garlandia place, but only because I want to know how to return these wings to wherever they've been hiding all these years."

I waited, watching as they mulled over my words. Finally, my mom said, "Okay, you have a point, but remember this: you will forever be our child, but in Garlandia you are Tanker and Maude's child, which means you have an obligation to that family as well. We cannot guarantee that you can just come right back to your old life."

"But it's a possibility?" I said quickly, as a piece of chandelier rolled across the table and fell to the floor.

"It's possible," she said.

I looked up at them expectantly, and without even allowing myself to entertain the possibility that things would *not* go my way, said, "That's good enough for me. What are we waiting for?"

8

Before we walked outside to the mailbox, my father rounded up some rope from the garage, and even though they weren't very cooperative, managed to tie my wings to my back so I wouldn't go flying away.

"They are like ghosts," my mom explained. "They are both transparent and solid. They are their own energy. This is why you can fit your clothing around them, but they can still be tied down because they are, in actuality, as solid as your heart."

"I don't get it," I said, as she wrapped one of her old shawls around my shoulders.

"You don't have to." She smiled, patting my arm.

As always, I needed to ensure that I was one step ahead of the plan, so I managed to run up to my room just before my mother and I headed out and jotted a few things down into one of my spare notebooks. This was going to be the list to beat all lists:

-Get into Garlandia.

-Meet birth parents. Hug.

-Learn a defensive spell or two. (This is for good measure, to make it look like I care. Because let's face it—all of this sounds completely ridiculous. It doesn't even sound like there's a smidgen of evidence that anyone was ever after me to begin with. With names like Maude and Tanker, I don't think it's too far off to say that these people—or whatever they are—overreacted to something miniscule.)

    -Remember initial defense spell to get rid of wings.

    -Wave good-bye and get out of Garlandia.

    -Forget all about this nonsense and apply to Yale.

    -Send formal apology to Lucy Armstrong. (It is always good to set oneself up for acts of greatness.)

    -Get back to the office and try to forget any of this ever happened.

    -Show new designs to the team and launch new bag line before Fall.

    -Go over to Cee-Cee's house and watch season two of *Grey's Anatomy.*

With the edge of my pencil at the next empty line under the last task, I tried to decide whether I should write down what I was thinking. In the end, my longing for the act and the fear of living a life without love won me over.

    -Experience your first kiss before it's too late . . . be it girl or boy . . . or whoever.

I'd been thinking over Jeremy and Cee-Cee's rationale that I was a pan-sexual teenage girl. Honestly, I had no idea what or who I was attracted to. Though I had a feeling that when I met the soul my heart was meant to desire—I would know. And I wouldn't care what sort or what gender that soul belonged to. Therefore, I guess I was pan-sexual. And I wasn't bothered by this realization in the very least. If anything, it made me stronger.

A blue broom in his hand, preparing to sweep up the pieces of crystal, and no doubt tidy up the remnants of our living room area, I hugged my dad good-bye; ensuring him I would see him again very soon while ignoring the uncertainty lingering in his embrace—a squeeze that was just a little bit tighter than usual.

It was evening when we left our house, but the sun was still out as we walked up to the mailbox at the end of our driveway. Lucky for us, no one was outside.

"So, we just put those things inside and wait for this Mort character to come out?" I asked. "Doesn't it look a little strange?"

"No one's ever noticed," my mom said, slipping the tray of mud cakes inside and putting up the little red flag. "You never noticed for that matter."

I made a face, crossing my arms over my chest. My wings were getting anxious, and I was beginning to worry my dad hadn't tied them down tight enough. I wondered what would happen if I lost control of them out here. Would I go galivanting up into the atmosphere—into space? I shuddered at the thought.

We stood there waiting for what began to feel like a *very* long time. I was about to open my mouth and ask where this little box dweller was, when the front flap fell open and a little man with a stout nose and a pot belly walked out—a glob of mud cake in his hand and a piece of moss hanging down from his bottom lip. I wasn't one to be around babies all that often, but I could still assume that if a two-month-old baby could stand up and walk, and if it had dirt smeared across its face and was dressed in rags, that this is what it would look like. The whole thing was rather creepy.

"Oh, it's you," he said nasally and unenthusiastically. "What do you want?"

"We need to get in. Can you please take us to the Abberwockey's home?"

The little gnome stuffed the rest of what was in his hand into his mouth and then licked his fingers. "You know, the Millers chop up earthworms and sauté 'em with onions before bakin' ther mud cakes." He pointed a grubby finger at my mom. "Somethin' you should think about. You always burn yers."

"Mort, this is an emergency. We need to get in, right now," my mother replied quietly, but with urgency.

The little man stuck a portly thumb into his mouth and picked at his teeth, looking from her to me.

"Who's she?"

"My daughter—well, not by blood—"

"She's fey. Why can't she get ya in?"

"She doesn't know how. It's a long story, will you please just let us in?"

The little dweeb then proceeded to visually inspect me as though he wasn't quite sure about my intentions.

"Is that an Erwain?"

"Mort," my mom said sternly, "I don't have the patience today to deal with you, and if you don't let us in, I will use other transportation and deal with you once I'm inside."

The gnome finally looked away from me. Then, what felt like ages later, he said halfheartedly, "Why do cats wear sweaters in Garlandia?"

"Because they don't like short sleeves," my mom answered.

"Fine. I'll let ya in, but it's curfew so get to where yer goin' quick," he retorted, turning around and starting to walk back into the box.

"Curfew?" my mom questioned, as though this was a new concept for her.

"Yeah," he said without offering an explanation. Before he disappeared completely, he poked his head out and said in a threatening manner, "Next time, earthworms sautéed with onions . . . and pickles." And then he was gone.

"What just happened?" I asked, watching the mailbox close on its own. But there wasn't time for an answer, because in a matter of seconds everything around us transformed.

Ivy grew up around the mailbox, enormous trees sprouted from out of nowhere—our house disappeared and in its place was a stream surrounded by both large and small wildflowers, red and white mushrooms—and in the near distance I could see a medium-sized cottage. The sun was setting in this world, just as it had been in front of our house, so the windows inside the home were lit up.

As we stood there, a fluttering of butterflies swarmed passed us, a missing person's photo floating along with them of what looked like a tiny faery, listed as: Vicky Rodgers, Gone Missing three weeks ago. I followed them with my eyes until they were gone, then continued to survey my surroundings. It was like an illustration straight out of a child's storybook, except—I couldn't quite put my finger on it—there was something strange lingering in the air. A kind of foreboding energy that didn't match the magic of the forest.

A small pair of gnomes scurried off towards a log lying on its side and entered a small door.

"Garlandia?" I whispered.

My mom took my hand. "Yes." She was frowning as though trying to figure something out. "I don't remember there being a curfew before."

"Great," I said sarcastically. "So, is this it—where they live?" I nodded towards the cottage.

"Yes. 17 Serendipity Lane."

"17?" A blockage manifested itself into my brain. I hated uneven numbers; they weren't clean. This was already a bad sign.

Playing off the concern flowing from my mother's energy, I said, "Maybe this was a mistake. We could just go back."

"No." She shook her head and began pulling me towards the cottage. "We must go in there. Hello Maynard."

"Maynard? Who are you talking to—holy shit!" I exclaimed, watching as a tree to our left opened its eyes.

Speaking extremely slowly, *frustratingly slowly*, the tree said, "Always a pleasure, young Naomi. And who is this? Wait, don't tell me that's the—"

"Yes," she answered. "She's found her wings."

"Wow," the tree said, with way more expression showing than I'd ever thought I would see out of a tree.

Once we'd gotten out of ear shot, I whispered to my mother, "So, like, trees can talk here?"

"Yes. You're going to find things are a little different in Garlandia."

"I think that may be a bit of an understatement," I retorted.

We were almost to the front door of the stony cottage when what looked like a large insect flew in front of me, levitating in front of my nose. It only took me a second to understand that this was a faery. A small one like the one in the missing person's picture, except it was male. I had always only thought of faeries as females.

"What do you want?" I asked, swatting it away.

"Oh no you didn't!" it squeaked, getting in my mom's face. "Does she belong to you? She just swatted at me!"

My mom pulled me closer as she apologized profusely. "I am so sorry, this is her first time here, uh—what's your name?"

"Larry!"

"I am so sorry, Larry. I'm Naomi and this is—"

But the faery was pissed off and had already flown away, a cacophony of curse words trailing behind him. "As if it wasn't already bad enough—dark times I tell ya! Then those mindless gnomes just let anybody in . . ."

"What was that?" I asked.

"One of the grumpiest Ardeens I've ever met," my mom retorted.

"Ardeen?" I repeated, but she wasn't paying attention to

me. Raising my eyebrows, I repeated the faery's last words. "Dark times?"

Ignoring my comment, her voice raised about an octave too high as she said, "Tanker and Maude don't know we're coming. But I suspect they have had an idea this was going to happen sooner than later." Before we stepped up to the door, she stopped me and squared my shoulders with hers. "Remember, these are the faeries who gave birth to you. They never stopped loving you. I need you to handle this situation with respect—no matter what."

Temporarily forgetting the maddening situation I was in, I crossed my arms over my chest. "God, you have, like, no faith in me. I think you are forgetting that I deal with international business affairs daily—or I used to before you took away my life. I can handle meeting strangers."

"They aren't strangers."

"Whatever," I said, "let's just get this over with."

My mom opened her mouth as though she was preparing to say more but stopped herself. "Fine, let's just do this." And then she prematurely pasted a fake smile onto her face.

We walked up the porch steps and rang the doorbell, at which point an obnoxious bout of laughter bellowed from inside the house. Prejudging the kind of people who had such a doorbell, I scoffed and looked over at the sign next to the door. It said, "No soliciting. But you can talk to the frog. He enjoys debates."

"The frog?" I questioned, but my query was left unanswered as the door swung open. Standing on the other side was a very well endowed, curvy, red-headed faery with purple butterfly wings, wearing a long, flowing dress that looked like something one might see at a renaissance festival—a dumbfounded look on her face.

Oh no, is that her? Please don't let that be her.

But it was her. Maude Abberwockey. It took her only a

second to gather her words; looking first at my mother, she then stared directly at me before framing her cheeks with her hands.

"Oh, my gawd!!!! Tanker!! Get your sweet bottom down here!!! It's our Lala!!!"

My head ticked and my mouth twitched. "It—it's Makayla," I whispered. But I don't think she heard me, because she'd already jumped through the door and was squeezing me so hard, I thought my insides would ooze out.

❧ 9 ❧

The Abberwockey's home was, well, interesting. It was nice, but rather messy. There were piles of newspapers in almost every corner, and I saw more than a few random socks and tutus thrown carelessly onto the floor. As soon as we'd been led in, a floppy-eared basset hound came sniffing around my ankles.

"Oh, that's just Kevin," Maude said, clinging to my side.

Maude was small, but fiery, and proving to be much like a leech; barely pulling herself away to give Tanker a chance to wrap his long spindly arms around me. He appeared a little older than her, but not much—if I hadn't known they were hundreds, if not thousands of years old already, I would've pegged them to be around thirty-seven.

Tanker had a handlebar mustache. He looked like a professor, or maybe it was the sweater he had on—one of those awful renditions with leather patches on the elbows; it was completely mismatched against his plaid red and blue pants, bunny slippers, and giant blue wings. When he'd leaned in, I could've sworn I saw a pearl necklace around his neck, but

I couldn't be sure. Regardless, Maude and Tanker were the most ridiculous things I'd ever seen.

"BRAT, BRAT, IT'S THE BRAT!"

I flinched as a bright green bird came sailing into the kitchen, its screeching voice bellowing into my ears. Then just seconds later another flew in, but red this time. "BRAT!" it screeched.

"Yes, yes, it's our little brat," Maude sang to the birds. Then turning towards me, she said, "Don't take offense, Pinch and Asshole don't mean to be rude."

"Their names are Pinch and Asshole?" I asked, visibly appalled.

"Yes, the red one is Asshole, and the green one is Pinch. They are Sun Conures. Beautiful, aren't they?"

The green one sat on my arm and squeezed my skin together with its talons.

"Ouch!" I yelped, stopping myself from swatting it away only because everyone had their eyes on me.

"Shut up, brat!" it squawked.

"Shut up!" the red one mimicked.

Perhaps they should've named both of them Asshole.

"Um, do you have any other animals in this place?" I hardly managed to hide my scowl.

"No," Maude answered with a silly grin. "Let's see, Kevin has been with us for ten years." She lifted her hands up and visibly counted each year on each of her fingers. "And Pinch and Asshole, they came to us just before you left."

"Pets pick their owners here," my mom specified.

Pinch cocked his beak to the side as he studied me for another minute before flying away. I rubbed the place on my arm where he had pinched me and toughed out a fake smile. "Well, they are all very nice," I lied.

"Thank you!" Maude replied excitedly. I could already tell; she was a sap.

"Where's Philip?" Tanker asked, leaning in and rubbing my mom's shoulder affectionately.

"Oh, well, there was a bit of a mess to clean up back at the house." She gestured towards my backside. "Lala's wings didn't quite come back to her as quietly as we might've hoped."

Tanker tucked in his chin and looked up at me, making me feel more on the spot than I really cared for. "Well, I'm not surprised. She's got Abberwockey blood, and we don't like to do anything half-assed, do we Maudie?"

"Absolutely not," she said, tugging on my arm and peering into my eyes with a wonky grin.

"Well then, let's have a sit, shall we." Tanker gestured towards the yellow kitchen table. It matched the lighting in the house. "Maude just made some lavender lemonade."

Pulling me down into a chair and scooting herself right up next to me, Maude looked up at my mom and said, "Naomi, would you mind getting that for us. It's in the fridge."

"Of course," my mom said. She moved around the kitchen as though it was her second home. Pulling down four glasses —all mismatched and of various colors—she said, as she poured the purple liquid into each one, "You are going to have to excuse Lala, this is all coming as quite a bit of a shock to her."

"Um, you can call me Makayla," I said to Maude and Tanker.

"Pish posh, where'd you come up with that?" Maude looked at my mom. "Naomi, where did she get that?"

My mom shrugged her shoulders. "She started calling herself that when she was four years old. She's always had this thing with names."

Maude turned back to me and placed a hand on the side of my head. I wanted to swat it away, but apparently faeries didn't care for that, so I sucked it up.

"Well, that's not right, is it? We named you Lala."

I felt my stomach curl. Very carefully, I placed my hand over hers and brought it down to the table. "Well, Mrs. Abberwockey, uh, Maude—it's just that the world we live in, if you want to have a reputable career it helps to have a professional name. I think Makay—"

"I like it!" Tanker said, holding out a giant cherry red pipe. "Very good choice, if I do say so myself."

Maude looked over at her husband, and then back at me. "Well, I'm going to call you Lala."

This was already a nightmare. I was trapped inside a children's fairy tale—though perhaps a bit darker around the edges than what one might find in a set of Little Golden Books. A vision of that fat baby looking Mort popped into my head . . . And maybe just a little more twisted. I opened my mouth to argue with my faery birth mother but was cut off.

"There are so many things we have to talk about!" Maude continued without pause. "All the things I always wanted to teach you! Like how to knit with red licorice, and learning to call the butterflies, and gardening, and—"

"That is all very nice," I interrupted, accepting the glass of lemonade handed to me by my mother before she sat down in the chair next to me. As soon as she did, I scooted next to her, at which point, Maude did the same to me. "But, well—"

"No need to go any further," Tanker said, sticking out his chest. "I think, my love, that what our daughter is trying to say, is that *Makayla* here needs some time to soak things in. Am I right?" he asked, nodding at me as he took a puff off his ridiculous contraption, puffing out indigo-colored bubbles that smelled of blueberries as they popped.

"Yes," I said, nodding my head, and as I did my shawl fell off and my restricted wings made their debut.

"Oh!" Maude shrieked, causing me to jump as she literally flew from her seat. "Your wings! Look at them,

Tanker! They are so beautiful—we were so worried they would never come back!" She immediately started ruffling them.

"Wait!" my mom and I yelled together.

"Maude," my mom said, placing a hand in the air. "Makayla is still having a bit of trouble controlling them, that's why they are tied down."

I was nodding profusely, silently begging her to sit back down and leave me and my wings alone.

"Oh dear, well we can fix that," she said, pulling out a purplish glowing stick of some sort and pointing it at my backside, causing a bright purple stream of light to envelop my wings until they seemed to deflate.

Had that been a wand?

I lifted a lifeless wing and held it in my hand as though it were a wet towel. "Did you break them?"

"No silly," Maude giggled. "Let's just say I turned them off for a while."

"Oh . . . okay."

Gripping my left wing tightly, she caused me to jump again as she screeched, "Tanker! It's still there, that cute little birth mark! Not so little anymore, is it?"

"What?" I immediately cringed at the idea of an imperfection anywhere on my body. "What is it?" I asked, trying to peer at it along with my mother, who had moved in to get a better look.

"A star of course! It's just the cutest. Isn't it, Naomi?"

Cranking my neck, I searched for it, finding a white five-pointed star broken into the pattern of my wing. It was about the size of my hand, and it actually—well, it was kind of cool.

"Beautiful," my mom said, smiling down at me and slinking back into her seat.

Maude finally sat down again, her curly hair bouncing around as she did. It was then that I noticed she had strings of glittery purple hairs strung between the red. It reminded me of Cee-Cee's green strip.

Noticing me looking at them, she pulled at one and stared at it awkwardly, crossing her eyes in the process. "The curse of getting older. Everyday there's more purple."

"Are you telling me that instead of going gray, you are going purple?" I asked.

"Gray? Whatever do you mean?"

"You know, when your hair starts to turn—" I looked across the table at Tanker, who was sitting a little more forward in his chair. "Never mind. So, I was wondering—I mean, we can't keep them turned off forever, so when do you think I could learn how to manage my wings?"

My mom jabbed me in the side with her elbow. "Why don't we visit a little longer before we get to that, okay Makayla." That famous plastic grin of hers was planted firmly on her face.

"Fine," I replied, copying her expression. "So . . . Maude, Tanker. What is it you do? I mean, do faeries do anything— ouch!" I glared at my mom who had jabbed me again.

Tanker laughed. "No, that's quite all right, Naomi. The poor girl has just found out she's a faery—let's cut her some slack. But yes, Makayla, we have careers."

"We're critics," Maude said proudly.

My mom cleared her throat and sipped her lemonade.

"Critics? Really?" I leaned forward attentively. "In this world or mine—uh, or the human world?"

"Both," Tanker said.

"Oh wow, that's exciting." I could handle that; it was a fairly respectable trade. "So, what is it that you review?"

"All sorts of things," Maude answered.

"Yes, from restaurants to the theatre. In fact, we just saw *Hamlet* with your parents not too long ago. Remember that,

Naomi?" Tanker asked, lifting his pipe back up to rest in his mouth.

"Oh yes," my mom said, nodding too quickly.

"It's a shame Philip had to leave halfway through the show. I daresay our commentary aided them in their next performance." Tanker was staring expectantly at my mom.

"Oh—why yes," she said. "I agree."

Tanker focused his attention on me again. "And then of course, we write for *The Garlandian Buzz.*"

"Is that the paper here?" I asked.

Nodding, Maude raised her perfectly shaped red eyebrows. "But we have to be careful about what we write, because of the restrict—"

Tanker cleared his throat. "Because not all faeries have gone into the human world, so we have to be careful that we translate the differences between the worlds."

"I see. Well, it is just so refreshing to know that you have reputable careers."

My mom's lips twitched. Ignoring her, I took a sip of lemonade, but as soon as the liquid hit my tongue, I had to cringe not to spit it back out. It must've had ten cups of sugar in it.

"Oh dear," Maude said, misreading the look on my face. "This must all be so much for you to take in."

"Well . . ." I searched my mind for a polite response, but really all I wanted was to get through the chit chat and figure out how to get rid of my wings again. "It's just such a relief to see that I come from intellectuals."

"Oh my! Tanker, did you hear her? What a sweetheart, she called us intellectuals."

Tanker nodded his head at me in approval.

This was going better than expected, perhaps I had judged them too harshly, too early. Regardless of what my mom said, I decided it wouldn't be a bad idea to start moving on to the next bullet point on my list; and I was just about to ask when a good time might be to begin the faery reversal when a riot broke out. Kevin started howling and Pinch and Asshole started yelling, "Shut up!" as whoever it was knocked furiously on the front door.

"Oh no," Maude said. "The word must've spread already of Lala's homecoming."

All the muscles in my back contracted. "What? We just got here."

"Well yes," Maude said matter-of-factly, "but those trees are worse than the flowers. I'm sure they've been whispering about your return all the way into the kingdom."

"King . . . dom?"

"Yes, you know, past the forest and through the tulips to the castle. Most of the elves live there though, and we don't really mix with them anymore, so—"

I cut her off. "Whoa, whoa, whoa. Elves? Castle?"

Tanker had stood up and was checking to see who was pounding on the front door, when he returned, he had an annoyed look on his face. Staring at his wife, he said without enthusiasm, "It's your sister."

Everyone, minus me, groaned.

The knocking and racket had settled, allowing for a rush of wind to soar through the house, bringing with it a tall, thin, faery with dark blue wings and beady eyes. She wore a short black and navy dress over fishnets tights, her hair was jet black, and her cheek bones sunken in; she was pretty, but in a frightening way.

"THE BRAT'S BACK! THE BRAT'S BACK!" the birds screeched, circling around her head.

"Is it her?" she asked, panicky almost. "Is it really her?"

"Of course, it is," Tanker said. "Look at her hair, at those wings. Besides, do you know any other Erwains her age?"

"Shut up! Shut up! Shut up!" the birds continued to squawk.

"Get out of here!" she screamed back at them, pulling a dark blue glittery wand from her side. Immediately the birds flew away.

"Would you like some lemonade, Helene?" Maude asked, handing her a purple beverage.

The two didn't look anything alike. If Maude was a cheerleader, then Helene was the smart girl who sat in the corner of the gym, plotting to kill all the cheerleaders. Instead of receiving the offering as any polite individual would do, Helene simply lifted a hand and waved her sister away before walking around the table to get closer to me.

"I thought you said she was lost." Helene looked up at my mother—my human mother. "You've had her this whole time, haven't you? Of course!" Looking from her back to Maude, she seethed, "You two always were chummy. Why didn't I think of that?" Focusing her attention on Maude, she said, "Why wouldn't you tell me? I'm *family*—I'm her aunt."

"We didn't tell anyone," Maude answered.

Pointing a long white finger down at me, she stammered, "So you just let me believe she'd been stolen! Just like you let the rest of the village believe. You've been lying to me all this time?"

"It was for her safety, Helene," Tanker said, his voice lacquered with fatigue. "We knew you wouldn't understand, and it was safer to keep her whereabouts a secret."

"Was there ever even a break-in?" Her fierce gaze was bouncing violently from Maude to Tanker.

"Yes," Maude said, "but she was never abducted." She explained how they'd found me and then sent me into the arms of my adoptive parents. I was still trying to wrap my head around the idea of my mother being best friends with not only my birth mother, but a faery. "Her wings just exploded an hour ago, this is all still a shock to her as well."

My aunt looked down on me, inspecting every inch of my body. I could nearly *feel* her doing so, like little pin pricks digging into my skin.

"You don't have any idea how you did it? How you spelled your wings away? Do—do you remember anything about what happened?"

"No—and look—I don't even know how to use my magic. Which leads me to what I was about to say a while ago. When do you think we could begin some lessons? I don't mean to be inconsiderate, but this couldn't have happened at a worse time."

"Makayla," my mom warned under her breath.

I paused, staring at her in disbelief. Then, looking up at Maude and Tanker I decided to lay it all out. "I'm really sorry. I know you're probably thinking that since my wings came back that I should spend some time getting to know you guys and digging into my fa-fa," I choked on the word, "my faery roots. But here's the thing, I'm happy with my life. I am an organized person, and quite frankly"—I scanned my surroundings—"this place is the opposite of that. It doesn't mean that someday we can't get to know one another better, but right now I just really want to get back to the way things are back home. And to be honest I don't need another set of parents right now."

I paused, surveying the faces around me. Maude looked as if she'd just been gutted. Tanker had a straight face, but I could tell he was disheartened by my abruptness, and Helene—well, she still looked appalled by my mere existence.

Finally, my mother stood up, and laying a hand over Maude's shoulder, said, "She has this habit of being terribly straight forward."

"*She's* sitting right here," I said, annoyed.

Ignoring me, my mother continued as Maude stared down at me. "But I'm afraid we can't entirely blame her. We decided to let her build her own life. We were the ones who didn't tell her the truth. Frankly, being a faery is the last thing on her—"

"Stop," Maude said.

Hesitating, my mom started to speak again, but was cut off as Maude raised her hand in the air. "No, you're right." As she spoke, her tongue got sharper. "It was silly of me to think I still had a daughter. She was yours, Naomi, practically from the moment she was born. Clearly, she's not a faery . . . except for her wings, and Tanker can help her with that. All I did was bring her to life, after all." Then she turned away and escaped the kitchen, leaving an awkward silence in her wake. That was until, of course, Helene spoke up.

"What does she mean, *clearly she's not a faery*? Looks like a faery to me! And once the council hears about the *lost Erwain* being found, you're going to want to bet they will be wanting to meet her. Let's not stand here and pretend like the little pet has a choice in the matter."

Tanker and my mom shot each other strange looks.

"What do you mean *the lost Erwain*?" I asked.

Helene propped her hand on her hip and cocked her head to the side. "That's what they've been calling you ever since you disappeared. When you are the only one of your kind born in two hundred years and then you go missing, it tends to get talked about."

"Oh, right," I answered. I suddenly found myself worrying that this would put a damper on my quick escape back into reality. "Who are the council?"

"King Loral and the forest representatives, of course," Helene said impatiently.

"*Okay*, that sounds perfectly normal. If not a bit cartoonish . . ."

"Makayla," my mom warned.

"Fine. I'll meet them. In the meantime, why don't you teach me how to do some magic tricks and I'll be on my way back into my own world."

Helene looked appalled. "Wow honey, you've got nerve."

"Helene," Tanker said quietly.

"No Tanker! Listen to this little brat—"

"Where do you get off calling my kid—" my mom started, but Helene's wings lifted and before anyone could stop her, she was standing over my mom with her wand out by her side.

"She's not your kid—she's my sister's!"

"That's funny, because I've been raising her for the past seventeen years!"

"Everyone, shut up!" Tanker yelled, causing all three of us to stare over at the corner he'd backed himself into. "Good," he said, once Helene had backed down. "This is what we are going to do. Naomi, you are going to go back home. Makayla, you're staying here."

Suddenly it felt like I'd swallowed a golf ball. I began to stand and argue his point, but Helene pushed me back down with the flick of her wand. "Listen to him."

With his gaze fixed on mine, Tanker continued, "It's plain to see you don't want any part of this life, but Helene is right, the council, or the king, will want to meet you. The fact of the matter is that you can't go back into your world until you learn enough to at least hide your wings again anyway. It seems to me that the best plan is to begin teaching you how to access your magic straight away. That way when you are called on by the king you can leave as soon as he gives you permission."

I took only a second to absorb his statement. There was one word in particular that didn't resonate well with me. "Permission?"

"So *what*?" Helene asked, digging her fingernails further into her hip bones. "You would just let her go again? The first

Erwain born in two hundred years, and you would just send her off to pretend she's a human?"

"If that's what she wants," Tanker said quietly.

"That is just the stupidest thing I have ever heard you say, Tanker Abberwockey. Not to mention the fact that it's not going to happen. Do you really think the king is going to just let her saunter out of here?" She scoffed. "Not bloody likely!" And then she stormed out of the house, but not before leaning in and giving my mother one last sneer.

After a moment of silence, allowing each of us to absorb that last tantrum, I looked up at my mother and Tanker and muttered a given question, "*What in the hell* did she mean by all that?"

They didn't respond. Instead, my mom, leaning against the sink with a hand over her heart, muttered to herself, "I see Maude's sister is just as eloquent as she always was."

Tanker cleared his throat. "In her defense, we've all seen better days. But that doesn't make up for her behavior."

"Better days?" my mom questioned. "Tanker, why is there a curfew in place? Is there something you need to tell me?"

Tanker's expression softened and he exhaled a deep breath. "It's fine, Naomi. The curfew was set in place by the neighborhood watch. It is just a precaution."

"Precaution for what?"

But Tanker didn't answer her.

"I need to know," she said, her motherly instincts front and center. "Will Lala be safe here?"

Tanker closed his eyes. "Maude and I would never let anything happen to her; you must know that."

My blood boiled in my cheeks. I just wanted someone to address me directly, instead of speaking about me like I wasn't sitting right there.

Slowly, my mom looked over at me. "I'm sorry baby, but Tanker's right. I need to go."

"Please don't leave me here," I said, my lack of patience transforming into an unsteady posture with trembling limbs. I stood, my hands out before me as if I were getting ready to scoop up sand. I could see Tanker's saddened expression in the corner of my eye, that his own daughter didn't want to be left alone with her biological father and mother—but at that point I didn't really care.

My mom walked over and grabbed my face in her hands, kissing my forehead. "I'll be back. I'll come visit all the time," she said, that fake smile plastered back onto her face.

"But what about the company?" I said, reaching for any excuse to go back with her. "I just came up with some really cool designs for some new handbags and—"

"Baby, you've got wings. Even if you didn't have certain obligations to this world, you would still need to learn how to manage them."

I didn't disagree with her, but I didn't give any indication that I was accepting the situation.

"We can cover them up," I whispered. "And what about Jeremy and Cee-Cee . . . they'll wonder where I went. They said they were going to bust me out if you didn't let me out of the house soon. They're bound to start asking questions."

"Your dad and I will come up with something."

"Please, Mom—you can't leave me here. These people are strangers to me, and" –lowering my voice, although not so low it was inaudible— "Maude is such a flake."

She pretended as if she hadn't heard that part as she broke away from me and started backing away towards the door. "You just worry about you right now. Listen to your parents."

"But you and Dad are my parents," I mumbled.

"Here, take these," Tanker said, holding out what looked like cake pops. I could smell the dirt in them from where I stood at a distance. "In case Mort is in one of his moods."

"Thanks," she said, blowing me a kiss and stepping out of the kitchen door before I could lunge forward and stop her.

And just like that I was all alone in a strange land with faery parents, in a messy house with live-in birds. So far, this day was beginning to really suck, and I had thought after my Harvard interview things couldn't possibly get any worse. It was not an ideal situation, and the only way I could deal with it, unfortunately, was to cry.

Tanker cleared his throat uncomfortably and pulled out a blue wand, pointing it at the door. When I looked up at him in question, he apologized, "I'm sorry. We can't take any chances that you might try to go after her. It's uh, it's not safe for you to go running around at night alone."

I just stood there, crying, unable to stop crying. My new wings were draped sadly behind me, spelled into paralysis.

"Why isn't it safe?" I whispered.

I caught an indecisive look appear on Tanker's face. "It's not as cartoonish as it appears."

We met eyes and a foreboding energy curled around me like a snake readying to feed.

"When will they, the council or the king or whatever, when will they want to meet me?"

Tanker shrugged his shoulders. "I'm sure you'll meet some of the members as soon as tomorrow, but it is really the king who will give the end all." Tapping his wand repeatedly into the palm of his hand, he stalled a moment before saying, "If you want to come with me, I can show you to your room."

I continued to stand there, unmoving.

"All right then, come on," he said, tucking in his wand and leaving the kitchen.

I looked back at the door, and even though I knew he'd locked it in some weird faery way that I wouldn't be able to undo, I still tried; immediately a shock of electricity shot up my arm before I could even wrap my hand all the way around the doorknob.

"Ouch!" I yelped, jumping away, the jolt causing a rash to run up my arm. I whimpered before turning around to find Tanker looking away.

He'd said it was for my protection, but I definitely felt imprisoned.

"Are you coming?"

"Yes," I finally muttered, laying a hand over my injured arm and rolling my shoulders forward, following him through the doorway. As we started up the stairs, I noticed a red and purple spot in the corner, shaking. It was Maude. She'd been just outside the kitchen the entire time, listening.

Suddenly I didn't feel very well.

Once upstairs, Tanker led me through a small, uneven hallway, littered with black and white and colored portraits of various faeries, hanging every way but straight. I was too mentally exhausted to reach out and fix all of them, but it was an act I would inevitably find myself doing if I was going to be staying here more than a few days.

At the end of the hall was a room that looked like it already belonged to a teenage girl, just not this particular breed. Inside was a twin bed surrounded by a pink canopy and a few brightly colored pieces of furniture. There was even a poster on the wall of what looked like some sort of musical group. The kids all had pointy ears.

Tanker reached up and scratched the area over his eyebrow. "Well, this is your room. We sort of thought we'd have you back a few years ago, so we um, we—"

"You decorated it for me," I said softly.

"Yeah." He looked away.

I walked over to the bed and picked up a framed picture sitting on the table next to it—a portrayal of Tanker and

Maude and what looked like a very large butterfly in their arms. "Is this us?"

"Yes," he said. "We took that just after you were born. We lost you three weeks later."

"Oh."

"It's been a long night, and I'm sure you're exhausted. Why don't you try and get some sleep and we'll talk again over breakfast."

"Okay," I said, watching him as he walked out of my room, his giant blue wings quite a bit lower than when I'd first met him.

After the door was closed, I laid the picture back on the table and walked around. I couldn't believe this was where I would've grown up if things had been different. I had to wonder, if I'd grown up as a faery, would I still be this driven, organized individual? Or would I be a giggling goober like Maude, or a mismatched fool like Tanker.

I leaned in closer to the poster on the wall. There were two girls and two boys, all dressed like punk rockers, and above their heads in big red and black letters it said, *The Dizzy Elf Circus.* Elves. So weird.

I then made my way towards the window and sat down in the little nook provided, draping my wings over my lap. This place was surrounded by trees, and brooks, and flowers. Most people would think it was magical, but I found myself already homesick for concrete and the sound of cars. Did they even have those here?

I took a deep breath and looked up at the moon. It looked the same as it did in my world. Or my parents' world. I wasn't sure where I belonged anymore.

"Don't cry, don't you dare cry again," I whispered to myself, allowing my gaze to fall back down into the trees.

Luckily something white caught my attention and robbed me of my frustrations. I leaned in closer to the window and stared past the darkness to where the moon shined on what appeared to be a statue.

Upon closer inspection, I rationalized that it was a faery statue. It wasn't like me though, not as big—but it was quite a bit larger than the small faery named Larry who I'd seen earlier.

The longer I studied it, the more I came to realize that it looked terrified.

I was just about to pull away from the window, realizing of course that the night's activities had probably started to play tricks on my mind. There couldn't be a statue of a frightened faery in Maude and Tanker's backyard . . . that would just be weird. I'm sure it was just an ordinary statue and the way the moon shined on it distorted its features.

But just as I was about to stand up and attempt to close my mind and body off from all the madness I'd endured that night, I witnessed something very peculiar. If it hadn't moved at all I wouldn't have noticed it. But it must have seen me staring its way, whatever it was; because just as I was about to pull away from the window, a shadow backed away from where it had been standing next to the white statue, almost as though it had been watching me.

❧ 10 ❧

I woke up the next morning to a large wet tongue licking my mouth and chin. When I opened my eyes, Kevin retracted his slobbery weapon and immediately started panting. I hadn't the vaguest idea of how he had even gotten on the bed with those stubby legs of his.

"Oh no," I groaned, staring up at the purple ceiling. "It wasn't a dream."

Kevin sighed and lowered his chin down onto my chest.

I very carefully eased him off me and started to get up. I was careful not to make too much noise, because I wasn't yet ready to face the Abberwockeys after all that had been said and done the previous night. I knew the things that had come from my mouth were not only juvenile, but terrible. Still, none of this was my fault. *They* had been the ones who had given me away. I couldn't help it if I didn't all the sudden desire to be like them, just because these frustrating wings had erupted from my back.

I walked carefully and quietly over to the window; the same one I had been looking out of the night before. There was music playing somewhere in the forest, but far enough away that I had to stretch my ears to hear it from inside. Now that it was light out, I could see that the backyard was full of gardens. Everything from various colors and breeds of flowers to squash, watermelon, and tomatoes. Tons of tomatoes.

I tried to see past the Abberwockey's property into the forest, but the trees were too thick. My gaze drifted down to the statue I'd seen the night before . . . it was definitely some sort of faery, and it did seem to have an unpleasant look frozen onto its face. After studying it for a bit longer, I decided that the shadow I'd thought I'd seen backing away from it the night before had to have been nothing more than a branch moving in the wind.

Before long Maude walked out into the garden with a bucket, collecting vegetables. Her red hair was braided down the side, and she wore a long flowing green dress.

She leaned down by a large rock and patted its side, then proceeded to talk to it. She nodded her head, as though agreeing with it, when a stoutly little creature walked up to her. I'd seen him before—it was Mort.

For a second, I got my hopes up, thinking that perhaps his reappearance meant he was escorting my mom back into Garlandia, but there was no sign of either of my parents. Instead he pulled a piece of paper from his grubby little pocket, and Maude made as if to grab for it; but just as he was about to let her have it, he pulled it back, pointing a stubby finger at her collection of corn and tomatoes.

At first, she shook her head, but when he started folding up the piece of paper and stuffing it back into his little green pants, she sighed and held out the biggest, reddest tomato. Mort accepted the fruit, inspecting every aspect of it, and when it appeared he was satisfied he handed her the paper and walked away.

Once he was gone Maude set down her basket and opened the note. Whatever the message contained, it must not have been very good news because her shoulders immediately slouched, and before I had a chance to hide, she turned and stared up at my window. For a second, I just stood there—both of us aware of the other—before backing away.

Slowly retreating to the bed, I sat down on the edge and ruffled Kevin's floppy ears. I wished more than anything that I was back home with my mom and dad. I imagined what I'd be doing right now, if instead of coming home that day after my interview with Lucy Armstrong to find that my world had turned upside down, that we had gone on to meet my dad at Rogue like we had planned. That he had met us there and ordered his favorite steak dish, while my mom and I had started with a cup of curry coconut soup. That we'd raised our glasses and cheered to my success. That instead of the last couple weeks making me feel like a zero, I'd been working out how to be both Co-Founder of Sewn Back Together and Harvard law student.

But none of that had happened, and the heaviness in my gut was a reminder of that.

I thought of the list I'd made last night right before leaving my house. If I was going to stick to what I'd written down then I had no choice other than to play along while I was here, and part of that was going to have to include playing nice with Tanker and Maude.

I had to remind myself I was a businessperson, and if there was one thing I'd learned it was that to get something, you have to give something. I needed these people—these faeries—I needed them to show me how to be something I was not, so that I could undo my current situation.

"That's it," I said, jumping up. "I mustn't mope any longer; it is unprofessional and childish. I am Makayla freaking Wood, and I do not hide in my room."

I then marched defiantly out of the brightly splattered bedroom, stopping to fix three or four of the portraits—

staring strangely at a tall, muscular male faery with a rigid jaw line, purple wings, and a face I saw every time I looked in the mirror—before heading downstairs to where Maude was now back inside with Tanker.

Pausing just outside the kitchen, I balled up my fists by my sides and took a deep breath. When I entered their space, I lifted my chest and smiled.

"Good morning, Mr. and Mrs. Abberwockey," I said, choosing to address them in such a way that made me feel more business-like. If I could just stay in my element then I could get through this. I knew as soon as I laid eyes on Tanker, however, that this was all going to be a struggle.

Maude stood over her husband, who sat over a breakfast of leafy greens with a runny egg over the top, dressed in a slinky black dress with red pumps on his feet and several beaded necklaces hanging around his neck. He was essentially dressed as a flapper from the 1920's. Upon hearing my voice, they stopped what they were doing and looked over at me. It was then I realized that Maude was showing him the piece of paper she'd gotten from Mort.

"Oh, hi there Makayla," Tanker said pleasantly. Maude chose to remain silent.

I tried very hard not to gawk at my birth father and his strange choice of wardrobe. Instead I moved forward with a grown-up conversation starter. "I wanted to apologize for my behavior last night. It was unacceptable and childish." Then looking over at Maude, I said, "And I am very sorry if I hurt anyone's feelings."

Maude looked down at the piece of paper in her hands while Tanker simply smiled.

"That's very nice of you to say, Makayla. We know this must feel very strange to you—"

"And to you," I cut in. "I don't know what it must feel like for you to see me after all these years, and then I'm not what you expected—"

"You are."

"I'm sorry?" I asked. But Tanker just nodded his head and repeated himself.

"You are what we expected. We had our ways of watching you grow up. We knew you'd turned into an anal-retentive git."

I wrinkled my forehead, both confused and insulted. "How do you mean?"

Tanker cleared his throat and then took a hold of Maude's pale, delicate hand. "You wouldn't have recognized us, but we—"

Maude suddenly looked up; her eyes were glossy. "We couldn't just stop loving you. You were the child we never thought we'd ever have the chance to give birth to. That very short time we had you with us, I never felt luckier, and I was the envy of all the fey." She lowered her gaze once more as she pulled her hand away from Tanker's. "Neither Tanker nor I had anything to do with this," she said, walking over and putting the note in my hand. "If it were up to me, I would send you back straight away. It seems very obvious that you do not belong in our world, and you should not be punished for something you have no control over."

I thought I saw a sparkly tear run down her cheek before she left the kitchen, but she didn't give me much of a chance to be sure. Once she was gone, I looked down to see my mother's handwriting.

Dear Lala,

Please don't take this as an insult towards our love for you, but it is with a heavy heart that I must inform you that your father and I have decided that we should not come visit you for a while. You need this time with Tanker and Maude so that you can better get to know where you came from. Our presence there would only be a distraction. We'll be here waiting for you when you come back.

Love always and forever,

Mom and Dad

P.S. I wasn't snooping, but I found your sketches of the new bag line for Sewn Back Together lying on your bed. They are excellent, and I will be showing them to the design team at this Monday's meeting.

I looked back up at Tanker. "What is this?"

He pressed his lips together and then pushed away from the table, leaving his breakfast only partially eaten. "It sounds as if they realize that you need some time to digest this world. Naomi and Philip are great friends, I know they are doing this because they love you."

Oh, how cliché. I began to debate him on the subject, but quickly stopped myself. I needed to stick to my guns, to maintain my composure so that I could get out of Garlandia before I too, was speaking with rocks.

"Fine," I said, folding up the paper and sticking it into my pocket. "When can we get started on my lessons?"

There was an air of indigence about Tanker as he stood there, but I ignored it. A good businessperson, a good lawyer always sticks to their agenda. So what, my parents weren't going to be by my side—they weren't supposed to leave me here overnight either.

"I suppose this morning is as good a time as any," he

answered. "Suppose you grab yourself something to eat, and then we can—"

Ignoring my growling stomach, I said over him, "I'm really not hungry. I would prefer to get going right now if that's okay."

"Of course," he said after a doleful moment. And then he reached for a sequined purse and pointed towards the kitchen door. "After you."

❧

"Faery dust?" I asked in disbelief. I don't know why I was still surprised by anything. I was a fictional character for god's sake, and I had what looked like a giant dead butterfly attached to my back.

"Yes," Tanker said resolutely, standing across from me in the forest, his blue wand in his hand. He had just explained to me that it was this dust that allowed us to use magic. "As I've already said, you cannot do anything without a wand. A faery's wand is nothing more than a piece of him or her, a bit of their soul. We use them to conjure up the dust swimming around our bodies, and it is the dust which has the ability to manipulate the elements and conjure spells."

"Is it also how we fly?"

"It is part of it, yes. It's swimming around you as we speak, and once you become aware of it and are able to access it, flying will become much easier."

"Right. I think I understand."

"So, Makayla, to your knowledge have you ever made anything happen without physical force?"

"No—" I started, but then thought back to the previous day. "Actually, yesterday I caused the chandelier to fall down in the dining room."

Tanker snickered, placing a hand over his mouth as his

shoulders started bouncing up and down uncontrollably causing his necklaces to swing. "Well it's about bloody time!"

Confused, I retorted, "I'm sorry?"

"That wasn't you I'm afraid. If it was, you would've noticed your wand, wouldn't you?"

"Oh. I guess you're right. But how did it happen then? I was thinking about grabbing it down and then it just came."

He wiped a laughing tear away from his left eye. "That was just a coincidence. Maude and I unscrewed that thing three years ago—it was supposed to be funny!"

I was flabbergasted. "Funny? That's not funny at all—it could've hurt one of us!"

"Oh relax, you ditty," a small voice said from the circle of creatures who had been forming around the two of us. I looked down to find a miniature faery scowling up at me. "It was just a joke."

I sneered down at our audience; the likes of Snow White's creatures gone rogue. Talking animals, plants, and flowers . . . if I had ever known that they were to exist, I would not have pictured this lot. I was about to spout off about how my opinion of a joke was a little less dangerous, when there was a rustling of twigs and pinecones as yet another critter made its way to the circle of onlookers. A raccoon wearing wire rim glasses and a hot pink tie, in desperate need of a washing machine, scooted between a deliriously happy flower and what appeared to be an angry gnome. He had half of a dead lizard in his hand, which I quickly gauged was the remnants of a snack.

"Gross," I whispered.

"Have I missed anything?" the raccoon whispered to the flower.

"Nope," the flower said in a voice licked by sunbeams. "She hasn't even got her wand out yet. She doesn't know where it is."

"What kind 'er faery don't know where 'er wand is?" the scruffy little gnome—another fat baby—asked in a gruff voice.

"The kind who only just found out who she is," answered the flower. "I think it's romantic and exciting—all this—the lost Erwain, after all these years. She's alive!"

"Oh, shut it, you bubbling Betsy," barked the gnome. "You's been down right annoyin' e'er since ya started yer cross-pollination regimen."

"IT HELPS ME!"

Everyone, including myself, jumped back from the flower's explosion. Two rows of sharp teeth had become exposed, and her petals, like a lion's mane, were now sticking out in every direction as if she'd just been electrocuted. Upon the realization that she had, for lack of a better description, lost her shit, the flower recoiled. Using a leaf to smooth out a frazzled petal, she lowered her voice and chirped in a more pleasant tone. "One cannot help if they are born with a depressive disposition. The Bizz Buzz factor has saved me from my own detrimental mind. I thank Gaia every day for Daisy Delamonte's self-help propaganda."

My mouth hung halfway open when Tanker brought me back to Earth . . . or wherever this place was.

"All right, Makayla, eyes on me."

I slowly shifted my gaze away from the overmedicated flower and returned my attention to my birth father. "Riiigghhhhht. *So* how do I get my wand?"

"You a'ready 'ave it, don't ya, ya bare ass!" the gnome yelled at me.

I immediately shot him a disgusted look. "I'm sorry, I don't remember asking *you*."

The dirty little vermin was about to retort, invariably with some sort of insult, when Tanker hollered over us yet again.

"Ignore them, Makayla. I need your full attention if this is going to work."

I stood straight up and did as I was told. Even though everything about him screamed frivolous, I very much appreciated Tanker's urgency. As the forest dwellers continued to offer their commentary, I did my best to shut them out.

"As for your wand, Arnie is right. You've always had it. Like I said before, it is a part of you." He lifted his wand in the air as though this was some sort of demonstration, and with the smallest of flicks, made it disappear. Waiting just a moment for dramatic effect, he then reopened his hand and it appeared inside it once more. "It is just like that, you see. We call on it and it comes to us." He pointed the wand down at Arnie, and suddenly the gnome was purple.

"'AY!" Arnie yelled, balling up his little fists before extending out his purple fingers. "Wha' you do tha' for?!"

Tanker flicked his wand in the direction of the gnome once more and returned him to his original peach color. "Sorry Arnie, just needed to provide an example."

"Oh, alrigh' then," he said, resigning back down to where he'd been lounging. "Gla' ter help then, Tanker."

"Okay," I said, wringing my hands out in front of me. "So I just need to figure out how to retract it from my soul. No big deal. I've done it before, right?"

Tanker winked at me. "I highly doubt you'd be standing here if you hadn't. You wouldn't have been able to ward off whoever was after you that night if you didn't have your wand."

Suddenly an uproar lifted out from the circle of onlookers.

"You *were* attacked then!"

"Do you remember who it was?"

"Was it an elf?"

I looked down at the assorted wildlife and talking flowers, but I didn't have to give an answer, Tanker was already on top of it.

"Quiet, all of you! Makayla has only just found out who she is! She doesn't need you bombarding her with questions that even she doesn't have the answers for. If she wants to tell you anything, she will."

There was a very small bit of silence before a tree off to the side, said very slowly, "Why is she calling herself Makayla? You named her Lala."

"Because that is what she likes to be called," Tanker answered, preparing to move on with our lesson.

"Well that is just the silliest name," the raccoon said, licking some blood from his lips.

Offended, I looked down at him. "Oh really? And what do they call you?" Yes, I Makayla Wood, was arguing with a raccoon in a pink tie. What the actual . . .

"Named after my father, I am. And he was named after his father. I'm none other than Dangelo the third."

A righteous laughter broke out.

"Dangelo is your name? And you think Makayla is silly," I ventured to ask.

The raccoon, looking insulted, stood up and began to argue, but changed his mind, barking back at me instead. "Fine, but at least I am proud of what my parents named me." He dropped the dead lizard's head on the ground, and the flower, revealing a set of sharp teeth that should belong to no such hybrid, swallowed it whole.

Letting out a foul belch, she giggled.

"Don' think that be on Daisy's plan, sweetheart," the gnome teased.

Letting down her guard for the second time, the flower spat back, "IT'S A CHEAT DAY!"

Once more, I just stood there, mouth gaping. Where the hell was I?

Shaking away the strange distraction, I returned my

attention to Tanker. "Maybe I should be reading up on all this stuff first. Is there a book on this dust that I might skim through—investigate the origins of such madness?"

"No, no, Makayla. The answers are already within you." He tapped his heart with his finger. "There is nothing you can learn from a book that will teach you about your own soul."

"Really?" I asked, dropping my hands to my sides. This wasn't going to be quite as easy as I'd thought it would be.

After three failed attempts to conjure up a bit of dust, including standing on a tree stump—an action I was told was disrespectful by a nearby cedar tree—and reaching for the sunlight as though I could find my faery dust in it, Tanker and I made our way back to the cottage.

"It will be okay, Makayla. We will get there. You must have faith and patience."

Faith and patience. No, what I needed to have were bullet points, a highlighter, and notebooks. This was not the way I preferred to learn, and I found myself warding away another serious panic attack just thinking about how long this might take.

I was doing everything in my power not to say this out loud, because I was still of a professional mind. Be excellent, I kept saying to myself. In order to achieve greatness, I must overcome! These thoughts were running avidly through my mind, like a bunch of motivational posters hanging on an office wall, when we passed a tiny stone faery looking out from a tree. Her mouth was wide open, and her eyes so enlarged that they appeared nearly half as big as her whole body.

"Hey," I said, pointing at the small figurine. "What is that? It's like that strange statue you and Maude have in your backyard."

Tanker glanced at the faery for no longer than a second or two before returning his attention to the path in front of him.

"Never mind those. They've been put here and there by order of the king. Pay no attention to them."

I gave him an odd sort of look. "Why would the king have statues of horrified creatures placed around his kingdom?" That was a sentence I'd never thought I'd say.

Tanker scratched his chin and let out a nervous laugh. "You think they look horrified, do you? Nonsense. That's just how they look. Now, I bet you're starving after all that. You'll find utilizing your magic may tempt your taste buds to things you're not used to eating. Faeries, especially, require more sugar. When we get back how about we go out for some lunch. Or would you rather stay in?"

"I suppose we could go out."

"Great. There's a wonderful little place on the edge of the forest. Run by a retired kitchen witch. She really does make a good jambalaya."

"What's that?"

Tanker looked at me like I'd gone mad. "Have you never had jambalaya?"

"No. We had a personal chef at the house for a while, but all he ever really made was French cuisine. Other than that, we do a lot of take out."

"It's settled then, we will check up on Maude and then head out."

Just the mention of her name made me feel uneasy. I had to say something.

"Tanker, what I said about Maude last night—I didn't mean it. I mean, I sort of did, but I never meant to hurt her feelings. I know she's upset today."

"You are going to have to wait for Maude to come back around, I'm afraid. She's a giddy soul but takes everything to heart. She's never thought of you as anything less than her daughter; the reality of what's really happening is just a little too much for her to handle."

I nodded my head. "That's understandable. I really do feel bad, though."

"Good, that means you have a heart." He smiled feebly. "And if you get to know us, you might find you even have some faery in there. Just so you know, Makayla, being an Erwain isn't something to balk about. It is something truly beautiful, and honorable."

His speech sparked my next question. "How—How did we originate?"

Tanker's eyes widened. "That was many years ago. And not too long ago Garlandia was swarming with us, but as you may soon find out, there are fewer and fewer of us now."

"But why? Are the faeries moving away or dying?"

"Both." He adjusted the sequined clutch he'd tucked under his armpit before laying a hand over my shoulder. "Perhaps, though, this is a conversation better suited for another time. For now, I want you to simply soak in the magic of the land and worry about finding your faery dust. As soon as you can do that, we can venture on towards teaching you the important things, like how to make yourself appear human again."

I thought about arguing with him, because I wasn't very impressed with his answers . . . I wanted more. On second thought, though, he had a point. I was the one who wanted nothing more than to get my life back, and if I asked too many questions about other things, it would just delay my progress.

"Right," I said. "I totally agree. So, jambalaya then."

"Yes, you are in for a real treat," he said, rubbing my shoulder.

However, as we came upon the cottage and passed the medium-sized statue I'd seen from my bedroom window the night before, there was no denying that it had a terrified expression on its face.

Stick to the list, Makayla, I said to myself. *This is about getting rid of these wings, not anything else.* But part of what made me a good candidate for becoming a lawyer was because when I began to ponder something, I couldn't let it go. These statues were sketchy, and it made me curious about what kind of king was ruling this land.

W hen we walked into the kitchen Helene was lounging in one of the yellow chairs around the kitchen table, sipping on what looked like coffee. Her dark hair was braided down her shoulder like Maude's, and she was wearing a dress the color of fresh blood.

As soon as her gaze met mine, something fluttered inside my chest, as though I were watching a tornado begin to move in my direction.

"Oh good, Helene's here," Tanker announced flatly and in a nasal tone, causing her to wince in his direction.

Pinch flew in from the other room followed closely by Asshole, both screeching, "SHUT UP! IT'S THE BRAT! SHUT UP, BRAT!"

They circled around Helene's head, causing her to spill some of the hot liquid from her mug as she tried to push them away from her.

"Quiet you two!" Tanker yelled, but his grin couldn't be hindered by the upset they were causing Helene. Finally, the birds retreated to wherever they'd come from, and Kevin waddled into the kitchen in their place. He came right up to me and sat at my feet.

"Don't act so excited to see me, Tickety Tank," Helene said bitterly, clearly exasperated from the birds as she tried to put her now stray pieces of hair back into their braid. "Of course I'm here, I wanted to see my niece—the one *you* took away from all of us." She softened her lips, returning her gaze to rest over my shoulders. "How's our little lost Erwain this morning? Maude tells me you went out to fetch your magic. Did you find it?"

"Um, no. Not yet," I said, looking over to where Maude stirred around some herbs with her wand. She tried to keep her head down. I wondered how long it would take before she started speaking to me again.

"Well, I am just so appalled that you didn't ask me to come with you, Tanker. We all know my skills are much more refined than yours. I can offer the girl things you can't."

"How you cast and how I cast have nothing to do with each other, Helene. I wouldn't say one way is more skilled than the other—only that you lack ethics in your practices."

Helene placed a hand over her chest. "That is a strong accusation to say to someone during these times, Tanker."

But he didn't seem fazed by her reaction, instead he walked over to Maude and kissed her on the cheek. "Ah, what do we have here? Licorice extract?" He picked up what I thought was a coffee pot and sniffed the contents.

"Yes, fresh this morning," Maude said delicately.

"Very good, I'll have some when we get back. Makayla and I are starving and are going to head over to Cajun Cathy's for lunch. Would you fancy a meal, dear?"

Maude continued to mix herbs in a little bowl with the tip of her wand. Without looking up, she said, "No thank you. I've got some remedies to tend to."

I could tell Tanker was a little disheartened. I felt horrible

—this was my fault. Maude was only acting this way because she'd heard me call her a flake. Wanting to shield myself from her upset, I bent down and ruffled Kevin's ears, at which point he decided it was a good time to roll over onto his back and let me rub his fat little tummy. When I looked back up, Helene's attention was geared on me once more.

"What did you learn today?" she asked pointedly, taking a sip from her cup.

"Um, well, I learned about faery dust, and that I can't really do anything until I figure out how to acknowledge it."

"Yes, yes, that's a good beginning, but it could take weeks, even months for someone like yourself to find awareness."

"Wait—what? Nobody told me that."

"Stop it, Helene," Tanker warned. "Don't go giving her anxiety. Everyone is different."

"Yes, and you said it yourself last night, she's not a faery. She's been raised as a human. My god, I can feel the nerves tightening within her even now. She's not cut out to learn from someone like you. She needs structure, this one." She placed her attention fully on me. "Detailed explanations, roots. She is not going to learn from intuition alone."

"Why not?" Tanker asked, stepping between us. "She's done it before. May have been a while ago, but I don't know any other swaddling who has ever been able to perform magic like that? She shed her wings when she was just three-weeks-old."

"Swaddling?" I asked.

"Newborn faery," Helene clarified, before sitting back in her chair. "I just think she could use another pair of wings helping her, that's all."

"We will be just fine on our own," Tanker snipped. "Come on, then, Makayla. Let's get going before lunch is over." He stared down at Helene one more time, and I could tell it killed him to ask her, but still he did. "Would you like to join us?"

She smiled deviously, as though she was taking pleasure in his pain. "No, but thanks for asking. I've got prior obligations with the neighborhood watch. Apparently, there's been another abduction."

Tanker's irritation with his sister-in-law quickly dispersed. "Another Ardeen faery?"

Helene sipped on her drink and nodded.

"Damn," he whispered under his breath. "That makes . . . how many in the last month?"

"Three," Helene said, looking down at her cuticles. "And the king isn't listening to the rest of the council's pleas that they get extra security out at night."

"Of course, he isn't," Tanker said, his right hand balled into a fist. "It's always been up to us. Well, I will surely be hearing from Contessa very soon, then. Especially now that I'm sure word has spread about our daughter's—I mean, about Makayla's return."

"Who is Contessa?" I asked, standing up.

"The Erwain's representative for the council," Helene retorted. "Not that it matters, the king hasn't listened to anything we've had to say for years—"

"That's enough of this," Tanker cut in. Then turning to me, he asked, "Are you ready?"

"Sure," I said, looking over at Maude while she continued to ignore my presence. It almost hurt, watching the woman who was my biological mother give me the silent treatment. As we left, I felt Helene's needle point eyes on me, as though she knew she wasn't through with me yet.

⚜

Tanker's high heels clacked away as we strolled along a cobblestone path on our way to Cajun Cathy's. We passed many homes of various sizes, but I only saw two others as large as the Abberwockey residence. The other ones were either half as tall and wide, or what looked like deluxe birdhouses. I hadn't yet seen a single vehicle, but before I asked if there was such a thing here in this world, I remembered the giant purple and blue wings attached to my backside. They already had means of transportation.

"What is an Ardeen faery?" I asked Tanker, once the silence we'd been sharing had grown from uncomfortable to slightly more nerve racking.

"Ardeens are the smallest of the fey, and also the oldest. Their lineage goes so far back, it can't be documented. Then there are the Sheridan faeries, and those range in height anywhere from one to four feet. They've also been around for a very long time. Then of course there is us, the Erwains."

"And we all live amongst elves—but I haven't seen any of those yet. Is there just one type of elf?"

"No, there are many kinds, but the two most prominent living in Garlandia are the Wood elves and the Aeronian elves. King Loral is an Aeronian elf."

"King Loral? This is your ruler?"

"Yes."

"Does he rule alone, or is there a queen?"

"No queen."

The more we spoke of this, the more fidgety he became; but I didn't get to dig much further because just then we came upon a small stone cottage with rickety old tables and chairs of all sizes strewn around the premises, and a large, tilted sign that read Cajun Cathy's. Part of the sign looked as though it had been pulled from a fire. The place looked a little foreboding and there was a strange weed with purple flowers all over it growing around the stairs to the place. But even I had to admit the smells coming from inside were amazing.

"Looks like it's emptied out quite a bit," Tanker observed. "Good news is there should be ample seating, bad news is there might not be much left. Watch your step, the Zappyweed is out of control over here."

My head snapped in his direction. "Zappyweed?"

"Yes. It'll climb around your limbs and cause quite the itch, and it'll laugh itself to sleep as you scratch."

"Right . . . Hey Tanker?"

"Yes Makayla?"

"Is there a karaoke bar around here? Some place called the Knight's Club, or something to that effect?"

"Used to be. Was off Octopus Lane and Shadow's Love Affair. Afraid folks just haven't been in the mood to sing all that much lately." He quickly cleared his throat and redirected his speech before I had a chance to jump on the statement. "Then again, I think we'd all heard "I Will Survive" enough times that we are all just fine with the intermission."

"I Will Survive," I muttered. "Marge the Beaver."

"Why yes—it was her who sang that song. Do you remember that? You were just a few days old when we took you to that place."

I pushed past the idea of my faery parents taking me to a karaoke bar when I was just an infant and replied to my birth father. "I don't remember it, but—well, never mind."

I was suddenly too famished to explain. Between my stubbornness and everything else that had ensued, I hadn't had a bite to eat since lunch the day before.

We sidestepped the vinery of purple-headed Zappyweeds and entered the restaurant. There were a couple gnomes sitting at a very small picnic table in the corner, and a table of faeries of all different sizes. Two of each, actually. The Ardeens were perched on the shoulders of the Erwains, and the Sheridans were sitting on booster seats. As soon as we walked in everyone stopped talking and stared at me.

"My god, Tanker! Is that *her*?" asked one of the Erwains, a blond man wearing a tattered newsboy cap, with green wings, and very light skin.

The female Erwain who sat across from him stood, the Ardeen on her shoulder fluttering down to the table. This Erwain had darker skin but red hair, orange wings, and her eyes were very blue. I blinked twice while taking in her costume—er—her clothes. She wore black and white striped tights under a purple tutu and a peasant shirt with puffy shoulders, covered by a corset.

"No, it can't be. I thought everyone was joking . . ." Her hand came up to her mouth. "Is it? Is it Lala?"

Wanting to squash this whole name fiasco before it got out of hand, I took a few steps towards the faery and held out my hand. "You can call me Makayla." I smiled. "And what's your name?"

Tanker snickered behind me as the female Erwain gawked at my hand.

Pointing down at it with a bright red fingernail, she asked, "What's wrong with it?" When I didn't answer, she looked at Tanker. "Why is she doing this?"

I looked back at Tanker who was chuckling under his breath. "It's a human thing, she's been raised as one."

There was a low humming throughout the small cafe as everyone took in the new information. I could hear little snippets from the creatures.

"Oh my, raised as a human?"

"I wonder if she knows Stella Ferguson, good old gal who I used to check in on when she was a child."

"That's a long time to shield your wings."

"In my world this a greeting," I explained to the she-faery. "It's how we introduce ourselves to one another."

She continued to inspect my hand for a moment before beaming with recognition. "Oh! Of course!" Then she slapped it, hard, before introducing herself. "My name is Contessa."

I retracted my hand and frowned.

"What's wrong, then? Did I not do it right? Oh wait." She pointed a finger at me. "I bet this is one of those actions that's supposed to be reciprocated, isn't it?" She held out her hand, but then quickly pulled it away. "It's probably supposed to go on my face, isn't it," she evaluated, leaning her cheek into me.

I wasn't really sure what to do. I could go ahead and nip this whole thing in the butt and tell her that she'd done it wrong, but at this point I felt like it would be demeaning to do so. So instead, I slapped her cheek.

"Oh yay!" she yelled, clapping her hands together and jumping around, her giant orange wings raising up behind her. "Did you see that, Owen? I did something human!"

The blond Erwain faery nodded his head, but he didn't look nearly as excited.

"You two should have a seat with us," Contessa said as she continued to beam. "We've just finished lunch, but we can hang around while you eat. Cathy! Two more specials please!"

There was some clinking and smashing of pots and pans coming from the small open window between what I assumed was the kitchen and the restaurant, and suddenly the face of an old woman with light purple hair—like a dye job gone wrong—stuck her head out.

"Just two then?" she asked. One of her eyes was cloudy, like it was dead, and the other one floated around as though it couldn't focus on just one thing.

"Yes please," answered Contessa.

Cathy's head disappeared back into the kitchen and Contessa grabbed my arm, ushering me to a place at the table. I sat down, feeling oddly uncomfortable about having to socialize with all these strange faeries, and watched as Tanker pulled up an extra chair and squeezed into the space across from me—laying his sequined purse next to a half empty glass of some sort of bright green liquid that was making bubbles like witch's brew.

"This is Sabrina," Contessa was saying, pointing to the little faery who had flown back up to her shoulder. The tiny Ardeen smiled and bowed her head. "These two are Todd and Grady," she pointed to the two Sheridan faeries, both about three feet tall. "Todd and Sabrina are both on the council with me; and then that is Jerry perched on Owen's shoulder. Owen is my husband."

The blond faery nodded his head at me. He didn't seem as friendly as Contessa.

I looked around at all the new faces—out of all of them I would remember Contessa's name for sure. That was a classy name.

"I hope we aren't interrupting a council meeting," I said, automatically trying to reach for a napkin to lay over my lap, but there weren't any.

"Oh no, this isn't a formal meeting. Puck, Adlar, and Teagan are all absent, and if I dare say King Loral, but we *are* discussing Larry's disappearance."

That name I remembered. Wasn't that the first faery I saw in Garlandia, the one who I swatted away?

"Oh dear," Tanker said, lowering his head into his hands. When he looked back up, exhaustion was painted into the lines of his face. "I just heard about the latest abduction. It was Larry?"

The Ardeen faery named Jerry, who was perched on Owen's shoulder, nodded gravely. "I don't know who we're dealing with here, but to kidnap that son of a goblin, well, it has to be someone very unsavory."

"Any leads then?" asked Tanker, his elbows on the table.

"Nothing, not a thing," Contessa said. "Just like all the other ones. Poor chap."

"And of course, he lived alone, so there's no one to

interview," said the Sheridan council member named Todd. "Wasn't very easy to get along with . . . I just don't understand who would want to take him."

"Here we go dears," a raspy voice said over the table, as an old spotted hand laid down a silver tray before me with what looked like slop on it. I immediately backed away, and in the process, I rammed my wings too hard against the chair back and yelped. I still forgot they were there sometimes. As I sat back up, pulling my marked wing over my lap and petting it as if to make it better, I noticed Contessa gazing at the star. All of them were for that matter—until they caught me staring back at them, at which point they all looked away.

Paying no mind to the sudden awkwardness that had enveloped us all, Tanker rubbed his hands together in front of him as Cathy the kitchen witch laid down his plate of brown mush.

"There you are, then," she said, placing her hands on her hips and moving her traveling gaze to rest over my shoulders. I was pretty sure she was looking at me, but it was hard to tell. "This is her, then? The little lost Erwain. Well, welcome back," she said, sounding a little winded still.

"Thank you," I answered politely, wondering which eye to look at.

"This one," she said, pointing to the dead-looking one.

"Oh!" I exclaimed, super embarrassed.

The Ardeen sitting on Contessa's shoulder buzzed next to my ear. "Don't worry, she's used to it."

"Bit of an explosion in the kitchen, I'm afraid," Cathy said. "It was years ago, a jinxed jalapeño—never buy produce from a gnome."

"Hey!" one of the gnomes in the corner protested.

"Sorry, but it's true," Cathy said, shaking her head and heading back to her kitchen.

"She's used to people staring at her funny," Sabrina

squeaked. "Don't worry about it. Now eat your jambalaya before it gets cold."

"Oh right," I said, staring down at the pile of what looked like something I had already eaten and regurgitated. "Um, where are the utensils?"

One would think I had asked if I could go to the bathroom on the table from the expressions on their faces.

"What are utensils?" Contessa asked.

"You know, spoons, knives, forks. Things to eat your food with." I looked up at Tanker. "You're a food critic, you know."

He stared at me quizzically for a moment before a look of realization washed over him. "Oh, is that what those things are for?" Looking up at the rest of them, he said, "Do you remember one of the first pieces Maude and I wrote—"

"About the humans and their eating weapons?" Todd asked.

"Yes! Oh goodness, well that explains a lot," Tanker said, and then to my horror grabbed a handful of slop and smeared it across his face. I think some of it got in his mouth.

"Go on then," Contessa said in my direction. "Eat up!"

"You all—just—eat with your hands?" I asked.

They all nodded as though it was a silly question.

"And you don't have any of the *food weapons* available here?"

Tanker swallowed a mouth full of food and reached down to grab some more. "Of course not. If we had those, we wouldn't be able to lick our fingers clean, and that's the best part."

"Right," I said, sounding a bit exasperated. "Well then, I guess I should just go ahead and—" Oh, it felt so disgusting! So warm and slimy, and uncivilized! Had my parents endured these sort of eating habits with the Abberwockeys before? My sophisticated, savvy parents.

They were all waiting for me to taste the food—all their

wings raised in the air in anticipation. Ever so slowly, I lifted my hand, caked in goo, up to my nose and sniffed it. It smelled spicy, and a bit earthy. Suddenly I was worried it was made of dirt.

"Go on then," Tanker said with his mouth full.

I exhaled a shaky breath, then carefully placed two fingers into my mouth, preparing myself for the worst—but what I tasted wasn't terrible. It was actually . . . well, it was actually quite good. Digging my fingers gingerly into the jambalaya I pulled out a shrimp and stared at it.

"The flavors are almost alive," I noted appreciatively. "What is that? Tomato, perhaps some chili pepper?"

"She keeps her recipes secret," Todd advised. "You don't want to crack her code either, or you'll feel her wrath. Looks like a sweet old witch, but she can get feisty, that one."

I placed the shrimp in my mouth and nodded, but as I allowed the complex flavors to break down around my taste buds, I thought to myself that Cathy looked nowhere near that of a sweet old witch.

❧

Tanker and Maude had to meet with the neighborhood about Larry's disappearance that afternoon, so I decided to go for a walk into the forest and practice searching for my dust. On my way out of the house, however, I'd heard what I could only assume was a burp. When I looked down, I saw that there was a large bright green frog wearing a faded purple bow tie.

"Oh dear, you'll have to excuse me," he said. "Try not to mind me, then, Miss Makayla."

The fact that everything and everyone in Garlandia had a voice was starting to feel normal . . . and that was weird. I took a seat and pointed to the sign near the Abberwockey's door. "Are you the frog who enjoys debates?"

"Right-O, Herbert the intellectual frog here at your service. What's your pleasure? I hear you've been raised human, so I'm sure you've got some rather laughable ideas about the afterlife."

"I was just asking. And I haven't given a lot of thought to that matter to be perfectly honest. Perhaps you *can* fill me in on something else though."

"Would be my pleasure, love—BURP! Oh no, please—BURP—excuse me, it's such a vulgar ailment."

The burping was amusing but I could clearly see that Herbert found it extremely revolting. The poor creature looked absolutely embarrassed.

"Don't worry about it," I said, trying to keep a straight face. "We all have these hiccups in our lives, don't we?" I pointed back to my wings.

"Ah yes, I've been hearing all about *you*." He lowered his head in my direction and said quietly, "And I agree with your name change. It suits you."

"Thank you, Herbert."

"What was your question, then—BURP."

"Do you mind if I get personal?"

"Shoot."

"How is it you can talk?"

"Ah, of course. The intellectuals in your world are keen to keep their heads down, and I daresay they never wear clothing. However would you know about us before now?"

"Intellectuals?"

He nodded. "Yes. Just like everyone else, we have evolved from simple-minded beings into creative and complex-minded individuals. In every species there are intellectuals and ninnies."

"You are calling the simple folk idiots?" I accused.

"No, not at all. You see, some people define the word ninny as innocent, and that is what they are. I'm sure you can think of a few ninnies from the human world that aren't animals, am I wrong?"

I smiled. "No Herbert, I don't think you are."

BURP.

I tried to contain the smirk on my face. "I should be going. I have to practice looking for my dust. I'm sure you've heard of my predicament by now—it seems the whole forest knows of me." Because there wasn't a rock or blade of grass that seemed to be absent from knowing how to talk, or even raise a brow.

"Yes, yes. And if you don't mind me saying, Miss Makayla of the Erwain descent, it is hard for intellectuals to see past what our minds are telling us and listen to our souls, but the truly brilliant ones learn how."

I began to stand up, adjusting my large wings behind me as I did so. "How do I do that? All I've ever known are books and concrete evidence. I don't know how to search for something that I don't believe in."

Herbert bowed his head and nodded. When he returned his gaze to me, he said, "Perhaps my debates would be beneficial for you, young one. For what is a god or a goddess other than something one must search for? An entity that only exists if you believe in it."

"A god *or* a goddess. Do you believe that there are multiple higher powers out there?"

"Like I said, I believe there is anything as long as you breathe life into it."

"Interesting . . ." I stood there for a moment, mulling over his words. And then he burped. "All right Herbert, I'll think about that."

Before I could walk away, he gestured to his head. "Do you mind giving it a scratch—I can't reach, and it's a terrible itch."

I bit my lip as I smirked. I guess I could cross off 'scratch a talking frog on its head' from any future list. Then, I bent down and scratched his head with the tip of my finger. "Thanks for the talk."

Relishing in my touch, he said, "Anytime. Oh, smells like someone's been to Cathy's. Ran right through me the first time I had it. Good luck with that—BURP."

And then I was off into the woods, waiting until I got far enough away to release the laughter I'd accrued from speaking with a chronically afflicted burping frog. In fact, it was the first time I remember laughing that hard. Possibly ever.

The days ticked by and I wasn't getting any closer to seeing even a hint of faery dust. The harder I tried and the faster I failed, the more anxious I grew.

Days could easily turn to weeks, and weeks to years in the blink of an eye. If I didn't hurry, the crisp white paper of the last list I'd written—lying on my desk in the house of Wood—would begin to turn yellow, and my ink would inevitably fade. I was going to outlive my human parents by centuries. That piece of paper I'd used to write down my goals could very well be buried under heaps of dirt by the time I returned to that world.

My anxiety was also fueled by the curiosity of how I was the first Erwain born in such a long time; and though I was very much concerned with getting back to my old life, every second that I was here in Garlandia, I found myself thinking more and more about what all that could mean. But then, of course, nothing was going to happen until I figured out how to manipulate my soul's energy into dust.

For a split second, the previous day, I'd caught a glimmer in the sun that I'd thought had been the beginning of finding my magic, but it had only turned out to be a naughty Ardeen faery playing a trick on me by blowing dandelion fuzz my way. And that was another thing I'd learned over the short time I'd been in Garlandia. Faeries were ornery. It didn't matter how big or small they were, they were feisty, and at best, playful. I had found that some of their 'occupations' were nothing more than causing mayhem.

Todd for instance, the Sheridan faery I'd met at lunch, was a weeder. Not like someone who pulls weeds from people's yards—no, Todd was responsible for planting them and making sure they got plenty of fertilizer via his own excrement. He made a living squatting in people's lawns! I'd also heard one say that he was a resolver. When I'd asked what that might be, my jaw dropped. Evidently there were lots of 'resolvers,' and most of them were Ardeens. Their sole purpose in life was to follow humans around, and if their assigned individual was found guilty of any sort of earthly destruction—such as littering or cutting down a live tree—they ensured that he or she lost their hair, their wallet, or worse. I just didn't understand it, nor could I fathom the idea that I had the same blood running through my veins (and wings for that matter) as these troublemakers.

"Humans are the worst," Sabrina had mentioned, when describing why she'd become a resolver at a picnic lunch one day. "Of all the worlds *theirs* is the dirtiest, and they don't even have Scaldrons to pick up after. Don't they realize that if their world fails, that it will affect everyone else's?"

I never did ask what any of that meant—it was far beyond anything I could comprehend.

And then there was the issue of faery fashion. Over the last few weeks, before my 'explosion', I'd been learning to dress a bit more casual during my forced early retirement; but shorts and t-shirts were one thing—tutus and renaissance dresses, well, I just couldn't make myself do it. Not yet, anyhow. The problem was I was beginning to understand that faeries used magic in place of more than a few things . . . like laundry. And as part of my training, Tanker had advised everyone and anyone not to help me out. I guess he figured it would push me harder in the direction of gaining back my dust.

But Garlandia had a faint mugginess about it, enough so that I was most definitely aware of the stink beginning to accrue on my clothing. Not to mention that the previous night, during our silent and awkward dinner—as Maude was still not speaking to me—my faery birth mother had made an unpleasant face while reaching for my plate to clear the table, and the next thing I knew there was a pile of strange faery clothes on my bed. I'd entertained the idea, but after trying on my third tutu—orange—I'd decided to send away for my clothing. After all, it was what I was always used to. Within no time at all Mort showed up with a large bag full of clothes and necessities sent from home.

"How did you get this through the mailbox?" I asked.

"Just give me somethin' fer the delivery, would ya," he answered rudely. "My services ain't free, and yer Naomi can't cook to save 'er life."

Tanker and Maude had already stepped out for the day, and it was only then that I realized that I'd given away the last of the gnome treats when I'd sent him to my human home. "I'm sorry, Mort. It looks like I don't have anything for you."

"Then make somethin'. You's got fingers and toes."

"Does it look like I've been versed in the fine culinary world of mud cake baking? *I'm* a business woman."

With a scowl on his Garbage Pail Kid face, he replied curtly, "And *I'm* a business gnome. Bet I can fetch a pretty penny for these human clothes down at the farmer's market. Doin' me a favor really."

"Wait!" I yelled, as he started marching back into the forest. "Give me a second!"

I ran inside to the fridge and searched one more time for the earthly pastries, but there was still nothing.

"Shit," I said to myself, continuing to search the kitchen. Then I paused, looking out the window into the gardens.

My eyes widening, I ran out outside, picked a tomato and brought it back to him. But I had barely extended out my arm when he began shaking his head.

"I's already had one today. I wan' a treat. Somethin' good."

Exasperated, I just stared down at him.

"Better 'urry! Getting bored," he said nasally.

"Are you kidding me?" I asked in disbelief.

But he clearly wasn't, and unless I wanted to raid my birth father's closet—because at least he had an affinity for human women's clothing, even though the fashion was still not my style—I had to do as this little twit of a creature requested.

"Hang on! Don't you dare run off with my clothes!" I yelled, running back into the house and out the back door and diving into the carrots and zucchini. "You want a treat," I huffed, as I violently pulled out the veggies from their roots. "I'll give you one hell of a treat."

Hurriedly, I pulled out an onion, a carrot, and some sort of squash. Then on my way back into the kitchen I started to yank a pink flower out of the ground, but immediately let go of the stem when I saw a pair of blue eyes well up in pain.

"What are you doing? Are you *insane*! What have I done to you?" The male flower's voice was like that of an aggravated taxi driver in New York.

"Oh my god, I am so sorry!" I exclaimed, backing away. "I was just trying to grab some ingredients to make—"

"Ingredients! Is that what I look like to you?"

"No, absolutely not. I didn't realize you were an intellectual—"

"Just get outta here, would ya."

I felt terrible. The flower's head tilted off to one side from where I'd pulled on it.

"Is there anything I can do?"

"No," he scoffed. "A bee will come along soon enough and patch me up. Go on, get—you've done enough."

"S-Sorry," I repeated before retreating to the kitchen, managing to grab a handful of dirt on my way back in.

"You about done in there? I got things to tend to!" Mort yelled.

I scrunched my fingers up into my hair, looking down at the vegetables I'd thrown onto the counter, and the dirt I'd slung into a bowl. With his obscenities continuing to stream into the kitchen, I screamed back at the antsy, needy gnome. "Hang on, Mort! If you want something good, then you have to wait for it!"

I had to assess the situation, think judiciously as though I was attempting to piece back together an international affair gone haywire—like the time our Kenya office of Sewn Back Together got ransacked and we had to figure out how to get more supplies to the workers before their wages got cut. I figured *that* out, I could do this.

Once I'd found a cutting board and knife, I set them aside and boiled some water. I chucked the squash into the pot, then quickly but concisely, began chopping up the carrot and onion. I took pride in everything I did, and that wasn't going to change just because I was making pastries from dirt.

When that was finished, I searched through the cupboards for some salt and any other spices I could find. A reddish powder caught my eye. Paprika.

Without a second's hesitation, I pulled down the spice and sprinkled it into the mud concoction. It was all dry still, though, and I needed it to make a paste. I supposed water would do, but that just seemed sort of, well, boring.

Sticking my head out the front door, my fingers now

darkened by the dirt, I asked Mort, "Are you lactose intolerant?"

"Wha? I don' even know wha' that means."

"Never mind—almost done."

"All righ'," he said, with a bent forward neck and a cocked eye.

I ran back into the kitchen and checked on my squash. It seemed soft enough, so I pulled it from the boiling water and peeled away the skin. It was purple and tasted a little sweet. Nodding my head in approval, I spooned out the squash and added it to my mud paste along with all the other ingredients, mixing in a bit of milk to make it smoother.

I knew I didn't have time to bake it, so instead I grabbed two bowls, filling one with ice and then placing the other inside of it. I cranked my arm quickly, manually mixing the concoction together until it became more solid and eventually turned into the stinkiest, most revolting ice cream I had ever seen. When I was finished, I found a cute little bowl and placed some of it inside. Then, cocking my head to the side, I realized it wasn't finished—that I couldn't in good conscious serve it like that just yet. I ran over to the fridge one more time and searched for something to top it with.

"Perfect," I said, finding a bit of mint in one of the drawers.

Snipping just a sprig or two, I gently laid the herb on top. If one hadn't known what it really was, it would have looked pleasing enough to eat.

"Wha' is that?" Mort asked, once I reappeared with the creation—a scowl on his face.

"It's iced mud cream," I said, wiping away a bit of sweat from my forehead and most likely leaving a dirty streak across my skin.

"I don' know abou' that," he said, eyeing the bowl as though I'd added poison.

"Come on, Mort. Just try it, I worked really hard on it."

The mailbox gnome continued to eye the bowl in my hands, but eventually he dropped my bag of clothes on the ground and reached a grubby hand in my direction. "All righ', but if it's anything like yer mom's cooking, then this deal is off."

"Fine," I said. Deep down I knew I couldn't do any worse than Naomi Wood.

Mort stuck his chubby fingers into the bowl and pulled out a glob of the dirty dessert. "Whatcha got in here? Is those carrots?"

"Um-hm," I said, my hands behind my back as though I was waiting to get critiqued by a world-renowned foodie.

"That's rather nice, never get those," he said, sniffing the ice cream. "Well, here it goes, then." He sucked up the glob.

I held my breath, waiting for the outcome. Oddly, I found myself not even worried about my clothes as much as his approval.

"I'll be damned," he said, staring down into the bowl.

"I'm sorry?" I questioned, my heart beginning to race. "Is that a good thing, or a bad thing."

"Why this is . . . it's just . . . how'd you do this? It's the best thing I've ever 'ad."

A huge smile began to take over my face and I knew I was blushing. "Naw, you're just saying that."

"No, really. Wow. All righ', you can have yer clothes, but I'm keepin' the bowl."

"Okay," I said, watching as Mort stalked off, his face immersed in the iced mud cream.

Feeling glorified for the first time in weeks, I bent down and retrieved my clothes and reentered the Abberwockey home.

My mom had managed to send me a litter of tank tops and

four pairs of shorts with a note that simply said, "We miss you, baby. Hurry up and find your magic."

I'd folded up the note and slipped it into the drawer next to my bed. I wondered if my parents knew how long this was going to take. Thinking back on the way my dad had hugged me, just a little tighter than usual before my mom and I left, I had a feeling they did.

I'd now been in Garlandia for over a week. I wasn't any closer to figuring any of this out, and Maude *still* hadn't forgiven me. When they'd left earlier to go gather supplies, she hadn't looked up at me when I'd said good-bye. I suppose I deserved it, even Pinch and Asshole knew I was a brat.

After that I went for a walk and somehow ended up further into the forest than I'd ever been. The further away I got, the larger the tree trunks seemed to get. I'd even seen a door or two on the outside of a couple trunks, as though they had been made into homes.

I quickly learned the necessity of being alert, and not just because I saw more than a few flowers show me their teeth as though they were hungry wolves taunting their prey—it was because I'd been warned by a snake wearing the smallest top hat I'd ever seen, trailing a package attached to the end of his body. He'd snuck up on me so quickly I'd almost wet myself when he spoke.

"Oops, didn't mean to scare you! Would you be the lost Erwain, then?"

"Yes . . . that's me," I'd said, my hand over my chest. "I apologize for jumping at you."

"Quite all right, quite all right," he'd said. "Word of advice though, young fey. It may be dangerous past the trees and into the castle, but I assure you it is not any safer this deep into the brush."

"What do you mean?"

"Do think about it, won't you? If you were going to

practice forbidden magic, would you do it in the open? Or would you find somewhere hidden . . . like the deep darkness of the forest?"

"What are *you* doing here then?" I'd questioned.

Gesturing back to the package, he'd said, "Got my own delivery service. More often than not I find myself having to go this way, but I don't judge. A snake's got to eat, too." And then he'd slithered away, deeper into the woods, leaving me wondering what he had exactly meant about the castle being dangerous.

I hadn't even seen this monstrosity yet. As far as I knew it was far enough away to be in its own zip code—not that they had those here. What I did know was that something strange was going on in Garlandia, and my curiosity of what that was interfered with the concentration I needed to find my dust.

Upon the intellectual snake's advice, I hadn't gone any further into the forest, but I'd wandered in pretty far, so it was taking me quite a while to get back. Judging by the sun's position in the sky, I'd guessed that it was nearing five in the evening. I had to thank my lucky stars that there were cobblestone walkways everywhere with 'street signs.' There were also signs on top of the trees, which made sense for those who preferred to fly rather than walk.

I was finally getting through the thicker part of the forest and coming back up on to Serendipity Lane when I heard the beating of large wings and the sound of feet hitting the cobblestone, slowing to a walk. In the hopes that I might meet another Erwain I slowed my own pace, waiting to see if it was someone new. Moments later, Helene's face popped up through the trees.

"Lala—er, I mean, Makayla," she said. There was a quality in her voice that I connected with. She was a very strong individual, and the way she held herself, with her shoulders rolled back and her chin lifted, well, it made me wonder if *she* wasn't my birth mother instead. In a world full of childish nonsense, she felt real to me.

"Helene," I replied, greeting her with a smile, admiring her long black locks as they fell freely around her face. "I was just heading back to the cottage."

She caught up with me and the two of us continued toward 17 Serendipity Lane.

"Any luck today?" she asked.

"No," I replied sadly. "But then again, I don't know what I'm doing. Tanker says I'm supposed to listen to my heartbeat and wait for it to happen, but my mind is too full and the only time I hear my heart is when I'm about to have a panic attack."

She smacked her lips together, and from her snappy little eyebrow raise I could tell that she felt justified. "I knew it. This is why I told him that I should be the one to help you."

I stopped walking and turned to her, my hands out to the sides. "Why doesn't he listen? I think you might be able to help me in ways he can't. I don't want to sound ungrateful towards him, because he has been nothing but understanding towards me, but I feel like it is you who I can relate to the most."

Helene smiled, her perfect lips thinning as she did so. "Well then, perhaps I *should* teach you."

"But Tanker said—"

"Who cares what Tanker said. Do you want to learn how to make those wings of yours invisible or not? Because my dear, at the rate you are going, the next Erwain will be born before you can manage that, and that could be two hundred more years from now."

A look of terror registered on my face. "I do not want to wait that long."

She laughed. "Then let us begin to do this the right way, shall we."

I was about to throw my arms around her and hug her,

when a Sheridan faery, about three feet tall, came running past, followed by three Ardeens. They all looked perfectly frantic.

"What's all this?" Helene asked of the little faeries.

"It's the king's heir!" squeaked an Ardeen. "He's come into the forest!"

My ears perked up. The king was an elf. That had to mean that his heir was an elf, or at least I supposed so. I turned towards the direction the little faeries had come from, but before I could listen for sounds of approaching elves—not that I knew what that sounded like—I felt Helene pulling me slowly away from the path and into the trees. When I turned to her, she had her wand in her hand and a finger up to her mouth.

"Pellucido," she whispered, whirling her wand around our heads.

"What did you just—" I stopped short, where had she gone?

"Shh," she said into my ear. But she wasn't there, and neither was I for that matter.

I held out my hand, but I couldn't see it. She'd turned us invisible.

I wanted to ask her why, but my attention was stolen by the sound of horse hooves hitting the forest floor on the other side of the pathway. In front of us, the Sheridan and Ardeen faeries bent down on their knees, bowing their heads.

"Helene?" I whispered, turning my translucent head from side to side. A finger laid itself over my lips.

"Quiet," my aunt whispered. "They must not hear us."

Just then a tan horse came walking up through the opposite side of the forest, followed closely behind by a white mare. On their backs were what looked like human teenage boys, except their ears were pointy. I struggled against Helene's fresh new grip on my arm, not to take a step forward and get a better look.

"Here's some fey," the one with darker hair and riding the tan horse said. I noticed that both were wearing white suits under long pale blue cloaks.

"Get up," the elf riding the tan horse demanded of the faeries.

"Yes sir," the Sheridan said in a rather shaky voice.

"I was just escorting Sir Toby into the forest in hopes that we might meet the lost Erwain. We knocked on the door of the Abberwockey home, but no one was in. Have you seen them?"

"Why, they are just right here," said the Sheridan, holding out his hand and turning to his right, jumping slightly when he realized Helene nor myself stood there any longer. "Oh dear, I must be losing myself," he whimpered. "I could've sworn."

"They was just there a minute ago, sirs," said one of the Ardeens.

The other elf, the one I supposed to be named Toby, looked over in the direction we were hiding.

As soon as my eyes met his, my lips parted. The world seemed to shrink. The sound of wings fluttering, the far away music of a flute being played, the water in the creek—it was all put on hold. Nothing around the elf—with his light brown skin, translucent blue eyes, and bleach blond hair which he'd secured in a ponytail behind his head—seemed to matter.

"I know him," I whispered. My gaze was securely on his, but he didn't seem to be staring directly back.

It was Helene's nasty retort that brought me back from where I'd floated away from my invisible body. "You *don't* know him," she spat into my ear, "and you need not *ever* know him."

The faintest whisper left my lips, "But I do."

Back on the path, Helene's and my disappearance caused quite the disturbance.

"That's odd," said another of the Ardeens. "Suppose they went off in that direction," she said, pointing deeper into the forest.

Toby raised his eyebrows and looked ahead. "All right, we'll check it out. Thank you for your kindness."

"Yes sirs," all four of them said at once, watching with their lungs full of air and waiting to release it until the elves were out of plain sight. As soon as they were gone, the faeries lifted into the air and flew away as fast as they could.

Pulling away from Helene's grip and ignoring her whispered curses towards my back, I tiptoed over the grassy area of the forest floor, trying as hard as I could not to make a sound. The elves had gotten a bit further ahead, but I could still hear them.

"I think we should turn around," said the one with darker hair. "If King Loral finds out I took you into the forest instead of Lauslin he'll have my head. I don't see what we're doing in here anyway; why do you want to meet this faery so badly?"

"She's the lost Erwain, aren't you curious?"

"Not really. She's just another useless faery to me."

I had to hold back from running over and frightening the elf's horse so he'd get bucked off. What a douche.

"I just thought it would be interesting to meet her, and I don't care what my uncle says."

"I care."

"Don't worry, Rally, I won't let you get in trouble for this. Besides, the king has no reason to believe we are anywhere else but that awful ball."

The elf on the tan horse scoffed. "Can't say I blame you much for wanting to skip this one; I've seen the elfin princess King Loral means for you to court—worse than all the others.

She's got buck teeth, this one, and a bit of an acne problem." He snickered. "Good old Princess Louisa."

Sir Toby chuckled. "That old bat hasn't set me up with anyone worth seeing more than once yet—"

"OUCH! Watch where you're going, then!"

Horrified, I looked down to see a little blue flower, now crumpled and trying like mad to hold its stem back up. What was with me and these cursed flowers?

"Sorry," I whispered, backing away, but not before I noticed the elves' horses had stopped moving, and both their heads were turned in my direction.

"Who goes there?" Sir Toby asked, an authoritative ring to his voice.

I froze.

"Something stepped on me, it did!" the flower whined. "I don't see anything though."

A hand clamped down over my forearm and started pulling me away. "What are you doing?" Helene whispered into my ear.

I waited until we were a safe distance away, until the elves seemed to have given up on the prospect of anyone being there, to respond. "I just wanted another peek."

Once the coast was completely clear and we were back on the path, she lifted the invisibility spell, revealing a rather sour look on her face. "That was very stupid of you. What did you mean when you said *you knew him* anyway? That was a very odd thing to say."

I bit my lip, backtracking for a moment.

"I—I don't know. I guess there was something about his eyes maybe . . ." Like they belonged to a memory. I started to get lost in the thought all over again, but Helene's jagged, violent energy brought me back. Returning my attention to her, I stammered out, "Sorry, I—I've never seen an elf before. I was just curious, that's all. Why'd you make us invisible anyway?"

Helene rolled her shoulders back defiantly and began to lead the way back towards the Abberwockey's house. "If you want to learn from me, then you must follow my rules; and the first rule is, my little lost Erwain: we bow to no one."

My eyes widened. "So that's like a thing here, faeries bow to elves?"

"It is supposed to be. But not just any elves, we are supposed to bow to King Loral and his company."

We passed the same small stone faery up in the tree that I'd seen with Tanker when he took me into the forest for my first lesson. Helene glanced at the small frozen character. "I will not allow us to bow for him nor anyone affiliated with him, and if I see you so much as drop your chin in the company of an elf, I will rescind any promise of aiding you in finding your faery dust." She turned and her stone-cold eyes landed on mine, causing a chill to run down my spine. As this happened, I could've sworn I felt and saw a blue particle move in front of us. "Do you understand?"

"Yes," I said, although not very confidently. It wasn't because I wanted to bow to the king—of course I didn't—that sounded like a completely ridiculous thing to do. It wasn't civilized and it was demeaning. But the way Helene was talking all the sudden, and the deep-rooted anger radiating from her energy just at the mention of King Loral—until I figured out what exactly was going on here, I couldn't help but feel shaky about agreeing to anything. Especially to things I didn't understand nor know anything about.

"Do you think those boys are going to come back through? Do you think they are going to come back to Tanker and Maude's house?"

"No," Helene said positively. "Once they can't find us,

they will assume we've flown away. I swear, the attention span of royalty is thinner than an Ardeen's wings."

"Do you think they wanted to bring me to the king?"

Helene shrugged her shoulders. "I wouldn't know. But if King Loral did want to meet you, he would have you retrieved by someone in his company. He has not left his throne for two hundred years, since the moment he was sworn in."

"Two hundred years?" I questioned. "I assume elves have extremely long lives as well?"

She nodded.

Such a long time, I thought, not to leave a chair. Wouldn't his legs get tired of not moving? Then it occurred to me.

"Helene, doesn't it seem a bit strange that King Loral hasn't left his throne for two hundred years, the same amount of time our race stopped reproducing?"

"No," she said flatly, the cottage appearing before us in the distance. "In fact, if you keep your eyes open, you will soon come to find that it isn't strange at all."

🜲   13   🜲

I was right, as usual. This place was super shady, and I didn't mean because of all the trees.

No sooner had Helene insinuated that something was off about the king, than we'd seen Tanker and Maude appear before us, carrying baskets of groceries. One look at Tanker and Helene had decided she didn't feel like playing nice nice, so she'd taken off, but not before telling me to meet her in the forest the next day. On the corner of Rum St. and Cocker Spaniel.

I decided to keep quiet about running into the elves while in the forest and helped with dinner instead. I also bit down over my tongue and didn't bring up the subject of Garlandia's seemingly corrupt government, although it nearly killed me not to.

"Do you like Portobello mushrooms, Makayla," Tanker asked as we put away the groceries. Today he was wearing a tie-dye t-shirt with green corduroy pants, silver platforms sandals, and an eye patch.

"I do. I've never cooked them, though. We never really cooked back home."

Tanker laughed and elbowed Maude. "That's probably for the better. You remember when Naomi had us over when Lala was just a year old? Poor thing tried to make a meatloaf." He ran his tongue over one of his teeth. "Never did get that chipped tooth fixed."

Maude, who had at this point seemed to be trying *not* to smile or acknowledge me, simply nodded her head.

"What can I do?" I asked, once we were ready to cook.

"You could go pick a few veggies from the garden," Tanker offered. "Then, if you feel comfortable chopping, you could do that. I'm going to start sautéing the mushrooms."

"*Okay!*" I said a little too enthusiastically, causing both Tanker and Maude—and Kevin, who had just waddled into the kitchen—to look at me inquisitively. "It's just that I *can* do that," I said, feeling self-satisfied. I'd had practice from making the iced mud cream.

After I'd collected some onion, zucchini, carrots, and spinach, I meticulously chopped them all up—a little faster this time since I was getting the hang of it—and handed the ingredients over to Tanker. I suddenly wished I had a notebook so I could write down, "Conquer the world of vegetables," and place a check next to it. It wasn't quite the victory I was used to, but these days I'd take what I could get.

At some point Maude left the kitchen to feed the animals —and probably to get away from me. As soon as it was just the two of us, Tanker asked, "Did I see Helene with you earlier, just before you walked up to the house?"

"Uh, yeah," I answered casually. "We walked back from the forest together."

"You know"—he glanced over his shoulder before going on— "you really need to be careful around her."

Narrowing my eyes, I questioned, "What is it with the two of you, if you don't mind me asking?"

"It's just that, well," he took a deep breath, and then

searching out the windows as though he was making sure no one was eavesdropping, he whispered, "it's rumored that she is a member of L.O.A.R."

I scrunched up my nose. "What?" It sounded like a geeky roleplaying game. Then again, fantasy had become my real life in a matter of exploding seconds.

With his voice so low that I could barely make out what he was saying, he clarified, "League of Aeronian Reform. They are a group of Garlandians who wish to usurp the king."

"And why would they want to do that?"

"Because they don't agree with the law of the land—but that's not why they are frowned upon. It's because they desire for the roles to be switched, for the elves to bow to the faeries. Things would not be any better that way. Their leader is tainted and won't listen to reason—"

Just then the kitchen door swung open as though a large wind had pushed through it, and Tanker straightened his back out, running over and closing it again—peering through the window nervously.

"We shouldn't be talking about this," he whispered to himself. When he turned to face me again, he said, "Just be careful around her. I realize there may be some similarities between the two of you, and it may seem to you as though she is more relatable to who you are as a person and a faery, but please listen to me when I say she is not the right one to learn anything from."

I stared at him, cockeyed, dissecting his words.

"You do realize, without any information to go on other than these little spurts I'm given to observe here and there, that it is very hard to agree to what you are saying."

"This is not fatherly advice, Makayla. I am warning you. I have watched Helene change over the years. She's always been surly and disobedient, but recently she's turned from unruly to vengeful. She's not playing around anymore, she's plotting;

and even though I know you don't know that much about this land, I will tell you this, it is not wise to go out of your way to upset the king."

"But why?" I exploded, unable to keep it in any longer. "Nobody will tell me anything! Elves, faeries, talking animals —hierarchies—I don't understand any of it! And minus Sir Toby looking for me in the forest, I have yet to meet an actual elf!"

"Wait—what?"

Oops, I hadn't meant to say that out loud. *Oh well*, I thought, *I might as well own it*. Straightening my back and standing up taller, I replied, "Sir Toby and another elf boy were looking for me today."

Tanker leaned slightly forward. "How do you know this?"

I looked away, searching for a more suitable answer than the truth. He probably wouldn't be excited to hear that I'd let Helene turn me invisible and sneak me away, not after all he'd had to say about her. "A Sheridan faery told me just before we got back to the house. I guess I'd just missed them."

Tanker studied me, discernibly. There were wheels turning in his head, and I wanted so badly to know what thoughts they were churning; but before he could say anything Maude walked back into the room.

Taking a moment to absorb the uncomfortable energy we seemed to have created, she asked, "What have you two been discussing?"

Tanker backed away from where he'd been leaning over my shoulders and went back to blending vegetables together with his hands.

"Oh, nothing much." Then, changing gears, he sprang into song. "*I know a purdy girl named Maude. When I first met her, I felt flawed, but upon getting her kiss, I knew I was amiss, because who could ever be a true fraud, when falling in love with Maude!*"

She snickered, the most I'd heard out of her in days, and went over to the stove and flipped over the mushrooms.

Asshole swerved into the room and circled my head. "HELLO BRAT!"

Exhaustion fell over me like the faery dust I couldn't seem to summon. I just stared at the two faeries, and asked, "Can I wake up now?"

⚜

Per the usual, we ate in silence, which was fine. The food was delicious, thank god; it distracted me from missing my human parents, and my old life where everything was perfectly fitted together and made sense. But even though I was home sick and longing for any sense of normalcy, that juicy Portobello burger, complimented by the veggie patty Tanker had put together with my chopped veggies, was worth this temporary insanity.

"You two should really open your own restaurant," I said, licking my fingers, an act I'd slowly been getting used to. "You could give that old kitchen witch some decent competition."

"Naw," Tanker said bashfully. "We aren't that good."

"Yes, you are. This is great. I'd pay at least fourteen dollars for it in the human world."

"Really?"

"Tanker," Maude said quietly.

"Right—uh, no. We are just fine working for *The Garlandian Buzz*. And that reminds me, there is a performance coming up in the park, oh what is it? *King Lear*."

"No," Maude said, picking at her burger as though she was without an appetite. "Don't you remember, King Loral struck it from the roster. The company was forced to choose from one of the approved titles to replace it."

"That's right," Tanker said, staring past Maude's face. "What is it they chose then?"

"*RATS*."

"What was that, Maudie? Say again."

Maude lifted the bun of her burger and then let it drop back down. It seemed she was finished. "The musical. We reviewed it in the human world December 17, 1993. Eight o' clock P.M. Except there it was called *CATS*. They've made some revisions."

Tanker closed his eyes and pressed the pads of his fingers up to his temples. After another minute or so they flew open. "Yes, yes! Oh dear, the Garlandia Shakespeare Company is going to perform that? They don't fare so well with song."

Maude shrugged her shoulders and stood. "The king doesn't want Shakespeare read on his stage anymore, nor any of their usual scripts, so I've heard. They've had to completely redesign their sets." She reached for Tanker's plate, but before she could take it, he bent down and licked it clean.

I made a sour face.

Once he was finished, he looked up at me. "Everything all right?"

"Yes," I said too quickly, handing my plate to Maude. I had other things on my mind besides my birth father's atrocious dinner habits. "If you don't mind me asking, why would the king get involved with the local theatre? I mean, what about free speech?"

Maude looked directly at Tanker, who returned the daunting stare; but I wasn't allowed to hear the answer, because just then there was a knock at the door, giving Tanker the excuse he so obviously desired to run from my question.

"Who in the name of the king would be calling at this hour?" Maude asked, pointing her wand at a scrubbing pad, causing it to go madly to work on one of the dishes. "Haven't they learned to stay in their houses after dark?"

Suddenly my muscles tensed. "What if it's those elves again?"

A plate fell into the sink and when I turned to look at her, Maude had frozen stiff. Then in one fluid movement, she was standing behind me, a firm grip on each of my arms as though she was about to take off and pull me along with her. "What elves?"

"Uhhh," I stalled, unsure of how to answer her. "Today while I was out, there were some guys from the castle . . ." I bit down over my lip and looked to Tanker for some sort of help.

"I'm sure it's nothing," he said, looking directly at Maude.

"No, *it's never nothing*. Tank, we just got her back! I—no! I won't let them—"

"Maude," Tanker said, his gaze growing heavy over hers. "Let's just see who it is before we start flying off the handle, shall we."

Suddenly my heart was racing. Maude seemed to be insinuating that she was afraid the elves were going to take me away.

Nevertheless, as Tanker went to open the door, Maude—who seemed to have forgotten that she was mad at me—squeezed my shoulders even tighter. I held my breath as he turned the doorknob; but when he opened it there was no one there. Or at least it appeared that way.

Ever so slowly he dropped his gaze, and a second later his shoulders and his wings relaxed.

"Oh, it's just you," he said, relief heavy in his voice.

Maude loosened her death grip on me and the two of us leaned over to look out the kitchen door. Standing there, along with three other ugly, fat baby looking creatures, was Mort.

"What do you want?" Tanker asked. "It's well past curfew. After the last abduction the neighborhood watch decided that those out of their homes after dark will be getting fined with community service—herding daisies away from the west creek.

They've been taking residence and proving to be quite territorial."

"It's a real problem, it is!" one of the gnomes standing behind Mort exclaimed. "I couldn't cross the damn thing the other day."

Mort, nodding his head from the upset gnome back to Tanker replied, "I agree with ya's, but uh, please don' rat us out. We know it's late but we'll head home right after this, promise. It's just, me and me friends, we was just wondering, if uh, if uh—"

A different gnome, the one standing directly behind him, jumped up and shoved Mort out of the way. "We was wonderin' if we might be gettin' some more of tha' iced mud cream Miss Makayla made for Mort the other day."

Tanker moved his gaze so slowly in my direction, that when it landed on mine, I almost heard a thud. "Iced mud cream?"

"Oh, right," I chuckled uncomfortably. "Mort came by with some clothes from my mom, but you guys didn't have any gnome treats, so I had to improvise." I looked down at the trail of gnomes just outside the door. "I'm sorry, I don't have any made right now."

"Well when you 'spose you'll have another batch made?" Mort asked.

"Wait a minute," Maude said. "You can't expect us to just give you treats when you aren't doing anything for us."

"Oh really, I don't mind," I retorted. "I mean, come on, it's dirt."

"We'll pay for it," the gnome standing behind Mort said.

Maude and Tanker looked shocked by this information.

"You'll what?" Tanker asked.

"Yeah, we'll pay for that mud ice cream. Best thing we's ever tasted," Mort said.

"Well, in that case," Tanker replied, "I suppose we can

figure something out. Perhaps Makayla can whip some up in a few days.”

“Please don’t make us wait that long,” came the voice of yet another gnome. “Can’t it be sooner?”

Everyone turned and looked at me.

“I can have a batch ready by tomorrow evening,” I said.

“Oh yes!”

“Tha’ would be most excellent!”

“All right,” Tanker said, lowering his hand to signal for them to calm down. “Why don’t you all just come back over tomorrow—before dark. One rune in exchange for her services.”

There was gasping on the other side of the door.

“How badly do you want the iced mud cream?” he demanded.

There was more rumbling between the gnomes as they argued with one another, trying to reach a decision. Finally, after much squabbling over my fine culinary treats, Mort stepped forward and pointed a stubby thumb up at Tanker.

“Fine. We will give ya a rune, but we want six quarts, of which we’ll divvy up ourselves.”

Maude gasped next to me.

Tanker turned and stared at me with a wonky grin etched into his face. “I think that’s fair. Do you think that’s fair, Makayla?”

I hadn’t ever heard of a rune, nor did I care what it was. I was actually just kind of excited that something I made had these little gnomes craving more. I nodded.

“It’s a deal then,” Tanker said, his wings lifting behind him, an action that I’d come to realize meant he was happy or excited. “See you tomorrow.”

“See you,” I heard Mort say before Tanker shut the door.

When he turned around, he looked like he was going to explode. “Can you believe that?”

"They are going to *pay* for this stuff," Maude declared.

"I know, right," I said, happy to join in. "Who would pay for dirt?"

"No Makayla, you don't understand," Tanker said. "Gnomes are the stingiest creatures; they don't share their runes with anyone . . . ever."

"What's a rune?"

"A magic stone," Maude said. "And gnomes hoard them like crazy. They are extremely valuable." She looked up at Tanker with the first smile I'd seen on her face in days. "Our little Lala might've just found a way to strike it rich." She shook her head. "Iced mud cream, you funny little nymph." She patted me on the shoulder and went back to her dishes, manually washing them this time.

"A whole rune," Tanker said in disbelief as he walked out of the kitchen, his silver platforms clunking against the wood floor.

Left alone with my birth mother, I bit down over my lip—my attention unwavering from the wings on her back. It seemed, at least for the time being, that she had forgiven me; and I realized for the first time, there was nothing I wanted more than for her to do so. Banking on the assumption that I could mend things, I walked over and stuck my hands in the sink next to hers, grabbing for a dish to wash. My shoulder bumped into hers and she jumped a little.

"You know," I said, "when I came up with the idea for my company, I knew it was going to be great, but that I wouldn't be able to do it on my own. That's when my mom got involved." She paused from her work but didn't look up. "Six quarts is a lot of iced mud cream to make, I could probably use some help. Do you think you could help me?"

Maude closed her eyes, and for a second, I wondered if she was going to say no; but then I felt her hand touch mine under the water, just as I saw a sparkly tear run down her face. Without words, she nodded.

"Thank you," I whispered. "And I'm sorry." She opened her eyes, so bright were they that the only ones I'd ever seen to match them were my own. Then I said something else that I wouldn't have meant, not up until that moment. "I'm glad I'm here."

A slow, deep breath, left her lips, turning immediately into a gasp, because in that second, just as I'd seen for a very brief moment earlier that day with Helene, a very small particle flashed before us. This time it was purple, but it was gone before I could catch it or find more.

In a fascinated voice, she said, "You are finding your dust, Lala."

That night when I went to bed, I felt more torn than ever. Normally my frustrations came from business decisions—like which fabric company to choose. The more cost effective one, or the one who adhered to environmental concerns but cost an arm and a leg more.

"Our mission states that we are environmentally conscious," my mom had always said when it came to these matters. "Therefore, we must do as we say we do. You will get farther in this life with honesty and compassion, Lala."

I balled up the comforter and screamed into it. I wanted more than anything to meet with Helene the next day, but my mom's voice kept repeating those words into my head, along with Tanker's warnings. The question was, could I lie to these faeries, my birthparents, who I knew loved me still, just as much as they did the day I was born? I just didn't know.

There was also this new information about L.O.A.R. There were secrets all around me—and as far as Tanker went, well, I couldn't figure him out. He seemed like a smart enough faery, but from what I could gather he wasn't doing anything to fight what was clearly an injustice in this land. I had to wonder if L.O.A.R. was really that bad of an organization.

And then there was this thing with the elves. Why did Maude worry the elves would take me away? It was almost as though she believed they'd tried to do it once before. And it wasn't like there wasn't reason for worry, not when faeries were getting abducted left and right.

Small footsteps padding into my dark bedroom caused me to look over in Kevin's direction.

"I take it if you were an intellectual you would've said something by now."

The dog cocked his head to the side as though he were confused, then opened his mouth and started panting.

"Oh, all right you big ninny, come on over," I said, making room for him on the bed. He got a running start before jumping up beside me, and he sighed before laying his head on my side and quickly falling into sleep.

"Wish you could talk. You don't seem like the sort of creature who would keep things from me." I ruffled his ears. "Nobody seems to want to tell me anything, not right away anyway. It's frustrating, you know. Back in my world I was about ready to go to school to become the best lawyer in Washington D.C. Someone people paid to crack open cases and get down to the truth. King Loral wouldn't make it a day in my world, not with his theatre restrictions and god knows what else he's up to."

And then it came to me. Why was I sitting here whining about being left in the dark? Here I was in a strange place with obvious political imperfections, with a king who seemed sedentary and possibly prejudiced. I shouldn't have been frustrated; I should have been looking at this as an opportunity!

Granted I couldn't exactly put "Reforming the kingdom of Garlandia" on a resume—but I could allude to the fact that I'd assisted in legislative reorganization of a failing society. Yes, it was brilliant, and if anyone was qualified to sleuth into this corrupt world, it was me.

I rested my head on my pillow and stared at the ceiling. Finally, I'd found some motivation. I could make the silly gnomes their treats and act as though that was enough to satisfy me, while secretly investigating the goings on of what was really happening inside that castle. And in between all that, I was going to find my magic—with or without Helene.

❧ 14 ☙

The next morning, I woke raring to go. I'd decided I was going to go meet with Helene, but only to tell her that I'd changed my mind. I appreciated her offer, but I wanted to keep trying Tanker's way just a little longer. Partly because I felt guilty going over Tanker's head, but mostly because I wanted to dig into this L.O.A.R. business a little more before I questioned Helene.

With Maude's help in the kitchen I managed to get all the veggies for the iced mud cream prepped, so that all we had to do later was collect the dirt and mix the concoction with some milk.

When we were done, Maude left to go tidy herself up and I prepared to go meet Helene, but just as I was about to step out the door, Tanker caught me. He had a cup of what I suspected to be licorice root in one hand, an unlit pipe in the other, and a bird on either shoulder.

"Where are you off to with that spring in your step?" he asked.

"Stop it, brat! Shut up! Stop it! BRAAATTT!"

"Quiet you two!"

I stared at the three of them and wondered how it was that in such a short amount of time this had become my new normal.

"I was about to head out into the woods, you know, get a bit of practice in. I think I'm making some headway."

His eyes lit up. "Really! I told you all you needed was some time." Shooing away the birds, he prepared to set down his pipe and coffee cup. "Let me just get these things out of the way and I'll come with you."

"No!"

He jumped at my sudden objection.

"I mean, no offense but I really need to do this alone. It's hard for me to concentrate with other people around."

"STOP IT, BRAT!"

Tanker rolled his shoulders back, ignoring Asshole's strong conviction, and his wings lowered softly back down. "I suppose I can't argue with you on that, everyone has their own way of doing things. But when you do start to see colors, it would be wise to come get Maude and me." He shrugged his shoulders up by his ears. "I know you're older now, but Maude has this thing, you see. You finding your dust and learning how to fly, well . . ." His words drifted away and he lifted his eyebrows as if I could figure out the rest.

I stared at him, a bit lost for a moment. "You mean to say that me finding my dust is like me taking my first steps?"

"Yes, like that," he said, retrieving his mug and gesturing towards me with it in his hand, as he did a bit of the black liquid jumped out, causing me to change gears.

"Tanker, what exactly is that stuff?" The smell was extremely strong, but it also made my mouth water.

"This?" he asked, staring down into his cup. "Oh, yes. This is homemade licorice root extract. Maude makes it. Costs a pretty penny more—most faeries go with molasses because of that—but she's always sprung for the good stuff. Would you fancy a taste?"

"Um . . . sure," I said hesitantly, taking the mug from his offered hand and giving it a sniff. It smelled quite good, but I wasn't sure how much I would like straight licorice root.

"Faeries looooove licorice," Tanker said, nodding his head. "Gives us a bit of a buzz, like caffeine does to humans—but better."

"You don't drink coffee then?" I asked, looking up from the cup.

He made a disgusted face. "Goblin stink! No. No, no, no."

"I see." I swirled the concoction around in the cup. It was thick, like agave, but dark like coffee. Ever so slowly I lifted the cup up to my lips and took a very small sip. Immediately my taste buds became alive, and as it slid down my throat, I felt a warmth come over my entire body. Suddenly I was more alert. "Wow."

"Right." Tanker nodded. Then he grabbed the cup from my hands before I could drink anymore. "Best to start out with little bits at a time, wouldn't want your heart to explode."

I grinned. "Why, is it like wine? If I have too much, will I start seeing pink bunnies again?"

Immediately his smile faded. "Makayla Wood Abberwockey, how would you know about that?"

I blushed. Pulling one of my wings out from behind my backside, I petted it gingerly. "I may have had a few sips over the past few weeks."

"You didn't?"

I dropped my wing. "Don't worry I got in loads of trouble for it—"

"Makayla, faeries can't have wine!"

As if the situation couldn't have gotten any worse or awkward, just then Maude came fluttering into the kitchen wearing another of her renaissance dresses.

"What's all this?" she asked, a dolly look on her face.

"Makayla has had wine recently," Tanker said, crossing his arms over his chest.

"No," Maude gasped.

"Yes, she has."

I was beginning to get annoyed. "I told you; my parents already scolded me. I don't plan on drinking it again . . . for a while."

"Ever! You don't plan on drinking it again *ever*!" Tanker shouted, his face red and the licorice root swishing violently out of the cup. Setting down his mug, he moved in on me while sticking a finger in my face. "You will not even entertain the thought of drinking wine as long as you are living under this roof, do you hear me!"

A fire lit up under my wings. I was not someone who got in trouble—I was someone who got praised. Now, in the past few weeks I'd managed to get grounded, scolded, and told I was acting like a teenager.

I balled up my fists and held them behind me. Squinting up at Tanker, I shouted, "I don't need you to yell at me! My parents already have! My *real* parents!"

"We are your real parents!" Tanker barked back without missing a beat. "And we've been with you just as long as they have, you ungrateful little—"

"BRAT!" Pinch sang out.

Tanker continued to rant without pause. "Wine is like heroine to our kind—it is highly addictive and affects us differently than humans!" His face was burgundy, and his whole body shook. "The more you have, the more addicted you will become."

By this point, I was sure my face matched his. "Well maybe if somebody told me that, I wouldn't have had any. Nobody tells me anything around here!" I stopped for a moment, huffing and panting, and then stretched out an arm to point outside. "Like why there are so many odd statues, and who you think might be abducting the faeries—or why you worry that elves are out to get me! I'm an intelligent being, if you don't tell me, I will find out on my own!"

I crossed my arms over my chest, catching my breath and waiting for one of them to answer me. Tanker looked as though he was about to combust while Maude appeared terrified. Turning to her, Tanker said with a shaky voice, "I just don't know what to do with her." There was a faint dark orange aura surrounding his body and wings all of the sudden; it had a shimmering quality.

"Seriously!" I screeched. "I'm right here!"

"Tanker, you need to calm down," Maude said, rubbing his arm. Then looking at me, she said, "Why don't we sit down and discuss this like rational fey."

"Rational!" I exclaimed. "There is nothing rational about this place! Talking trees, flowers, frogs! Everybody and everything talks, but nobody says anything that is worth a damn!"

And with that, I gave them one final stare before storming out. I didn't look back; I just dragged my useless wings behind me and marched as fast as I could along the cobblestone path until I reached the crossroads of Rum and Cocker Spaniel.

Helene was waiting for me when I got there, a sly smile on her face. "Ready for some answers, Makayla?"

I had planned to tell her to bug off, but that was before Tanker decided to treat me like a child.

"You have no idea how ready I am," I retorted, still fuming.

❧

Helene took me down Rum Street until we reached a tree that looked a little worse for wear. By this time, we were quite deep into the forest. Deeper than I'd been when I'd met the snake wearing the top hat.

"Good morrow, Miss Helene," the tree said very slowly in a raspy voice.

"Hello, Frederick. I would like to access the basement, please."

"Of course." He choked on the words, coughing up some dust. "Would you like the door locked after you're in?"

"Yes please," she answered.

"Very well, in you go."

Helene grabbed my arm and pulled me to the side, and as she did the tree's roots lifted from the ground, raising the tree up at least six feet. As the trunk rose, a door appeared. It was old and moldy.

"After you," she said.

"Do you, um, live here?" I asked, hesitantly.

"God no, only scroungers live in trees. This is more like my office."

"Oh, sorry—didn't know." I looked from her to the door and then back to her again. "I just go through there then, into the tree?"

She looked impatient. "Where else would you go?"

"Right," I said, my heart still racing from earlier.

I pulled the heavy door aside and walked into the wide trunk, directly into a spiral staircase.

"Go on, then," Helene said, as she shoved me gently inside.

Dampness clung to my skin and earthiness filled my nostrils as I took the stairs down into the basement into a small, dark room, with a single desk and a table lined with glass vases—some of them full of what looked like potions. Another door resided along one of the walls, and on the other side was a blank blackboard.

"Have a seat," Helene said, pulling out her wand.

"Does anyone know we're here?" I asked, staring around at the dark walls. It was a little frightening to say the least.

She scoffed. "Of course not. Tanker wouldn't be all too thrilled if he knew you were here, would he now." She made a face and said in a mocking tone, "He wants you to learn your magic intuitively, from within—that's poppycock, and it takes too long. Now, the first thing we need to go over is the basics of your faery dust."

I crossed my legs and pulled my right wing over my lap. "I already know that. My dust is my essence, and it is what I use to manipulate the elements . . . to make magic."

"Right, but everyone's dust is different. For instance, you could have three different shades of dust, or hundreds. Each color is specific to your soul and represents *your* different emotions; it is used for particular manipulations, or spells. Also, as dust is a very personal part of who you are, nobody can see your dust unless you allow them to do so." She flicked her wand over towards a shelf in the wall and a small notepad came flying onto my desk, along with a very small pencil. "You will use this to write down the colors you begin to notice in your dust, and what feelings you are having as these particles appear."

"Wait," I said, stopping her. "Let's say I already saw a very small piece of dust, and someone else saw it too—that means that I wanted them to see it?"

Helene, who had started writing something down on the board with the end of her wand, stopped and turned towards me. "This happened to you recently?"

I nodded. "Last night."

She narrowed her eyes. "With Maude?"

"How'd you know?"

"She's your blood mother, of course you would feel affection towards her in some way." Her gaze lingered over mine for another cold minute, before she returned to what she was writing. "Faeries also use their dust to communicate affection; like humans blow kisses to one another, faeries send their dust to those whose hearts they wish to touch." The way she'd said this, it made me believe that love was the last thing on her to do list.

"Helene, if you don't mind me asking, do you have a boyfriend or anything?"

She scoffed. "I don't have time for that sort of thing, Makayla."

"Right," I answered softly. "It's just that you're so pretty."

"Whatever. Looks don't save you here, and neither does love."

My intestines knotted together. It was like I was looking at my future self, that is if I never ventured towards that first kiss. A vision of Sir Toby floated through my mind all of the sudden, causing me to fidget in my seat. I hadn't much thought about the elf, other than being frightened that the castle thugs might be coming to abduct me for some unknown reason; but when I did think about him, I felt my body soften and my balance unsteady.

I gulped and returned my gaze to the board. In dark purple letters, it read: The three principles of activating faery dust: Emotion, Fight or Flight, Spellcasting.

"Should I be writing this down?" I asked.

"Either that or memorize it."

"Right," I said, quickly repeating the script into my mind.

"First things first." She stepped away from the board and lifted her arms out to her sides. "Let's show you what it really looks like." And then a very soft light began to emanate around her.

"Whoa," I muttered, watching as the light began to shimmer and transform into so many different colors that I couldn't count them. Colors that I didn't even know existed. The dust radiated out from where she stood and eventually took up all the space in the room, but she was careful not to allow it to touch me.

Once she'd retracted it, she held out her wand and began to point it at the board behind her, but I stopped her before she could continue with her next thought.

"How come your dust flew around me?"

Her sharp gaze settled over my shoulders. "Allowing someone to feel your dust is letting someone read your soul. We don't know one another that well yet."

Interesting.

"How far can you make it go?"

"As far as your soul is big. The measure of one's dust is an example of how powerful he or she is."

"Okay. So how far can yours go?"

She smirked, but instead of answering me, she tapped the words on the board. "Emotion, Fight or Flight, and Spellcasting. These are the reasons we use our dust. The *only* reasons. What you've experienced already is emotion. What color was it?"

"Purple."

"Write it down." She pointed at the small notebook. "Then add the way you felt when it happened—which was probably sympathy. My poor dear sister, so dumb."

"Actually," I said, almost defensively, "I think it was affection."

Helene chuckled scornfully under her breath. "Isn't that cute. Whatever, write it down."

I did as I was told and then wrote down blue under it, for I had seen a spec of blue the day before while I was with Helene. I'd felt and seen it when she'd been talking to me about the stone faeries in the woods. But I didn't yet write down the meaning because I wasn't sure what it meant.

Continuing, she explained, "Your dust surrounds you always, but grows and vibrates more strongly when your emotion rises. Whether you are happy or angry, your dust will expound from around you. Now, the second principle is Fight or Flight. This is not a new concept for you I hope."

"No, I've heard of this."

"Good. If you feel threatened, like the hairs on a dog sticking up along his spine, as will your dust. It is what lifts your wings and allows you to flee or gives you the strength to take on your attacker—and this leads directly into spellcasting, which branches out into hexes."

I raised my eyebrows. "Hexes?"

"Oh yes, there are dark forces all around you, Makayla. You must know these things in case you ever need to use them. As far as spellcasting, we know already that you have the ability to spin great magic, for if you didn't you wouldn't be here. My job is to help you remember how to do this again. But considering your situation"—she glanced at my lifeless wings— "the main thing we are going to be focusing on is finding your dust, so Maude can release those wings of yours again. Spellcasting we can worry about later."

For two hours, I listened to Helene spout off boring material about dust. I suppose it was what I'd asked for, but after seeing her actual dust, and watching her use it to move materials around the room, I was more impatient than ever to find my own.

"Maybe you could teach me just a few small spells," I suggested after a while.

"I thought you only wanted to access your dust so you could remove your wings again—so you could return to your *own* world undetected," she said condescendingly. "I thought these minute details didn't mean anything to you."

"Well—they don't," I answered half-heartedly. "It's just that once I find my magic, I still have to locate the spell to remove my wings completely, and that could take some time. And I'm a faery, I might as well be able to use my magic."

A dimple appeared in her left cheek, and I knew I'd been busted—that the idea of magic was starting to appeal to me. "Either way, Makayla, if you want to learn from me you are going to learn the correct way. You are welcome at any time to go back to Tanker and wait it out—"

"No, it's fine," I said, recrossing my legs. "I can be patient."

"Good, but I'm afraid this is all we have time for today. I have a meeting I need to get to—"

She was interrupted by a noise coming from the small door in the wall. From where I sat, it sounded like something had crashed to the floor. Helene and I both turned and looked at it at the same time.

"What's in there?" I asked.

"I don't know?" She looked at me and grinned. "Maybe it's a ghost."

"Oh whatever," I retorted, getting up out of my chair. Then, because the opportunity seemed to have arrived, I asked without hesitation, "So this meeting you have to go to . . . does it have anything to do with L.O.A.R.?"

The playfulness I'd just seen in her dissipated as her sharp eyes pierced mine, and she replied in a tense manner, "You really do have some nerve."

I pressed my lips together, refusing to back down from my inquiry.

"And who told you about that organization? Was it my dear brother-in-law?"

Again, I chose not to answer.

She gave her head the smallest of shakes and then motioned for me to get up before she led me towards the stairs. As she nudged me up the unfinished wooden slats, she said, "Figures, thinks he's got it all figured out because of that silly mark."

I opened my mouth to question the statement, but she

talked over me, continually forcing me to ascend back up to that moldy old tree door.

"And by the way, the name of that organization is something I wouldn't say too loud out of doors if I were you."

"Are you part of it?"

"What if I was? Would you stop coming to see me?"

I halted at the top of the stairs and turned back to face her. "No—I don't think so. From what I've observed this land could use some reformation, but I'm not so sure I understand what L.O.A.R. intends on doing to repair the damage that has been done. I still don't even know what the king looks like, and—"

At the mention of King Loral, Helene burst into laughter. "How cute, you really think you're going to meet him."

"Why is that amusing? You're the one who suggested that he would want to meet me in the first place."

"That's because on paper he does." She moved in so her nose was almost touching mine. "King Loral is a coward, Makayla. He fears everyone and everything, especially those he doesn't understand. I would wager that you scare the quintessence right out of him. He's not going to meet with you—he's going to sit back and observe and have others spy on you for him."

I wanted to question the appalling statement, but found myself unable to form words.

As Helene took a step back to the stairs behind her, she said, "Stop worrying your pretty little head with the details of this world. You don't belong here. That's what this is all about, right?"

My voice cracked when I finally spoke again. "I—I don't know where I belong exactly. But Helene, I am not the kind of person who can just turn away from something like this— watch as innocent creatures are forced to live amongst tyranny."

"And what is it you claim to know about our government? What leads you to believe it needs to be reformed?"

Standing taller, I pushed out my chest. "I believe the citizens of Garlandia are living in fear for their lives, and it appears as though no one is doing anything about it—except for maybe this organization that *you* may be a part of."

Helene studied me for a hard minute, and for a second, I thought she might cave and fill in some of the holes I'd been stumbling over. But instead, she gently pushed me towards the door and rapped on its surface. "It seems to me, Makayla, that this is a conversation best suited for another time."

My stomach filled with lead. "Wait! Won't you tell me something—anything! I don't care what side you're on, I just want some answers."

Her expression softened, but I could still feel her hesitance lingering between us like an immovable fog. I clamped down, hammering her with more questions before she could push me further away.

"Just tell me. Do you know what's with all the faery abductions? Does it have to do with the elves? With the king?"

"Of course, it does," she muttered. Leaning in, her eyes growing smaller and darker, she said, "The fey have magic King Loral cannot compete with, not as long as there are enough of us. He's already managed to deplete our numbers."

"By stopping the reproduction of our race?"

Helene bit down over her lip, her hand shaking idly at her side. Finally, she said, "If you were the king and something was in your way, wouldn't you want to get rid of the smallest and easiest component first?"

A heavy feeling settled into my chest. "The Ardeens."

Helene took a deep breath, and I could tell she was about to blow me off. I couldn't let her, though. Grabbing her wrist, I looked her deep in the eyes. "You think it was him who tried to take me when I was a baby, don't you? They all do.

Everyone here thinks that King Loral sent the elves to abduct me from my crib, don't they?"

I could see my questions settling into her mind, and there was an inexplicable quality about her facial reaction. Looking down at my hand over her wrist, she pulled away. "Have you not noticed, Makayla, that those who speak out of turn here have a way of never speaking again?"

My eyebrows danced. "If that's true, then how does L.O.A.R. get away with meeting and discussing their ambitions of overthrowing the current government?"

Her lips slowly curled into a sly grin. Crossing her arms over her chest, the door blew open behind me. "You, I like. It's a shame you'll be leaving us."

"Why don't you answer me then?"

"We'll finish this later," she said, causing my heart to sink.

"Wait—not yet! Just explain this one thing to me!"

Leaning in and dropping her voice so that it was barely audible, she whispered, "We have those who can speak, deliver our messages for us." Then she pulled away, a contented look on her face as though she enjoyed watching me squirm. "Go on now, get back to your adorable family. They'll be wondering where you are, I'm sure."

And with that I was pushed backwards, landing on my rear end as the door slammed shut and the tree sunk back into the ground. But I didn't even care about that. What had my thoughts reeling was this: if I'd been told continually to watch what I say about this or that, who then would be safe from speaking?

Next to me a flower opened its creepy mouth and licked a very sharp incisor. Jumping away from it, I stumbled my way back onto the path that would lead me out of this part of the forest, and even further away from any viable explanations.

When I returned to the Abberwockey's, Tanker sat at the kitchen table wearing a flowered muumuu with black socks and a scowl on his face. There was a book lying on the table next to him titled, *So You've Decided to Watch Over a Human —The Ins and Outs of Dealing with Rationality* By Polly Pinhead Periwinkle, Ardeen Doctor of the Mind.

Picking up the book, he turned to a page that he'd dog eared and pointed at a paragraph. "This here says that I should ground you." He then pointed his wand at me, and a showering of dirt shot at my chest before falling to the ground. "You're grounded."

I rolled my eyes as I dusted the remnants of the dirt off my shirt. After the information I'd just been handed before being dumped on my ass, I was not in the mood for this.

"You're too late. Philip and Naomi beat you to it. I've been grounded for weeks."

Laying the book back down, he said matter-of-factly, "Well, now you're grounded here, too."

"I really can't take you seriously while you're wearing that."

He sat forward in his chair and held out the fabric of his house dress. "I'll have you know that this is quality workmanship. The tag says it was made in Indonesia."

"Yeah, and the person making it was probably treated unfairly and paid a quarter of a penny. Sewn Back Together has a plant there for that reason."

"Oh really, well—" He searched for something to say back but couldn't seem to come up with anything. Standing abruptly, quite red in the face for the second time that day, he pointed a finger at me and shouted, "You are not to leave this house!"

"Fine!" I shouted back childishly, watching his large wings trail behind him through the hallway. Not even a second later Maude appeared.

"Everything okay?" she asked, walking in as I pulled out a chair and sat down in a huff.

"I'm just sick to death of being treated like a juvenile when I've been an adult my entire life. My restlessness has coaxed me into the role of a teenager, and I hate that too."

I scooted up to the table and rested my forehead in my hands. Maude pulled up a chair and scooted up next to me, petting my wings.

"Lala, you mustn't be mad with Tanker. This isn't easy for us either, you know."

"I know, I know, I'm an ungrateful little brat. Even the birds know that."

"Please don't think we taught them to say that. That started soon after we took you to the Woods' home."

I lifted my head. "That's strange."

"Not really, they are the naughtiest birds. So, Tanker *grounded* you, then." She snickered. "How cute."

I looked at her in disbelief. "What about that is cute?"

"Him. Grounding our daughter—never thought it would happen." She giggled again and stood up. "That doesn't mean you're off the hook for making all this iced mud cream. I don't have the vaguest idea how you did it."

"Oh . . . that's right," I muttered. I'd forgotten about my latest and greatest venture (heavy with the sarcasm). "We should probably get started," I sighed as I stood up and assessed the kitchen. Pointing to the cabinets, I began delegating. "If you want to begin pulling out some bowls and lining them with ice, I can go collect some—" I was cut off abruptly as Maude's arms suddenly surrounded me, a calming sensation falling over my shoulders along with bubble gum colored faery dust. I was instantly filled with the feeling like this was the happiest I'd been in my entire life; and as I remained in her grip, I caught a glimpse of someone staring down into their arms, holding out their finger for a gleeful swaddling to take and squeeze. The swaddling was wrapped in purple and blue butterfly wings, and she had tufts of red sparkly hair coming out of her head.

"I'm just so glad you're here," Maude whispered, then pulled away, taking her pink dust back with her.

I was suddenly slightly off kilter, and as I steadied my stance, I whispered, "Emotional dust."

Maude flipped back around on her toes and stared at me. "What did you say?"

"Oh . . . nothing." I smiled. "It's just, you let me in, and showed me what you were feeling."

"Why wouldn't I? You're my Lala."

A ragged breath fell from my lips. All my life I'd forced myself to be tough. I didn't ever have time, nor did I ever allow myself to wonder where the color of my emerald eyes had come from, and now I was face to face with them. I pressed my lips tightly together, warding off the emotion rising in the back of my throat.

"I'm just, uh—I'm going to go outside and gather the dirt." I scooted by her and grabbed a few bowls. "And some mint as well." And then I hurried out of the kitchen before things had a chance to get any sappier.

An hour later we had six quarts of iced mud cream ready and prepared. It helped that Maude had sped up the process with a few flicks of her wand. Once we were finished and the cream was in the freezer, awaiting its anxious feasters, Maude and I slumped down at the kitchen table to split a bowl of actual ice cream.

I shook my head at her, digesting a large bite of molasses swirl. "You and Helene are nothing alike."

"Thank you," she said, a small shimmer of dust falling from her wings. It was hard to believe that just yesterday she hadn't been speaking to me.

"Do you come from the same parents?"

"Yes. She's a lot more like our father. He moved away a long time ago."

I thought of the faery in the crooked frame in the upstairs hallway, the large one with purple wings. There'd been something about that picture that had made me wonder.

"Is that him in that photo upstairs? The big faery, the muscular one?"

She nodded, staring down at the bowl as she bent down and pulled out a large bite of ice cream with her tongue.

"Where does he live?"

"Somewhere over the mountainside."

I remembered Sir Toby and the other elf I'd eavesdropped on speaking of another village. "Does he live in Lauslin?"

Maude lowered her chin and lifted her eyes. "How do you know the name of that place?"

"I overheard someone speaking of it in the woods," I answered casually. "Is it another village like this one?"

She sat back in her chair. "Yes. It didn't used to be, but now it is." The way she said it was kind of sad, like Garlandia wasn't the kind of place to be modeled after. "But your grandfather doesn't live there. I don't know where he is, but I assume it's somewhere very far away. I wouldn't plan on meeting him anytime soon."

I entertained the idea of having more living faery relatives, but I could tell by Maude's blunt description of her father that this wasn't a subject she wanted to discuss further. So, I decided to dig where I really needed to dig.

"So how big is this place anyway? I haven't even been out of the forest yet and I'm curious about what the castle looks like."

Maude sighed. "Garlandia is quite large. You've only seen a very small part of it, I'm afraid. Perhaps tomorrow we can go to the Farmer's Market—oh wait, Tank and I have that awful musical to review."

"I could go with you," I piped up. "That is if I am allowed to leave the house."

Maude took another lick from the bowl. "You would want to come with us?"

"Of course. What am I going to do here besides make more iced mud cream?"

"Hmmm. Why don't you let me talk to Tanker about it. I bet all he needs is some time to cool off. In fact, I bet he's soaking in an ice bath right now."

I snickered, but then realized she was being serious.

The gnomes arrived as they said they would, and in exchange for the six quarts of the foulest ice cream known to mankind, I received what looked like a rock with a symbol etched into it. I tried to offer it to Maude, because really, what was I going to do with it? I didn't even know what it would buy—but she insisted I keep it.

After we'd cleaned up the kitchen Maude announced that she was going to bed, at which point I decided to follow suit. I was cozied up in my canopy covered bed, staring at the little notebook Helene had given me, letting the moonlight caress the words I'd written down so far, when I heard a pair of muffled voices coming from outside. Pushing Kevin out of the way, I crept out of my bed and neared the window, holding my wings up so they wouldn't drag along the floor.

"This is so f-ing weird!" someone whispered.

"This straight crazy, yo. I think we should go back."

"No way! This is where she lives—that angry little man told us so."

It sounded like a boy and a girl, but I wasn't sure because their voices were so low.

"Holy shit! That flower just screamed at me for stepping on its head!"

"No, it didn't. You probably just have low blood sugar or something. Come on, I see a light coming on in the kitchen."

A light? Tanker and Maude must've heard the voices too.

I stood away from the window and backed up against the wall. As I did, Kevin jumped down from the bed and scuttled out of my bedroom.

Downstairs I heard the front door open, along with a ruckus as Pinch and Asshole woke up and alerted the neighborhood to our visitors.

"THE BRAT'S UPSTAIRS! SHUT UP! SHUT UP!"

I held my breath, uneasy about someone coming here unannounced at this hour. It could've been elves, or perhaps someone had seen me with Helene and was tattling because they, too, thought her a bad egg.

I strained my ears but all I could hear were more muffled voices, and then the sound of footsteps coming up the stairs. Before I could duck and hide, my door swung wide open and Tanker stood there in a white robe with red polka dots, a purple and silk turban wrapped around his head, and his bunny slippers.

"You've got company," he said, looking rather unimpressed.

"What? Who?"

"They say their names are Anastacia Montgomery and Jeremy Love."

I had visitors! I'd never had visitors before in my entire life! I mean, I'd had appointments, but those were all business related. I was so excited that it hadn't even occurred to me how Cee-Cee and Jeremy had gotten in.

It was now well past midnight, and the three of us were sitting around the kitchen table, while Tanker stood with his arms crossed in the corner and Maude floated around refilling purple lemonade whenever anyone took a sip. Cee-Cee was ranting non-stop, and Jeremy had his head in his hands, goggling dreamily in my direction.

Cee-Cee, losing it for about the tenth time since I'd come down the stairs to greet them, screeched, "Shut up! I mean, like, shut up! You got me trippin' all up in here. You're a freaking faery, girl!"

"She's fabulous. Just fabulous," Jeremy said hypnotically.

"Tell me again how you two got in here," Tanker said, after heaving a sigh.

"Tank*er*," Maude said, shooting him a dark look. "Don't be snippy with Lala's friends."

"It's okay, Mrs. Abberwockey," said Cee-Cee, curling her finger around her emerald strip.

"Oh honey, that is just the prettiest color," Maude cooed.

"Not as pretty as yours but thank you."

Maude blushed.

"Okay, it goes like this," Cee-Cee stated. "Mr. and Mrs. Wood said Makayla was grounded and she couldn't hang out, but we knew something was off, because she wouldn't answer the door even when her parents were gone. So, we started thinking that something was fishy, you know, like someone's dead, fishy. Anyway, we started snoopin' around and keepin' a closer watch on the house, and then we see the strangest thing. We see Mrs. Wood, *Mrs. always all put together*, come out of her house with what looked like the nastiest cupcake in the world, and a bag of clothes. Makayla's clothes. Then she proceeds to put that nasty treat in the mailbox, and a second later a little man appears." She looked over at Jeremy, who was nodding his head. "So, Mrs. Wood starts talking to this little guy, and when he leaves, she sets down the bag. And this is where we get all sorts of messed up, cause before we can even look away, the bag disappears—like, out of nowhere. It was gone."

"It was," Jeremy said, still staring at me. "Gone."

"So then, I was all like, we got to go and see if we can get that little man to come out again—but he wouldn't."

"No, he would not," Jeremy shook his head.

"And Jeremy was all like, why don't we try putting some mud in the mailbox—and oh what a mistake that was."

"Ooooo," Maude shook her head. "He doesn't like that."

"Apparently not, because the mailbox flap opened and he threw that mud right back in our faces," Cee-Cee said. "Before he could disappear though, he said something about upping his standards now that he'd had the best mud ice cream in the world."

I snickered.

"We ain't so thick that we couldn't put together what that little man wanted, so—"

"So, she made *me* make a mud pie," Jeremy cut in, finally looking somewhere other than at me. Sitting up and placing a hand over his chest, he said, "Do I look like someone who wants to put mud on anything other than my face?"

"You're the one who always says he wants to go to culinary school," Cee-Cee countered defensively.

By this point, Tanker, minus his silly robe and silk turban, was beginning to look more like Philip than ever, and I could tell he'd had it with Cee-Cee's story. Even though it was him who had asked how they'd gotten in.

"All right," he said, "we get the point. Did anyone see you?"

"Whatchu mean?" Cee-Cee asked, tucking her chin into her chest.

He sighed. "Did anyone see you coming through your world into ours?"

"God no," Cee-Cee retorted. "It was all dark, and everyone in our neighborhood is lights out by ten."

"What question did you answer to get in here?" I asked, remembering that my mom had to answer something about cats and sweaters.

"He asked us if we were intellectuals." Jeremy said, "And I answered, 'Of course we are, can't you tell by my glasses?'"

I smirked.

"Where do your parents think you are, dears?" Maude asked, looking rather maternal.

"At Cee-Cee's."

"At Jeremy's."

Tanker shoved away from where he was leaning. "That's it, you kids need to get going back home."

"Oh Tanker, stop it," Maude said, the jug of lemonade

levitating next to her. "I think you've done quite enough parenting today." She leaned into him and patted his arm, lowering her voice for a second. "And I find it very handsome on you, but don't you think it would be nice for Lala to have her friends over for a night. They could go to the farmer's market tomorrow and—"

"Maude," he said, "she is grounded. How can you advocate her going out with her friends tomorrow? Not to mention how *irresponsible* it would be for us to allow these children to stay here when they are clearly lying to their parents."

Jeremy, Cee-Cee, and I sat up straighter, waiting to see the outcome of this argument between the two winged creatures. I'd thought for sure Tanker was going to win, because he'd been stretching his fatherly role all day. It only seemed fitting that he would reinforce my punishment.

But just then, as the three of us anxiously waited to see if Jeremy and Cee-Cee could stay the night in Garlandia amidst Tanker and Maude's very long stare off, the two of them burst out into laughter.

"What the—" Cee-Cee started to question.

I lowered my forehead into one of my hands for just long enough to rub at the questions that were appearing over my skin.

"Oh, you're right Maudie, I *have* done enough parenting today. It was kind of fun though, and I really got into character with it, didn't I?"

"You sure did, Tank!" Maude exclaimed.

And at that, he kissed the top of her head, and pointed a finger at me before signing off. "If you remember why I was mad at you, will you tell me please. I forgot five minutes after you left."

"Uh—okay," I replied unsteadily.

"Good to meet you two," he said to Cee-Cee and Jeremy.

"Maude will take care that you have everything you need for the night. Now I'm going back to bed. Kevin has probably already scooted into my spot by now."

"Good night, Mr. Abberwockey," Jeremy said, waving at his winged back as Tanker left the room.

"That was weird," Cee-Cee said.

"You haven't seen weird yet," I assured her. "Just wait till tomorrow."

After everyone was sufficiently pumped with enough sugar to equal the amount one might need for a year, or possibly two, I prepared to lead my friends up to my bedroom for my first official sleepover—better late than never. However, we didn't make it out of the kitchen before there was a tiny knock on the kitchen door window.

"Oh dear," Maude said, wiping her hands on a dish towel. "What would Sabrina be doing here at this hour?"

I stared out the glass partition of the door to see the small Ardeen levitating. She was wearing purple pajamas with fish printed on them, and her silver hair was in curlers.

"Sorry to call this late," Sabrina squeaked, fluttering into the kitchen as Maude opened the door.

"Sabrina, it is dangerous for you to be out after dark," Maude scolded.

"I know, but I was alerted by McGraph that there were some strange noises coming from your backyard, and I personally wanted to make sure everything was in order." Her sparkling green eyes landed on Cee-Cee and Jeremy, and her little head cocked to the side.

"Humans?"

"Sabrina, these are Lala's friends; they broke in from the other side," Maude explained. "I'm sure it was them your patrol overheard."

I stood. "What patrol?"

"The one watching to make sure those wings don't get

ripped from your back," Sabrina said pragmatically. "Or do you not see the importance of extra protection when there is someone out there abducting faeries? Probably plucking their wings before skinning them, and slicing them up into little pieces, draining their blood and drinking it—"

Maude stepped forward and cut Sabrina off. "Yes dear, I think she gets the point."

Ignoring Cee-Cee and Jeremy's reactions to the tiny faery's gruesome account, I said, "I didn't realize there were people—er—Garlandians watching the house."

"Well there are," Sabrina said. "So, mind your P's and Q's." Then she stuck out her tongue at me.

Really mature.

"All right, sorry to bother you for nothing."

"No worries, better to be safe than sorry," Maude replied.

"Um hm," Sabrina retorted, prepping to leave. But just as she was about to flutter away, she stopped short. "Wait a tic, is that your famous lavender lemonade?"

"Yes!" Maude said happily. "Would you like some?"

"Do you mind?"

"Of course not, just give me a second."

Maude grabbed a regular sized glass and filled it three quarters of the way full, at which point Sabrina went over and dove into it, completely immersing herself in the purple drink.

Jeremy, Cee-Cee, and I were all sitting on the edges of our seats, watching with mouths wide open.

"Is she going to come out of there okay?" I asked.

"Yes, she always does this. Likes to smell like it later. There she goes!" Maude said, clapping her hands together excitedly as the lemonade started to lower down into the cup. Sabrina was taking giant gulps of it.

When it was gone, all that was left was her little body inside of the clear cup, so bloated she could barely fly out.

"Thank you," she said, nodding to Maude, "ever so

delicious." And then she burped, louder than Herbert, and returned to her normal size. "I'll be off now. Will I see you all at the market tomorrow?"

"Yes indeed," Maude answered.

"Good." Then looking at the three of us, she added, "Nighty night, then. Don't let the red bed bugs bite because they will kill you and your innards will fall out everywhere. The blue ones are okay though."

"Thank you, Sabrina," Maude said as she opened the door for her.

"You're welcome—oh, what's that?" she said softly, peering out into the garden.

"What's what, dear?" Maude asked, following her gaze.

"Oh, nothing. Just thought I saw a shadow over by that Sheridan statue—no matter. I might just have a look see just to be safe." And then she flew out the door without saying another word.

"Be careful, Sabrina!" Maude yelled out to her. "Go straight home, now!" She stared out into her gardens for another minute, a cautious look on her face, before closing the door and pulling out her wand—securing the lock.

"She's a violent little bugger, isn't she?" Cee-Cee retorted after she'd gone.

"Don't call them bugs, dear," Maude said, turning back to face us, "they don't like that."

❧ 16 ❧

The next morning, I woke up and smiled down at my friends. Cee-Cee was lying on her back, snoring, and Jeremy was on his stomach, his glasses on the other side of his head. Maude had pulled out bean bag beds for them to sleep on.

Once everyone was up and around, Maude made a giant breakfast with everything from quiche to white chocolate chip raspberry pancakes.

"Um, Makayla," Jeremy had said, after Tanker had already scooped up a handful of eggs and stuffed them into his mouth. "I don't suppose there's any forks around here, are there?"

"No, we don't use food weapons," I answered seriously, before sopping up some gravy with a biscuit and eating it. His expression was priceless.

"I could get used to this," Cee-Cee was saying, taking a drink of strawberry juice before devouring a pancake. "Mrs. Abberwockey, you've done this meal justice."

"That's so sweet," answered Maude. "Although I'm afraid I've made too much again."

"We could give the leftovers to the gnomes." I winked at Tanker. "Maybe get another rune out of it."

"No, no, no, you silly little Erwain," Tanker replied, bits of egg flying from his mouth. Turning to his wife, he said, "What do you think, Maudie? Has our little girl loosened up any since she's been here?"

What was that supposed to mean?

Maude, sipping on a mug of licorice root, placed a hand on her hip and stared at me. "She's tried, but I can still detect hints of snootiness. What do you think, Tanker?"

"I think she needs to know what we do with leftovers in this house."

"What are you guys—" BAM! And there it was, a buttered pancake stuck to my face. As it peeled off, Tanker stood and gathered as many biscuits as he could fit into his arms.

"Food fight!" my birth father yelled, jumping up and down with glee.

"No way, your faery parents are so cool!" Cee-Cee yelled, shoving her plate out of the way and lunging for the sausages.

Within seconds, food flew everywhere. I didn't have a chance to freak out—didn't have a chance to decide whether I should run or participate. My white tank top was already splattered with quiche and gravy.

"Hey! Maybe we should cover ourselves first!" I yelled out, a hesitant grin wavering on my face, as Cee-Cee got Tanker in the nose with a blueberry muffin.

"Give it up, ya old fart!" Tanker hollered, getting both Cee-Cee and Maude in the back with orange slices. "You're a faery, Makayla—time to act like one!"

The kitchen was already covered in pieces of wadded up pastries, and eggs filled with cheese and tomatoes. My heart was racing at the thought of having to clean all this up when a jam-filled donut landed square on my nose and blew up.

Wiping away the red goo, I looked over at Maude who

almost looked fearful of me. "Oh, it is *so* on now," I fumed, picking up four slices of toast from my plate and sending them towards my birth mother like they were ninja stars.

"There she is, Tanker!" she screamed through her laughter, dodging my bread bullets. "Our daughter has finally arrived!"

At some point the fight ended. I, of course, chucked the most pastries and hit the most targets. As if it hasn't been clear by now, I don't fail when I set out to do something. It wasn't until we were cleaning up that we found Jeremy Love cowering under the table, shaking. Apparently, I wasn't the only one who didn't like to get dirty.

I was pretty excited about the prospect of getting out of the forest for the first time. As we walked along, Maude and Tanker relayed to us that the farmer's market was held in a valley between the forest and the castle, just past Bernice and Edmond—a couple of unhappily married trees.

As we continued to stroll along, I took pleasure in introducing Cee-Cee and Jeremy to a few of the forest creatures I'd met over the past few days, including an anxious tree who wouldn't sit still, and moved daily between the streets of Rapture and Tequila.

Once the trees began thinning out and the sound of flutes being played grew louder, Tanker and Maude pulled us aside and gave each of us a bottle of honey—incidentally ignoring the statue of a Sheridan faery with her hand out as though pleading. She was just a few feet from the main path.

"What's this for?" I asked about the honey.

"In case you want to buy anything," Tanker said. "Your moth—Maude and I need to get going if we are going to get good seats for the musical. I'm afraid we are going to skip on ahead of you, but the market is right through those two." He pointed to a couple trees whose branches were tangled together on top as though they were holding hands. "The stage is just past the venues. Perhaps you can come catch the last part of the show if you all get bored."

"Maybe," I replied, looking to my friends for signs of what they might want to do. They both looked quite out of their element, so I just nodded and hugged Maude and Tanker good-bye before they flew up into the trees, each of them carrying a stuffed bag over their shoulders.

"This place is so cool," Cee-Cee said, watching the two of them disappear.

"You've got to learn how to fly soon," Jeremy added.

"With Helene's help that should be any day now."

I'd filled the two of them in on my super-secret lessons before we'd fallen asleep the night before. It was good to talk about all the things I'd learned, and to vent about the discrepancies I'd come upon in the short amount of time I'd been in Garlandia. And even though I'd refrained from mentioning L.O.A.R., they both agreed that something was off about all these crazy statues.

Following Tanker's instructions, we took our bottles of honey and walked through the two trees. As our heads bobbed underneath their branches, a very slow female voice said, "Somedays I like you less, Edmond."

"Then why don't you move?" an equally depressed male voice answered.

"Because you're my husband, you fat-bellied twig—"

"Not in front of the children."

"Is that the lost Erwain, then?"

"I believe so . . ."

As we crossed out of the forest, Jeremy turned to me. "*Everyone* knows who you are. You're, like, famous here."

"It's really not that glamorous," I retorted. "It's like being a famous celebrity of a reality T.V. show you never knew you were on all your life."

After that we only had to walk a couple more steps before the sun hit our eyes. The three of us stopped, staring into the valley, so full of tents and booths, music and food. There were faeries dancing in the air and on the ground, and crony old women with baskets hanging around their arms, haggling loudly with vendors. The sky was filled with what I could only describe as faery traffic. Erwains, Sheridans, Ardeens, along with witches and wizards on brooms; they were flying back and forth as though there were invisible byways paved in all directions.

"Whoa," Cee-Cee and Jeremy said together.

"Yeah," I agreed, just as the buzz of the world surrounding me faded. For the first time, I saw it—the castle, as it appeared in the distance.

"This is, like, *so* renaissance right now," Cee-Cee said, not waiting for us as she took off in the direction of a booth manned by a wizard, full of magic wands.

"I think we should stay together," I said to Jeremy. He nodded and laced his arm through mine.

"Come with me, my fabulous lady," he said in a knightly voice. Although he looked anything but in his black skinny jeans, nerd glasses, and tight plaid shirt.

The market was amazing. I'd never seen so many colors in one place, nor heard so many different voices. Faeries, witches, wizards, and plenty of elves were selling everything one could think of and much more. We quickly realized that the single bottle of honey we'd each been given to barter with, wasn't going to add up to very much.

Jeremy found a Wood elf who was selling everything leather. Initially he had his hands on a leather goblet, but quickly changed his mind when he spotted a high-quality belt and handed over his honey—just before he caught sight of some orange shoes that he just *had* to have.

The Wood elf, a stern looking character with dark eyes and

light hair, asked dryly before trading with him, "Are you sure? There's no exchanges."

Jeremy innocently nodded his head, and graciously accepted the shoes.

"Guess you're done then," Cee-Cee said flatly, when we had finally left the tent. "We aren't even halfway through this place yet and you blew all your honey already."

"I don't care," he said, stroking the sides of the shoes. "Just look at this workmanship."

"What's a Wood elf anyway?" Cee-Cee asked, eyeballing a stand of crystal balls. One of them turned the color of her hair extension as she passed it. The young witch manning the station studied the three of us as we walked by, and as I met her pointed stare, I felt an icy chill run down my spine.

"I think it just means they live in the woods," I answered, returning my gaze forward, away from the maiden-faced witch. "Oh my god, look at these dresses!"

I unhooked my arm from around Cee-Cee's and ran over to a table littered with gowns like Maude often wore. Long and flowy. Though they weren't anything 'Makayla the lawyer' would be caught dead wearing, the winged part of me was beginning to grow slightly fond of them. And if anything, they were much more my design than the fluffy tutus I'd seen other faeries adorned in. Lifting a light blue and silvery one from where it hung on display, I held it up to my chest. The stitching appeared to be made of pure gold thread.

"That's beautiful," Cee-Cee said, as she reached out and felt the fabric.

"Everyone wears these here. At first, I thought they were silly, but I'm starting to kind of want one. This one is super pretty."

An Erwain faery browsing the selection inside the tent popped her head out and surveyed the three of us, her gaze landing on me last. "Son of a giantess, are you the lost Erwain?"

I looked up at the faery. She had blonde curly hair and looked to be about the same age as Maude—whatever that meant. Maybe she was like, oh I don't know, a thousand.

"Yes ma'am."

"My goodness, I honestly didn't believe the rumors."

"Well, they're true," I said a bit uncomfortably. I was getting sick of this lost Erwain nonsense. "Hey, do you happen to know how much these dresses go for? All I have is this honey."

The Erwain stared at the dress in my hands, and then sighed. "You've got your hands on a ball gown, dear." Then aiming her voice into the tent, she shouted, "Esmerelda is a real hag! She's bound to laugh in your face if you try to trade honey for that!"

Just then a frail-looking Erwain popped her head out of the tent, her hair a sparkly green, and her pale pink wings saggy. "What's your problem, Wella? I told you, if you don't like my prices, then go over to Mim's. That witch is giving her crap away."

"Just warning our little honey trader here, that's all," the faery named Wella said, before curtsying in my direction and flying away.

The elderly Erwain took one look at the dress in my arms before her hands began to shake, and her jaw became unhinged as though she was about to yell at me for even picking it up—but just then horns began to sound down the row of tents.

Jeremy, Cee-Cee, and I all looked at one another alarmingly as everyone in the vicinity fell to their knees. Soon after a voice shouted out to the crowd.

"Hear ye! Hear ye! Make way for Sir Toby, the Aeronian heir of Garlandia!"

There was a heavy murmuring as everyone stopped what they were doing and waited for the heir and his company to pass by.

Something tapped me behind the knees and I looked back to find Esmerelda poking me with her shimmering wand. "Get down!" she whispered. "All of you, you must kneel before royalty or you'll get us all in trouble!"

Cee-Cee and Jeremy looked over at one another, heavy amusement lining their faces, whereas I was finding this anything but funny.

"Oh yes, let us now bow to Sir Toby," Cee-Cee said sarcastically, falling to her knees.

"Oh yes, lets," Jeremy agreed, lining up his knees beside hers.

I turned towards Esmerelda. "Why would we get in trouble if we refused to kneel?"

"Just do it, you stupid twit!" Then she pointed her pink wand at my knees and they fell out from in front of me. I landed roughly on the grass, still clutching the ball gown.

Sneering back at the old faery, I quickly returned my gaze back towards the sound of footsteps making their way through the villagers. Before long, I saw the same elf who I'd seen in the forest the other day, the one riding the tan horse. Then, just behind him, waving at the attendants bowing their heads for him as he passed by, was Sir Toby.

"Oh my stars, I would bow to him any day," Jeremy whispered.

I looked over at the starry-eyed look now on his face, and then towards Toby.

"He's all right looking," I muttered, causing Cee-Cee to snort under her breath.

"He's wearing a cape," she snickered.

Yes, he was. But I found myself looking past the oddity, and instead began recording every little thing about him. He was of average height, and his chest was fairly broad. Although he *was* still wearing that silly light blue cape, I could tell his arms were rather defined, and his cheekbones were very strong. And his soul...I could feel it, even though he was a good distance away. It was like a sun beam coming through a window on a chilly day.

"Don't freak, Makayla," Jeremy whispered frantically, "but he is looking right at you."

He walked past three more tents coming upon us, and as he did Jeremy and Cee-Cee both bowed their heads.

"Seriously?" I murmured into Cee-Cee's ear.

"What?" she whispered, her head still bowed. "Everyone else is doing it."

I wanted to tell her that this was case and point why the king and his company were getting away with this treatment, but I never got the chance, because just then Sir Toby paused right in front of me—studying me as though I was a struggling Ardeen whom he'd pulled from the bottom of his ridiculous white leather boot. I felt like lead pellets were raining over my shoulders.

"You are to bow in front of me, faery."

"Why?" I asked.

Immediately a hushed murmur broke out around me, and Esmerelda sighed as though the end was near. Nobody, however, lifted their heads.

Sir Toby appeared taken aback, and quite unsure of what to make of my question. The elf with the darker hair, who was now standing behind him, began stepping forward, but Toby pushed him back.

"No. It's okay, Rally." Toby then held out his hand for me to take.

"Oh shit, what did you just do, girl?" Cee-Cee cried softly.

Completely unafraid of anyone in a cape, I took Toby's hand and allowed him to help me up. His skin was soft and warm, and his eyes were like translucent blue glass. As I dared to search inside them, I felt something flutter inside my stomach.

Once I was standing, his gaze drifted away from my face to my hair, and then to my wings.

"You're her."

"Excuse me?"

"The lost Erwain."

"Oh yes, that," I said exasperatedly. "You may address me as Makayla Wood."

"Sir Toby may address you however he pleases," said the elf named Rally. His tone wasn't very nice at all.

"Is that so?" I questioned, rolling my shoulders back, and folding the gown I was still holding carefully over my arm.

"You are on thin ice, Miss Lala Abberwockey. I happen to know that's your real name," Rally spat out.

"That's my birth name, but when I was adopted it changed. I'm Makayla Wood, and that is final."

"Adopted?" Rally said, a queer expression materializing onto his face. "Explain how that is possible. The king is already curious as to how you escaped our tracking system all these years. If your parents willingly gave you away—"

"They didn't," I said, jutting out my chin. I could tell he was aggrieved by my interruption. "I sent myself away, they had nothing to do with it."

Rally had slipped his hand under his robe and was reaching for something. I couldn't tell if it was the end of a wooden wand or some kind of spear. Did elves even have wands?

"I don't believe that," said Rally.

"Well if you'd chosen to get to know me before judging me, which is the civilized thing to do where I come from, then perhaps you would find out that I'm no ordinary being. I've achieved great success at an early age, for a human or a faery. It is completely feasible that I was intelligent enough at just weeks old to find my way out of Garlandia and onto the front steps of my human parents' home. Parents I chose because they are both intellectual and caring people."

After I was finished, I held my breath, fully aware that I had crossed some sort of line. Rally looked positively ready to slice me open, but Sir Toby on the other hand appeared amused.

Placing a sturdy arm between Rally and myself, he turned to Rally and told him to back off. Rally stood down but stayed on edge. Toby lowered his arm and squared his shoulders with mine one more time.

"Well, Miss Makayla Wood of the Erwain descent, you are a very brave faery. None-the-less there is a hierarchy here that we expect those who live under our rule to adhere by."

Though there was something about this elf that caused my heart to pump out extra blood, and my limbs to lose all feeling, this was all still too much for me. One cannot strive to become a lawyer and ignore the desired chance to argue with what doesn't seem righteous or fair.

"And what if one doesn't agree with the hierarchy?"

There was more indistinct chatter coming from those with their heads bowed, but Toby kept his cool, even though I could tell he'd never been challenged before.

"I think, Miss Wood, things are much different here than what you're used to."

"You can say that again. But I assure you, I won't be here long."

At that, Rally couldn't contain himself. "We'll see what the king has to say about that! He is the one who ultimately decides whether someone can leave Garlandia or not! If you leave without permission, you will be a fugitive!"

"Or an escaped convict," I said, eyebrows firmly crossed.

"What's that supposed to mean?" Rally countered.

But Toby didn't give either one of us the chance to go on. Once more separating us with his arm, he moved in so that his chest blocked Rally.

"This is neither the time nor place for a shouting match. Miss Makayla, I apologize for my company's accusations. You need time to adjust to this world, just as any of us would require that of your world, I am sure. As for King Loral, he has plans to meet you—"

"And when might that be?" I interrupted, thinking back on what Helene had insinuated—that the king would never meet with me face to face.

Toby smiled. "From what I hear he has been waiting for you to find your faery dust again."

My tone became even more accusatory. "Has he been spying on me?"

"Spying, no. But word travels quickly around here, and just so you know, Miss Makayla Wood, my uncle knows everything." Noticing the dress in my arms for the first time, he asked, "Are you planning on attending a ball while you're here?"

"Oh this?" I lifted the dress in question, before placing it back where I'd found it. "No. I was just looking." Returning to the subject at hand, I said, "What if I wanted to meet with your uncle before I found my faery magic? Maybe I have a few questions for *him*."

Again, Toby appeared to be entertained by my complete disregard. He didn't answer me, though, instead he nodded at the dress. "You shouldn't have put it down; it would have looked nice on you."

I cocked an eyebrow at him, at which point he chuckled before backing away.

"Miss Makayla Wood of the Erwain descent, it was nice to meet you, wings and all." And then something happened that made the crowd gasp. He placed a hand behind his back and bowed slightly towards me. Towards *me*. He didn't seem to even notice he'd done it until Rally snagged his elbow and whispered haughtily into his ear. Immediately he straightened and attempted to retract the bow.

And then he was off again. The horns screeching out for the next group of Garlandians to prepare for his arrival. Rally stared me down as he began marching behind Toby again, and then spit at my foot.

"You little—" I started, preparing to lunge forward and wring his neck, but Cee-Cee and Jeremy grabbed hold of me and pulled me back before I could do anything that would get my wings plucked from my back, or worse.

After all that, it couldn't be clearer—Garlandia was *not* free. This was a government ruled by a king who seemed to crave power, and the injustice flowing through the ranks was like an angry river through a busted dam. It was enough to keep me grinding my teeth for hours. I unlocked my jaw only once for the rest of the day, and that was only because the three of us had made our way over to the stage where *RATS* was being performed.

As soon as we got close enough to see the actors, I dropped the licorice soda I was drinking onto the ground— at which point a flock of Ardeens came flying over and rolled around in it as though it were a mud bath. But it *wasn't* the elaborate costumes that had me struck dumb— the cast had transfigured themselves into humanoid rats— and it *wasn't* the very off-key singing either (they really didn't fare well with singing). It was the flying tomatoes being chucked onto the stage. Dozens of tomatoes, along with the angry yelling that the cast was terrible and should go running back home to cower in the corners of their homes as soon as possible.

"Your mothers should be ashamed!" Maude yelled.

Another tomato directly into one of the singer's whiskers.

"The only "Memory" I hope to take from this production is the one of you sulking off the stage!" Tanker shrieked.

SMACK. Another tomato.

"I thought you said your parents were critics," Jeremy said, as awestruck as Cee-Cee and myself, watching Maude and Tanker chuck tomatoes and yell obscenities at the cast.

"That's what they said..." My words drifted away.

"Well, they *are* sort of critiquing them," Cee-Cee offered, sticking a piece of cotton candy into her mouth. She was wearing a giant pair of fake faery wings she'd used her honey to buy. The Erwain she'd bought them from said if she came back later with something more substantial than honey that she'd make them work.

I, being the smart businesswoman I was, had refused to spend all my honey on one purchase. Instead, I'd given it away in small amounts, feeding my friends and I with sugar and more sugar. It was a substance that I'd found I'd needed more of—ever since I'd had these blasted wings.

In regards to the travesty unfolding before us, I could only stand to watch the display of horror my birth parents were creating for a moment longer before advocating our departure. It was just too much for me to take. I had to wonder, did they do this when they reviewed the theatre in the human world? What were they like at restaurants? I mean, my god, they didn't even use utensils. That was not something I could think on for too long without bringing on another one of my panic attacks. I'd had fun during the food fight, but this—this was a whole new level of crazy.

By the time we arrived back to 17 Serendipity Lane it was beginning to get dark, so faeries and various creatures were scampering quickly into their homes before curfew. I was completely exhausted from trying not to call out my birth parents for their more than odd behavior at the farmer's market. Apparently, I was the only faery who found their tomato slinging appalling though, because as we passed another group on our way back to the cottage, I heard a Sheridan faery yell out, "Great commentary, you guys! Can't wait to read what you have to say in the paper!"

"Thanks, Bob!" Tanker called back.

I kept my head down, shaking it gently to myself.

"I'm sad you guys have to go," I said to my friends at the closing of our day, the three of us standing before Maynard the tree. Mort was already there, impatiently waiting for his bribe; which was a carrot cake mud eclair I'd made in an effort to see what else I was capable of.

"We'll be back," Cee-Cee said.

"And with more honey," Jeremy added.

"Well, all right," I said, wrapping my arms around the two of them. "Try not to wait too long though, okay."

"We won't," they said in unison, before backing away and moving towards the tree.

"All righ', all righ', the three of ya done yet? Give me tha' cake," Mort grumbled, jumping up and snagging the treat from my hands, before stuffing it greedily into his mouth, his eyes rolling back in pleasure.

"Gross," Cee-Cee said.

"Okay, good-bye," I said, backing away, watching as the three of them faded from this world and returned to theirs— to mine—to the human world.

When I turned back to the cottage, I could see Maude and Tanker dancing in the living room through the windows. I stopped for a moment to appreciate the sight of them. I suppose I was going to have to forgive them for being 'critics.' Evidently what they did made others happy here, or at least the ones not getting hit in the face with tomatoes. Providing laughter during dark times was a gift . . . perhaps my initial judgements had been skewed.

I was just about to head back inside when a long, thin arm

reached out and pulled me back into the trees. Before I had a chance to act like I knew how to defend my wings I turned to find myself face to face with a pair of fierce eyes, and a mouth turned down into a scowl.

"Helene! You frightened me!"

"Oh, shut up," she snapped. "What is this I hear about you getting friendly with Sir Toby?"

I gave her a look as if to suggest she had to be joking, but when she didn't budge, I said, "I was hardly friendly. In fact, I demanded answers that I never received. Something that is becoming frustratingly routine around here."

"You kneeled before him," she accused. "What did I tell you about that?"

"An old faery forced me to, I didn't want to!" I pleaded. "And what does it matter to you if I did or didn't? I am old enough to make my own choices."

She crossed her arms and leaned in towards me. "I already told you—if you want my help, you have to do as I say."

I bit my lip in place of barking back at her.

"And just so you know, it would be inadvisable to be seen speaking with the heir like that ever again. His bowing to you didn't help either. From what I've heard the king isn't happy, and he's ordered his nephew out of the kingdom for the next few days."

"What do you mean?"

She scoffed. "Makayla, it is illegal for faeries and elves to intermingle any more than trading goods."

"What?"

"Do you need me to talk slower?"

"No." God, how rude. "I heard what you said. I just, well, that is segregation."

"Duh."

I did my best not to sneer at her. "What you are saying is that elves and faeries can't, like, be friends . . . or fall in love?"

"If a faery and elf are found together, they are put to death . . . or worse."

I gasped. Every time I thought things couldn't get any bleaker, they found a way.

"Look," Helene said, uncrossing her arms, "just stay away from Sir Toby. The last thing we Erwains need is another reason for the king to—just stay away from him." And then she flew up through the trees before I even had a chance to retort.

"Hey! Wait!" I pleaded, but it was of no use, she was gone. I really needed to learn how to fly.

Herbert was perched in front of the house when I walked up, I caught him mid burp.

"Good evening, Miss Makayla," he said, once he'd gathered himself.

"Hello, Herbert. How's it going?"

"It's been a fulfilling day if ever there was one."

"Oh? Did you get to engage in one of your debates?"

"Sort of, although I may have gone a bit off the Aeronian paved path." He gave me a strange look and then quickly turned his head away. "A group of solicitors came along while you all were out and I had a lovely conversation with them about *Titania*." He emphasized the name, saying it loud and proud.

As soon as he'd said it there was a strange crack from somewhere in the woods, like a tree branch snapping. Looking back down at him, I asked, "The faery from *A Midsummer Night's Dream*?"

"No—well, sort of. Will used the idea of her—she probably whispered her character into his ear," he chuckled. "Did you know, Miss Makayla, that Titania was actually an Erwain faery?"

Again, I thought I heard a strange noise, and even thought I saw something blue flash in the distance, but it disappeared before I could get a closer look. "I, uh—well, no. I still don't know who she is exactly."

Moving his gaze to rest on mine, he said, "She's the daughter of Gaia, the goddess of everything, the mother of us all."

"Gaia."

"Yes."

"How can a faery be born of a goddess?"

"We all came from something at some point."

I stared down at him in confusion, but he didn't offer any kind of explanation.

Returning to the subject matter, I asked, "What happened to this faery? You speak of her as though she's gone."

His eyes drifted away, and as they did, they glazed over. He gave a half-hearted burp.

"They say she's gone, but she's not. In fact, I believe she's closer than she's ever been. It was said she had the power of creation at her fingertips . . . something I believe as well. BURP. Well, if you don't mind, I need to rest, and I think it's time for young Erwains to get to bed. It's been a pleasure, and do remember what I said to you when we first met."

"Remind me."

"Just because you cannot see something, doesn't mean it doesn't exist. Now, I suggest you go inside. I am very happy I had the pleasure of meeting you." And then he bowed his head, in the same manner as the Garlandian's had for Sir Toby.

"Okay, I'll see you soon," I said, quite unsure of the statement. Then, just as I had before, I bent down and scratched the top of his slimy head. He cooed with delight.

Once I was inside, I said goodnight to Maude and Tanker and quickly excused myself up to my room. Tucked in beside Kevin, I pulled out my small notebook and flipped to a middle page and wrote down, "Titania, daughter of Gaia. Gaia, the goddess of everything."

Without the internet, I was at a loss for information, and as a future lawyer I was a research junkie. I was dying to know who these characters were.

Staring at the names for a moment longer, I then closed the notebook and slipped it back under my pillow. Perhaps I could speak with Herbert more about Titania later, I thought, as I drifted to sleep. He'd been shallow with his information, but I bet I could persuade him to be more forthright later.

But that was something that wasn't ever going to happen, because when I woke up the next morning, it was to Maude shrieking; and when I ran downstairs, I found the front door opened and my birth mother cowered over what looked like a rock, her hands over her whimpering mouth.

It wasn't a rock though, far from it. It was Herbert, his mouth open in what looked like a burp, and he had been turned to stone.

❈ 17 ❈

Petrified. Mortified. Mournful. I'm sure there were more words to describe what I was feeling, but the shock I was in wouldn't allow me to find them. Tanker, Maude, and I were sitting around one side of the kitchen table, our hands wrapped around three piping mugs of licorice root extract, with Owen and Contessa on the opposite side.

"I don't know where Sabrina could be," Contessa kept saying, fidgeting with her own cup of brew. "We were supposed to meet at Cajun Cathy's last night and she never showed."

"I'm sure she's just running behind," Owen said, rubbing Contessa's shoulder. "You know how she gets when she's involved with something, she probably forgot."

"No." She shook her head. "She said she had something very important to tell me, and she hinted that it had to do with the abductions. I think she knew something."

"Puck and Adlar are heading to her apartment right now, Tess," Maude said, sounding very motherly. "Owen's right, she probably just lost track of the time."

Tanker, completely oblivious to any other conversations,

mumbled, "I just can't believe it . . . Herbert. I really loved that damn frog."

All I had been receiving from the moment we found our little friend in his frozen state, were desperately sad looks whenever I asked any questions. Tanker had spoken up only once—when I had started to lay my hands on Herbert to move him, at which point he had pulled me immediately away, a look of warning on his face as he said, "No one must touch him. King Loral will know if you do."

"Will somebody *please* just attempt to make sense of this to me," I demanded. "I know this is the work of the king." Everyone looked away. "This is maddening! Herbert was like a friend to me—granted I didn't know him all that well, but he opened up to me more than anyone else has. I deserve to know what happened to him!"

Just then a knock came at the door and Maude jumped up to answer it, revealing Todd, the Sheridan faery I'd met at Cajun Cathy's, and a little gnome I didn't recognize.

"Oh yes, of course, come in," Maude said, ushering the little creatures inside.

Contessa, struggling to stand, nodded her head towards the two. "Teagan," she said to the gnome, "this is Makayla."

"Oh righ', the little lost Erwain. Nice to meet ya'," he said. "Word's been spreadin' 'bout that mud cream stuff." I could tell he was trying to sound enthusiastic, but under the circumstances it didn't come out very well.

"Teagan is also a council member," Contessa said, sitting back down and curling back into Owen's arms. Looking up at the two new arrivals, she asked, "Have you heard from Sabrina?"

"No," Todd said, watching as Maude set some books on a couple chairs for him and Teagan. When she was done, he flew up onto the pile and accepted a small cup of licorice root. "We thought she would be here already." He used his eyes to trace the star on my wing, causing me to feel self-conscious. It was beginning to feel like a hairy mole people couldn't unsee but did all they could not to address.

"No." Contessa looked down; her eyes unfocused.

"Here you are," Maude said, helping Teagan up onto the chair and then laying down a mud éclair in front of him; it was from my latest batch of gnome treat creations. He nodded to her in appreciation.

Meanwhile, I'd been weaving together small pieces of information with the little I already knew, and I couldn't hold back any longer.

"Contessa, you were supposed to meet Sabrina at Cajun Cathy's last night, right?"

Everyone shifted their attention my way.

"Yes," Contessa answered.

"Who else was there?"

"It was after dinner service, so no one. Once the food runs out, so do the customers."

I couldn't get the vision of that creepy kitchen witch out of my head. "Was Cathy there?"

"Of course, she was," Contessa answered. "She went with me to look for Sabrina after she didn't show up. But there were no traces of her, and she wasn't home."

"How well do you all really know Cajun Cathy?"

The entire table gasped.

"Makayla," Tanker warned, shaking his head.

Owen, a stern look written upon his face, retorted, "I know she's a bit frazzled looking, but trust us, that witch couldn't hurt a fly . . . unless it was staring at her funny."

"Well she's a kitchen witch, ain't she!" Teagan piped up; a piece of mud eclair stuck to his teeth. "The only menacing that ol' bat gets into is with an onion slicer."

"Right," I said, sensing no one at this table was willing to speak ill of their precious jambalaya queen. But inside I was still reeling, because the fact remained that it was *totally plausible* that Sabrina got to the restaurant first. Perhaps Cathy was working for the king. It would be the perfect guise—hearing the conversations of all the villagers' day after day, eating her grub with their dirty fingers.

As I continued to stew over those thoughts, Owen returned to the matter at hand: Herbert. "What was it he said? What could he have been saying that landed him in this situation?"

"We don't know," Tanker said, wiping his nose on the sleeve of his bright pink satin button up shirt; it had little red hearts for buttons. "He seemed well when we got home, quite happy actually."

"I always told him to be careful," Maude said, shaking her head. "All that talk about the afterlife—deities even! It is not a safe time for such talk."

Before anyone could utter another word, a burst of darkness exploded from the corner, and everyone—including me—jumped in our seats. Dark blue glitter faded away and Helene stood in its place.

"Son of a dark wizard, Helene!" Tanker shouted; licorice root now spilled down the front of his shiny shirt. "How many times have we told you *not* to Pop inside!" He pulled out his wand and removed the stain.

"Sorry Ticker," she said without sincerity, before moving towards the table and pulling up a chair. I noticed a scar on her left cheek that I hadn't seen before. The skin was very pink, like it had been recently healed. "So, what's this, an informal council meeting?"

"Herbert's been frozen," Owen said, a bit of a bite in his bark.

"The frog? Why on earth—"

"Is this because of Titania?" I asked, causing every single pair of wings at the table to extend. Teagan had brought his hands up around his neck and was wringing it as he choked on his filthy snack.

"Maude," Tanker said in a hushed voice, as Owen reached over and pounded the gnome's back—a bit of mud eclair flying out onto the table, "did you protect the walls?"

"Of course," she said, looking aghast.

"Protect the walls?" I asked.

"So no one can eavesdrop from the other side of the cottage," Helene whispered in my ear.

"Where'd you hear that name?" the gnome asked, pounding his chest with his fist.

"Herbert mentioned her to me before I came in last night. He said she was the daughter of—"

"Gaia," Contessa whispered. Then, sitting forward, she geared all her attention over me. "Why—What did he say about her?"

Everyone was leaning forward now. "Nothing really. He just happened to bring her up, but when I asked to know more about her, he said that was all he could say for the time being."

Silence. The entire room was filled with complete and utter nothingness; and Tanker was staring at me with such peculiarity, that it began to make me feel uncomfortable.

"Well that settles it," Todd said, leaning back into his chair. "We know why he was turned."

"I knew it!" I said, my muscles contracting. "This *was* the work of the king. He's punishing—"

"Makayla, you should go to your room," Tanker said, staring down at his hands.

"No! I may not have chosen this for myself, but I'm one of *you* now, and I deserve to know what is going on here!"

Owen, staring at me in the same manner as Tanker had been just seconds ago, stated so softly I could barely make out his words, "You are more than one of us."

My gaze fell upon his shoulders, but before I could question the bizarre statement, there was another knock at the door.

This time Tanker answered it, and when he did there was a dirty elf wearing brown leather pants and a leather vest, standing in front of a large brown bear. The bear had a leather pouch drawn around his neck.

Tanker nodded his head and stepped aside, allowing them in, both their expressions rather grave.

"What is it?" Contessa asked, standing up. She had begun to shake all over again.

"It's Sabrina," the Wood elf said.

"Did you find her? Was she home?" Contessa was pleading for the right answer, because there was only one word she wanted to hear in that very moment.

The elf looked at the bear and lowered his head. The bear spoke quietly, and in a gruff voice, just as he opened his paw to reveal the smallest curlers I'd ever seen . . . the same curlers Sabrina had had in her hair when she'd stopped by the other night. "We found traces of a struggle . . . we have reason to believe she's been taken."

After that there was a sudden eruption of wings raising and a fountain of tears pouring out from Contessa. Before I had a chance to even reach out to the distraught faery, Helene took me into her grasp, and within a matter of seconds she dragged me through the front door before flapping her giant wings and lifting us into the air. My adrenaline rose so high that I didn't even have time to acknowledge my first flight.

She sped upwards through the trees, and she kept flapping even after we were far above the forest. If my heartbeats hadn't already been preoccupied, I would have begun to worry that she wasn't going to stop until the oxygen supply was cut short. But just as the sky was beginning to darken into a deep blue, she turned us around and began taking us on a nosedive that didn't end until we hit the forest floor.

When we landed, we weren't anywhere I'd been before. Gasping for air, I fell to my knees as though I'd just ended a sprint race, and when I looked up, I saw what looked like a very old gazebo with vines wrapped all around it, and the statue of an elf—an alarmed look frozen onto his face. I took one look at him and glared at Helene.

"Why did you take me away?"

"That was no place for a child," she said, rolling back her shoulders and dusting off her wings.

"Why do people keep calling me that? I am *not* a child!"

She filled her chest before letting out a long exhale, then pulled out her wand and pointed it down at my face. "Stop this insolence. You have no idea what is good for you and what isn't; and until you can learn to defend yourself, *niece*, I would stop asking questions unless you want to end up like this." She turned her wand on the statue. "Now stand up and show me that you've learned something."

I looked at her as though she was mad.

"You want to work today? Are you insane?" I pointed an arm out into the forest. "You can't expect me to concentrate with everything that is going on."

"I thought you were a smart girl, Makayla."

"I am."

"Then why would you balk at the opportunity to gain back your magic during a time when you need it the most? If you want to stand up to your enemies, then you have to learn the proper way to do so."

I continued to sneer at her, but her point was valid. So even though it felt wrong, because there was an entire group of mourning creatures back in that cottage, I stood up and faced my teacher.

"Fine. What do you want me to do?"

Holding her wand horizontally between her forefingers and thumbs, she neared me. With a subtle, yet evil quality escaping from her eyes, she said, "Run."

"What?"

A blackish sparkle began to emanate around her head, swirling down around her long black locks until it enveloped her entire body. Without flinching, she repeated the word. "Run."

My heart rate picked right back up, and for the first time I looked at Helene and saw a predator. My shoulder blades twitched. I'd only felt that sensation once before—just before my wings grew back. They wanted to fly, but they were still immobile from Maude's spell.

I began to back away. Was this real? My heart was beating as though it was. Or was she just trying to get me to dig up my dust? Either way, my gut told me not to chance it, so I turned around and did as she said. I ran.

It was difficult to run fast with my wings lifeless and dragging behind me. That and we were so far deep into the forest that there was barely any space between the trees. As I ran, the shadows moved—chased me even—and every now and then the face of a wizard or a witch popped out from one of the cold, dark spaces; but even over the sound of my breath and the heartbeats that had moved into my ear canal, the beating of Helene's wings overhead remained constant.

At some point I tripped and fell face first into horse manure. Cursing, I stood back up and continued to run.

Fight or flight, I thought to myself. That's what this was. She was trying to get me to utilize my fears to gauge my magic. As I ran, I dug deeper, trying to play on the beating of my heart, trying to muster up the intuition of holding my wand in my hand and directing it at Helene. My feet were pounding into the soft earth—it was all I could do not to roll an ankle; and then it happened. I lost sight of the last bit of light and moved directly into the darkness.

A chill enveloped my body and the ground became more solid. I stopped running and tried to catch my breath, reaching around to see if I could hold on to anything. There were no trees . . . there was nothing, it seemed. I'd crossed over into a part of the forest I didn't feel comfortable in at all.

"What are you going to do now, Lala?" a creepy voice sang out from no particular direction, as though I were inside of a well.

"Helene?" My voice was strong, but shaky.

The tip of her wand lit up, and I saw her face. She was standing just feet away.

"Where are we?"

She lifted a finger and shook it at me. "Little Erwains shouldn't ever be this far into the forest. Not safe."

"Is this still part of the lesson?" I asked, my breath shallow.

The glowing tip of her wand moved as she turned around, cupping her chin with her hand. "Oh Makayla, enough with the questions! Show me some skill!" And then she swung back around and pointed her wand directly at my heart. Holding me still with the end of her wand, she reached up and yanked a necklace from around her neck, revealing a small vial at the end of it. Uncorking the bottle with her teeth, she sucked its contents into her mouth and then blew it towards me.

"Take a deep breath," she said wickedly.

It swirled around me, like wind with hands, lifting me into the air; and as I stared down at my aunt in horror, a clear ball encased me. I kicked my feet, trying to poke through it, but it was like some kind of unbreakable ectoplasm.

"Shall I just leave you here, then?" she asked, from where she was standing below me. "With the darkest of magicians all around you. Is this the only way to teach you? Will you allow yourself to die with fear in your heart?"

I tried to scream at her, but my words only came bouncing back to me inside of my shell; and the harder I kicked and punched, the more I screamed, the more I felt my lungs constrict. The air in here was depleting quickly.

As I struggled, Helene's laughter grew as she pointed her wand up at me, and bounced my body up and down, shaking me up inside the ball. My fear quickly began to transform into anger as fury rose inside me.

"My god, Makayla, you are so pathetic," she said, dropping the ball to the ground and letting it pop.

I rolled out onto the frozen ground and crawled up to my knees, once more gasping for air. The scent of animal feces was drying on my cheeks, fueling my rage. Helene's face was still lit from her wand and all I wanted to do was wipe that snarky look off her face.

"I am *not* pathetic!" I screamed, jumping up and ramming into her, pushing her backwards until I felt her back hit against a tree. As soon as it did, the darkness disappeared and we were back in the light; and not only did I have one of my hands around her throat, but I was pointing a purplish, blue wand directly at her nose.

Her gaze darted from the wand in my hands back to my eyes and she smiled. "I thought so."

Upon the realization of what I had conjured, I backed away and looked down. It was still there, *my wand*. I lifted it, inspecting it. It was heavy with life.

Helene hadn't moved from where I'd slammed her into the tree, but instead of looking exasperated by what I had done, she seemed very proud of herself.

"What do you mean, *you thought so*?" I asked.

"I wanted to see what would really get you going. What did we learn last time about motivation?"

"The three principles?"

She nodded.

"Fight or Flight, Emotion, and Spellcasting."

"Yes, and since you can't learn how to cast until you conquer fear and emotion, I wanted to know which one of those would most motivate you. Just as I suspected, fear you put up with, but what truly drew that out"—she signaled to my wand— "was your temperament. You are not a creature who can be played with. Now we know."

"I could've told you that," I muttered, staring down into the swirling colors inside my wand. I couldn't believe something so solid could be conjured from my soul.

"I think that's enough for today," Helene said, wrapping an arm around my waist and guiding me towards a path not far from where we were standing. "We can go show Maude and Tanker. I think they could use some cheering up today, don't you?"

I smiled for the first time since I'd woken that morning. "Yeah. For sure. Thanks, Helene," I said, watching as another blue fleck crossed my line of vision.

We were quiet for most of the way back to 17 Serendipity Lane, but as we got closer, the excitement of what I was holding seemed to fade as I thought about Herbert and Sabrina. I was still chomping at the bit for some sort of explanation, and since Helene was more forthright with details, I decided to try and get something out of her.

"So, do *you* ever eat at Cajun Cathy's with the others?"

"Cathy's?" she replied. "No. I prefer to eat alone."

"Oh . . . okay." That shouldn't have been surprising.

"Why are you asking me about her?"

"I was asking about her restaurant, not her."

"No, you weren't," she replied stiffly.

"*Okay,* I guess I'm just curious about her is all. Has she always just been Cajun Cathy, or is there a history there?"

"Everyone has a history, Makayla. Cathy used to be the

king's chef, but then she injured her eye and he said he didn't want a half blind witch in his kitchen."

"Cathy used to work for the king?"

"Yes," she answered simply.

"How long ago?"

"Oh, let's see—fifty—eighty or so years ago. I don't know." She paused for a moment before posing her question. "Where are you going with this?"

I stopped short and turned to her. "Don't you think it's a little strange that Cathy used to work for the king, and now she's planted directly in the spot where all the Ardeens keep going missing?"

Helene screwed up her lips as if she were on the brink of speaking but couldn't think of the words to say, and for a moment I thought she was entertaining the idea that I was on to something, but she just as quickly shut me down. "You need to be more careful, Makayla. Throwing around accusations like that will turn Garlandians against you quickly, and everyone needs allies during these times."

"But what if she's a spy?"

"Enough!" She grabbed my shoulders and drew me in close. "You are going down the wrong path. I'm not going to pretend that there aren't some shady characters living amongst us, but those of us who have joined hands and have prepared to fight, have already stripped our neighbors of any suspicions."

"You mean L.O.A—"

She slapped a hand over my mouth. "Shut up! How many times do we have to beat this into your head, that you don't say certain things out loud!"

My wand warmed and turned blue in my hands.

Taking a deep breath and backing off, Helene looked towards the cottage of number seventeen in the near distance. Huffing, she said, "You are like me, you require answers. I daresay this makes me proud, but you must realize you are teetering on a narrow bridge. You may know how to swim, but the water is shallow and you don't yet know how to fly. You have one thing to worry about while you are here, Makayla, and that is finding your dust. Let those of us who know what we are getting into, do the dirty work." She brushed away a strand of hair that had fallen over her cheek and revealed the mark I'd seen earlier. When she caught me staring at it, she frowned and looked away. "Even those of us who know how to fight can't win them all."

Furrowing my brow, I asked, "What happened, Helene? Was it an elf who did that to you?"

She flipped her head back around and in a cautionary tone, said, "I am not discussing this with you."

"Fine, but what about what Herbert told me last night—"

"Don't say her name," Helene warned before I could even think about muttering Titania's name out loud.

"I'm not, but you all insinuated that was why he was turned. Does *she* have something to do with all this?" I lowered my chin and looked up at her. "Does your little club—"

"Quiet!"

"I know, I get it—but does that group have anything to do with *her*?"

Helene bit down over her lip as she continued to stare at me. Finally, she took my arm and started leading me back towards the cottage. "Of course, she does. There is reason to believe she is the key to unlocking the doors of this prison. But once again, I must advise you to stay out of it."

❧ 18 ❧

It had been a few days since Sabrina went missing, and although finding my wand had indeed lifted Maude and Tanker's spirits, it had failed to negate the truth: something sinister was going on beneath the already infected surface of Garlandia, and every time I walked past Herbert's statue I was reminded of that fact.

"What could the king be doing with Ardeen faeries?" Tanker had said to Maude the night before last, only after they'd thought I'd gone to bed. Apparently, it didn't matter if it was my birth or adoptive parents—I wasn't going to get any answers unless I eavesdropped.

"I have no idea," Maude had returned. "It just doesn't make any sense—and Sabrina was on the council. I mean, you don't think—"

"That he's trying to get rid of the council altogether? Wouldn't surprise me. Perhaps he no longer needs a guise."

There was a small bout of silence before Maude replied, "I realize King Loral has never respected those of us living in the trees, but would he really go so far as to begin killing us off?"

"It's not like he hasn't tried that before."

"I suppose he could be going after the council members," Maude said, "but that still doesn't explain the rest of the missing Ardeens."

I hadn't gotten much more from that conversation, other than the fact that the king was more dangerous than I could ever have imagined. Upon hearing of the council when I first arrived, I thought perhaps Garlandia was governed by a democracy, but the longer I stayed, the clearer it became. The king was a dictator, and the council was only for show. If only I could've gotten more information out of Helene, but even she was shallow on handing out details.

Maude and Tanker had been extremely preoccupied with the neighborhood watch over the next few days and had little time to spend with me. They apologized profusely, but it was fine; I needed the extra time to concentrate on learning to call on my dust. Helene had been right, in times like these I really needed to know how to defend myself, and typical of my character I'd skipped ahead. I had figured out how to summon my wand, but not my dust, and one was useless without the other.

Against Helene's demands that I discontinue my sleuthing, I went ahead and decided to survey Cathy over a late lunch. Staking out a table close to the kitchen, I ordered a plate of jambalaya and folded my hands over the table, nodding in the direction of two giggling Ardeens who were finishing up with a food fight.

"Here ya go, dear." Cathy panted as she laid down my food.

"Thanks Cathy. Hey," I said casually, "it looks like I'm the last customer. You should grab a plate and keep me company."

Her dancing eye bounced from my nose to my shoulder and towards the door. "Oh, why not." Then staring at the Ardeens covered in spicy sauce, she hollered out, "You best be licking all that up when you're finished!" She shook her head and mumbled under her breath, "Filthy little pests." She pulled out a chair and sat down, a plate materializing in front of her. "Thanks for having me sit with you, I forget to slow down sometimes."

I forced a smile, her 'pest' comment now on my radar. "I would think you should know how to slow down—you're retired, aren't you?"

She laid her hands flat on the table and stared at me with her foggy eye. I got the sinking suspicion that she was searching me over. "You're an interesting specimen, aren't you? Not very faery-like, minus those wings behind your back." She pointed at them with a fork in her hand—a fork!

"Hey! I thought you didn't have any food weapons."

"This? Of course, I do. Witches and wizards don't like to get their hands dirty."

"I don't like to get my hands dirty, either."

Cathy paused, she'd speared a shrimp with her fork and was about to put it in her mouth. She seemed to entertain my justification for a moment, before shrugging her shoulders and taking a bite. Next thing I knew there was a flash of silver next to my plate and I looked down to find a fork.

I smiled in gratitude. "Thanks."

She shrugged her shoulders again.

"So, I heard you used to work for the king."

She stopped mid chew.

"Who told you that?"

I took the fork in my hand and shoveled some red sauce with sausage onto it. "I can't remember, I think it just kind of came up. I was curious what it was like, though—working in the castle."

"Ah," she nodded, chewing on a large bite.

When she didn't offer any other explanation, I pushed a little harder. "So uh, did you know him very well? The king, that is."

"I suppose. One begins to get to know someone quite well when they are cooking for them. King Loral was always a bit guarded—well" —she got a funny look on her face— "you know, I just don't remember that much about him, or being there at all for that matter."

I furrowed my brow, ignoring the heat enveloping my entire mouth from the bite of food I'd just taken. "How can you *not* remember?"

She scraped her fork along her empty plate. She'd finished her meal in about three bites. "I don't know." She grabbed a napkin from her lap—one I hadn't seen before she'd sat down —and dabbed the corners of her mouth. "I just don't."

"How many years did you work there?"

She scratched the inside of her ear and turned her cloudy eye to the ceiling. "Gee, I don't know, maybe twenty, fifty, a hundred years or so."

That was a wide range. "And you don't remember being there?" Something was definitely off about that.

"Not really. I remember cooking in the kitchen, and blurbs here and again, but not much else." She stood, signaling to my fork. "Keep that. A gift for letting an old witch eat lunch with you. I don't get much company these days, I'm afraid."

"Wait," I said, holding out my arm in an attempt to delay her departure. "Um, did you like the king? While you worked for him—was he a descent employer?"

Once more she got a wonky look on her face, and after a moment, nodded her head. "Yes. I believe so . . . but like I said, it's all a bit foggy." Then she turned and walked away, leaving me completely unsatisfied.

Why couldn't she remember? She could just be old—*or* the king had her under some sort of spell. Perhaps he was using her to do his bidding, to collect Ardeens and dispose of their bodies. A whole lot of assumptions that would have been easier to connect if I had even the vaguest idea of what King Loral was actually like.

The forkful of food lingered before my mouth as my mind jutted to the darkest of places. I wondered, how could Cathy be disposing of the Ardeen bodies if it was in fact her who was doing the abductions? Suddenly the bite seemed repulsive.

I looked up at the Ardeens now licking themselves off from their food fight.

"Don't be ridiculous, Makayla," I muttered to myself. But I still decided not to finish my lunch.

I needed to get back to my faery education, so after that I returned to my special spot in the woods. I was surrounded by the usual audience of forest creatures, trees, and plant life; and I was currently flicking my wand around in the air aimlessly, trying to conjure up even the faintest of sparkles.

"I see a yellow one!" a Sheridan faery passing by yelled.

"Really?"

"No, but I made you look!"

"Stupid little Sheridans," I grumbled, dropping to the ground and pulling out my notebook.

I still only had two colors listed and was without an explanation for blue. I'd seen blue twice and both times had been with Helene. I set the tip of my pencil against the paper and wrote, "Adrenaline?"

After that I flipped to the middle of the book, to where I'd written down the names Titania and Gaia. Without hesitation, I wrote down Cathy and King Loral's names with a question mark, then made note of the missing faeries and frozen Garlandians. I needed to figure out how these hideous acts were related, and after speaking with Cathy, I was more convinced than ever that she was somehow involved. If she wasn't, I had to imagine there was something in her memory bank covered up by old age that could somehow point to a finding.

Helene had insinuated that the king was trying to get rid of the Ardeens because they were the easiest to capture. Because we had magic that he couldn't compete with.

Suddenly my thoughts were interrupted by a rustling through the trees. I looked up just in time to see all the animals jet off in different directions, and the flowers and trees close their eyes as though they were asleep.

I closed my notepad and tucked it into my pocket before pulling out my wand—even though I didn't know how to use it—and held it confidently in front of me. I didn't have to wait long until I heard a familiar voice yelling at someone to go ahead and that he would catch up. My heartbeat immediately picked up. It was Sir Toby, and as soon as our eyes met, he froze.

"Makayla."

"Toby," I answered, lowering my wand. I thought Helene had said he'd been sent away.

Staring at me for a few seconds more before relaxing his shoulders, he asked, "Haven't seen Petal, have you?"

"Petal?"

"Sorry, you wouldn't know. She's my horse. A spunky white mare."

"No, I'm afraid I haven't. When did you last see her?"

He hesitated for a moment before starting towards me—his white boots crunching over pinecones and fallen branches. He was still wearing that ridiculous cape.

"About an hour ago," he said.

"That long?"

"Don't worry, she always comes back. She does this when I'm out with Rally for a long time—doesn't really care for him. Also, she likes to lead, and since Rally is supposed to guard me, we always end up in the back. She'll return as soon as he has gotten further enough away."

I smirked. I couldn't quite tell him, but I agreed with Petal on that one. I didn't need to get to know Rally to understand that the two of us would never get along. One doesn't tend to make friends with those who spit at their feet.

"I see," I said, instead of all that.

Toby looked down at my wand and raised his eyebrows. "I see you are getting closer to acknowledging your magic. Have you found your dust yet, Miss Makayla?"

"Not yet." I suddenly realized how close he'd gotten to me. He smelled woodsy, and like incense. The scent caused me to feel slightly light-headed, and I could've sworn the air around us was beginning to glisten as though it were wet.

"I hope my question wasn't too forward, but ever since your arrival the entire kingdom has been talking about your progress from human into faery again." Very slowly, he lifted a hand to my cheek, causing my chest to rise too quickly. "You've gotten some sun, though, being out here." The corners of his mouth turned up as he said the words, brushing my skin with the back of his knuckles. "A bit red." Then, as though he'd just realized he was touching me, he immediately dropped his hand away.

I stumbled over my next words. "Yes. The sun. That's why they're red."

The silence quickly grew thick between us, along with another form of energy I wasn't accustomed to feeling every day. I found myself searching for something to say to break the ice, but there was only one thing I was really good at . . . being a businesswoman and all.

"What are you doing?" he asked, looking down at my proffered hand.

I looked down. I hadn't even realized I'd extended it.

Feeling even more blood rushing to my face, I tried to make sense of my bizarre behavior in faery land. "I—well, it's just occurred to me that the way we were introduced was a bit strange, and where I come from—"

"Oh yes, I've heard of this. Faeries and elves all over the kingdom are doing it—introducing themselves the *human* way." And then he slapped my hand before leaning forward. "Go on, then."

It was clear this false handshake had become a sort of endearing activity to the creatures of Garlandia. Even though I felt like it was wrong on several levels, I hesitated for only a second before slapping his face.

"Sorry," I said automatically.

He reached up and rubbed his cheek, a funny smile forming along the lines of his cherry lips. "Why are you sorry? I thought that was kind of fun."

Still, I held onto my slapping hand with the other as though it was now in jeopardy of being sliced off. "You haven't ever been to the human world, have you?"

"No. I've been under my uncle's care since I was very young, and before that I lived with my parents in Cavita." He pronounced the name of the village with a strange accent. "Uncle has kept me quite busy traveling all over the country since the moment I arrived here. In fact, I'm supposed to be over the other side of mountain right now, but Rally's been covering for me. He tells the old goat we're on these lengthy trips, when really we're out fishing in the next village."

"Because the fish here are intellectuals?" I asked, unsure of where the question came from.

"Yes."

God, his grin was catching.

Studying his lips, I asked, "Where is Cavita?"

He took a deep breath and searched the sky, before pointing northeast. "Very far away, in that direction."

"And why is your uncle raising you—I'm sorry, that was incredibly forward of me," I said, realizing that must have meant his parents were dead.

He studied me only for a second before responding.

"Forgive me, but you don't come across as someone who apologizes for being forward."

I blushed. "Normally I don't."

He remained still, his posture elegantly refined. "A baby dragon came into our village and destroyed nearly everything and everyone. I was the only survivor. King Loral had no choice but to take me in; and since my mother, his sister and the last of his siblings, died, I became the next heir."

"Your mother was the next in line? But she didn't live here —I mean, I'm so sorry about your parents."

Toby stalled, studying me, his expression unwavering. "It's okay, death is only of the body—and yes, my parents moved away before I was born. Pardon me for asking, but you seem very curious about my uncle. From what I've heard, you want nothing more than to return to where you came from, so why do you care?"

"Words do travel fast here, don't they?"

"Trees aren't known for keeping secrets."

I glanced at a cedar tree and caught it with one eye open— until it saw me looking, at which point it crammed it shut again.

"Okay fine. I'm interested in King Loral because there are quite a few things around here that seem suspicious to me. You see, back home I was working towards being a lawyer—"

"What's that?"

No kidding. They didn't have lawyers in Garlandia, they had executioners. "It's someone who stands up for what they believe in. Doing service for others and bringing justice to where it's needed."

His expression slowly began to harden. "Justice?"

"Yes." My breath shortened as he moved in closer to me. "I'm sorry Sir Toby, but I can't just watch a talking frog get turned to stone for expressing his opinion and sit back as Ardeen faeries get abducted left and right."

"Now hold on just a second, my uncle swears up and down that he has nothing to do with the abductions."

"Does he say the same about the statues?" I asked, without missing a beat.

He paused, mulling over my pointed question.

Unwilling to hold back, I took a chance. "Where I come from, there is this thing called free speech. It seems my friend Herbert was turned to stone after the mere mention of Tita—"

Wrapping an arm around my waist, Toby pulled me into him and covered my mouth with his hand before I could finish saying the name. "We do not say it out loud," he whispered.

I teetered on my feet, somewhere between light-headed from his embrace and jolted from his reaction.

He removed his hand from my mouth, his eyes diving inside mine as I exhaled my next words. "Then he *was* punished for saying her name?"

I took it from his silence that I was correct.

"And if I were to say her name, I would also be turned to stone?"

"He can't hear you right now—I've put up charms." He gestured to the twinkling sunbeams and glistening shadows. "But you should know it is illegal to speak of the goddess's daughter. King Loral fancies himself the only higher power you ever need to follow or know about."

I scoffed. "You're messing with me, right?"

Toby's arms were still around me, and without my permission my knees began to weaken.

He tweaked his neck to the side, looking at me inquisitively. "Messing with you?"

"It's an expression."

"Oh, right," he said, still trying to sort out the words. After giving up on figuring out what I'd meant he lowered his mouth so that his lips were close to my ear. Once more, I took too quick of a breath. "Listen to me, Makayla. I realize this world is much different than the one you came from, but please do try to keep your head down, and don't lift veils where they don't need to be lifted. Not yet."

"But what if they need to be lifted? Wait—what do you mean by *not yet*?"

He pulled away just enough to peer directly at me, and as he did, I could hear my heart beating in my ears.

"It is all about timing. If you provoke the king now it will only destroy your path. Your impatience isn't worth giving your life. Don't you see that?"

I frowned. "No, I don't *see that*. Every moment that we stand aside, another innocent life might be ended unfairly."

"We aren't standing by. We are waiting until the time is right."

"What are you saying?"

His tightened expression slowly melted. "It's all in one's heart."

I continued to gawk at him. "Can't you just speak plainly? Where exactly do you stand in this world? You are Loral's nephew, his heir—not to mention an elf, and elves aren't supposed to care about faeries."

I may not have had a lot of education in this area, but I was pretty sure acquaintances, or even friends, didn't hold one another the way he'd held me.

His gaze was relentless, so deep into the ocean were his eyes as they dove into mine. And as they continued to soften, I felt his thumb begin to stroke my cheek.

"We are different, Makayla, but that doesn't mean we should be apart. Elves see things differently than faeries. Your kind sees the sky, we see the earth. The first time I saw you I knew at once—you see both. You are the sunbeam on the forest floor, as well as the warmth between the chilly winds crossing through the deadened leaves in autumn. You are a reminder of what could be."

A very light breath escaped my parted lips.

"I must tell you something, Makayla Wood."

"What's that?" I questioned quietly, suddenly not caring that he was talking in circles instead of answering me directly.

"Before my mother died, she used to tell me stories to put me to sleep at night. She often spoke of an Aeronian elf boy who one day met a faery with hair as fiery as her soul, adorning wings so beautiful they had to have belonged to a goddess. This untamed beauty saw not the body—for when she fell in love, she fell in love with the soul. The faery had the boy's heart before it ever beat, and the boy knew when he met her that one day the tear that had ripped them apart lifetimes ago, would be once more sealed together."

"Lifetimes ago . . ."

"Yes."

I opened my mouth to try and compete with whatever it was he'd just said, but he placed his thumb over my lips so I couldn't speak.

"If you must lift veils, Makayla Wood of the Erwain descent, do not do it without your magic. You are still too human to understand what you're up against."

His thumb slipped away and I whispered, "Why do you care?"

"Isn't it obvious?"

"No." The word rode along the wisps of my breath.

The corners of his lips turned upwards. "I've been preparing for this moment since I returned to the kingdom. I've always known that at some point I would meet my faery with goddess-like wings, and yet when I first saw you a moment ago, I almost didn't near you—do you know why?"

I furrowed my brow and shook my head, frustratingly confused.

"One day you will."

What the hell? "Nothing you are saying is making sense."

"Of course it is. And when the time comes, you'll remember, and you will know."

My lips parted as I remembered how I'd felt when I'd first seen his face. Like I'd known his eyes before. In another time; in another body.

Still, I shook my head at him. "How do you know your mother was referring to me?"

"I know," he said, staring at the white star on my upper left wing, my birthmark.

A warm breeze ran over my heart, and then it happened—as he looked into my eyes, I *felt* his soul, like a warm fire on a cold night—and in an instant, an explosion of red faery dust occurred. Like it was actually leaving my heart from a vessel I never knew existed, it streamed out from my chest and flew up into the air, dropping down and circling around our shoulders.

My mouth opened in awe as I stared around at the shimmering dust. Toby tried to follow my gaze, but it seemed he couldn't see it. But then, of course, why would he? Faeries showed their dust to others when they *wanted* them to see it, and as of right now, I didn't want him to know how I felt—anymore than he could already see.

Gathering my wits, I backed away, forcing his arms to fall away. "I think your mother was just telling you a bedtime story, and because you miss her very much, you've put too much stock into what was clearly a fairytale."

Toby studied me for a moment, smirking as he began to back away. "It *was* a faery tale, and you are exactly how I thought you would be."

"You've only just met me. You don't know me at all, Sir Toby."

He climbed over a rock and pulled a branch up out of his

way as he started back through the forest. "I should be getting back to finding Petal."

"Just like that—you're leaving? What if I have more questions for you?"

"Ask them of me tomorrow."

"Tomorrow?"

"Yes. And the charm is lifting now, so please, do watch what you say, my lost little Erwain."

"*Your* lost little Erwain?" I repeated, but he refused to answer me, simply bowing out and disappearing through the brush the same way he'd appeared. Somehow, though, in a very uncharacteristic way, I wasn't appalled, nor was I upset that he had labeled me as his. In fact, I kind of liked it.

I walked home that evening with red dust trailing behind my useless wings. I couldn't yet fly, but I felt like was floating over the cobblestone walkway.

When I reentered the Abberwockey home that night, Maude and Tanker were already gathered around plates full of spinach and strawberries. There was a plate sat for me, but I simply looked down at it and shook my head.

"I'm not really hungry."

Tanker frowned and tossed a large golden earring elegantly over his shoulder. "Is everything all right? You're quite flushed."

"Oh dear," Maude cooed, "you aren't coming down with that bug going around are you?"

Tanker gave her a destressed look. "What bug?"

"The Garth pack—you know, those blue and black striped bugs from the other village—they're getting into people's stomachs and making them so very ill."

My dolly look washed away. "No, I don't have bugs in my stomach. I just—I don't have much of an appetite tonight."

And then I leaned down and kissed Tanker's head, then

Maude's before heading to my bedroom, not paying mind to the odd expressions on their faces.

"She's acting very strange, our daughter," I heard Tanker say as I started up the stairs.

"Almost like a young fey in love," echoed Maude.

There were no words said after that.

❦   19   ❦

The next day I went back to the forest to the same exact spot. Part of me ached at the thought that I might not see Toby again. That he'd only been messing with me, or that he had gone away only to second guess our conversation. I tried not to believe that I would fall apart if he stood me up.

After about two hours of pretending to channel my dust instead of awaiting my actual prince, I decided I needed a change of scenery. Not to mention, I didn't want it to look like I'd been impatiently waiting for him.

I moved through the forest, searching for a different spot to pretend to practice. There was an anxiousness residing beside my heart, one unlike any kind I'd ever encountered; in fact, the pitter patter of my heartbeats jumping around in my chest were more than a little invigorating. And why couldn't I get the idea of that incense smell out of my head?

As I continued through the trees and scattered sunbeams, twirling my dust around with the tip of my wand, I passed a witch guarding what looked like a spell book close to her chest as she scampered away with her head down, and shortly after that I stumbled upon the gazebo

Helene had dumped me next to the day I'd conjured up my wand.

I walked past the statue of the male elf, studying him a little more than I had the first time. He was wearing clothes very similar to Toby and Rally and the other elves I'd seen associated with the castle. Was this an Aeronian elf? If he was, it was curious that the king would turn one of his own. Then again, I didn't need to meet King Loral to assume that he was completely rotten. No one was safe from his torment.

I began to reach out to touch the statue, completely disregarding the warning against such acts, because I had the strongest desire to place my hands over the elf's and tell him I was sorry this had happened—but before I got the chance I heard footsteps, and when I turned around I found Toby walking up to both the statue and me.

Immediately my heart rate began to race. In an attempt to act as if I hadn't been searching for his face all day, I leapt forward and entered the gazebo—because I needed that time with my back turned—the time to shield the stupid, giddy expression, that I couldn't wipe away. When I turned around, he was staring at me somewhat mischievously.

My dust grew the color of my cheeks, and I looked down. Someone had carved P.K. + H.V. into the wood.

I traced the initials with my fingertip, only affording Toby a small glance as I asked, "Why do you look at me like that?"

"Like what?"

"Like you aren't sure whether or not I'm real."

He chuckled under his breath. "Because maybe I'm not so sure you are."

"We aren't supposed to meet like this. You're an elf. I'm a faery."

"Is that something that bothers you?"

I looked up to find him gazing at the statue.

"I think you know my answer to that. But does it bother

you?" When he didn't respond, I continued, "It's curious. I've now met you three times, and still have yet to meet your uncle."

"To be fair," he said, as he lifted a white wand that looked like it could have once belonged on the forehead of a unicorn, and tapped the corners of north, south, east, and west, "I shouldn't have met you at all. Uncle still thinks I'm entertaining Princess Louisa of the Aeronian descent."

The air began to twinkle just as it had when he'd appeared the day before.

"And why aren't you there? Is she not your type?"

He tucked his wand back into his pants and neared the gazebo. When he reached the banister where my hand rested, he placed his hand over mine. "I've had only one type since I was born."

As soon as I felt his touch, my red dust curled out from behind my wings and swirled around his face. As it glistened in between the shards of light coming from the sun shining through the spaces in the trees, my chest rose, and I realized I could no longer keep the question burning inside me hostage.

"Toby, what do you really think of your uncle?"

"King Loral?"

I nodded.

"I think . . ." He seemed to be choosing his words carefully. "I think, Miss Makayla, that his reign is coming to an end very soon."

I exhaled a shaky breath, and for a moment I thought I caught the shadow of my ghostly queen lurking behind a cedar tree. "I think so, too," I whispered.

He gripped my hand just a little tighter in his own.

Matching my gaze with his, I asked carefully, "Your mother thought that, too, didn't she?"

Toby said nothing, but he didn't have to. I could feel it in him, his answer. I could feel it in his warm campfire soul.

"So," I said, my heart beats causing my breath to shake, "what other stories did she used to tell you before you went to sleep at night?"

He licked his lips, that damn grin reappearing, before removing his hand from mine. He stared over his shoulder at the surrounding trees, before saying, "That was the only one I can remember off the top of my head. The rest of the time she rather fancied showing me magic. She said a bit of sorcery before shut eye made it easier to gain access to the ether once we fall into sleep."

"What's the ether?"

He glanced back over his shoulder. "Where the souls dance."

His voice alone put me into a trance, and as I continued to watch him, I began to feel the child inside me fading away—a woman preparing to step up in her place. And she was starving, for I'd never fed her even the tiniest bit of physical love.

"What kind of magic did she used to show you?" I asked.

"You really want to know?"

I nodded.

"All right, well, let me see." He backed away and surveyed our surroundings, his gaze eventually falling onto a gray stone. "Perfect," he said, picking it up and bouncing it in his hand. Before continuing, he paused in his tracks and gave me an inquisitive look.

"What?"

"First, I need to know. Do you truly believe in love, Makayla?"

My cheeks began to burn, the queen lurking over my shoulders prodding me to be courageous. "What do you think?" I lifted my hand and sent a bit of red dust to swirl around his head.

He reached up and tangled his fingers in it. There was no going back now—I'd just let him in.

"Okay," he said, a hitch in his voice. "Let me rephrase this. Would you rather taste the forbidden fruit and know how it feels on your tongue, even if you can only taste it once, or would you choose to live your life without ever knowing what it tastes like—because if you don't know, you might not miss it?"

I relaxed my forehead. "Not knowing would cause me to feel more devastation, because what are our lives, our bodies, for, if not to experience the things we long to feel and touch?"

Toby's gaze halted over my person, studying me for so long that I began to feel uncomfortable. Finally, giving me the slightest of nods, he asked, "Do you really mean that?"

"I had to grow wings to understand it, but yes, I do."

"Then so it begins," he said, lifting the stone to his lips.

A pale blue and silvery light came from his breath and seeped into it. When he was done, he walked back over and took my hand, placing the rock against my palm.

"What did you do to it?" I asked.

"I told it my secret."

I looked down at the rock, shook it, and then placed it against my ear.

Toby snickered. "You can't hear it that way. You have to use magic to get it out of there."

I unintentionally took a step back as he jumped over the balcony to get to me. "But I don't know how to use my magic yet."

He placed his hands around mine, and his eyes fixed onto my lips. "That's why it's a secret stone. In order to hear what's inside, you must break through the magic. It's kind of like you."

My breath was shallow. "And you think you can do this, Sir Toby? Undo me?"

"It's not me who has to break inside, I already see you for who you are. It's you who has the task of undoing things," he said, his lips slowly lowering down to meet mine.

In the amount of time it took me to close my eyes, I forgot about everything; and even though I didn't yet know how to use my wings, I felt like I was flying. His lips were wet and hot, and his tongue tasted sweet—like ginger candy. I don't know how long we kissed, but the longer we did, the more I forgot all about the world I came from and the discrepancies of the one I was supposed to belong to. I couldn't even think of what my name was—until he said it out loud.

⬥

Two days later, upon returning from the forest, encircled by purple, red, and orange dust—the orange of which I'd associated with feeling spicy, after arguing with a sexist snail for an hour about the proper way to treat a lady—I walked past Herbert's statue to find a package waiting for me by the door.

I hadn't seen Toby again, not since the day at the gazebo, but he'd told me his uncle was sending him away for a couple days, and that he couldn't get out of it because Rally wasn't the one escorting him. He'd promised to get in touch as soon as he was back. It was almost cruel, this separation.

When I went inside Maude was prepping vegetables for our next batch of iced mud cream, and she set down her wand as soon as she saw what was in my hands.

"Light blue wrapping paper? That surely must be from the castle. Where did you get that?"

I set the box on the table, revealing my name written on a tiny scroll. "It was on the porch. Did you see who delivered it?"

"No. It must have been dropped by some of the castle's Ardeens."

I paused. "There are Ardeens working at the castle?"

"Of course," Maude replied distractedly. "The king has a various employ working for him under his throne."

"Huh," I mused. I would've thought he would've gotten rid of all the Ardeens closest to him first . . .

As my thoughts drifted, Maude burst out in excitement. "Well go on then, open it!" She'd grabbed a washcloth and was wiping off her hands in anticipation of what was coming.

I slipped my finger under the wrapping and carefully began pulling it away, but obviously not fast enough for Maude, who was whimpering in impatience. After watching me for about ten seconds, she pulled out her wand and stripped the box clean as she yelled at me to "Open it quick!"

"Okay, okay, calm down, woman," I said. Then, after lifting the lid, my lips parted, and I gasped. "Oh my god." Picking up the small note lying on top of the folded-up gown, I read softly to myself, "For when next we meet."

Maude raised her hands to cover her mouth, taking a step back and gawking at me.

"This is not from the king."

"No." I gently lifted the dress up out of the package. The same dress I'd been holding when Toby walked up to me at the market.

Maude's lips pursed tightly together before she reopened them and said, "That is a fine piece of clothing."

"Yes, it is." I could feel my cheeks coloring as they so often had been lately. As I held it, I imagined I was back under that gazebo with Toby, his arms around me, his lips moving against mine.

I was feeling so elevated that I forgot Maude was in the room, and when I looked at her it was obvious, she was not as excited about the gift as I was.

"You will send it back." Her voice deeper than I'd ever heard it.

"What?"

"Right away. You must send it back to the castle. If the king finds out this has been sent to you—"

"Then wouldn't he question it more than if I kept it and he didn't find out about it at all."

Leaning in towards me, she placed a finger gingerly on the shoulder of the dress. "This is a ball gown. If you keep this, you will never be able to lawfully dance with the one who sent it to you. Can you live with that?"

A bit of orange and brown dust radiated out from around my head, and I made damn sure she saw it.

"I can one-hundred percent live with it, but why should I?"

$$\text{❦} \quad 2\,0 \quad \text{❦}$$

That night Maude and Tanker demanded I sit down with them, and this time they didn't seem to be making light of their parental roles. As I sat before my opened package, Maude flitted back and forth via her wings, while Tanker sat cross-legged over the tabletop—blue bubbles streaming from his pipe as he stared down at me with pointed eyes.

"You can't date the heir," he said, once more making it nearly impossible to take him seriously, as he was wearing an orange bikini top and red-flowered board shorts—a conk shell necklace strewn around his neck.

"I'm not!" I exclaimed, slamming my fists down over the yellow table.

Technically I wasn't, I mean, we hadn't said we were going steady or anything. Honestly, I wasn't really very clear on the rules of dating in the human world, let alone in this one.

"Then who sent this to you?" he asked.

As she flew by my seat, I shot Maude an unhappy glance. Why had she told him? I'd thought we'd settled this argument earlier after I'd stormed out of the kitchen and stalked off to my room. I was getting rather good at being a teenager.

"How am I supposed to know?" I asked, with my arms crossed tightly across my chest. "Maybe the dress shop owner thought I should have it. I *am* the famous lost Erwain after all," I added sarcastically.

Maude scoffed. "Esmerelda Waukine wouldn't even give the king a free robe if he requested it, let alone send you this dress out of the kindness of her heart."

"No, she wouldn't." Tanker was frowning at me. "We know that dress is from Sir Toby, Makayla, so why don't you just come out with it."

"So what? I'm not allowed to see people here? What if I said I wanted to start splitting my time between Garlandia and home?" Maude looked over at me expectantly. "If I did that, it would be unfair to tell me I couldn't have friends, or *boy*friends."

"Sir Toby cannot be a boyfriend! *Elves* cannot be boyfriends!" Tanker exclaimed, pounding his fist on the table so hard that the package bounced.

"Who do you expect me to date then? A ten-hundred-year-old faery! Oh, I know, how about a gnome, they *love* my cooking."

"Don't be ridiculous, Makayla," Tanker argued, "there are plenty of younger fey than that." Signaling to Maude, he said, "Why Ericka Blume is two hundred and thirteen if you fancy a she faery, or Jerome down off Skyway is only two hundred and fifty-three!"

"Gross!" I stood up and swiped both the package and my wand up into my arms. Yellow, orange, and brown dust had begun radiating from my shoulders, and as it did Maude and Tanker looked at it, wide-eyed. "Who cares who sent this to me anyway! It's beautiful and I'm keeping it!"

I was upstairs when Tanker knocked on my door, playing with the two runes I'd collected from my little side business—

the dress hanging from a hanger on the outside of my closet, and Kevin on my lap.

"May I come in, Makayla?"

"I don't care," I retorted, shaking my head.

The door opened slowly, and he walked in.

"You know the rules of this land; I know you do."

I laid down the runes next to the secret stone Toby had given me and sat up, readjusting Kevin so his head wasn't digging into my stomach. "I've been informed, yes. But I think it's absolute shit."

"What you *think* about it doesn't matter. Keeping you alive does."

I took a deep breath, and then instead of arguing with him, I simply let it all out. "Back in the human world I didn't even have friends my own age until just before I came here. Not ever. I didn't think I cared, not until I met Cee-Cee and Jeremy. And until I met Toby—I just, I've never done anything that kids my age should be doing. It's stunted me, which is bizarre because I've always thought myself light years ahead of my peers." Wrapping my fingers around Kevin's floppy ears, I muttered, "What kind of girl grows up thinking more about a handshake than a first kiss?"

Tanker's wings lowered from where they'd been raised over his head.

Looking up at him, I tried to reason. "I know the rules here, but what if someone had told you that you couldn't marry Maude? Finding someone who I feel this way about . . . it's not a small thing to me. And I don't really care what he is or who he is, because when I'm around him I could care less about making lists, or how much work I'm missing by being here, or—or about odd or even numbers, or whether the hand towel and the pictures hanging in the hallway are straight or not—"

"Is that who's been doing that?" Tanker said in revelation,

suddenly forgetting about our argument. "Do you know how frustrating it is for me to dry my hands when the towel is hanging straight?"

"I have trouble breathing when it's not."

He looked down at me as though I was some strange new breed he'd just discovered.

"Why does everything have to be so perfect all the time, Makayla?"

I looked away from him, a hot tear manifesting in my right eye. "I don't know. Maybe because I never felt complete, so I was trying everything I could to figure how to even myself out."

He lowered himself down to the edge of my bed—an awful lot like my mom did back home. Placing a hand over my ankle, he asked, "How many colors are there now?"

"What?"

"In that little notebook of yours, the one Helene gave you. How many colors of dust have you noted?"

My jaw dropped. "How do you know about that?"

"Come on, you don't really think we've let you go on entirely by yourself—not with someone out there abducting faeries. The only time we haven't had eyes on you is when Sir Toby comes into the forest, at which point our patrol Ardeens have been shut out. I'm assuming he's been using elfin magic to secure the perimeter around the two of you so word doesn't get back to the king."

"You already knew about him . . . and that I was getting help from Helene?"

He inhaled through his nose and nodded.

"Are you mad that I went behind your back?"

"Mad, no. Disappointed, yes." He looked down at his hands.

"I'm sorry," I said, and I meant it. "For what it's worth, I think Helene ditched me. I haven't had a proper lesson in almost a week."

He repeated his initial question. "How many colors?"

"Oh . . . right." I leaned to the side and pulled out my notebook. "Let's see. Purple, orange, brown, blue, red, green, and now," I pulled out my pencil, "yellow."

"You've been busy." He smiled. "I think you're ready."

I looked up from the list. "For what?"

"To learn to fly."

I straightened right up, causing Kevin to groan. "Really?"

"I think so. But this time you're going to let your mother and I teach you. It's only fair."

I nodded, and I didn't even care that he'd called Maude my mother. "Of course, yes. When can we start?"

He patted my ankle. "Tomorrow. Meet us in the garden at sunrise."

"Okay," I said enthusiastically as he stood back up.

He glanced at the ball gown on his way out.

"And Makayla—"

"Yes?"

Lowering his voice considerably, he said, "I'm not saying I agree with the law, but you've seen what happens to those who ignore it. You may call us Tanker and Maude as much as you like, but we remain your mother and father, and you, our daughter. We are prepared to do whatever it takes to keep you from making the biggest mistake of your life . . . to keep you safe."

"I get it, but surely you must—"

He cut me off, holding up his hand. "It's not up for debate. Have you ever considered that Sir Toby is baiting you?"

"Baiting me? For what?" I was appalled at the mere suggestion.

"He *is* the king's nephew, and I daresay there isn't an elf in King Loral's company who hasn't turned someone to stone."

"Are you insinuating that Toby has murdered—"

"I'm only stating the obvious. I know you think you have feelings for him, but elfin magic is powerful too. He could be making you feel this way so that he and his uncle can better get to you."

"For what?" I hinged forward. "What could he possibly gain from pretending to like me?"

Hesitating, he lowered his voice once more. "Those wings of yours were almost taken once, and the only creatures who have ever harmed others in this kingdom have been under the king's reign."

"But why would he pretend to like me when all he or the king have to do is pluck me from this forest? It all seems like a giant waste of time if what you are suggesting is true."

"I'm only warning you, Makayla, that is all. It is one thing to get your heart broken, but another thing altogether—"

"No . . . That's—that's ridiculous. Toby isn't baiting me and he would never turn a living creature to stone. He doesn't have it in him."

Tanker just stood there, staring at me, for what felt like a lifetime. Finally, he retorted, "*Sir* Toby most likely already has used his wand on a living creature. In fact, I would bet my dust on it." And then he slipped out of my room, leaving my tongue coated with the foul taste of repression.

$\mathscr{K}$ 21 $\mathscr{K}$

I didn't sleep well that night, and I couldn't even get excited about the prospect of learning to fly; I was too frustrated. So instead I stayed up swirling my dust around with my wand, thinking about what Herbert had said before taking the plunge into stone land.

As I recalled our conversation about Titania and Gaia, it seemed more and more apparent that the frog had known what he was doing. Almost as if he were setting himself up on purpose. Especially now that I knew that the mere mention of Titania's name was an act punishable by death. But why would Herbert have done such a thing? Unless he believed the information was important for me to know.

Relentlessly anxious, I fought off my insanity by trying to access my magic; because if I could fly, then I could cast. But with no other direction as to how to use my dust, I was left with only Tanker's old school of thought: intuition.

At this, I wasn't very successful; but I did manage to levitate Kevin about a foot off the bed. Of course, without understanding how I'd done it, he came back down just about as quickly as I'd gotten him uncomfortably up into the air.

Interestingly enough, though, the second I'd managed to conjure his flight, a small blue star glimmered at the end of my wand, and for a second, I could have sworn it was encased in a diamond.

After several failed hours of trying to make the star and diamond reappear, I settled for the good old-fashioned insomniac habit of staring listlessly at the dark ceiling. I may have closed my eyes for a bit, but if I did it was for a very short time, because when the sun began to rise, I rose with the sort of headache one gets from unrest. Passing my beautiful ball gown, I strode out from my bedroom and through the house, making my way towards the gardens.

"Right on time," Tanker said, as I walked up, placing an arm around my shoulder and leading me, along with Maude, further into the forest. They seemed in good spirits this morning, almost as if the dress hanging in my room had never arrived. I decided it was a good idea just to let the subject fall away and hope it never resurfaced.

"Why are we doing this so early?" I asked, covering my mouth as I yawned. They hadn't made any licorice root extract that morning, and coffee was about as accepted in the Abberwockey residence as Sir Toby. I wasn't used to getting up without a coffee mug in my hand.

"Silly girl," Maude sang, she was flying softly over the ground. "The air is at its best this hour."

"The air traffic will be low as well," Tanker added. "Most witches and wizards prefer to sleep until the sun has had its second cup of tea."

We trampled on for about a mile until we came to a meadow. We must've hiked higher into the forest than I thought, because if one looked hard enough through the trees they could see the castle in the distance. I squinted in the direction of one of the towers with a light blue flag hanging from it.

"The king hasn't demanded to see me yet. He must know I've found my dust. I thought the whole reason I couldn't leave was because he had to give me permission to go."

"He does," Tanker said, clearing away some fallen branches. A flower thanked him profusely for getting it off her head. "King Loral does things his own way, and he hasn't come out of that castle in a very long time. But I wouldn't worry, he has spies everywhere—he'd know if you'd tried to leave and you would've found yourself brought back in a jiffy."

I suddenly felt like I had rocks in my stomach.

"He wouldn't abduct me from my other home—"

"Yes, he would. The only way you would be able to get away is if your wings were spelled away just as they were before. That's the only way he wouldn't be able to find you or track you."

"Right." That had been my initial reason for agreeing to come here. To figure out how to get rid of these things . . . that's what my list said in my desk back home anyway. A list that was beginning to fade from my thoughts more and more every day.

"Are we ready, Tanker?" Maude asked. She was flapping away over our heads, making me dizzy as she flew in circles, and her wand was out as though she couldn't wait another second.

"Hang on, hang on, Maudie," Tanker said, scouring the ground for any other obstructions. "Okay, looks clear." Matching his gaze with mine, he explained with an ornery smile, "Don't want you getting impaled if you fall before we catch you."

"No, no—don't want that," I replied nervously.

"Okay, here we go!" Maude exclaimed. I looked up just in time to see a purple light hit me in the backside, and as soon as it did, my wings released from where they'd been held down by magic for so long.

"Whoa," I said, glancing behind my shoulders. My wings were extending behind my back like a peacock spreading out its feathers.

For a second, I prepared for them to begin beating out of control, like they had at my parents' house. But they didn't.

"Like stretching out your legs, isn't it?" Tanker said, slapping my shoulder before lifting into the air to join Maude. The two held hands and began spinning over my head. I was grateful that Tanker had gone with pants today.

"Now then, Lala, listen to your dust! What color is excitability?" Maude yelled down to me.

I scratched the skin over my eyebrow. Excitability . . . What color *was* that?

"Green!" I shouted, once it came to me.

"Right, then. Get it out!" Tanker hollered down to me.

Their flapping was causing quite a bit of wind to blow around my shoulders, but just seeing them like that, happy and in love, flying over my head—it made it easy to manifest my green dust.

"There it is!" Maude shouted. "Now you must address it along the bottoms of your wings, all four parts!"

"And as you feel it gravitating, pull out as many other colors as you can!" Tanker added. "Anything that makes your heart beat—beat in all the right places!"

Puffing out my cheeks, I concentrated on my feelings, pulling out my dust. A slight wind accrued beneath my arms and I cranked my head backwards, watching as my dust accumulated under the borders of my wings. As it did, they began to flap, like when a fan is very slowly beginning to spin after being charged with electricity.

"Now focus, Lala!" Maude shouted from above. "It's just like walking, but more like swimming! Keep your hands and arms by your sides, until you are more confident that they won't get in the way of your wings!"

The flapping was getting faster, but it wasn't strong enough to pick me up. Perhaps I was concentrating too hard on not becoming an Erwain bouncy ball, like I had when the wings first appeared.

"You need at least three colors to get off the ground, Makayla!" yelled Tanker. "I see purple and green—what else have you got!"

And then, as though I'd been saving it for some kind of special reserve, a flood of red dust poured from my heart and circulated around my wings, lifting me instantly from the ground and raising me higher than my birth parents.

"Oh my god!" I screeched, my heart beating out of my chest as I zipped into the air, and over the trees to where I had a clear view of the castle.

"Great!" Tanker yelled, flying up to meet me, Maude just behind him. "Now keep your focus!"

They each took one of my hands, levitating next to me as though all three of us were in the ocean treading water. It *was* like swimming.

A couple wizards, looking quite like a pair of rabbis on broomsticks, tipped their hats in our direction as they flew by.

"Morning, Harold! Bart!" Tanker shouted their way.

"Morning Tanker!" one of them hollered back.

"Just teaching the kid how to fly!"

"Fair job, young Erwain!"

"Thanks!" I yelled as they passed us. "This is *so* cool!" I continued to shout over the beating of our wings, lifting higher into the sky.

"Stay focused, Makayla," Tanker warned. "If you get too excited your wings will take you away faster than you can control them."

At the mere mention of that, I freaked out; and realizing I

could lose control any second—my concentration wavering—I dipped, hard. I managed to lift myself back up, but I lost their grips as I did so. I was reaching out for Maude again, like a toddler finding herself in a room without anything to hold onto, when I heard a loud popping noise issue from below. I heard my aunt's voice before I had a chance to see her.

"Well, it looks like someone found her dust."

I stared down long enough to find Helene with a queer smile on her face and her arms crossed over her chest. Every color of dust encompassing me turned to blue, and as it did, I lost focus and fell instantly to the ground.

Luckily Helene had stuck out her wand just in time to break my fall, an inch from the same flower Tanker had just freed from an obstructing stick, and I was brought back up to my feet before I could break my tailbone. The flower huffed a sigh of relief and then picked up its roots and ran away.

"Thanks," I said to Helene, straightening myself back up as I took in my aunt's disheveled appearance.

Her slick black locks were frazzled, like a girl at the end of prom night; and her long black and blue dress was torn up the side, revealing a thin leg covered in fish net tights. Upon catching me staring at it, she pushed some of the fabric over the tear.

"What happened to you?" Maude accused, landing next to me and pulling me to her side. My dust turned bright purple.

A thump landed near my feet as Tanker set down next to me, a nasty smile on his face. "My god, Helene. Rough night, ay? Pan's Poison?"

Helene returned their comments with a scowl, and looking at Tanker, replied, "For your information I haven't been to that poor excuse of a bar since I was one thousand and forty-eight." Petting the backside of her hair and pulling out a twig, she said, "Got in a tussle with a raccoon who I thought was a ninny. How was I supposed to know he could understand me? That's why they are supposed to wear clothes."

"You should respect *all* creatures, Helene," Maude said.

"Whatever," Helene snipped, then returning her attention to me, continued. "So, we are learning to fly. How do we feel?"

"Good," I said. "I literally just got into the air, but—"

She waved her hand around as though that was unimportant. "So, now we can start incantations." Setting her beady eyes on Maude and Tanker, she said, "Oh come on, you know I do a better job with her than you ever could."

"Why are you here?" Maude asked, a gray, shimmering dust emanating around her wings.

"I'm sorry, am I interrupting family time?"

"As a matter of fact—" Tanker began.

"Whatever. I have things to do." Then, looking directly at me, she said, "You know where I'll be if you want to learn how to do more with your dust than just twirl designs in the air."

I wanted to acknowledge her with a nod, but I didn't want to upset my birth parents. I needed Helene; not just for learning purposes, but I needed to pick her brain about all the new questions I'd been accumulating in my notebook. With a little more information, I felt I could begin to form a solid investigation based on my theories.

"Bored," Helene said, after another moment of silence, and then—POP! she was gone.

"How'd she do that?" I asked, stepping away from Maude and Tanker and looking around the spot where she'd been.

"Not important right now," Tanker said. "Are you done flying, then?"

I turned and looked at him, and as I did a rusty color began to emanate around my shoulders.

"What kind of question is that, Tanker? I have Abberwockey blood, don't I?" And then I lifted from the ground, my purple and blue wings beating rapidly behind my back.

I aimed for a tree in the distance and felt the moisture from the morning air hit my face as I sped along, Tanker and Maude's laughter along with the beating of their wings just behind mine.

At some point I got close enough to the castle to observe the highest balconies. As I lingered in the air, a male figure wearing a blue robe stepped out from a set of shadows. He only afforded me a glimpse at the side of his face before turning and walking back to where he'd come from, but I couldn't help but record the observation that he had light brown skin, like Toby's—and bleach blond hair. As I flew away, there was no doubt in my mind that I had just been given my first glimpse at the king of Garlandia.

After a full day of flying, I could hardly stay awake. And after a dinner of trout that a gnome wheeling around an old radio flyer sold us—caught from the village of Lauslin of course, because of the intellectual fish situation here in Garlandia—I barely made it back up the stairs to my room before crashing out. In fact, I'm fairly confident I would have slept well into the next day if I hadn't woken to a strange tickling sensation on my nose.

"Kevin—seriously. Can't you go sleep with Tanker tonight?"

"Who's Kevin? Should I be jealous?"

The unexpected male voice caused me to jump, and I nearly fell off the bed. When I rolled over, I found Toby grinning down at me while holding a feather. I took less than a second to gather my wits, and as my vision came into focus, I judged by how dark my room was that it was sometime after midnight.

"How did you get in here?" I whispered, appalled at the disheveled state in which he'd found me.

"I heard *you* learned how to fly today," he said, in place of an answer to my question.

"Oh, did you?" I replied, feeling as though I'd been caught with my retainer in my mouth . . . luckily for me I hadn't thought to bring it with me.

He stood back up, and with the moonlight reflecting off his pale hair, he gestured to the dress hanging next to my closet. "Do you like it?"

I rolled my eyes. "How could I not like it?"

His expression wavered. "I'm sorry? Is there a problem—does it not fit?"

I hadn't even tried it on yet, but I knew it would.

"Toby, you sent me a ball gown."

"I know."

"You can't *do* that," I affirmed. "My parents—Maude and Tanker—they don't understand this . . . whatever *this is* that's going on between us." I looked up at him expectantly, as though maybe he could define what I couldn't yet understand.

"They became angry with you?"

"Of course they did."

"How could they know it was from me?"

I shook my head. "It was wrapped in pale blue paper, it was pretty clear that it came from the castle. And . . . they may have had their suspicions before that."

He raised his frosted brows.

I held my breath for a moment, weighing out whether to admit to my trail. Finally, I decided just to come out with it. "They've been having me followed—only because of the recent faery abductions, and because someone tried to take my wings once before. They just got me back and now they're, like, freaking out."

His demeanor changed. "What do you mean someone tried to take your wings before?"

"You know, when I was a baby. That's why I went missing—"
I stopped myself short, realizing my mistake. Just days ago, I'd told
Rally that I'd left of my own accord, and that Maude and Tanker
hadn't had anything to do with my absence from Garlandia.

"I thought you said—"

"Yes," I interrupted, trying to cover my tracks. "*I* left this
world, but only after our house was broken into and someone
tried to take my wings."

"And you remember this?" He didn't seem very
convinced.

"Bits and pieces," I lied. "You, um, you don't think anyone
working for your uncle would've had anything to do with—"

"With trying to murder the first Erwain born in over two
hundred years? No. Makayla, my uncle was absolutely relieved
when he heard of your return. So much so, I was worried the
old bat was going to tip over in his throne."

"He was relieved?"

"He keeps very close tabs on those living in his kingdom.
The fact that one of his faeries went missing nearly drove him
insane. Did Maude and Tanker not tell you all they went
through after you'd gone?"

I shook my head very slowly.

"It was lucky they didn't seem to know where you were."
The expression on his face led me to believe that he didn't
believe that assumption. "My uncle expelled their dust to see if
they'd sent you into the mountains—to live with the rebels."

"Expelled their dust?" *Rebels?*

"Forcibly exhausted it from them, then had it read to him
by one of his guards. Luckily all that they *seemed* to know was
that you'd slipped from this world into another, and they
didn't know where to find you."

"*Forcibly exhausted their dust*? That sounds torturous," I
murmured, cupping my hands over my mouth.

"It's no woodland stroll, that's for sure."

"I guess it could've been worse . . ."

"Yes, it could've been way worse." Arching his brows, Toby said, "Good thing not all the king's men are actually the king's men, if you know what I mean."

"The guard lied? They lied about the information they found in their dust?"

Toby shrugged his shoulders, but I could tell that's what he meant.

"I wonder why they never told me any of this."

"Probably not something a parent wants to ever have to tell their child," Toby offered.

"Right."

I waited for the information to settle into my brain, then pulled him down so he was sitting on the bed next to me. When I felt his gaze rest over my shoulder, I turned to him. My breath was growing warmer as it exited my lips, and in an effort to try and relax, I reached for the vial dangling around his neck from a silver chain. It felt heavy with something I could not yet define.

"What is this?"

His hand clasped around my fingers and pulled them down slowly. "The last gift my mother ever gave me."

"It's full of magic," I whispered.

"Yes."

I met his gaze again. There were two winds colliding inside me, both hungry. One, for information, and the second, for Toby's touch. Pushing past the second, I repeated a question that had been simmering in my mind for days. "Toby, is your uncle trying to get rid of the faery population in Garlandia? And if so, is he starting with the smallest of us first."

He took a deep breath and laced his fingers through mine. He pulled my arm over into his lap and stared up at the ceiling as if his head had just gotten heavy. "King Loral isn't the one abducting Ardeens. We have no idea who is doing that."

"You didn't answer my question."

All I could hear was the sound of my heart beating as I waited for him to respond, but he didn't. It was as if he was waiting for the moment to pass.

"Don't run from me, Toby. I'm not the kind of girl you can sway. It sounds to me like you aren't backing his insane rulings, but still you jump when he says jump. What sort of hold does this king have on you? If there is anything to what is transpiring between us, I need to trust you."

He exhausted an exasperated breath. "You can more than trust me, Makayla. As far as my uncle goes, in order to outsmart someone, sometimes you have to act as though you believe as they do."

Immediately a small voice in my head began shouting, *or Toby is the one who is trying to outsmart you, and make you think he loves you when in actuality he's going to take you straight to the king to chop off your wings and your head!*

Even still, I didn't trust people, I trusted facts. But facts were hard to come by here and there were no people. That left me with my heart . . . and my heart said that I needed to trust Toby.

"You *aren't* following your uncle's rules, then?"

Leaning in so that his lips were nearly touching my ear, he whispered, "I don't think we should talk about this here. Let us save this conversation for another time. Perhaps when you are closer to learning how to undo the spell I placed on that stone."

My eyes leapt from his to the stone resting on my bedside table and back. "But you *are* willing to tell me things—like what is actually going on here in this wicked excuse for a kingdom?"

He nodded his head. "I will tell you everything. I ask only for your patience."

I waited a few beats before replying. "Fine."

I wasn't backing down. I was evoking a trait I hadn't used for weeks: tolerance. Shooting another glance over towards the secret stone, I asked, "What did you say into it anyway?"

The air grew thicker, and his hand came to my chin, pulling me in towards him. "It wouldn't be a secret if I told you, now would it."

As soon as I felt his breath on my skin, all my tension melted away. I reached for his face and his lips found mine quickly. In a very short time, the kiss we shared had found a rhythm, one that I couldn't believe I had lived without for so long. In his arms, it felt to me like we'd been kissing one another every day for the past seventeen years.

Nothing around the two of us mattered anymore. His hands explored my body as the kiss deepened, and my hands traveled down to his waist. As I laid down into the bed, I pulled him over me like a blanket. The heat was growing around us like a hungry flame, and the yearning desire to feel him inside me was beginning to change from a whimper to a roar. I didn't care that I was inexperienced, I only cared that I took care of this itch that needed to be scratched. I'd ignored my sexual energy for seventeen years, and now that it was out of its box, it was completely untamed.

Kneading my fingers into his shoulders, I rocked my hips against his. I could tell he wanted me, and the weight of him on top of my body sent me into a euphoric state. He moaned, pressing his body harder into mine, and as he did, I gripped his pants in my hands, ready to rip away anything standing in the way between his bare body and mine.

"Makayla," he whispered, grabbing my wrists and pulling them to the sides.

My chest constricted, along with every other part of my body, and as he pulled away from me, it almost felt cruel. The longing I was left with was nothing more than sexual torture.

"What's wrong?" I asked, a pleading in my voice I didn't realize I was capable of making.

"Nothing. It's just—we shouldn't. Not yet," he replied, sitting on the edge of my bed, brushing the hair out his face. There was just enough moonlight coming through the window to show that he was flushed.

I pushed myself partway up. "Is this some sort of elfin chivalry thing? Because if it is, I don't—"

"This is me not wanting to move too fast," he whispered.

Well, he definitely wasn't a *human* boy, that was for sure.

"Are you afraid? I mean . . . are you . . . have you ever been with anyone before?"

Suddenly he looked amused. "No Makayla, I have not. And I'm not afraid, not at all." He reached for my hand. "We only have the beginning once. We should treasure it."

He must have seen the aggrieved look as it colored my face, because he chuckled softly to himself as he said the next part. "I want this, too. But you must remember that you aren't from here, not really. You're a faery—but let's face it, you're still so very human."

I made a face, unsure of whether this was an insult.

"What I'm trying to tell you, Makayla, is that mating is different here than what you're used to. Elves and faeries, well, we tend to mate for life."

"So do humans," I said, leaning in closer, as I twisted my lips into a seductive smile.

"No—I mean, I realize they do, but—Makayla, what I'm trying to say is that once we do this, there really isn't any going back. From what I know of the world you're used to, if something doesn't work out then you can move on. It's not quite the same here. We will be each other's forever. My magic, fused with yours, will make it so."

I paused from where I'd been leaning into him, the fire inside me suddenly dying down a little.

"Huh?"

Toby chuckled. "That's what I thought."

"I—I—" My tongue was tied into a knot.

Forever. Each other's forever. And we lived for . . . ever.

Toby stood up and held out his hand for me to take, a wide grin on his face. "Come on, why don't we slow it down a bit. Dance with me."

"Dance with you? Here?" I looked down at what I was wearing. A ratty old t-shirt—a peasant compared to his get up.

"Yes," he insisted. "Come on, Makayla. I want to dance with my future queen, for there will be no balls where we are going."

And that was when the mood changed . . . and not because he'd referred to me as his lifelong partner to be. As I allowed him to pull me up, I felt as though a dark cloud was falling around the two of us. "And where are we going?"

"We don't know yet," he answered seriously. "In time we will find out."

And then, taking a step backwards, he bowed to me.

"In time?"

He nodded, leading me into a dance I was sure he'd danced a few times before. I followed his lead, and as I did the walls changed into the gazebo where we'd had our first kiss. I could better hear the creatures of the forest stirring and there was a slight chill in the air. When he twirled me around, a flash of gold spun with me—encasing me in its glow—and when next I looked down, it was to find that I was wearing the ball gown.

"How did you do that?" I asked, staring down at the light blue fabric. It was as translucent as my wings.

"Have you not figured out yet, Makayla, that I am an elf?"

"Right," I said. "Magic, it still baffles me from time to time."

"Any progress in that department?"

"It's a bit more complicated than I thought it would be."

"But it's inside you, it always has been. You let me feel your dust last time we were here, so now I see you clearly. You've spent your entire life encased in an armor; one you wore because you didn't have your wings. Now that your wings are back, the armor is gone. The only one standing in the way of you getting what you need, is you. Before moving forward, you need your magic, and all you have to do to get it back is accept that it is a part of you. Once you begin to use it again, it will become as natural as breathing air, as flapping those beautiful wings."

"You are saying that once I learn how to hone my skills, utilize my dust, that I will be able to understand everything else?"

"Yes."

He twirled me again, then pulled me into his chest. Studying him, the way he looked at me, I couldn't help but ask, "You don't think I'm going to return back to where I came from, do you?"

Very slowly, he shook his head.

"You've called me your future queen—you already know you want me forever. How can you know that?"

"That's a question I've already answered for you."

I opened my mouth to reply but couldn't. Because I didn't know what to say. He spun me around so that his hands were resting on my hips, my head and wings resting against his chest.

The last time we were in this place, the day he made me the secret stone, he'd asked me—had I believed in love. Would I rather taste love and have it taken away, or never have it at all? Now he was telling me that ours was a love that would last, literally, forever. And if I was correctly translating everything he'd said thus far—ours was a love we'd shared lifetimes ago. It was a lot to take in. All I'd been after was a first kiss.

My gaze wandered and fell to the statue of the Aeronian elf on the other side of the balcony. The way the moonlight was shining on it, it was like he was staring directly at me. Pleading with me almost. Suddenly I was reminded of what Tanker had insinuated a few nights ago. His doubts of Toby's true intentions. That Toby, this elf who I was madly falling for, had most likely murdered under the king's reign.

"Toby," I whispered. "I have very strong feelings for you —" He pulled me in tighter. "But I—this is all so very foreign to me. I mean, even if this was happening in the human world, it would be new." I flipped around to face him. "If I am going to give you any more of my heart, I have to know something." As I reached for the words, I found they'd become stifled. Perhaps because I didn't want to know the truth.

"What is it?"

"Have you—do you—" I couldn't say it out loud. Scrunching up my nose, I pointed back at the elf. "Do you know what that elf did?"

"What do you mean?"

I nibbled at my lip, then adjusted my gaze so it was on Toby's chest. "Do you know what that elf did to get turned to stone? He appears as though he worked for the king."

Toby was silent for a moment. When he spoke again, he was very serious. "I have no idea what he could've done."

"Do you recognize him?"

"No. He must've worked for the king before I was old enough to remember. Makayla, what are you getting at?"

"It's just that this place is, like, haunted. Don't you feel it? It's like he's not gone. It's like King Loral's nasty charade is bleeding down from the stars that align directly over this poor soldier's frozen shoulders."

Toby's lips grew thin as they pursed together. It wasn't the reaction I wanted. I needed him to appear more upset, more in *agreement.*

I let go of his hand and took a step back. "I need you to be honest with me . . . because I have to know." My heart rate picked up again as I stared into his glass blue eyes. "Have you ever done this to someone?"

"Makayla," he said, raising a hand in the air as though he could put an end to my demands. "This is not the time nor place—"

"Have you?"

He stared at me as though I'd ripped out his heart. "I refuse to answer that. There are things you cannot understand as you are right now. Things you aren't prepared to hear. I've had to do things—horrible things—in order to—"

"Have you done this?" I lashed out, pointing a shaking arm at the statue. "Have you ever turned an innocent villager to stone?"

"Mak—"

"Don't say my name. For once, *just once* in this fantastical, *cruel* place, I would just like an honest answer."

He dropped his hands to his sides. "Yes."

As soon as he said it, I felt my chest constrict. The chorus of woodland creatures stirring desisted, leaving only the kind of silence that makes one feel more than empty inside.

"You—you've murdered—"

"Please listen to me," he said, lunging forward and grabbing my arms, pulling me into his chest. I tried to pull away, but he was too strong. "I am not on his side, Makayla. You have to believe me."

"You're no better than any of the rest of them," I sputtered out, as I wretched and twisted until I was free from his grip, backing away into a post. With my chest heaving, I practically spat at his feet. "I *trusted* you. How could you make me believe that you were someone I could actually love?"

He looked so hurt that I almost believed him. "You *can*

trust me." He strode towards me again, but I quickly manifested my wand and held it out.

He halted before it. "You don't know how to use that."

"Don't I? You're the one who just said I already have all the magic I need, right inside of me. One step closer and you'll be sorry."

"You're not going to hurt me," he whispered.

"Please just go."

"Let me explain, at least."

"There is nothing you can say to me right now that will make me think you are anything less than a murderer."

He started to reach for me again, but I swiped my wand in the air. Nothing happened of course, but he still pulled away.

"You seriously want me to go?" he asked softly.

"I don't know how much clearer I can be."

"All right," he said, taking a step backwards. "I'm a knight, I have no choice but to do as a lady says. Take some time and cool down." And then he disappeared, almost too quickly.

Tears began to well up in the corners of my eyes, and as I pushed away from the post, the gazebo transformed back into my bedroom. I only made it a couple steps before collapsing onto my bed.

How had that happened? Everything had been going so well—my sheets even still smelled of him. Incense and orange peels. For a split second I thought I'd reacted too brash, that I should have given him a chance to explain. But no—no, he'd admitted to being a party to stoning innocent villagers. For all I knew he could've been the one who murdered Herbert. It didn't matter to me whether he was on his uncle's side, there had to have been ways around the killing of faeries and elves. As these thoughts continued to swirl around my head, my shoulders began to shake as I lost control.

This was all the result of poor judgement. I'd allowed myself to become vulnerable for the first time, and in the process, I'd completely come derailed from my stringently aligned set of goals. Toby was right, I'd taken off my armor; but perhaps I'd always had it on for good reason. Either way, the only thing I was sure of as I cried myself to sleep, was that love was a dangerous thing. I mean, I could've given myself to him forever—in a heart's beat, I would've done it. No wonder Helene looked so hard. It all made a lot more sense now.

I woke up the next morning with a terrible headache and an aching desire for everything to have been a horrible dream. But then Maude came busting into my room, a worrisome look on her face and a letter in her hand.

"Lala, wake up! Wake up!" She came to a halt, staring down at me, strewn across the bed, still wearing the ball gown. "Why are you wearing that?"

"Oh this," I said, playing it off as though it was nothing. "I just wanted to try it on, that's all. I laid down in it and must've fallen asleep." Interpreting the look on her face, I said truthfully, "Don't worry, there is absolutely no reason for me to wear it ever again."

"Well," she said exasperatedly, lifting the note, "you might as well keep it on for a little longer. You'll need to look presentable. King Loral has requested your presence at his throne."

A porcupine might as well have crawled under my skin and exploded. Every nerve in my body was on fire. There was no way I could tell Tanker and Maude what had happened the night before, but I was so desperately worried that the timing of this meant that the king had found out about Toby and me.

"Now, when you meet him, Lala, remember to bow," Maude was saying to me in the kitchen as she straightened out my dress. Her mouth was full of bobby pins, and I winced as she stabbed one through my hair with enough force to meet my skull.

Annoyed, I asked, "Why are you even bothering with my hair—aren't we flying there?"

"Flying? No!" She loosed a high-pitched nervous laugh. "The carriage will be here any moment."

"Carriage?"

"Yes."

Tanker was sitting at the kitchen table with his hands folded over one another, looking rather tense. He was wearing a green tuxedo, cubic zirconium clip-on earrings, and a cowboy hat. "He's probably heard of her progress. Knowing the king, he didn't want to meet her until she'd gotten used to Garlandia a bit."

"That's right, dear," Maude said, wearing the same plastic smile I was used to seeing my other mother wear when she was worried. "He's just been waiting for the proper time."

"Why can't you guys come?" I asked.

"Because the letter didn't have our names on it. But we promise we aren't going anywhere. Isn't that right, Tanker?" Maude said, ramming another pin into my head. "Oh dear," she fussed, pulling out her wand and pointing it at the skin above my cheeks. "Why are your eyes so puffy?"

"She looks as though she's been crying all night," Tanker said, suspiciously.

"I'm just tired, that's all."

"Crying yourself to sleep in a dress given to you by an elf," he added. "I spoke to McGraph this morning, apparently there was a strange spell around the house last night. I don't suppose you know why, Makayla?"

I sneered at him but refused to answer his question. There was still a tear in my heart from where it had ripped apart the night before.

"BRAT! BRAT!"

Maude and I jumped as Pinch and Asshole came swooping into the kitchen.

"Tank, would you go check out front. I think they're trying to tell us that the carriage is here."

"Right," Tanker said, getting to his feet and heading for the front door. It was then I noticed he was wearing black stilettos. A second later he reappeared, removing his hat and holding it by his chest. "They're here."

Fumbling with the rest of the pins, Maude quickly stuffed them into my hair, and when she was done, she blew something white and sparkly into my face. Immediately I felt the skin tighten around my cheeks like I'd just gotten a Botox treatment. "All right, then. That should freeze her smile. How does she look?"

"Beautiful," Tanker said.

"This feels funny," I said, poking the skin around my cheeks.

"Leave it," Maude said, shuffling me towards the door. "It doesn't matter, it's how you are presented that does."

"Helene didn't seem to think the king would actually meet with me in person," I said as they pushed me forward. "Should I be concerned?"

Maude let out a high-pitched squeal and shook her head far too quickly. "Helene doesn't know anything, Lala. This is simply protocol." But the inflection in her voice, and the nervous look she gave Tanker—which he returned—said the complete opposite of that. What could they say or do, though? Here, in Garlandia, there was no one to see to it that I would be safe.

After Tanker and Maude had to practically throw me over the threshold, I looked up to find that there was an actual carriage waiting for me; another thing I could check off my mental list of possible outcomes I never could've imagined facing. I could only hope that list didn't end today.

My transportation was a pale blue cab lined in white leather interior, drawn by two white horses. Standing by the open door was an elf wearing a pale blue uniform. Every little girl, it seems, dreams of becoming Cinderella . . . every little girl but me. Even if I had spent a heavy portion of my youth daydreaming about this dress and this carriage, I still wouldn't have been excited. For what laid before me was anything but a ball.

It was sort of ironic. I'd spent *my* youth envisioning standing before a judge, so I guess depending on how one dared to look at it—my childhood fantasies *were* coming true.

"His royal highness has requested your presence, Miss Makayla Wood, also known as Lala Abberwockey of the Erwain descent."

I nodded my head, then turned towards Maude and Tanker. Anyone could plainly see that they were terrified.

"I'll be right back." And anyone with half a brain would know that my statement was clearly a question.

"Of course you will. We will be right here, waiting for you," Maude said.

Tanker grabbed my hands and pulled me in. "Just smile and be polite," he warned. "That is all you have to do. We will see you in a few hours." His gaze separated from mine only long enough to attach to the elf escorting me to the castle. "And you will be seeing to it that we *do* see her back here in a few hours?"

"Of course, Tanker," the elf replied. "By the sword in my hand." I thought I saw his right-hand form into a kind of salute down by his side, but my nerves were causing my heart rate to raise so high that I wasn't sure what I was seeing.

"Right then," Tanker said, "off you go."

I nodded my head again and then swallowed a big gulp of air before turning around and letting the elf help me inside the carriage. I waved to Maude and Tanker until they were out of my sight, and then sat back with my hands folded anxiously over my lap as we made the journey out of the forest and towards the castle.

The castle hadn't looked that far away, but in hindsight it was further than it appeared. It took us two hours to get there. It was a lot of time to be left alone with my thoughts, which were bouncing back and forth between heartache, to the perturbation of what King Loral would say to me once I was in front of him. Or worse yet, what I would say to him. I wasn't so sure that I could play along—bow to the feet of someone capable of so much hatred. But then again, if I said the wrong thing, what good would I be to anyone if I were dead? Suddenly Toby's words returned to me from the night before . . . that sometimes one had to pretend to follow their leader to take them down.

"Shit . . ."

The word escaped my lips, my thoughts circling around Toby's statement and our fight that had followed shortly after. In this wretched place, how far did one have to reach into the darkness to play a role?

My thoughts continued to spin in dizzy circles until we got closer to the castle grounds, at which point the sound of hooves pounding the earth became so loud that they were all I could hear. After we crossed the drawbridge, I saw that we were surrounded by knights. Half of them were wearing armor with pale blue crests and the other were wearing bright red; and as they were carried towards each other via horses, each holding jousting sticks, they bellowed out before knocking one another to the ground. At first, I jumped in my seat—thinking I'd just witnessed a mass murder. But as the grounded knights slowly began to stand back up, I realized their weapons must've been props.

"Don't worry, hon, it's just practice."

Again, I jumped. Levitating next to where I was seated, was a tiny Ardeen faery wearing a pale blue maid's outfit.

"Wh—Who are you?"

"Gwen," the faery squeaked, a large grin on her face.

"Hi . . . Gwen. What are you doing in here?"

"Buggin." A burst of purple and orange dust burst from her wings.

"Buggin?"

"Uh-huh."

I wiggled my jaw back and forth before responding. "Okay. So, did you just fly in to say hi?"

"Oh no, I came to bug you," she said, floating over to my knee.

"Bug me?"

"Yeah, you see, I'm his nanny."

"Whose nanny?"

"Toby's, duh."

"Toby has a nanny?"

"Yes, and even though he thinks he's too old for me anymore, it doesn't mean I don't care about him. I've been with him since he was a baby. Brought him all the way here from Cavita, and *you*," she said, flying up and pointing a finger at my nose, "hurt his feelings."

My eyes crossed as I tried to look at her. I wanted more than anything to swat her away. "What unfolded between Toby and I is absolutely none of your business."

"Yes, it is!" she squeaked. "He was an absolute mess when he got home last night and—" Suddenly she stopped short, her attention wavering as her gaze fell to where one of my wings was draped over my shoulder. "No," she whispered.

"What?"

She looked back up at me. "*You're her?*" She said the words as though she couldn't believe it, almost as though the truth of what she was seeing offended her spirit.

I stared down at my wing, at the star printed into the pattern of blue and purple. "What is it—my mark?"

But she didn't answer, instead she fluttered around as though she were mad, muttering nonsense to herself as she did so. "Oh dear, I must go. I have to get it—" And then she fled the carriage before giving me the chance to snag her into my hands and force her to tell me what was going on.

I didn't have long to think about the strange occurrence though, because just then the door swung open and my driver held out his hand for me.

"Miss Makayla Wood, also known as Lala Abberwockey of the—"

I put up a hand. "You don't have to say all that every time you open a door for me."

The elf bowed his head in acknowledgment, before proceeding to help me out of the cab. My feet hadn't even hit the ground before the main doors opened and another elf was standing there in the same uniform. This one was wearing a white powdered wig.

"Will you be here when I return?" I asked the carriage driver.

The elf nodded.

"Thank you, uh, what was your name?"

"My name's not important, Miss Makayla."

"What?" I asked, appalled. Even in these dire moments, names meant something to me. "I believe names are quite important. They aid us in our identity—set us apart. We are not all the same, after all. What do they call you?"

The elf looked over towards the other elf wearing the wig, then very quickly whispered as he leaned into me just enough so I could hear, "Jude."

"Jude! I like it. What's your last name?"

"You should go," he said, looking very uneasy. It was not the same reaction I'd gotten when I'd told Cee-Cee and Jeremy how much I liked their names. That felt like forever ago.

My smile faded internally, still frozen on the outside from whatever spell Maude had dowsed me with. Looking around, I realized that all the chirping and sounds that had been going on around us from the moment we pulled up to the castle had ceased, and everyone and everything was staring at us.

"Right," I said, "thanks for the ride, Jude."

Looking over at the elf with the powdered wig, I began my way towards the castle doors, hearing the carriage door close and the horses whinny as it pulled away.

The elf manning the wooden doors nodded to me as I passed through the marble walls. "King Loral welcomes you, Miss Makayla Wood, also known as Lala Abberwockey of the Erwain descent."

"Thanks," I said, giving him a brief nod. I decided not to ask him his name.

As soon as I was in, another elf wearing the same uniform met me, again this one was wearing a wig. Offering me his arm, which I took, he led me through a vast marble hallway, which bent around into another great room.

"His majesty will see you now, Miss Makayla Wood, also known as—"

"Yes, you don't have to say it."

"My apologies, Miss Makayla Wood, also known as—"

"It's fine," I said.

The elf, crossing his hands behind his back, bowed his head before dipping out from the room, leaving me alone in the giant foreign space.

I turned and faced a single chair on top of an elevated marble platform, covered in light blue velour. It must have been the king's throne, but it was empty.

I scanned the room. It was quite large—lighter and far less dreary than I imagined the inside of a castle to be. The energy lingering all around me, however, was anything but light. In fact, I felt as though I was standing in the midst of a graveyard.

Holding my hands tightly together, I neared the throne. There was a long rectangular box in front of it, filled with water.

"What is that?" I asked, mesmerized by the colors swirling together inside of it. I was nearing it, trying to get a closer look, when I heard footsteps.

"Miss Makayla Wood?"

My heart stopped beating.

I turned around just in time to see Toby standing there, mere feet away.

"What are you doing here?" I asked.

His gaze drifted towards the door where I'd already noted many elfin guards on duty, and he immediately signaled for them to leave.

"The king would like me to speak privately with Miss Makayla."

The elves bowed their heads, then took their exits. Within seconds, Toby and I owned the room.

"Where's King Loral?" I asked.

"The king is unwell today."

"I was told he never leaves his throne." Although I'd seen proof that this was not true just days ago.

"He never leaves the castle," Toby corrected.

"I see." His eyes were bloodshot, like he hadn't slept. My insides wretched just looking at him. I wanted to tell him that I was sorry—that I had overreacted. But the truth was that I still wasn't sure what I believed when it came to Toby. Except for that it was inevitable the elf would one day break my heart. If not today, tomorrow. "What was it he wanted to say to me, then?"

"Only that he releases you."

"What?"

"From Garlandia. As soon as you can hide your wings from the humans, you may go back to your own world. He sees no reason to keep you here. Although, you should know that you will be tracked wherever you go. He will not lose your location ever again." Lowering his voice, Toby stated very seriously, "And it is in the best interest of those around you, that you remain trackable."

"Wait—what? After all this hype about the king needing to tell me whether I can go or stay, he's just going to let me go without even meeting me?"

"Yes."

I leaned in, and in a softer voice, asked, "Is this because of last night?"

Toby's shoulders relaxed for a moment, and he cleared the space between us. Whispering, he said, "Of course not. He's probably just seen all he wants to see of you for now. This is a complete coincidence, that's all."

"If I go, what happens with us?"

Toby prepared to reach for my arm, his mouth open, ready to answer me; but just as he was about to, Rally barged in through the side doors, causing Toby to immediately separate himself from where I was standing.

Rally came to a halt, staring suspiciously at the two of us.

Toby hesitated for a moment and then turned on me, a false temper residing beside his energy. "I said you will bow to me, faery."

"What?" I asked, staring at him questionably.

Shooting me a rather nasty look, Rally moved forward and grabbed Toby's elbow. Speaking curtly, he said, "What are you doing? If the king finds out you're here instead of me—you're not even supposed to be in the castle right now."

"Toby?" I whispered.

Rally flinched and whipped his head towards me. "How did you just address your heir?"

What was going on? I felt as though I'd seriously just taken a pill that had altered my reality from one moment to another.

"I—I—"

"On your knees, faery," Toby stammered, and through the fierceness he was portraying I could tell that he was pleading with me just to do as he said. "Before you force me to call on the guards."

Still I was struck dumb, and though I knew what I needed to do, I couldn't find it within myself to act fast enough.

Rally cocked a brow, inspecting the way Toby was looking

at me, and then without hesitation pointed his wand at me and screeched, "On your knees!"

Immediately my legs unbuckled, and I fell to the ground, forced to kneel before the one who I would've willingly given myself to the night before. I cried out in pain as Rally continued to point his wand down at me, threatening me from saying anything else. Turning his attention back to Toby, he said in a hushed voice, "Are you mad? If the king finds out you're here at all, let alone with *her* it will be both our heads. What reason do you have for this?"

"I simply thought it my duty to deal with the Erwain myself, seeing as my uncle was too ill—"

"It was my duty. He sent *me.*" Rally shook his head. Then looking suspiciously from me back to Toby, he said, "There's nothing else going on here that I need to be aware of, is there?"

Toby looked wronged. "What are you insinuating?"

Rally hesitated before going on. "It's just that when I came in here, sir, it looked like there was something going on."

"Careful Rally. As someone next in line for the throne after me, your accusations could be construed as that of someone who is trying to get another out his way."

Rally looked offended. "I am a servant to the king, Sir Toby, and to you. I would never plot to get you out of my way."

"Then you would be forewarned to drop this now." Toby lifted his chest and backed away; but before he could get too far Rally caught him by his cape.

"I would never plot, but I *would* stand up for what I believe in. And if there is something intolerant going on under the king's nose, I would make damn sure he knows about it."

Toby tightened his jaw as the two stared one another down. Finally, Toby stepped away and addressed me directly. "The choice is yours where you live, but if you live in

Garlandia, *faery*, you will need to begin following the rules of this land."

I choked on the word as it came from my mouth. "Faery?"

Rally stepped in line with his heir. "That is what you are. A large insect."

"Shut your mouth," I snapped, knowing the second I said it that it was a mistake. Toby's eyes flared up in my direction and two perfectly round red circles found his cheeks; his blood was surely boiling.

Rally's wand pointed down at me once more, and he began to yell, "Bow, faery! Bow to the heir or face the dungeons!"

My face burned as I scowled up at Rally—thank god, the spell Maude had placed on me had finally worn off so I could show this foul entity how I really felt. I stood, balling up my fists. "I will not bow my head. It is no more an act of respect as much as it is a practice to demean those who serve you. I won't be a part of it."

Rally's pupils centered in on me. "Guards!"

Immediately the doors flung open and at least ten elves wearing pale blue armor marched in and lined up all around me. They all had porcelain masks covering their faces—each one of them indistinguishable from the next. I gulped at the sight of them.

"Take her to the dungeons! Force her to expel her dust!" Centering his full attention on me, Rally spat out, "Let's see what you're *really* made of, faery. How it is you kept yourself untraceable all these years?"

Three guards hammered down on me right away, and I had to fight the urge to pull out my wand; not that it would have done me any good.

"Stop!" Toby shouted, just as the guards started pulling me roughly towards the doors. At his command, they came to a halt.

"Sir Toby, what are you doing?" Rally barked.

"She's not going anywhere, let her go," he replied softly. "You all may go back to your stations."

"Sir?" the one closest to me questioned.

"I said let her go!" Toby exclaimed.

"Yes sir." This time the guard didn't argue, and I was released instantly. The guards left as quickly as they'd come in.

Rally, looking as though a murderer was getting freed, pleaded with Toby. "I beg of you, think about what you are doing. She is disobedient, and the king has no tolerance for—"

"Rally, shut up," Toby said, looking fiercer than I'd ever seen him. "She's allowed to go, and if I hear that you are causing her any trouble, I will tell the king you allowed me to see her." Then, with no more than a fleeting look in my direction, he turned and slipped out from the room, his cape fluttering behind him.

As soon as it was just the two of us, Rally pointed his wand at me as though it was a gun. "I'm on to you."

I turned back to look at him; I despised him more than ever. "Oh look," I said, holding up my purple and blue wand, "I have one, too."

"You better watch it."

"Why?"

Rally lowered his wand, but kept his eyes invested on me. "I never believed for a second that those idiot parents of yours didn't know where you were. There's something brewing in that forest and I don't like it, and I won't look the other way. As far as King Loral goes, I don't know what it is about you that has got him soft, but I took an oath to protect my king, and I will die keeping it."

"Well, everyone makes mistakes," I said condescendingly. "It sounds to me like the king doesn't want me to meet his heir. I don't suppose you know anything about why that is?"

"For your information, it is the elves in general he doesn't want you to meet."

"That doesn't make any sense. I've been around elves from the moment I got here practically. You're an elf."

"Mostly."

I cocked my head to the side, but he didn't explain further.

"Everyone else can be monitored. Toby, however, shares his uncle's blood. He can camouflage himself. The king isn't a fan of knowing he may be blinded from his nephew's actions."

"The king doesn't trust his own heir?"

"In the end, *Lala*, the king doesn't believe the species should mix, and he needs to give no reason for his decisions. He is the king," Rally hissed.

"Long live the King of Serpents then, right Rally," I said, still holding out my wand.

"You better watch it," Rally repeated, taking a step forward. "I'll make you a garden ornament if it is the last thing I do; and whether or not he's mine to guard, if I catch Sir Toby slipping up with you, he will find himself turned into a cozy little bird bath."

"I wish *I* could aspire to be a monster when *I* grow up," I said sarcastically, still backing away. I couldn't let him see that his words actually terrified me, that if Toby and I weren't careful both of us could be turned to stone. I slipped through the doorway and let the nearest guard escort me away, but not before hearing Rally's last words.

"It works in both worlds, faery! A fine statue you will make here or there!"

Refusing to look back, I let the elf guiding me take my arm.

"Miss Makayla Wood, also known as Lala—"

"Would you *stop* that!" I yelled. "Just please get me out of here!"

"Yes, of course."

Once outside, I saw that Jude was waiting for me with the carriage. Separating myself from the elf who had my arm entangled with his, I ran over to him.

"Thanks, but I think I'll just get back on my own if that's all right." I didn't have time for a carriage ride, and I needed to work off some of this built-up anxiety.

"Anything you want, Miss Makayla," Jude answered. Thank god, he'd learned not to say the whole thing. Then he said so softly that I wouldn't have heard him if I hadn't seen his lips moving. "You have my sword, my queen."

I lowered my chin. "What?"

But he was off and moving again before I could question him any further.

As the carriage moved along, I stared around at my audience for only a second more before gathering my dust around my wings, lifting further into the sky than ever. It was a little different flying with the weight of the ball gown, but I didn't care, I just wanted away from that castle as soon as possible.

I threw my frustrations to the wind, quite literally, and I didn't allow my wings to stop beating until I came to the sign in the tree that read Serendipity. Only then did I allow them to slow as my feet drifted down to meet the cobblestone pathway.

Much to my surprise, Helene was leaning against Maynard the tree as I strolled over towards 17 Serendipity Lane.

"That was quick," she said, a sharp look in her eye.

"Helene? What are you doing here?" My breath was shortened from the flight.

"I heard you were summoned. I came to wait for you to return with your parents, but they had to go."

"Tanker and Maude aren't home?"

"Afraid they got called out, Contessa needed them. Something about a pickle jar. Anyway, how'd it go?"

"Not very well," I said, preparing to head back to the house. I needed to find a way to speak with Toby.

"Hey, where are you going?" Helene hollered at my back, a slight alarm to her voice.

"I'm changing out of this, and then I need to—" I didn't know what I needed to do. Perhaps I could return to the gazebo, maybe Toby would be there.

"I can change that faster than you can," Helene said from behind.

And before I could question her, I heard a snap and looked down to see that the ball gown Toby had given me had suddenly transformed into a short black dress over fish nets and red pumps.

"Hope you don't mind borrowing from my closet."

"Whatever," I said. I was too distraught to bother with the fact that I looked like a cheap hooker with wings.

Helene studied me for a moment. "That bad, huh? Did they say you couldn't go back?"

"No. They said I could."

"Why the long face then?"

"It was their delivery, I suppose. I don't like being told how to act."

Helene smiled devilishly. "There's no question about it, then. You *are* my niece. Come on," she said, grabbing my hand and pulling me up into flight with her before I had a chance to hit the brakes. "Looks like you could use a good, stiff drink."

"I'm sorry, Helene, but I really need to attend to something." I pulled away, my wings beating in place over the tree line, preparing to head back down.

"Whatever it is, is it more important than learning how to use that?" She gestured to my wand. I hadn't even realized I'd pulled it out.

"You're willing to show me how to use my magic *now*?"

She rolled her head in a circle. "Yeah. And I suppose I could share with you a little of the information you so desire."

"You mean, you'd tell me about—" I couldn't say the organization's name out loud, but she nodded at me as though she knew what I was insinuating. Sneering at the castle in the distance, I pictured myself holding Rally down with my wand. If I mastered my magic, that dream could one day become a reality. "Fine, but I do have something important I need to do before we—"

"Don't you worry. What I have planned won't take too long. So, how about that drink?"

I hesitated only a moment before following her lead. As we flew above the trees, I said, "No offense, but I don't think licorice root is going to cut it right now."

"Oh honey," she said, reaching down and pulling an ankle flask from the inside of her boot. "This ain't licorice; if it was, I wouldn't be the cool aunt. A little birdie told me you fancy something a bit stronger."

I gave her a disbelieving look as we flew deeper into the forest, away from the castle, and then I accepted the flask, sniffing its contents. "Merlot? But I thought faeries weren't supposed to have wine."

"Pish posh, who told you that—Tanker? Hell, everyone drinks the stuff, Makayla. Just because he can't handle his liquor!"

The mature side of me, the one who had given up fun and friends, and romantic notions her entire life, looked down into the flask and thought, *no, you should not drink this.* But the faery inside me, the one named Lala who had just had a wand directed at her head—that side of me was drawn to the wine like a glass of ice-cold water in the desert.

Whether or not it was the right decision, I decided to listen to Lala, and just as I said to hell with it and tipped back the flask, I saw and felt blue dust all around me.

"*Must* mean adrenaline," I mumbled, the wine entering my system, immediately flowing into my veins.

"What's that?" Helene asked, shoving the flask back in my face when I tried to hand it over.

My lips felt swollen as I spoke, my tongue thick inside my mouth. "Blue dust. I haven't figured out what it means yet, but that's got to be it. Adrenaline. My heart is beating so fast."

"I see," she said, her voice distant. "Drink up, kiddo, I've got a killer night planned for us."

When I looked at her again, half her face seemed to slip away, leaving only a black skull. That's all I remember.

❧ 24 ❧

I don't know how many hours passed before my head
cleared, but when I finally opened my eyes, I awoke to a
musty smell and my body ached as though I was full of fever.

"Oh god," I muttered under my breath. My head felt like
it had gotten hit by a train. "What time is it?"

But as I lifted my head, I realized that was all I could move.

"Blue. It probably doesn't mean adrenaline."

"Helene?" I tried to sift through the haziness clouding my
vision for the root of my aunt's voice.

"I would venture that it was your intuition telling you that
you were in danger."

"What's going on?" I blinked, trying to shake away the
dizziness. When my vision came into focus, I saw that I was
back inside the tree basement Helene had brought me into for
our first lesson, and that I was chained to the wall. I looked up
at my aunt, who was standing near the chalk board, pointing
her wand at something hovering just above her head.
"Helene?" I repeated.

"Sorry about the extra reinforcements, but you're a
fighter," she said, signaling to the clunky chains around my

wrists. "But even with that fiery soul of yours, and the part where you disappeared for seventeen freaking years, you made this far too easy."

"The wine, it was laced—you drugged me!"

"No, the wine was just wine. You were simply *juvenile* enough to believe me. Faeries are allergic to that stuff, you stupid twit; plus it's already been in your system, so it hit you hard."

Suddenly I felt as if the staticky white noise of an old television set had been drained from the screen and poured into my body. In an effort to collect my thoughts, my gaze wandered to the small door that had been shut last time I was down here. It was open now, and inside it was what looked like hundreds of levitating balls of yellow light, and one large ball filled with an orange glow.

Helene's voice entered my ear canal as though it were coming through heavy insulation. "Two hundred of them. That's how many the spell called for. I never quit collecting them, even after you'd gone—somehow I knew I would still get a chance to finish what I started."

"Two hundred what?"

"Ardeen souls."

Bile immediately crept up the back of my throat.

"Well, one hundred and ninety-nine. I have the last one right here. Like you, she was a bit of a fighter, but she's finally losing."

I already knew what I was going to see. Acid filled my gut as I looked back up at the ball Helene was holding still with her wand. Inside was a very small body gasping for its last breaths. It was hard to make out the features but there was no denying that it had silver hair.

I battled a wave of nausea and gulped. "Sabrina."

"Yes, Sabrina," Helene said in a nasty voice. "Spoiled little princess brat. I wasn't going to use her because I knew it would be too much work, but then the brat caught on to me so I didn't have a choice."

Sabrina's tiny little head rolled to the side and her eyes met mine. She looked defeated.

I dug down deep and utilized what was left of my strength to stare down my aunt. "What is all this for?"

"Funny you should ask, my little lost Erwain." She chuckled. "Or should I say *Toby's* lost Erwain."

Every single muscle in my body tensed. "Why would you say that?"

"Oh, come on, honey. I've been on to you like the black spots on a ladybug's backside ever since I heard you were back. I must admit, your little boyfriend is very good at memory charms, so almost anyone who thought they saw the two of you together lurking in the woods, or occupying *my* gazebo, would pass out or forget all about what they'd seen; but I was prepared. As soon as I heard about your little encounter at the market, how he bowed to you—I had a feeling you were stupid enough to let him court you. So, I concocted a little potion which made me immune to his charms." While keeping her wand pointed at Sabrina, she said, "I saw everything."

I pulled at my chains but only managed to bruise my wrists. Glaring harder at her, I asked, "What do you mean, *your gazebo?*"

"It must run in the family—falling in love with the wrong sort."

"Falling in love with the wrong sort? What's that supposed to—oh my god." My words drifted away as I thought back to the night of Toby's and my first kiss. "The initials."

"Yes, the initials! My god, you *are* a prodigy," she mocked.

I pictured them as they were engraved into the banister. "P.K. + H.V."

"Peter Kiln plus Helene Voss."

"The statue of the Aeronian elf—that was—"

"Peter! My Peter!" she shouted, so enraged that she lowered her wand for just a second, but not long enough to allow Sabrina to stand up and fight. I think it was safe to assume that Sabrina was wasted. The ball she was in didn't look as if it had air inside it, not by the way the tiny faery was gasping for breath. Sabrina was suffocating.

"We were going to be getting out of here—head to the north. We weren't hurting anybody, we just wanted to be together. But just before we were about to leave, they showed up and turned him into stone. One of their own!"

She was beginning to shake, dark dust enveloping her. It didn't take long for me to realize she wasn't just angry but insane. The injustice of this land had broken her.

"He was a knight—*he was their brother*—and still they froze him!"

"Because they are brainwashed! Helene, don't you see? I mean, isn't this what L.O.A.R. stands for? Or was that all just a lie? Are you even really a part of that?"

"Of course I am," she snipped. "But what good has it done me? My father would have me forget all about Peter, wouldn't he? Have me just continue to do his bidding from down here until the day when he can—"

"Your father? What does he have to do with any of this?"

"He's only the leader of L.O.A.R.," she said as if I was an idiot. "Or did old Tanker forget to mention that part when he was telling you about it."

"No, he—he didn't say that," I whispered. Was that why Maude didn't like to speak about her father?

"Never mind. That's not what this is about. This is about bringing Peter back."

"But murdering innocent faeries isn't the answer!"

Suddenly the violent look on her face transformed into one of twisted lunacy. "That, dear niece, is where you are wrong." Pointing back to the room filled with Ardeen souls with her free hand, she spoke with a vivacious tenacity. "Murdering innocent fey is exactly how I'm going to get him back. I've been collecting these beauties for years, along with that dragon's breath—which was an absolute nightmare getting a hold of even for a dragon dancer. But I needed all this, because once I have all my ingredients together, I mesh them with my heart's beat and the dust of my lover, and he will come back as alive as he was the day we were to be married."

My thoughts were racing. "What exactly is the dust of your lover?"

"The statue."

"But as soon as you touch it, the king will know—that's what Tanker said—"

"And that is what the dragon's breath is for. You see, its fire is so hot, it will burn off any enchantments that threaten to get in my way. For years I've had everything I needed in order to bring Peter back, everything but that one rare component, and now I'm standing before the final piece. The wings of an Erwain faery, not yet of age. Sorry it had to be family, but there is only one of you." Making a nasty face, she said, "You understand, it's nothing personal."

"No, I don't understand. And oh my god," I said in realization. "It was you."

"Oh my god, it was you," she mimicked maliciously.

"You broke in and tried to take my wings when I was a baby."

"Gee, you just keep getting smarter, don't ya kid. Yes, it was me—but then you sent those loud-mouthed birds in to fly at my head."

"Pinch and Asshole?"

"Yes, and the stupid little brat you were just laid there and laughed."

"Shut up, brat," I murmured.

"You wouldn't shut up!"

That's why the birds kept repeating that—they were trying to tell me this whole time.

"And then you figured out how to hide your wings. I still don't know how you did that."

"I can't believe this—you were going to kill your own sister's child."

"Correction, honey. I *am* going to kill my own sister's child. Could have done this a lot sooner if my idiot sister hadn't clamped down your wings. Stupid spell made them inaccessible. But things still worked out just fine. You learned how to fly before you ever learned how to defend yourself— and I made sure I got a hold of you before you remembered how to access your magic. Now you're all mine." Then, with one swift flick of her wand, she moved the ball Sabrina was levitating inside of to the middle of the room. I gasped as soon as I saw that her body was gone—all that was left was a yellow orb, her soul. She'd died while we'd been talking, and now her spirit was imprisoned.

I screeched, but Helene didn't give notice; instead she lifted her wand, the whites of her eyes clouding over as Sabrina and the rest of the orbs crashed to the ground, and all the souls began merging, meeting at Helene's feet. The dragon's breath not far behind.

"Don't be scared, little Erwain," she said, her voice deepening. "Just a few moments of silent suffocation and then your wings will join us, and your soul can return to the ether." Then, just as she'd done in the woods, she pulled out a vial and blew its contents towards me.

"NO!" I screamed, twisting around violently as a nearly transparent ball encased me and my chains.

I squirmed as Helene pointed her wand at her arm and opened it so that she could bleed onto the floor. The blood flowed into the souls like it was finding a body to circulate into, and as it did her head fell back and a stream of words in a language I hadn't ever heard before came from her mouth.

Shackled, defenseless, and beginning to feel the air around me grow stale, I continued pulling on my chains, my wings unable to fully extend because of my encasement. I began shouting up at the ceiling in case anyone was out there, but I was sure if Helene had gone to this much trouble, that she would have soundproofed the tree.

She continued to chant, her wings extending out to the side, and the spell she was casting came to life as her blood began to swim in newly manifested veins that were extending out before her like branches of a tree.

"Okay Makayla," I said, coaching myself as I attempted to slow down my breath; I had no choice but to conserve the air I had. I crammed my eyes shut and then reopened them, peering over at my wand; it had appeared in my hand. "You know everything you need to know. It can't end like this." I replayed the words Toby had spoken to me before everything had turned topsy turvy—*my future queen*. My jaw stiffened. "I can't *let it* end like this."

On the other side of my prison, the converging souls and dragon's breath were beginning to wrap around Helene and the blood-pumping vessels like a snake, and as they did her words grew louder. The dragon's breath could burn away any enchantment . . . If I could only get it to work for me instead of her, then it could dissolve her spell. But how in the world was I supposed to do that? The magic unfolding on the other side of where I was being held captive was growing. It didn't care that I was struggling, and it wasn't going to wait for me to figure out how to escape. The longer I did nothing, the more of a chance it was that Helene was going to succeed with the villainy she'd worked so hard and so long to achieve. I had no choice, I had to try something.

Determination . . . that was all I had. All I'd ever had. I gulped before looking up at the wand in my shackled hand. Fully aware that my time was growing increasingly short, I imagined using it to cut a hole in my encasement.

"It's always been inside you," I muttered. "You were never a human. You've always been *this*. You've always had magic at your fingertips . . . in your heart."

A slow, ragged breath left my lips and I pointed my wand at the ectoplasm shell.

"It's always been inside of you . . ." I repeated to myself.

Ever so slowly, I let go of everything I knew. I released the idea that everything in life was meant to line up in a perfect, orderly fashion. I threw away any and all lists; I connected with a different side of myself. I paid attention to my breath— its heat, and how it felt against my chin as it was exhaled. There was something more to it than just air. It contained something from within—it knew what my blood felt like, and it had been with my heartbeats, with my dust. And that's when I finally understood it. The cognizance of sorcery lay in belief alone. *Feeling* it, not trying to figure it out. Because it wasn't made to make sense.

Again, my chest rose, and as I steadied my wand in place next to the shell Helene had encased me in, I closed my eyes and let the heat flow from my heart through my palm and into my wand.

Immediately I had to fight back the urge to scream, for the sensation was like fire swimming in my veins; but as I bit down over my lips, so hard that I eventually tasted blood, the burning that was surging through my limb became euphoric.

After a few more moments had passed, I carefully chanced a look up at where I'd aimed my wand. I exhaled a small sigh of relief, for as though it was being burned from the inside out, an opening the size of my wand's tip appeared in the ectoplasm.

"Yes," I gasped. "Okay. Okay, okay, okay," I repeated, attempting to calm my heartbeats and set my thoughts in order. My gaze flitted in the direction of the dragon's breath, still hugging Helene tight. As I watched it swirl around her body, I attempted to claim it as mine. As I did this, I slowed my breath, calling on my dust; just moments later the ball became filled with at least seven different colors, meshing together.

I took only a moment to center myself. When the blood moving through my veins ran steadier, I imagined the dust gathering back inside me—into its own veins—then shooting out of my arm into the wand, and through the wand out of that hole with enough force to bring Helene's spell to a close. As I did this, a boiling heat began to radiate from my chest into my arm—again, a shrill scream could not be kept from me.

Through the pain, I looked down as my magic penetrated my wand and shot out from the tip. As it flowed into the room, the breath of the dragon seemed to turn from Helene as though it was taking notice of my magic. The ghostly wisps of breath formed itself into the head of the creature it had been pulled from, and it began to move towards my magic as if hypnotized. I had it! I just knew I had it, and so I did the only thing that felt right. Holding my wand steady, feeling a connection with the dragon's breath, I began to chant through clenched teeth, "Release their souls . . . Release their souls . . ." My grip over my wand tightened and my voice rose; and as it did, Helene, now aware of the interruption, began to rage. And as she began to screech, a shadow came out of thin air.

I will never know for sure what I saw just then—if it was real or not. But I could swear that there was another Erwain in the room, and not just any faery. Up until I'd learned about Garlandia, this figment of a ghostly queen was nothing but that to me. I'd thought I'd seen glimpses of this royal entity over my shoulders now and again over the course of my life, and sometimes I would've bet my company on the fact that there was a winged woman with a crown on her head studying me from a dark corner. But as I sat in my ball, chained to the tree, I could have sworn she was there—nodding her head at me in approval.

Regardless of whatever ghosts had found me, the room looked like it was on fire with every color of my dust as the breath of the dragon combined with my magic, crawling into every crevasse of the basement and raging over Helene and her spell. She continued to try and fight it off, but she had been caught off guard. At some point she turned and looked directly at me. Every cell in my body went cold as I looked into her eyes.

"Release their souls," I repeated.

Helene, for the first time since I'd known her, looked terrified. Her lips moved around the words, "Dragon dancer." But whether what she'd said had any merit, I didn't have time to pause and find out.

The dragon's breath continued to ravage through the small basement, burning up Helene's carefully thought out enchantments. My queen had gone; it was just my aunt and myself. The flames began to die down along with the dragon's breath, returning to dust and wafting back towards where I was still caged, through the hole I'd created and back into my wand.

I was hit with a giant wave of fatigue, and it was all I could do to keep my head up, let alone think over what I'd just witnessed; to see that all that was left in the room was Helene and a shower of blood droplets as they fell from where they'd been spiraling in the air to the ground.

Helene, now fallen to her knees, let her wand fall between her fingers as she grasped her chest. Once she'd gathered herself enough to look up at me, she asked, "How could you do that? You—you don't even know how to—"

But her words quickly faded as she stared at the wand in my hand. The star was back, twinkling a brighter blue than before, encased in the diamond.

"No . . . Th-That's impossible. It wasn't ever real—it was just a story. S-Something to use against the king . . ." Her eyes drifted back to mine, but before she could say anymore there was a loud crashing noise above us followed by a flood of light. The star and diamond faded from my wand, and the shell Helene had encased me in evaporated.

I gasped for a breath of fresh air and cranked my neck to the side just in time to see a pair of white boots come running down the stairs, followed by three more just like it.

"They're down here!" an elf whose voice I recognized as one of the castle guards yelled at another pair of feet running down the stairs. He had one of those creepy porcelain masks over his face.

"Is she all right?" asked another of them.

"Yes," said the guard, walking over and lifting my chin. "A little worse for wear, but she'll be fine."

Toby emerged from the last stair, followed by two more guards. As soon as he saw me, he stopped cold.

Within seconds he was marching over to Helene, a white marble wand in his hand, which he pointed at her head as though it were a gun. "What were you about to do to her? Speak, faery!"

Helene didn't answer, instead she sat there, shaking. Her gaze still planted on the end of my wand.

"Peter Kiln," I said, my words heavy. As soon as I said the name, every elf minus Toby froze, as though they knew exactly what the name implied.

"What does that mean?" Toby asked.

"He was persecuted, sir, years ago," one of the guards said.

"For trying to flee with an Erwain. The faery got away before we could find out who it was, but I think we just found her."

"He did nothing!" Helene shouted, her eyes coming unglued from my wand so that they could trace the outline of every elf in the room. "All we wanted to do was leave peacefully and start our lives together! That was all we ever wanted!"

"Let her down," Toby commanded, gesturing at me with his chin as he kept his wand stiffly in place. My cage was gone, but I was still chained to the wall.

The guard closest to me flicked his wand in my direction and the shackles around my wrists disappeared. Falling to my knees, I stared across the room at my aunt. I know I shouldn't have, but I pitied her right then. She'd started out as a victim, just as anyone else. She'd just lost herself in her pain . . . I could see how one might do that.

One of the guards moved in on Toby and pushed him to the side. "I'll handle this, sir."

Toby, a dangerous look on his face as he stared down at Helene, backed away reluctantly; and as he did the other guard pulled out his wand and pointed it directly at her heart while reaching down and moving the fabric of her dress away from her collarbone. There, engraved in her skin was an upside-down crest.

"She's a member of L.O.A.R.," the guard said stiffly. "It is an automatic punishment."

"No!" I yelled out.

"Quiet, Erwain!" another guard yelled at me.

"She doesn't deserve to be turned to stone!"

"Makayla," Toby warned quietly.

"Wait," Helene said, pointing a finger at me. "Before you —" She paused, then staring right at me, she said, "Makayla, what you asked me before—the day you got your wand—the organization has everything to do with her. Listen for the butterflies, they will lead you to—" But whatever she had to say, she would never get the chance, because just then the guard froze her mouth shut. The area around her lips turning to stone.

"What did you do that for?" one of the other guards yelled at the one who had cut her off. "She was about to tell the other one where the headquarters was!"

The guard standing over Helene appeared unfazed. "No, she wasn't. She wouldn't have told her in front of all of us. She was giving her valuable rebel information if anything. Now shut up and let me finish her off."

"Stop!" I screamed. The importance of her last words lost on me as the terror unfolded. My eyes darted over towards Toby. "Please . . . don't let them."

The guard also looked to Toby. "Sir?"

Toby looked around the room, then rested his gaze on me. I could tell by his expression that he was caught between wanting to hurt her for trying to end my life, and not wanting to upset me further. It was this business of persecuting Garlandians that had been the reason for us fighting in the first place.

"Stand down," he said to the guard. Walking over to Helene and bending down, he whispered something into her ear and then pulled away. She blinked twice and then looked at me as though she was sorry. Toby looked back up at the guard. "Do it."

It was the most horrifying scene I'd ever witnessed, and as it happened, I found myself crying out from where I was crumpled up in the corner. My aunt transformed into a faery statue, right there on the ground. Even though she'd killed her fair share of fey, including Sabrina, it still didn't seem right. Somehow, it just didn't.

When it was done, the guards turned to Toby as though

they were waiting to usher him back out; but instead of leaving, he told them to go ahead without him.

"This is the lost Erwain," he explained. "She's not accustomed to this sort of thing. I need to make sure she gets home safely."

The guards shot unconvincing looks at one another.

"We should be bringing her to the castle, not home," said the one who had sewn Helene's mouth shut. "The king will be curious as to what was manifesting down here."

"Yes, of course," Toby agreed. "Go on ahead and alert him. The faery is weak, she will need assistance—I will carry this burden."

The elf crossed his brows, as though he was suspicious of Toby's true intentions; but unlike Rally, he did not speak back to his superior.

"As you wish, sir," he said, then nodded his head at the rest of them, before leading them from the tree.

As soon as he was sure it was just the two of us, Toby knelt to where I was crumpled up on the floor, lifting my chin and pulling a large purple strand of hair between his fingers. Oh, dear god, no. Was that on my head?

"You spun magic from your soul. It's effective, but ages you quickly." A blaring alarm went off in my head, which Toby must have observed. "Don't worry, you've many years ahead of you, Makayla, but we do need to show you the proper way to cast spells. We burn through the elements, not through ourselves."

"Right," I whispered. I was far too overwhelmed with what I had just been through to think too hard on his words. Gearing my attention to the top of the stairs, I said, "That guard didn't believe that you were going to take me to the castle."

"That's because I'm not going to," he answered. "Don't worry, they will be taken care of. By the time they return to the castle they will think they've spent the afternoon swimming down by the river."

I nodded in understanding, then attempting to sit up taller, I asked, "How did you know where to find me?"

He hesitated for a second. "I busted into my uncle's system and found your tracker."

"How did you get away with that?"

"Not important right now, I'm just glad we got here in time. This is an unregistered tree—it's been brought in from across the land. Helene must've been using it for years. I could barely get through her enchantments. We almost didn't make it." He took my hands in his, his voice trembling. "I was so worried that I would never get the chance to tell you that I didn't mean any of those things that I said at the castle."

I shook my head, resisting the dizziness I felt as I did so. "You don't have to explain. I get it now . . . or at least I think I do. What you said last night, it makes more sense." Staring at Helene's statue, I said, "In order to achieve our goals in this place, we have to hide who we are."

Toby ran a hand down my cheek. "Not for long. I can tell you that much. We won't have to pretend for long."

"Rally is on to us. He said he would turn us both to stone."

"Don't worry about him, I can handle Rally."

I bit down over my lip. I had no choice but to trust that he could.

Gesturing to my aunt with my chin, I said, "You gave her a choice, didn't you? You asked her whether she wanted to die."

"Yes."

I sucked in a quick breath.

"But you *wanted* to turn her."

"I did . . . but not for some sick twisted form of enjoyment. She was going to kill you, Makayla." He gripped my hands with his own. "I am an acting knight under the king,

I've had to do many things I'm not proud of, but if you let me explain, which I will as soon as we are out of this world, you will understand why I've had to do what I've done. Please, do not be angry with me—I've punished myself enough over the years."

"An *acting* knight?" I questioned.

He nodded.

"Are you saying you never swore an oath to the king?"

His gaze was centered wholly over mine. "I swore an oath, but never to him."

"Then who do you serve?"

He squeezed my hands harder into his. I waited for him to offer some sort of explanation, but he never did.

"Your mother, she was next in line for the crown, but she deserted her station. She was a rebel." He lifted his chin. "She told you more than you're letting on, didn't she? Her bedtime stories . . ."

Toby lifted my hands up to his lips and kissed them before coming to his feet and helping me up. I was still weak, and my legs were shaky. "There is much I must tell you, and although this is not the place for such words, this much I can say. Makayla, your life is not completely your own, nor is it mine nor anyone else's."

The image of the ghostly queen hung in the back of my mind.

"What does that even mean?"

"It means, what you feel in your heart—it has purpose. There is a reason you were born strong. To get past the king's curse put on your race, to be born at all, it means—" He was cut off as a chill ran down from the tree's opened door and circled us. Toby followed the wind with his gaze. Placing a finger over his lips, hushing me from saying anything, he whispered, "We must go."

I didn't move an inch. Had he really just said what I

thought he'd said? King Loral, *had* in fact, somehow managed to cut off the reproduction of the Erwain race? I wanted to slam Toby against the wall and force him to come out with everything he knew—but I was physically too weak, and the temperature *had* dropped. Whatever it was, I could feel it in there with us. Watching us, waiting for us to slip up and say something we weren't supposed to.

Suddenly everything became very clear. What we were up against was more than a judge or a jury . . . it was a dragon's den.

I managed to bite my tongue, nodding to him in understanding, and as I let him lead me out of the basement, I took one last glance at Helene. The expression left on her face wasn't the same as any of the other statues I had seen. Toby had to have been telling the truth when he'd said she wanted to die, for her eyes had never been that soft while she'd been living, at least since I'd known her.

"Come on," Toby said, his gaze flitting in all directions as though he knew we were being watched, "let's get you back."

❧ 25 ☙

Toby and I walked back to 17 Serendipity Lane in silence. For a brief moment I wondered if my birth parents had lived at 18 Serendipity Lane if this entire visit may have gone a whole lot smoother. But in the end, it was just a matter of a digit, and there really was no difference between odd and even numbers. It was at that moment I knew; the old Makayla was gone. The girl who worried too much about organization and getting into law school—she couldn't exist anymore. Not for real, anyway. I needed the new Makayla, the one who believed in magic and fell in love with elves. Because only she would be able to do what had to happen next . . . whatever that was.

As soon as we passed Maynard the tree, Toby stopped. "I must go."

I turned into him, wanting so badly to ask when we might see one another again—when he could finish what he had been saying down in that tree—but I could tell by his rigidity that he didn't feel it was safe.

"Where does this leave things?" I asked, praying for some sort of answer.

He opened his mouth to respond, but before he could the

trees next to us began to rustle, and as we backed away Petal emerged in front of us.

"Don't worry, Sir Toby, you may speak freely now. The sliver has passed."

My jaw fell open. Petal was an intellectual!

Toby's eyes were cross. "You are sure?"

"Yes, I saw it evaporate ten minutes ago. I've been watching for reappearances, but there have been none. Rally must have sent it—the git. But minus him, all the guards' memories have been wiped, even the ones who traveled with you to rescue Miss Makayla. You will be expected back any moment from Anemone. We must discuss how your night went with Princess Francine of the Aeronian descent, so you have a detailed report for the old goat. The king has no idea you were in the castle earlier. The potion we gave him really knocked him out."

"Yes, of course. Thank you, Petal," Toby said, petting her head and preparing to mount her. "And there is some left, I hope. I will need to cause him another black out so that I may visit Makayla in the other world."

"Of course, Sir Toby," said the horse. "It's hidden in my stall back at the castle." Looking at me, she clarified, "Elves are horrible at potions—had to get this off the black market, and it was hard to come by."

"Wh—What's a sliver?" I asked.

Petal blinked, her large, silky lashes coming together. "A bit of magic used to absorb conversations. They slip into the world and when they begin to wind down, evaporate back into the wand from which they were sent."

I shivered. So, the coldness we felt down in that tree, it had been Rally eavesdropping.

Petal continued to speak. "Rally will be a problem. He has stationed himself outside the king's quarters and is no doubt waiting for him to wake. I suspect he is going to try and breach our plan. Did you say anything that can be damaging?"

"I don't think so," Toby replied. "I stopped as soon as I felt it in there with us. But we don't have the luxury of worrying about Rally. Luckily, I've already got something lined up for him. He will be out of our hair before my uncle wakes; Loral will not know Makayla and I have spoken at all on this day. Let us head back to the castle, it sounds as if we have no time to waste. I *will* find you, Makayla. For now, wait for me in the other world—the king will be expecting you to go."

I wanted to reach for him, to keep him from going, but it was an impossible thing. I was going to have to learn patience. Petal whinnied and kicked up her front hooves as she prepared to take them back to the castle.

"Hurry," I said, watching him longingly as he disappeared through the brush.

I scarcely had enough time to turn around before the front door of the cottage opened and all four of my parents came running from it. I had barely registered the truth of what I was seeing—my adoptive parents in Garlandia—before there was an eruption as all four of them spoke at once.

"Where were you?"

"We were so scared, Lala!"

"Don't you ever do that again!"

"Is that *purple* in your hair?"

"What are you guys doing here?" I asked the first chance I got, looking up at my adoptive parents' faces. My mom's cheeks were tear stained, and my dad's face was pale and rigid. Looking at them, I couldn't believe all that had happened since last we'd seen one another. And I couldn't help but think how human they looked standing there . . . how out of place.

"We came as soon as they told us." My mom was shaking. "That you'd been summoned."

Maude was fussing away as usual, checking my wings over frantically as though she was searching for ticks. Tanker had stepped aside and was staring out into the forest.

"Was that Sir Toby that I saw here with you?" he asked.

My father—my adoptive father—stepped up between the two of us, a protective quality in his voice. "Sir Toby?"

Catching Tanker's gaze, I said over the fussing of my mothers, "It's not what you think."

"Oh my god, Lala," Maude said, lifting my wrists. They were bruised from the restraints Helene had wrapped around them. "What has happened to you?"

"I—" I looked around at everyone, realizing I was going to have to tell them that Helene was dead. "We should go inside and talk."

"Wait a minute," Tanker said. "What happened at the castle?"

"King Loral gave me permission to leave." My mom's shoulders released from where she'd been housing them by her ears, while Maude's wings seemed to flutter and lower sadly. "But I don't want to."

Maude looked up expectantly.

"I mean, I think it's best for me to return for a little while, and I'll explain why once we get inside, but it's important, I think, for me to split my time between the worlds."

My mom and dad looked at me as though I'd lost my mind, while Maude looked hopeful and Tanker apprehensive.

Tanker took my elbow, pulling me gently away from my mother. Then, addressing the group, he added, "She's right, I think it would be better to take this inside. If you all would like to head in, I just need a moment with my daughter, please."

My mom and dad nodded hesitantly, while Maude kept looking back as she made her way into the cottage, as though she was afraid I wouldn't be there if she took her eyes away for too long. Once it was just the two of us, Tanker let go of my arm and leaned in, scratching the skin above his eyebrow.

"I know you were with Sir Toby."

"Tanker, he's not what you think."

"I'm not scolding you, Makayla. I'm just—I'm concerned. One of his guards was here about an hour ago. An unfriendly looking fellow."

"What did he look like?"

"Dark hair, tan horse—"

"Rally." I tried not to spit as I said his name.

"Whoever he was, he planted himself in front of the house on top of his horse, and when I came out, he sneered at me. It was a warning, Makayla."

"I know it was," I whispered. Then, grabbing his arm, I looked into his eyes. "We know what we're doing. I promise you."

His gaze moved to the star embedded in my wing and he loosed a hesitant breath. "Are you *sure* you can trust him?"

I licked my lips. "Yes, because if he didn't love me, he would've let me die just now."

Tanker raised his eyebrows. Then reevaluating my appearance as though he'd just realized what I was wearing—still adorned in Helene's racy clothing—he asked, "What happened to the ball gown? Why are you wearing that? Did the king dress you like this?"

"I didn't even see the king; he sent someone else to tell me I was free to go. But that's not where I got into trouble."

He turned his head to the side, in question.

"I don't suppose you guys ever even left the house today, did you?"

"Of course not. Why would we leave when our only daughter was in such a perilous situation?"

"That's what I thought," I mumbled.

"Makayla," Tanker said, grabbing my forearm, "what happened today?"

Again, I scratched the area above my eyebrow, a habit I now knew the origin of, and exhaled a deep breath as I started pulling him towards the cottage.

"Let's go inside, I don't think I have the energy to tell this story twice. But I will say this, that Helene was damn good with her spells."

"Was . . .?"

"Yes. Was."

I thought, as we walked towards the cottage, that I saw a large purple butterfly levitating next to a nearby tree. For a second, I could've even sworn I heard it say my aunt's name.

❧ 26 ❧

Leaving Garlandia wasn't a permanent solution; in fact, I hadn't wanted to go back to the human world at all. But after only a day, Toby had sent word reaffirming that I needed to leave soon, and that he would meet me again on the other side.

I didn't tell Tanker or Maude anything about what Toby had insinuated about my life not being my own, but I had the sinking suspicion that Tanker already knew something was up. The way he looked at me before I left their house, it was different. Like he was looking past my soul and into another.

Before I left the cottage, Maude showed me a few practice spells to work on. I couldn't get my wand to work right away, but they both assured me that once my magic recharged—because I'd burned through it so fiercely when I'd spun from my soul—that in a few days I would be able to cast normally.

"Make sure you pull from the wind, flame, or whatever is at your disposal," Maude had told me while braiding my hair. "As much as this color suits you," she said of my new purple strip, "you should not get used to pulling from your soul. It changes you."

Just before leaving, Maude showed me the proper way to make my wings transparent, by lining the edges of them with dust, and whispering the same incantation Helene had used on us in the woods to make us invisible. They weren't erased, not like before, but the spell was enough to make me appear human.

I also ensured that the pictures in the hallway, which tended to fall crooked after every time I set them straight, stayed aligned. I knew it would drive Tanker crazy, but I wouldn't be a real faery if I didn't appreciate a good leg pulling now and again; and after the weeks and days I'd had, I needed a little humor in my life.

I'd only been back in the human world for a week, and I had to admit, it didn't feel as much like home as it had before. Everything seemed a little duller.

I'd managed to escape the fact so far that I wasn't planning on going back to the office. All I could think about was getting back into Garlandia and picking up where I left off. First, I needed Toby to finish what he had been saying before the sliver showed up, and secondly, I needed to meet my grandfather. Helene had said he was the leader of L.O.A.R., and I couldn't help but feel like he was the key to unlocking so many of the closed doors around me. She'd told me to listen for the butterflies . . . I needed to figure out what that meant.

"Have you begun the reapplying process for law school yet?" my dad asked over Chinese take-out.

I looked up at the new chandelier they'd had installed while I was gone. I was staring up at the screws, wondering how easy it would be to set this one up to crash in three more years— snickering as the thought ran through my head.

"Lala, your father is speaking to you."

I looked over at my mother, and then to my father, clearing my throat and trying to replace my grin with something a little more serious.

"Sorry, I was just—um, no, actually. I think I'm going to put law school on hold for a little while."

My parents stopped mid chew and stared at me as though I'd scraped out their stomachs with a melon baller.

"Well . . . if that's what you want," my dad said, clearly in shock.

"Yes baby, if that's what you want, then we will completely support you in that decision," my mom mimicked.

"Yeah," I said. "It's just, you know, I think I have some unfinished business in Garlandia. There are some things I feel obligated to do over there, and if I attended Yale or another school, I wouldn't have the time to go back and forth."

"Great," my mom said, a little too enthusiastically. I had the feeling that she was wondering what had happened to her daughter.

After dinner my parents went to their study to get some work done, leaving me to sift around the rooms of the house, my thoughts still unsettled. I just wanted Toby to show up.

I continued to meander around, making my wand appear and disappear in my hands as though I was juggling a set of keys. It was weird now, walking around without my wings dragging on the floor or extending behind me. They were still there, of course, but the spell Maude had shown me made them thinner than air. I missed them.

At some point I found myself back in the library, my fingers racing over the bindings of those faery books whose presence I hadn't understood just weeks ago. Pulling out the one about mythology, I leaned down into a chair and turned to the index.

Between Toby, my aunt trying to kill me, and now this threat hanging in the air from Rally, I'd completely forgotten about my yearning desire to find out about the goddess Gaia and her daughter Titania. I skimmed through the Ts until my finger lined up with the name I was so curious about and turned quickly to page 58.

I gasped. There she was, a large faery with goddess-like wings, and a face I more than recognized as my ghostly queen. I read the description next to her illustration:

Titania, queen of the faeries. Her soul was born of the goddess, Gaia, the goddess of the Earth. According to scholars, she chose her form because she adored the human female body as well as the magic of the faeries. An illuminated soul, Titania was one who strove for equality; and there have been rumors that her last words before her life was terminated, were that she would return and regain justice for the world she inhabited. She said her soul would ride the waves of someone merited of her expectations; that this chosen spirit would be marked with the stain of her mother's heart, and that that symbol would be protected by an unconquerable element worthy of warding away evil.

I looked up from the description. What was 'the stain of her mother's heart?'

I was just about to flip back to the index to find where I could look up the goddess Gaia when the doorbell rang.

Immediately I hunched down and covered my ears, preparing for Pinch and Asshole to begin their routine screeching of BRAT! BRAT! But when that didn't happen, I sat up only to hear my dad answering the door, without the pitter patter of Kevin's toenails against the hardwood floors. It was then I remembered those pets didn't live in this house.

"Makayla!"

Standing back up, I dropped the book onto the seat so I could go see who was at the door. When I saw Cee-Cee and

Jeremy standing there, popcorn in one hand and root beer soda in the other, I didn't waste another second before pushing past my dad and reaching for the two of them.

"Oh my god! What took you guys so long—we've only got, like, five more episodes!"

That stupid television series was the only thing keeping my mind at bay these days.

"Hi, Mr. Wood," Cee-Cee said, as I dragged her across the floor into the living room.

"Hello there, Anastacia. Jeremy," he said as he nodded at them.

Jeremy's face colored when my dad spoke. "Here," he said, handing me a pack of black licorice as we walked into the T.V. room.

"Thank god," I said, ripping into it as though it contained my next breath of fresh air.

"Your dad is, like, *so* cute," Cee-Cee said, popping a piece of popcorn into her mouth.

"He sure is," seconded Jeremy.

"Oh my god, gross." I grabbed at the remote control and began to search for where we had left off the night before on our quest to finish season two of *Grey's Anatomy*.

I had to know. I *needed* to know whether Meredith and McDreamy were going to get back together. Maybe it was because I still hadn't heard a peep from Toby, and being here —in a completely different realm than him—well, it was like he didn't exist again.

I was preparing to hit play on the episode we were at when my parents appeared at the edge of the room, my mom's purse slung over her shoulder.

"You kids be okay if we go out for a while?" she asked.

"Yeah, of course," I said. "Where are you going?"

She smiled. "On a date."

"Awwwww." Jeremy and Cee-Cee cooed together.

"That is just the cutest, Mr. and Mrs. Wood," said Cee-Cee.

My dad rolled his eyes and cleared his throat. "You ready, Naomi."

She nodded her head and smiled back at me before they left.

As soon as they were gone, Cee-Cee looked over in my direction. "I'm guessing we don't gotta dig out anymore wine for you," she joked.

I'd told them everything the minute I got back. They'd wasted no time coming over, laying over one another on top of my bed, listening to my dangerous retelling of what had happened.

"No way. I don't think I'll ever go down that road again." I shuddered at the thought. If Helene had done anything right, it had been scaring the desire to drink out of me before I became one of those faeries at the farmer's market who we'd seen, meandering around dizzily, asking for scraps of anything to barter with.

We'd only gotten through one episode of the five we had left when there was another knock at the door. I turned to my friends in alarm. "Shit," I said, distilling a sense of fear into them that might have not otherwise been there. I was a little jumpier these days.

"Who could that be?" Jeremy said, standing up and pretending as though he wasn't too frightened to defend his two girlfriends.

"I don't know," I said. I could feel my wings pulling at my shoulders. Manifesting my wand, I stuck it behind my back and shushed the two of them.

"What if it's that guy who wants your head, girl? That Rally dweeb," Cee-Cee warned, holding onto my shoulders as we tip-toed to the door—Jeremy Love, now hunkered down behind the two of us.

"There's no way," I whispered. "But just to be safe, stay back."

There was a second knock just as I laid my hand over the doorknob. Forcing a fierce look on my face that didn't match my fear, I held my breath and swung open the door. But as it turned out, there was nothing to fear but that of dying from laughter.

"Oh my," Jeremy said, gasping behind me.

"That's not—is that? No way," Cee-Cee said.

Standing there in a pair of blue jeans rolled up over black lace-up boots, a tight black t-shirt with a pack of cigarettes rolled up in the sleeve, and his hair gelled and pulled back into a ponytail, was Toby. His ears still as pointy as the last day I saw him.

There were two thuds behind me, and I turned around to see Jeremy and Cee-Cee on their knees, heads bowed.

"For the love of intellectuals, what are you two doing?" I asked, temporarily substituting my shock and excitement of seeing Toby for my friends' own idiotic reactions.

"He the heir!" Cee-Cee whispered, keeping her head bowed.

"I thought we were bowing cause he's so pretty," Jeremy snickered.

"Get up, get up you two!" I said, pulling on Cee-Cee's shoulder before turning back around to face Toby. I took in his appearance one more time, before plastering a hand over my mouth, trying to stifle a laugh.

"Not really the reaction I was hoping for," Toby said, leaning forward and unclasping my hands from where they were covering my face. "Is it the way I look? Tanker said this is how humans dress."

"Tanker said!" I laughed. Well at least he'd gotten an outfit right for once, even though Toby was the spitting image of a

1950's bad boy. "Wait—if Tanker dressed you that means you were at my house, in Garlandia."

Toby pursed his lips together. But instead of answering right away, his gaze moved over to where Cee-Cee and Jeremy were standing. "May I please come in?"

"Oh yes, you may," Jeremy said, practically pulling him in with his own hands.

"Thank you." Then addressing both Cee-Cee and Jeremy, he added, "I believe we've met, but not formally."

"This is Anastacia Montgomery and Jeremy Love," I said, closing the door. "They were at the farmer's market the first day we met."

"Right," he said, before slapping both of their hands.

"Ouch!" Cee-Cee exclaimed.

"Well, go on then, slap his face," I said, trying to sound serious.

"What—why—" Cee-Cee started, as Jeremy lunged forward and slapped Toby. It was all I could do not to pee my pants.

"Well then," Toby said, nodding his head at the two of them, before coming over to me and wrapping his arm around my shoulder. The room quickly grew quiet as he cleared his throat and stared at them as though he were waiting for them to leave.

"Yeah okay, we get it," Cee-Cee said, grabbing Jeremy by the hand and yanking him away. "You guys should be alone. We can finish watching this tomorrow."

"You guys don't have to leave," I said half-heartedly.

"Course we do," Cee-Cee replied, grabbing my elbow and winking, before heading towards the door, trying to reel Jeremy away from Toby.

"Bye-bye," Jeremy said, before Cee-Cee snagged him.

Once it was just the two of us, I wasted no time falling

into Toby's arms. It was like finally being able to let out a breath that had been held for far too long.

I was already dreading his departure, and he'd only just arrived.

My cheek to his chest, I said, "I know the king has trackers on me, but if you are here, I have to assume it's safe to talk."

He pulled his chest away so that we could look one another in the eyes. "We have a short amount of time before the king comes back to. And as for Rally, he doesn't know where you live, and he has no way of figuring that out."

"Can't he trace me by my wings?"

"Yes, but all that information is kept by the king; it's encrypted. I'm the only other soul who knows how to get into it—but my uncle doesn't know that." Looking over my shoulders, he appeared to be searching for something. "Are your parents home?"

"No, they're out for a bit."

"So, it's just us then?" He moved his hands onto my waist, where they fit so perfectly it was as though they'd been created for that sole purpose.

"Yes—but wait—why did you go to Maude and Tanker's house? Wasn't that kind of risky?"

"It's fine. My uncle doesn't have eyes on me at the moment and Rally is in Lauslin. He was invited by Princess Louisa herself." The serious expression he wore quickly faded into a smirk. "Rally doesn't remember this, but he sent the princess a love letter. The princess has now fallen head over heels for our dear Rally, and everyone knows that what Princess Louisa wants, she gets. Poor gent doesn't stand a chance of getting away." He chuckled sinisterly to himself. "Anyway, I took advantage of his absence and met with Tanker and Maude."

"What for?"

"It was time," he stated simply, staring at the space around my shoulders where my wings should've been. "Miss Makayla, you just don't look complete this way." Then, whispering something in elvish, my wings reappeared.

"How did you—hang on. You just messed with my magic, and I have yet to crack into that secret stone of yours."

"And you won't until the moment's right."

I tilted my head to the side. "For someone who is supposedly my ally, my *boyfriend*," I chanced, "you sure do have a lot of secrets. Come to think of it, I don't even know your last name."

His lips curled up in a way that drove me insane. "I do hope that you think of me as more than just your, what do you say—boyfriend. And for your information, it is Koehaias."

The constantly turning wheels in my head stopped cold. I didn't know quite what to make of a name like that. I was used to imagining what names would sound like in court, but suddenly I found myself wondering how it would sound attached to a title. King Koehaias. Oh yes, that had merit.

"Is that elvish?" I asked.

He nodded. "My father's name."

"And your father—where was he from?"

"The hills."

I studied him for a moment, trying to put the pieces together. My fate was teetering before me. I knew that being with Toby meant more in Garlandia than it did here. That he wouldn't just be my first boyfriend, that he would be my last.

Grown-ups always speak of first loves as just that—that one first love that tears you up and ages you—that gets you ready for the next. I'd been thinking about that a lot since I'd been back home. I'd also been doing nothing but missing Toby. The way I felt when he touched me, kissed me, held me . . . I knew down deep that he was all I would ever need.

Maybe I *was* just a stupid teenager, but I knew I loved

Toby. I'd fallen for him the first time he pulled me into him, when he'd spoken of two souls who had been torn apart lifetimes ago. So what was so wrong with this? The same people who say first loves prepare you for what's next, also say you never quite get over that first heart throb. It seems to me love is the last thing people should try to preach about. It's a feeling, a part of our souls, and our souls always know what's right for us.

"Makayla," Toby whispered, his eyes heavy in mine. It wasn't until I felt my wings hit the wall that I realized he'd moved us into the living room, his body up against mine. "We have much to discuss."

"I know," I said, my heart beginning to race.

Pinching my chin with his thumb and forefinger, he pulled my face up closer to his. His breath hot and short as it caressed my face, he whispered, "But even more than that, I don't know if I can wait until I make you my queen."

"Then don't," I choked out.

A short look of pain washed over him, but just as quickly disappeared again.

"You say this now—"

"I *mean* this now. The idea of not being with you forever is far more frightening than losing you."

"You are letting your physical needs speak for you." His breath was in my ear, and it was enough to drive me to insanity.

Pressing my ear closer to his mouth, the heat inside my body raising to a dangerous temperature, I whispered, "No . . . No, I'm absolutely not."

Squaring his hips with mine, grabbing my hands and holding them tightly against the wall, he kissed my neck. A small whimper fell from my mouth as he whispered in my ear, "My queen, you've had my sword since before I met you. When we become one—our strength will double."

"Your sword," I whispered, the words waking up a recent memory I'd forgotten all about.

"Yes."

Using all my strength, I pushed Toby away just enough to look him in the eyes. Mildly out of breath, I said, "The day I was brought to the castle, the elf who escorted me—he said those same words. 'You have my sword, my queen.' Toby, what does that mean?"

His expression relaxed. "It means he has already knighted himself under your name. It means they are preparing for the fight, and they've already chosen you as their leader."

My legs, which were already unsteady, lost all feeling. "What?"

"There are many who stand against the king, Makayla. Many who have been waiting for the king's spell to break so that they might fight."

"What spell? And why would they pick me for their leader? I don't know anything. I—I can barely point my wand in the right direction."

Shushing me, Toby let go of one of my wrists and ran his hand down the side of my cheek. "Stop. The explanations are all in here." He pointed to my chest. "The rest will come with time." And then, before I could accost him with more questions, he laid into me with a kiss laced with something other than just his tongue. In it, I felt and saw what he wasn't telling me with his words.

As he pressed his hips harder against mine, a vision appeared in my mind. I saw the two of us riding Petal along a mountainside. My wings flapping in the wind, and a long, thick silver sword hanging from a belt around my waist. In the distance there was the sound of water sloshing up against a tide, and the sky was as dark as night, but it was day.

"Toby," I said, coming up for air, "we aren't in the beginning anymore, are we?"

"No, my queen, that moment has passed us." His lips moved from my lips to my ear, then down my throat, causing me to gasp. All I wanted was to open up for him, to let him inside. Suddenly *any* doubts I still had secretly lingering in the back of my mind dissipated. I *was* his queen, and he was my king, and we were going to bind ourselves together, forever —until—

"Makayla! We're back!"

Immediately I shoved Toby away, and jumped from the wall so fast I thought my wings were going to pull me across the room all over again.

"Who is that?" Toby asked, pulling out his ivory wand.

"It's just my parents—my human ones." I fanned my face while trying to put myself back together, but the look on my parents' faces once they discovered us told me that we were already busted. "Put that away," I said, shoving his wand down.

"Makayla," my dad said, coming to a halt, his frown lines deepening the longer he stared at Toby. Both our faces were completely flushed. "Why is there a boy here with you alone? And why are your wings out?"

My mom walked up beside him, her eyes landing on Toby's ears.

"I thought you guys were going on a date," I said, trying to change the subject.

"The movie we wanted to see was sold out—are those cigarettes in that boy's shirt sleeve?" She dropped her purse down onto the end table closest to her. "And is he an elf?"

"Hello," Toby said, walking over and slapping my father and mother on the hand.

"Oh shit," I whispered.

"What the hell, son?" my dad said.

"Now if you would, please," Toby said, leaning his cheek in between the two of them. "Go on, then. Give it a slap."

My parents looked up at me in complete bewilderment. I bit down over my lip and nodded. "Just do it," I said quietly. And so, they did.

"Good. Now that we've properly met, let me introduce myself. I'm Sir Toby, heir to the Garlandian throne."

My mom reached for her chest as a look of shock washed over her. "Oh!"

My dad still looked like he wanted to murder him.

"Yes." Toby smiled. "I apologize profusely for not meeting with you before now. You see, there are certain restrictions in our world that make it difficult for Makayla and me to be seen together."

Both my parents looked at me in question. Not just because they had no previous knowledge of me being in a relationship with an elf—but because they had no inclination of what Garlandia was really like. Maude, Tanker, and now I had sugarcoated every last detail. As far as they knew, it was all frivolous dancing and honey trading. It was best, I thought, to keep it that way. At least for the time being.

"Maude and Tanker Abberwockey have filled me in on what it is you know—"

"Wait," I said, reaching for his shoulder. I couldn't let him tell them the truth, that Garlandia was actually dangerous. If they knew, they would fight against my return.

Toby held up a hand in my direction. "Makayla, would you mind giving us a few minutes, I need the chance to discuss a few things with your parents."

"What? Toby, I don't think—"

But he immediately began shaking his head, his glass blue eyes sharpening around the edges. "Please, Makayla. Just give me a few moments alone." Then, nearing me, he took my elbow and led me away and into the other room. Over his shoulder, I watched as my mother's brows furrowed deeper into her skull.

"Toby, what are you doing?" I asked as soon as we were out of earshot.

"Trust me," he said, near pleading. "Any day now things are going to start making a lot more sense to you, and as soon as they do, you will understand the importance of what I am about to do. The only agenda I have is keeping those who you love safe."

When I said nothing back, only because I was stewing over what was lurking behind his words, he backed away and walked back into the living room. I could have easily followed him, eavesdropped on what he was intending to do or say to my parents, but I decided to wait it out in the kitchen instead.

I had an inkling of what he was up to. If this was about keeping my parents safe, that could only mean one thing; and as soon as my mother reappeared in the kitchen, her eyes a little glazed over and a pair of tickets in her hand, I knew that my assumptions were correct. Toby was getting them out of here.

"Thank you for bringing him here, Lala!" she said, running over to give me a giant hug. "I can't believe this— your father and I have always wanted to go to Calonzia!"

My father sauntered in right behind her. He looked a little like he'd just gotten shot in the stomach but hadn't figured it out yet. I stared questionably at Toby as he appeared behind him, but he simply gave me a nod and smiled at my father as he turned around and shook his hand.

"Thanks again," my dad said, unaware of Toby's reaction to his hand being shaken, like he thought my dad was trying to pull it off. "Well, I guess we should start packing, right Naomi?"

"Yes!" she exclaimed, running over to Toby and kissing him on the cheek, before grabbing my father's hand and pulling him from the kitchen.

Once they were gone, I turned to Toby. "What was that? And where the hell is Calonzia?"

"That was something that had to be done. My uncle knows where you live now—we can't gamble with fate. He is someone who only knows how to use fear as a weapon; do you see where I am going with this?"

"Yes . . . I do. But how long are they going to be like that? I mean, you, like, stunned them or something. Not to mention I've never heard of such a place, and I am very good with my geography."

Laying his hands over my shoulders, he said, "Just know that they will be safe where they are going."

"What about their jobs—their lives here?"

"I said don't worry. Everything is taken care of. As soon as the king is out of our way, their lives will go back to normal."

I listened to the pitter patter of my parents' feet scampering around upstairs, the sound of my mother pulling out her Louis Vuitton suitcases and mindlessly throwing clothes into them.

My dad was asking strange questions. "Naomi, are we allowed to take socks? What color is the water in Calonzia? Shall I bring my slippers? Where's that old Van Halen cassette tape of mine?"

I pointed at the ceiling. "Are you sure they are going to be okay on their own?"

Toby smiled reassuringly. "Gwen will be with them."

"Your nanny?" I didn't mean for it to sound condescending, but I could tell he took it that way.

"She isn't my nanny, she is my keeper," he said defensively.

"Right. Whatever, as long as she keeps them safe."

"She will."

"Fine," I finally agreed. "So now what?" I knew the drill by now, and I could tell I wasn't going to get any more answers out of him. Not today.

"We wait until I'm sure the timing is right, and then you come back to Garlandia. And I'm afraid"—an apologetic look forming over his face— "that my time here is up. I must go back before the guard I was with wakes." As he spoke, he began pulling me to the front door.

"Wait," I said, tugging him to a halt. "You, spelling my parents into leaving for another world, *that* I will go along with because I understand why you are doing it; but the rest of this—me sitting here, waiting—"

"Like I've already told you, Makayla, everything you need to know is already inside of you. The answers are in your soul, just like your magic. It is something you will have to dig out, just like your dust."

I frowned. "Well then, answer me this at least. Earlier, when you kissed me, I saw the two of us riding Petal. I—I had a sword, and where we were headed didn't look anything like Garlandia. Did you see it, too?"

He wrapped his hands around my arms in a way that made me feel like nothing could ever hurt me. "Yes. I told you, together we are stronger. We used to be bonded . . . a long, long time ago. We were torn apart so that certain other forces could go on."

I thought on his words for only a second. "When does that day happen? The day I saw."

"I don't know any more than you do, I'm afraid. But I would venture that it isn't a day that far from now."

Grabbing his hands and gripping them tightly, I asked, "How much longer do I have to wait to understand what is going on around me?"

"That Makayla, depends solely on you."

Of course, it did. Why would any of this get any easier?

Once we were outside, I looked around, searching for Rally even though I knew he was nowhere near us. It was strange being out in the open with Toby—it was difficult to believe no one was watching us. I held his hands in mine, afraid of how long it would be until I felt the touch of his skin again. I just wanted to hold onto him forever.

Looking up into his irises, a color deep as the ocean, I said, "You said the neighborhood was safe, right?"

"Yes."

"What about the sky?"

He stared at me inquisitively. "That too."

"Good." I extended my wings behind my shoulders and grabbed Toby's waist, right before I pulled us into the stars.

Surrounded by red, green, and purple dust, we floated in the air, staring down at the streetlights below. "I can wait for you, Toby, but I just need to be alone with you, even if it's for the length of a heart's beat."

Framing my cheek with his free hand, his thumb resting over my bottom lip, he said, "My love for you is eternal, whether we be in body or soul. It always has been."

"The words you say, they are beginning to sound less strange to me."

"That's because your veins have filled back in with magic."

And then we kissed until our feet landed back on the ground.

❧

Once Toby was gone, I helped my parents finish packing. Someone had to make sure they stuffed more than socks and toothpicks into their suitcases.

They were leaving that night—Toby hadn't wasted a single second. As they lined up at the door like a couple of kids waiting to journey forth into Disney World, I studied their tickets.

"These passes are awfully strange," I noted. Whatever

form of travel they were about to embark upon, it didn't include an airplane ride.

"Toby said Roe Haertchec would be coming to retrieve us," my mom said, fidgeting anxiously with her purse. "Roe Haertchec, from Bathar. She's a dragon dancer."

Dragon dancer? Something about that phrase was oddly familiar.

I was fully prepared to question everything about my mom's statement, but I never got the chance. For a second later there was a knock at the door and I scooted past my parents to get to it first, my father mumbling something about striped socks and blueberry vodka. I had to wonder if Toby had had to tamper a little more with his brain than my mother's in order to get him to drop everything and leave.

When I opened the door, I found myself face to face with a slender female elf. Or at least whoever she was *looked* like an elf. The creature was average height, wearing dark green spandex pants and a tight shirt, revealing her chiseled form.

"I'm here for the Woods," she said. There was no emotion in her pointed, black eyes.

"Of course," I retorted, trying to reach my gaze around the elf to see what kind of transportation she'd arrived in—but there was nothing there.

"We're right here!" my mom piped up, excitedly jumping up and down, grabbing her suitcase and pushing past my dad. "You must be Roe."

"Yes," the elf answered unenthusiastically. "Come stand next to me please."

My parents did as they were told, my dad still completely unfocused and my mom so wound up she barely felt it when I moved in and hugged her extra tight.

"They will be fine, Makayla Wood," said the elf named Roe.

"Where are they going?"

"About two paces in and four out." And then Roe bowed her head, before the three of them disappeared completely out of my sight.

I stared out into the empty front stoop for a moment longer before closing the door again. I knew better than to think too hard on what had just happened; I could only trust that Toby had seen to it that they would be taken care of. There was nothing else I could do for them now.

It wasn't until they were gone and I'd walked back into our giant empty house, that I remembered the book I'd been reading about Titania. Grabbing it from where I'd dropped it onto the chair, I fluttered over the stairs and into my bedroom. Now that I was alone again, I'd pulled my wings back out; I usually slept wrapped inside of them like a cocoon.

I switched on my bedside lamp then flopped down on my bed, rereading the paragraph I'd read hours ago aloud.

"'She said her soul would ride the waves of someone merited of her expectations; that this chosen spirit would be marked with the stain of her mother's heart, and that that symbol would be protected by an unconquerable element worthy of warding away evil.'"

Flipping to the part of the book that highlighted Gaia, I read through the caption stating that she was "the goddess of all things. Her abundance plenty, her heart a star . . ."

"Her heart was a star," I whispered.

I pulled my left wing over my shoulder and cranked my head, staring at my birthmark.

"No. That's just a coincidence."

But just because my wings had a star, the wings Toby always referred to as goddess wings—it didn't necessarily mean anything. Besides, the description of Titania had clearly said the symbol of her mother would be protected by some sort of element. My wings were cool, but they weren't unconquerable.

"Shit." I turned towards my lamp as it flickered and died, leaving me in the dark amidst the most informative reading I'd found in a decade.

Pulling out my wand, I remembered the word Tanker had taught me to bring light to the end of my magic tool.

"Photizma," I said, imagining a shimmer at the end of my wand, and immediately a halo began emanating near the tip, bright enough to shed light on the pages of my book. I was still in awe whenever I was able to make actual magic.

Holding my wand near the description of Gaia, I smiled at the blue star and diamond at the end. So far, I hadn't seen any other faeries with anything at the end of their wands—

"Oh my god." I leaned forward, staring down at the star.

Diamonds. They were one of the strongest materials found on earth. If one were to encase something valuable inside of it, it would be nearly impossible to get it back out.

I reached down and felt the tip of the diamond . . . it was sharp. I'd never thought much about it because I'd never observed the star for longer than a few seconds, but as I studied it now, it seemed alive. Like it had a heartbeat.

The book slid from my hands, and I looked over at my vanity mirror, seeing the reflection of my wand in its glass. "That's what he was trying to tell me before he died," I said of Herbert. Titania wasn't gone, he'd insinuated she was closer than ever. And he was right, because she was riding the waves of someone's soul . . . mine.

⁂ 27 ⁂

Unbeknownst to Makayla, far from where she lay curled up in her bed, wrapped in a heavy realization, an elf with a face like Toby's rose from his bed. But unlike Toby, his eyes were weathered from deeply rooted sin. Sitting up, he clenched the space over his heart, wincing from the sensation of a chill separating its beats.

"Uncle?"

He looked up at his nephew, then down at the chain around the boy's neck to the vial hanging from it.

"What did you do to me?"

"Nothing, Uncle," the boy frowned. He was an excellent actor—had been all his life. "We were all very worried, you slipped away after having your carrot soup. This is the second time now. Shall we call a healer?"

King Loral tightened his lips before retorting. "Not necessary. Leave me now."

Sir Toby bowed his head before turning to leave.

"And have the kitchen witch fired."

His nephew turned around. "Why, Uncle? She has done nothing."

The king only lowered his gaze to settle on a bit of glass resting against the wall, a top his dresser. "There is but one witch who I can trust. I will have no more sorcerers in the castle—only elves."

"I daresay Uncle, the strength of our kind does not lay in the kitchen."

King Loral raised two beady eyes to meet his nephew's; there was more than mischief lurking in there—the boy's mother was in there as well. Whatever secrets his sister had left with, they were now living on in her son. It was why he'd stuck him with Rally the second the boy arrived—that son of a witch would be able to sense when and if the boy was going to strike. Rally was not merely an elf, after all.

"Does it look like I care?" the king finally answered.

"No Uncle, it does not."

"Go." His hands trembled as he pushed off from his bed. "I will be sending you to Anemone in the morning. The Knights of Ten Gables are ready to be trained."

His nephew stared down at the floor before nodding his head.

"Yes, Uncle," he replied, before taking his leave.

King Loral waited for his bedroom door to close to move from his bed, hobbling over towards the mirror on his dresser. It had been a long time since he'd needed to speak with the one on the other side of that reflection, but the chill in his heart told him that he had no other choice. The crone had warned him that it could happen, the spell he'd used to cut off the Erwain race could only harness his intent—it could not possibly debunk fate.

Years he'd gritted his teeth over where the lost Erwain could've gotten off to, her absence alluding to the possibility that the rebels were training her to invoke his enemy. But then, out of nowhere she'd shown up—nothing more than a developed human with wings. But being here had changed her, and he could feel it coming back to life—the ghost he'd always feared she carried.

He placed his hands on top of the dresser, steadied himself, then peered deeply into the glass. "Where light ends and darkness begins, hear me, Crone. I must speak with you."

Immediately a pair of eyes appeared, the color of their irises faded away to barely a hint of green.

"What is it you desire to know?" came a smooth, female voice.

"Makayla Wood."

The eyes in the reflection seemed to smile, if not a bit wickedly.

"Ahhh, yes. The one who got past our spell."

"She's been found."

"I've heard."

"When she disappeared, you assured me that she was of no concern."

"That was before."

"Before what?" The king was becoming increasingly agitated.

"Before *him*."

King Loral's frown deepened.

A low, seedy laugh began to emanate from the reflection. "There is love, and not just any love—one that was formed from two souls before they found bodies. Two souls who have been through the gamut in this world. It is what drew the soul of the lost queen to her in the first place. This is a love so strong that it dove past our spell, and into its destined body, so that it could find its counterpart."

The king, now growing impatient, slammed his fists down over his dresser. "What love do you speak of? There is no one here for her *to* love!"

"Come now, Sebastian. We both know even you are not so blind that you cannot see it."

King Loral cocked his head to the side. "Another faery?"

The eyes moved back and forth as though the face was shaking its head. "It is one who was born only a few years before her."

He swallowed hard. "An elf?"

The eyes moved up and down.

"It is impossible," he muttered. The second the girl reappeared into this world she was followed. The only elf around her age that she exchanged more than a few words with was when she'd been at the market and his nephew had—

"No," he gasped. "It can't be—Rally would've said something. Overseeing my nephew is his one job, and I assure you, he is loyal."

The eyes blinked. "Silly Sebastian, don't you think Toby knows that too?"

King Loral sneered, flattening his hands onto the hard surface of the dresser. "Speak plainly. I have paid you well, and I deserve fitful answers. If you are insinuating what I think you are, that I've been fooled by my own blood—"

"I warned you of this the day you came to me. Some things will never remain unbroken."

"But it is in your best interest that they do."

"My story is one that belongs to a much later edition, Sebastian. And I worry not, for I am not a whole being. To find me, is to lose oneself. You know that better than anyone."

The king's skin began to darken, his color shifting to more of a ripened plum. Breathing heavily through his nose, he asked, "If what you are saying has truth in it, then the queen *has* found a way to resurface through this girl."

"Not so much resurface, we cannot live the same life twice —but she can dance around the girl's soul, persuade her to finish what she could not. If this has truly happened, there will be signs."

"What signs?" he asked sharply.

"You know as well as I. It is why you had planned to assassinate the swaddling soon after receiving news of her birth."

"Because of the star on her wing? But you said after she disappeared that this was not the true mark."

"And it wasn't, but it doesn't mean Makayla Wood does not still carry the stamp of her predecessor."

The king's expression shifted into even more of a scowl. "There is no predecessor. The elfin gold used to make our crowns was never meant to sit upon a faery's head."

There was silence for a brief moment as the eyes inside the mirror remained still. "What will you do now, Sebastian?"

The king cupped his chin and turned his head away. His gaze darted into various corners of the room as his thoughts churned with enough force to make butter. "You say the love between Makayla and Toby is real?"

"Quite."

"It has nothing to do with that leech Titania?"

"Their love existed when they were souls, even before the faery queen was ever born, before she was ever killed. As I've already suggested, Sebastian, I very much believe that it was this love that drew the queen to the girl in the first place. She wanted someone worthy of her values, after all."

He bared his teeth.

The edges of the eyes inside the mirror lifted ever so slightly. "Since you are a paying customer, I feel the need to give you some sage advice. One might suggest that in order to undo something, one must first understand how it works."

The corner of the king's top lip curled upwards as he dipped his chin towards his chest. "I did not barter with you for those kinds of suggestions. Thank you for your answers, Crone. You may go."

The eyes blinked twice, then as quickly as they had arrived, they departed. The king turned from the glass, facing the red curtain that served as a wall, separating his sleeping quarters from the kingdom that laid outside the castle. Lifting his hand, he pulled away the heavy fabric and stood before all who served him.

Out in the distance, witches, wizards, and faeries flew over the trees. For years he had been preparing, gaining strength in his armies. Still, the faeries had magic strong enough to fight back, and he still hadn't located the illegal organization for which Helene Voss had just been terminated. Unfortunately, he knew their leader all too well, and nothing was going to pull *him* out of hiding, not even if he captured his last living daughter. In order to sink these creatures, he was going to have to come at them underhanded—deplete their numbers even more than he already had. And this was why he'd allowed them the freedom to which they'd had for so long . . . so that they wouldn't expect it when the hammer fell.

The king's gaze fell to a specific area in the forest where smoke was billowing towards the sky. If he concentrated hard enough, he could still smell the spices from his favorite dish. He'd requested it so often, it was no wonder the old bat could only remember that one recipe after he'd tampered with her brain.

Turning his chin towards his bedroom door, he shouted for the knight who stood guard over his quarters. A second later a medium-sized elf appeared inside his room.

"Yes, Your Highness?"

"Lionel, I need you to send word to the guard. From here on out there will be no travel in or out of the kingdom—except for the girl. Do you have wands on her yet?"

"We have just sent three guards into her world. She is alone. The parents are nowhere to be found."

"She is the exception to the rule. If she desires to get back in, then allow her to do so."

"Yes, sir."

"And air travel shall be shut down immediately."

The knight shifted where he stood uncomfortably. "Sir, how do you suggest we—"

The king pulled out his wand and held it stiffly by his side.

"Of course, Your Highness. I will go relay the messages."

King Loral waited until his guard departed before glancing one more time into the forest. Reaching into his robe, he pulled out what appeared to be a grey marble and studied it. But it wasn't a marble. It was part of a matching set, and its brother had been residing inside Cajun Cathy's eye socket ever since he'd put it there. As he stared into the ball, a scene began to unfold of jambalaya patrons gathered to feast, and inevitably to chat. Private meetings and illegal conversations.

He pulled out his wand and tapped the ball, making it grow to the size of a melon. Placing it to levitate in the space over his bed, King Loral sat back down and rested his head against the headboard. It was time, he decided, to begin bringing them in. One by one, he would find cause, and one by one the faeries and Wood elves would begin to drown. Because to take down their precious queen for the second time, he was going to have to first wound these Garlandians . . . make them bleed.

ACKNOWLEDGMENTS

Makayla Wood found me at a time when I needed a good laugh. I've learned a lot from her over the years, specifically that there is no such thing as being perfect. She's also taught me patience, and that everyone has magic if they believe they do. Yes, I am in fact thanking a fictional character.

Beyond the fiction, I am so obviously thankful to Jean Lowd and everyone at Creative James Media. I so appreciate this opportunity to share my stories with the world.

Thank you to my mother and sister for reading to me when I was little and raising me to believe in faeries. I'll never forget *Little Orphant Annie* or the 'Gobble-uns.' And most of all, thank you to my husband for not just believing in me as a writer, but for trusting in me when I insisted (even when it looked like it would never happen) that we would one day have a little imp of our own. And to Liv, thank you for being that little imp and for finally crossing the veil to get to us. Without the idea of you there would have been no Makayla, and if I know anything, it's that this world needs her.

ABOUT THE AUTHOR

Mariah Stillbrook, originally from Iowa, lives in Colorado with her white german shepherd, husband, and little girl.

She graduated from the University of Colorado at Colorado Springs. She spends most of her days writing, reading, and enjoying the occasional hike.

In her late twenties she realized that her writing was missing something, magic. She now focuses her writing on urban fantasy in both adult and young adult genres.